Ana had taken only a few steps into the room when Owen's voice stopped her in her tracks.

*

"Wait! Don't move! There's a broken fruit jar here."

Before she knew what was happening, he swung her up in his arms as if she were a child. Her arms went around his neck and she held on to him tightly. She had never been lifted and held like this. It was frightening, yet exciting.

"Oh! Put me down! I'm too heavy—"

"Too heavy? Good Lord! You don't weigh as much as a sack of grain."

As he eased her down, she held on to his shoulders to keep her balance. She thought he would move away, but he grasped her bare ankle in his big hand and lifted her foot.

"Did you cut your feet?"

Ana tried not to look at him. Every nerve in her body jumped to attention. The warm fingers curled around her bare ankle sent blood surging to her cheeks ...

"FIVE STARS! A special joy ... a unique plot.... Set in early times with earthy people, the overall texture of this book was gentle and heartwarming, with a wealth of layering in the characters. This story tugs at the heartstrings. I was impressed! Thanks so much, Dorothy ... THIS ONE IS A KEEPER."

—Julie Meisinger, *Heartland Critiques*

HOME-PLACE

DOROTHY GARLOCK

WARNER BOOKS

A Time Warner Company

WARNER BOOKS EDITION

Copyright © 1991 by Dorothy Garlock
All rights reserved.

Cover illustration by Franco Accanero
Handlettering by Carl Dellacroce

Warner Books, Inc.
666 Fifth Avenue
New York, N.Y. 10103

A Time Warner Company

Printed in the United States of America

First Printing: April, 1991

10 9 8 7 6 5 4 3 2 1

To
Marge Theiss
and
Mary Ann Hendricks
for
listening—

ACKNOWLEDGMENTS

A special thanks . . .

To Jean Reed for sharing with me the story of her great-grandmother, who did, indeed, marry her son-in-law after her daughter died in childbirth. This story, however, in no way parallels the life of that lady.

To Jay Anderson and Candace Matelic for their wonderful book, PIONEER IOWA—THE LIVING HISTORY FARM.

To Edward J. Lettermann for his book, PIONEER FARMING IN IOWA.

I wish to express my appreciation to all the talented employees of ARCATA GRAPHICS, Buffalo, New York, for their dedication to quality.
  A special thanks to:
    Kevin Clarke, Manager of Manufacturing/Books
    Robert Scheifflee, Manager Customer Service/Books
    Greg Boilard, Customer Service Representative

One

~~~~~~

S*pring* had come to the river town of Dubuque, and with it the long awaited letter. The happiness that brightened Ana's face when she received it faded quickly as she read:

April 10, 1885

Dearest Mama,
  I am so sick. I fear I will die giving birth to the child of my beloved. My feet and legs are so swollen I can hardly stand on them. I think of you often and weep for the worry I have caused you. My heart aches to see you one last time. I want you to take my baby and give it the love you gave to me. O Mama, my heart is sore. This is a dreary place. The Jamison's do nothing but work. Please come. Owen has promised that you will be met in Lansing. Make haste, dearest Mama.

Your loving daughter, Harriet

The sounds and the fragrant smells of an Iowa spring were in the air. The spicewood was in bud, the cottonwood in tassel and the shrill piping of the season's first frogs could be heard. Unending swarms of ducks, brant and cranes glided down to settle on the river while others soared aloft to continue their long journey northward. Hardy violets and yellow dandelions edged the path on which Ana trod to reach her small house backed against the river bluff. She neither saw nor heard these wonders of spring.

In the privacy of her home, she read the letter again and again and wept. After the weeping passed, Ana damned the man responsible for enticing so young a girl to do what she clearly knew to be wrong and then abandoning her, leaving her no choice but to follow him so that her child would not be born a bastard. Ana remembered the loneliness after Harriet left: the days long and empty, the nights a nightmare in which she wandered a vast open plain searching for a small girl who called for her mama.

The winter had been agonizingly long for Ana. She had spent a cold, lonely Christmas day sitting beside the cookstove in the rocking chair remembering other Christmas days when the house, filled with the smell of roasted goose, fruitcake and pumpkin pie, rang with laughter as a young child opened gifts left by Santa Claus.

During the weeks that followed the holidays, she had kept busy. In January she had been snowbound for a week, unable to climb the icy hill to go to work in one of the big houses on the bluff overlooking the city. Every spare minute of her time had been spent knitting or sewing. She kept one of the merchants down on Locust Street supplied with caps, scarfs, mittens and stockings. She put away the money he paid her. It was enough to pay her fare to Lansing and back with some left over to buy more yarn.

Holding the tear-stained letter, Ana recalled the unhappy late summer months that had climaxed in a terrible scene. Ana could still see the stubborn, defiant look on Harriet's face—Harriet who had always been so obedient and reasonable—screaming at her.

"For heaven's sake! I'm old enough to go out if I want to. A lot of girls are married at my age."

"Where are you going? You've been out three nights this week."

"To the ice cream parlor to meet Maud."

"Don't lie to me, Harriet. Maud's mother wouldn't allow her to go out with—"

"—with a servant? Is that what you were going to say?" Tears flooded Harriet's eyes as she crossed the room to the door and flung it open. Her plump cheeks were flushed with hurt and anger, and brown eyes that usually sparkled with laughter now sparkled with indignation. "Not everyone thinks of me as a servant."

"It's honest work, honey. Nothing to be ashamed of. I didn't want you working in the button factory."

"You don't think being a servant is a bad job because that's all you've ever been." Harriet must have known how hurt Ana was, yet she rushed on, "I'm just as good as Maud and a lot prettier."

"Of course, you are. That's not the point. I don't want you with that fast, reckless crowd Maud's brother runs with. I've seen the way they race their horses up and down the hills. One of these days there'll be an accident and someone may be killed or maimed for life."

"Oh, Mama—"

"That crowd has a bad reputation, Harriet."

"They're nice to me!"

"Someday you'll meet a nice man and be glad you've kept yourself above reproach."

"Like you did?" Harriet shot back. "You kept yourself above reproach and look what happened to you. Don't you ever wish you'd married someone else? Papa was old and grouchy and stingy—"

"That's enough! Don't say another word. Your father took

me and my grandmother in when we had no place to go. He
married me after Granny died so I could stay here and take
care of you. It would have broken my heart to leave you.
You were only four years old—''

''—and you were my age—fifteen. Did you sleep with
him, Mama?''

Ana, taken back by the question, could only stare at her
stepdaughter. Harriet had changed so drastically in the past
few months that she hardly knew her anymore.

''You know I didn't sleep with your papa. He never asked
it of me,'' Ana finally said in a low, trembling voice.

''I remember how it was. He treated you like his servant.
He paid you to take care of me. He married you so people
wouldn't talk about you living here in the house after your
granny died.'' Bitterness edged Harriet's tone and distorted
her young face. ''I'm not going to marry an old man and live
in a place like this. I'm going to marry a young man who
will love me and want to sleep with me and do all those *nasty*
things I've heard a man does to a woman in bed.''

''Harriet!'' If her stepdaughter had suddenly sprouted
horns, Ana couldn't have been more shocked. For a moment
she couldn't move, couldn't speak. ''Hush that kind of talk!
My word! If Judge Henderson heard you talk like that he'd
think you were . . . fast!''

''Judge Henderson! He's heard a lot worse things than
that.''

''But not from a fifteen-year-old girl.''

''Can't you understand that I just want to have some fun?''
Harriet set her lips to keep them from trembling.

''And I want you to enjoy being young and having the
young men pay attention to you. But I think you're going
about it the wrong way. The boy who delivers coal has been
trying to talk to you. He's a handsome lad. Give him a
chance.''

''Oscar Swensen! That stick! All he does is stutter and
stammer and twist his cap in his hands.'' Harriet raised her
eyes to the ceiling while buttoning her coat. She threaded her

fingers into her gloves and looked defiantly into Ana's eyes. "You work your fingers to the bone during the day and wear your eyes out at night sewing or knitting. I'm not going to work all my life. I'm going to find someone who will love and pamper me like Judge Henderson does his wife."

"Your papa left us this house but little else. We have a place to live, but we have to earn money for everything else. I'd like you to remember that my sewing and knitting paid for the material in that dress and coat you're wearing." Ana turned her head, hiding a face suddenly contorted with the pain of remembering her own lost youth and the time and love she had given this girl.

"I know that, Mama, and I'm grateful." Harriet hung her head, then raised it to glare defiantly. "You should try and find a man, Ana. This time get a young one with some life left in him."

"Is that what you've done?"

"That's exactly what I've done and I'm having the most wonderful time of my life. Please don't spoil it for me."

"If you've met someone you like, I'm happy for you. Invite the boy to come to Sunday dinner, honey. I'll cook a good meal—"

"Boy? He's a *man* with a smile like an angel. He laughs, he sings, he dances. It makes me happy just to look at him. I can't ask him to come *here*!"

"Oh, Harriet!" It hurt unbearably to know Harriet was ashamed of her home.

"Fiddle, Mama! I know what I'm doing."

"I hope you do," Ana said quietly.

With mixed exasperation and desperation, Ana followed Harriet out onto the porch and watched her go through the front gate and down the street. For the first time her step-daughter had called her by her given name, and to Ana it signified a new stage in their relationship. She loved Harriet as if she were her own daughter, although there were scarcely eleven years between their ages. She had tried to teach Harriet the same values that her grandmother had instilled in her.

Where had she gone wrong? What could she have done differently?

A buggy pulled by a slick sorrel came careening around the corner. It sped past the house, but slowed when it reached Harriet and kept pace with her. Then it stopped and a man jumped down. He lifted his bowler hat and bowed from the waist with a flourish. Ana could see that Harriet was laughing at him as he lifted her into the buggy. Seconds later they were down the hill and out of sight.

Remembering, Ana lifted her palms to her cheeks. She should have done something. But what?

Harriet had finished school two months before and had gone to work in Judge Henderson's home on the bluff. Maud Johnson's father owned a boat and the boiler works, and her mother had social ambitions that didn't include her daughter associating with a girl who worked as a maid in a home where on occasion the Johnsons were guests. Harriet and Maud had not been friends outside the classroom, and Ana doubted that it was Maud whom Harriet was meeting; perhaps it was her brother or one of his friends.

October arrived and with it another change in Harriet. She became increasingly quiet and moody. Her evening visits to town stopped abruptly. Since she worked only part of the day, she was often in bed by the time Ana got home from work. Ana was sure the young man who had laughed and sang, the one who had made Harriet so happy, had left town. She waited patiently for time to heal the young girl's heart.

One evening in the middle of October Ana came home to an empty house. A letter lay on the kitchen table.

> *Dear Mama,*
>   *Forgive me for taking the money in your*
> *sewing basket. I will write when I am settled. I*
> *do love you and don't want to cause you worry,*
> *but I must go.*
>
>   *Harriet*

Part of Ana's life had gone with Harriet. Now she had no one. Almost frantic with worry, Ana visited the boiler works to speak to young Franklin. He said he hadn't seen Harriet and that he did not know whom she had been meeting. With a cocky grin he assured Ana that Harriet was a big girl who could take care of herself. Ana had wanted to slap the smirk from his face. She called on Judge Henderson. Neither he nor his housekeeper could think of a reason why Harriet would leave so suddenly.

Work kept Ana sane. She worked harder than she ever had in her life, worked and worried and waited. Thanksgiving came and with it heavy snow, but no word from Harriet.

Just before Christmas a short letter arrived. Harriet said she had married Owen Jamison and was living on a farm west of Lansing, a small port on the Mississippi River in the northern part of the state. She said that she was happy and well and expecting a baby. She had signed it simply, Harriet. It had seemed to Ana that Harriet had cut her out of her life.

Not another word had come until now. Now Harriet needed her and she would go. Harriet had always been alarmed by the slightest illness. Ana could well imagine how frightening having a baby would be to the young girl.

Ana stood on the porch and looked toward the river where the black smoke from a river steamer shot upward and trailed behind it as it made its way upriver. In the years since the end of the Civil War, Dubuque had become lusty and ambitious with the large influx of immigrants to the fertile prairies of northeastern Iowa. Lumbering had replaced mining as the important industry. Huge log rafts were floated down from the north and converted into lumber and ties for the railroads that were opening new paths into the West.

Dubuque was home. Ana had never been more than twenty-five miles from it. Her father had worked in the lead mines. He had died in a fire trying to rescue her mother after he had carried Ana and led his mother-in-law to safety. After that there had been just she and her grandmother until they came to work for Ezra Fairfax and she'd had Harriet to love.

Ezra had been good to her in his own way. He had paid for her to attend school while her grandmother took care of his house. He was also a frugal man, and one who cherished his standing in the community. It would never do for a young woman to live in his home, without benefit of marriage, to care for his daughter. The customers who came to his tailor shop were church-going people. During the days following her grandmother's death, when Ana was overcome with grief and feeling lonely, Ezra offered to marry her. He gave her a home and security in exchange for taking care of the house and four-year-old Harriet.

Ana went back inside, lit the lamp, and picked up her knitting. Before she could leave she had to finish the order for two dozen pairs of mittens. They were almost ready for delivery as were the black caps and the heavy stockings the rivermen would buy.

While she knitted, Ana's thoughts went ahead to all the things she would have to do before she could leave. First she would go to the steamship office and purchase a ticket. Then she would write to Harriet and tell her the time of her arrival. The trunk in the attic was old, but in good shape and big enough to hold her best clothes as well as work dresses to wear while she helped Harriet. Her neighbor, Mr. Leonard promised to watch the house. Her garden had been planted and she hated to leave it. Fiddle! What did that matter when she was going to Harriet?

"Thank you." Ana smiled at the boatman who set her small trunk on the boardwalk in front of the steamship office.

The boat trip from Dubuque to Lansing had been exciting. The boat had tied up for the night at a place near Harper's Ferry and she had slept in a dormitory room with five other women. The morning had been spent standing at the railing with the other passengers watching the shoreline and waving at the people in the small villages they passed.

The fact that she was a lone woman disembarking caused raised brows among a few of the men who also left the boat at Lansing, but they tipped their hats as they passed her and headed for one of the weathered plank buildings that made up the little port town on the Mississippi River.

Ana's self-contained demeanor was discouraging enough that only the most brazen men would attempt to approach her with an intimate suggestion. Today none of them were brave enough, and she stood alone. She was not as self-assured as she appeared to be, here in this new place more than a hundred miles from home, waiting for a stranger to take her to Harriet. What would she do if no one came for her? Her heart sank. It was down-right scary.

Faint lines of strain that had appeared lately between Ana's brows deepened as minutes passed. Her head was high, however, and her shoulders straight, despite the pensive look on her face and the shadows of worry beneath her eyes. She turned to watch goods being unloaded from the boat onto a large dray. The friendly young riverman who had carried her trunk to the street, waved and ran back up the plank to the deck as the steamer prepared to lift anchor.

Standing alone on the street, Ana was unaware of the picture she made—handsome, willow thin, with a thick rope of blond hair twisted and pinned to the back of her head. The brim of her hat shaded her smooth skin and large, luminous golden-brown eyes which she considered her only singular claim to beauty in a face that was usually intensely serious.

She went into the stuffy, smoke-filled steamboat office and approached the clerk behind a glassed enclosure. He wore a visor cap and was busy scribbling on a paper with a stub of a pencil.

"Sir?" Ana tapped on the glass to get the man's attention.

"Yes, ma'am?"

"I'm Mrs. Ana Fairfax. Someone was to meet me here. Has anyone inquired?"

"No, ma'am. But likely they'll show up. You can wait in here if you like."

"Thank you. I'll wait outside for now."

Across the street, a man in a dark red flannel shirt watched Ana come out of the steamship office. He leaned against a building whose painted sign proclaimed in bold black letters that it was the billiard parlor. One knee was bent, and the sole of a heavy boot rested against the weathered boards of the building. His thumbs were hooked in the wide straps that held up his duck britches.

He studied the slender woman with hair the color of honey from bees that had fed on a clover field. It was rich and golden, and from what he could see, there was plenty of it. The hat atop her head was serviceable rather than one of the frivolous things he'd seen women wearing on his infrequent trips to Dubuque. At least it had a small brim for shade. It also kept him from seeing her eyes. Not that it mattered; she wasn't the one he was waiting for. He was waiting for a woman old enough to have a grown daughter. This one was mature and pleasant to look at, but she wasn't old enough to be the mother of a girl expecting a baby.

The man ran his thumbs up and down his suspenders and watched her, enjoying the way she moved, the way her skirt swished around her ankles. She was sure-footed as a cat even in her new, shiny black shoes with their high heels and bow-straps. She was trying to appear perfectly confident, but she was nervous. Otherwise why had she checked her hatpin three times during the past five minutes?

The blast of the whistle made the man aware that the boat was leaving and that this was the only woman who had gotten off the boat.

"What the hell?" he swore as he pushed himself away from the building. He had given up two days planting time to come get the woman and she hadn't shown up. Un-less—

Ana scanned the street with anxious, worried eyes. The only vehicle on the street was a loaded farm wagon. The horses with blinders attached to the bridles waited patiently, swishing their tails and occasionally stamping their feet to discourage the pesky river flies that appeared as if by magic each spring. Ana heard the chug of the powerful engines as the steamer pulled away from the dock and headed upriver once again. The crowd that had gathered to watch the lumbering craft arrive and depart was dispersing, leaving the street almost empty.

Ana's hands shook with something between anger and despair as she poked loose strands of hair into the knot on the back of her head with her forefinger. Surely Harriet had received her letter. It was sent almost two weeks ago as soon as she purchased her ticket and was sure of the day she would arrive in Lansing.

She began to walk restlessly up and down. The group of men who had gathered in front of the livery down the street were now examining a horse. One was holding a snub on its nose to control the frightened animal while another carefully lifted a hind foot. A few fishermen worked on boats at the water's edge.

A man, who looked to be either drunk or asleep, leaned against the building housing the billiard parlor. He was the only person within sight who wasn't doing something. Ana's glance honed in on him. He was tall and broad of shoulder with a straw hat pulled down low on his forehead. He lounged against the building as if he had all the time in the world.

With a sudden quickening of her heart, she realized that this stranger was looking at her and had been for some time. His gaze was so intense that it pulled her eyes back to him, and she looked at him for several seconds longer than propriety allowed even though it was impossible to see his eyes. The distance between them was too great for her to see anything of his face except that it was clean-shaven. She tilted her chin up as she turned her head away and continued her pacing. When she looked at him again, she found him staring at her as brazenly as before. He was no longer leaning against the building but standing away from it, his booted feet spread, his hands resting on his hips.

Ana looked toward the river trying to pull her scattered

thoughts together. She smoothed her skirt down over her hips for the tenth time and adjusted the hatpin that held her felt hat in place. Her stomach had not enjoyed the rolling motion of the boat and now it was tight with nervous tension. If the man by the billiard parlor was the one who had come to meet her, why had he stood there all this time watching her? She slanted a quick look at him and took a shallow, jerky breath.

He was coming toward her.

Two

*M*y goodness, he was big.

If this was the one who had come to fetch her, he certainly had made no effort to impress her by dressing up. He was tall and broad, looked to be strong as an ox, and watched her the way a hawk watches a rattlesnake.

"Mrs. Fairfax?" The voice was deep, strong and without hesitation even if it was a question.

Ana lifted her brows. He was only an arm's length away, and she did her best not to be intimidated by his size or the scowl on his face. She felt positively dwarfed and fought to resist the urge to lift a hand to ward him away.

"Yes. I'm Ana Fairfax."

"You're . . . Harriet's mother?"

"Yes. I'm—"

"Good Lord!"—he snorted with disapproval—"it's no wonder—"

No wonder what? Ana felt the blood rush to her face and was mindful of the thudding of her heart in her chest. But with chin up, shoulders straight, she gathered her splintered composure, locked her gaze with his, and refused to look away.

His frown deepened.

Cobalt blue eyes, fenced with thick brown lashes and topped with brows that were drawn together with displeasure, looked into hers. As they stared at each other, his eyelids drooped to half-mast and a muscle in one lean cheek jumped in response to clenched teeth. She was aware of the exasperation lurking in the depths of the bluest eyes she had ever seen. He pushed his hat back, and she saw the small white strip near his hair line that had been protected from the sun and the glint of gray strands among the dark clipped hair at his temples. His open-necked shirt revealed a strong sun-browned throat and nicks along his jaw line were evidence that he had shaved with a dull razor within the last few hours. By the grim set of his firm, wide mouth and cold eyes, he was obviously not happy.

Ana lifted her chin another inch and forced herself to look more confident than she felt, hoping the man would not notice that insecurity made the hands clutching her reticule tremble.

"Are you from the Jamison farm?" she asked crisply.

"I am."

"How is Harriet?"

"She hadn't had the youngun as of yesterday morning." The curt sentence was slapped at her. His gaze fell from her eyes to the soft and vulnerable curve of her lips, lingered long enough to send an unwelcome tremor through her, and then passed down the length of her. He made no attempt to conceal a look of savage impatience that twisted his face.

"Is she all right?"

He answered her question with one of his own. "How would I know?" He jerked up her trunk and set it on his shoulder. "Come on," he said and started off down the street as if the heavy trunk were no burden at all.

Ana felt nothing but shock as she followed him.

They reached the farm wagon parked in the street in front of the general store before she noticed that he favored his right leg. He placed her trunk atop a stack of sawed lumber, went around to the other side, and climbed up the wheel to the seat without offering to assist her. His stabbing eyes searched her face while Ana's amber ones stared up at him from beneath dark lashes and straight dark brows.

"Well? Are you coming or not?" His brows lowered and drew together until they almost met over his high-bridged nose. "It'll be dark by the time we get there as it is."

She shrugged her shoulders in exasperation, lifted her skirts, and put her foot on the hub of the wheel. She soon realized that she would have to accept his hand when he held it out to her, but was not prepared for the strength that hauled her up and onto the spring seat, or for the hard eyes that stared at her. There was no friendliness in their depths, only cold, quiet resignation.

An icy hand clutched Ana's heart and a knot of apprehension twisted her stomach.

As soon as she was settled, he stung the horses' rumps with a whip and the wagon moved over the ruts with a jarring jolt. Ana held onto the side of the narrow, low-backed seat and pulled away when her shoulder bumped into the rock-hard arm of the man beside her.

Ana had dressed in her best for the trip, wanting to make a good impression on Harriet's new family. Her dark serge suit was still unwrinkled. She nervously fingered one of the large pearl buttons on the tight-fitting jacket and adjusted the broach on the black ribbon around her throat. There would be dust on the hem of her skirt and on the shiny black shoes she had bought two days ago, but there was nothing she could do about that now.

The big-footed horses picked up speed as they left town and turned west. The trail climbed steadily to the bluff overlooking the town and veered off through spruce and pine that stood amid the early greening of the grasses lining the trail. They came down out of the hills amid huge oak trees whose leaves were the size of squirrel's ears this last week of April.

Flocks of robins rose as the wagon approached. Birds were

a source of delight for Ana. She loved to watch them migrating, following the great river south in the fall, and she looked forward to their return in the spring. She would have been delighted with the journey through the lush meadows if not for the worry about Harriet and having to endure this cold, uncommunicative man beside her.

An hour went by without a word passing between Ana and the driver of the wagon. Ana wondered who he was. It was certain that he was not Harriet's dancing, laughing man. The *grump* sitting beside her was probably one of the farm hands or a neighbor. He had said he was from the Jamison farm. Did that mean he was a member of the family? If so, which one? He wasn't old enough to be Harriet's father-in-law. A brother-in-law maybe? Or an uncle? Whoever he was, he needed to be taught some manners.

Ana turned her head to look at him and found him looking at her as if she were something wet and slimy he had dragged out of the river. She had a strange desire to stick out her tongue and bare her teeth. He stared at her from beneath furrowed brows; silent and disapproving. She stared back. He was not as old as she had first believed him to be. He was not much older than her own twenty-six years. His face was free of lines except for a few that fanned out from the corners of his eyes from squinting against the sun. Creases bracketed his wide mouth and his big square chin had an indention big enough to hold her little finger.

Unexpectedly, she wondered if his face would crack if he smiled. The thought made her want to giggle and amusement lit her amber eyes. As if he knew she was laughing at him, his expression changed from extreme disapproval to anger, and he stubbornly refused to break eye contact with her.

Ana turned her face away, opened her mouth to speak, then closed it and swallowed before the words would come.

"How far to the Jamison farm?"

Turning his face toward the horses, he grunted, "It'll be dark when we get there."

"Thank you very much," Ana said stiffly.

Farther down the road a huge hip-roofed barn came into view. As they neared, Ana could see that the big, solidly built barn dwarfed the house sitting just south of it in a sheltering grove of tall oak, walnut and evergreen trees. A farmer was plowing with a team of oxen. The rich black furrows lay like a ribbon across the land.

Coming across a field was a young girl driving two milch cows. Two children played hopscotch in the yard, and another child swung on a sack swing tied to the limb of a walnut tree. A woman in a dark dress and an old straw hat was taking clothes from a line stretched between two trees. With her arms full, she waited beside the line and watched the wagon pass. Ana lifted her arm and waved. The woman hesitantly raised her hand.

The *grump* on the seat beside Ana didn't so much as turn his head.

Evening came and a few stars twinkled in the still-light sky. Ana's back ached from sitting so straight on the low-backed wagon seat and jarring over the rutted road. When the air cooled after the sun went down, she wished for the warm shawl she had packed in her trunk, but she decided not to give the silent man beside her an opportunity to grumble by asking him to stop so that she could get it.

He seemed immune to the cold or the discomfort.

Just when Ana was sure she would be frozen in place, a long arm arced over her head. His hand dipped down behind the seat and came up with a heavy wool coat. He dumped it into her lap without so much as looking at her.

"Thank you," Ana said to his profile and swung the coat around her shivering shoulders. It took minutes for the warmth to penetrate. She burrowed her face in the collar, doing her best to control her shivering limbs. The masculine odor of tobacco came from the garment. It was a pleasant smell.

Ana wanted desperately to ask the man about Harriet, but she reasoned that if the girl's condition were serious, he would have told her. Still, uneasiness plagued her mind.

A faint light still glowed in the sky when they reached a small village. The white church on a rise above the village was enclosed within a white picket fence, and the tall spire seemed to reach to the sky. They passed houses that sat back from the road. A dog ran out from one of them and barked, setting off a chorus of barking dogs. A man came out onto the porch and shouted at the dog who slunk away with his tail between his legs. He waved a hand in greeting. The *grump* lifted a hand from the reins in acknowledgment.

"Is this a town?" It had been so long since Ana had spoken that her lips were stiff.

"Sort of."

She peeked at him. He sat hunched over, his forearms resting on his thighs, his booted foot on the front board of the wagonbox. The silence thickened and grated on her nerves. What made the man so rude? So crotchety? What had fueled his dislike of her? Was he angry because he had to make the trip to Lansing to get her? From the looks of the lumber in the back of the wagon he had probably had to make the trip anyway. She was here by Harriet's invitation. Perhaps the *grouch* didn't understand good manners. Assuming that was the case, she decided to try another approach to get his attention.

"You ration your words as if they were little gold nuggets to be doled out on special occasions," she remarked in a curt, haughty tone. "What exactly do you mean by . . . sort of? It is either a town, or it is not."

At her sharp words, his head swiveled slowly toward her. Ana was appalled at herself for speaking so sharply, but it was too late to back down now.

"Does it look like a town?"

They had passed four widely spaced buildings that appeared to be the business section. One was definitely a blacksmith shop and one a general store. She had no idea what purpose the other two served. Not one person was in sight. If not for the very few lights that shone from the windows of the houses lining the road as they approached, she would think it was a deserted place.

"It does not look like a *town*. It does not look like anything but a wide spot in the road. But even such a dreary place as this must have a name. Or is that some deep dark secret you're keeping to yourself?"

"White Oak."

"White Oak," Ana repeated. "Well, thank you very much for that very valuable piece of information. Harriet had not mentioned White Oak in her letter." When Ana received only a grunt for a reply, her jaw grew stubborn. "I sincerely hope that all the Jamison's are not as cantankerous as you are. If that's the case, I certainly pity poor Harriet having to live among them."

He studied her from beneath the brim of his hat. Even in the near dark she could see the disapproval in every line of his face. There was something hard and frightening about his size, his silence, and his gaze. The hard planes of his face were taut as if he were under some sort of strain. When he spoke, his words were tinged with bitterness.

"She wouldn't be here if you'd done what you should, instead of letting her loose to prowl like a common street woman."

The quiet words stunned Ana for a moment. Shards of pain pierced her heart; then anger flared.

"What in the world are you talking about?" When he didn't answer, she demanded in a louder, strident voice, "I resent you calling Harriet a common st—" She couldn't say the word. "I demand to know what you meant by that remark."

"Just what I said." He glowered at her for a moment before he turned away.

"I heard what you said. But I want to know the reasoning behind your insulting comment. You know nothing about me or Harriet. If you can't be decent, I'll thank you to keep a civil tongue in your head."

After a tense, heavy, waiting period, Ana knew from the

set of his face that he was not going to say another word. So much for a civil conversation! Once they reached the farm, she hoped never to see the uncouth bore again. But realistically she knew that was an impossible wish.

A half-hour of silence passed while Ana pondered his words. She had done her best with Harriet, or had she? During the long, lonely winter months she had relived the trying days of last September and wondered if she should have done something differently. But what? Lock the girl up? Harriet had been determined to meet her laughing, dancing man. For a few short weeks she had been so supremely happy. The scoundrel had used the young, innocent girl! He had made her pregnant, left her to face the consequences alone, and had returned home.

Poor Harriet. She must have been desperate to follow him. Ana knew why the girl had been unable to confide in her: she had known how disappointed Ana would be. How lonely and frightened the child must have been. Harriet had been scared each time she had a cold, thinking it would turn into the lung sickness. If she cut her hand she would be sure her arm would have to be taken off. Now she was afraid that she would die in childbirth. It was a natural fear, but she was young and strong.

When the wagon turned into a lane, the tired horses picked up speed knowing they were close to home. Ahead, Ana could see a house. It was two-storied with lights shining from the long, narrow windows on both floors. The shadow of a huge barn with a dome-shaped roof was behind the house, but she could see nothing more.

"Is this the Jamison place?"

"It is," he replied curtly.

"Well, thank goodness!" Ana said in the same curt tone. She glanced at his dim profile with a look of utter disgust on her face and shook her head in dismay. At last the journey was over. The rest of the Jamison's couldn't possibly be as unfriendly as this one.

As they passed close to the front of the house, Ana could

see a porch with fancy wooden grillwork spreading across the front of it. On the side, light from an open door made a bright path across another porch. They turned into an area between the barn and the house. Ana heard the squeak of a windmill and the lowing of cows as they gathered around a watering tank. She sniffed the air; there must be a hogpen nearby. A dog came bounding out of the darkness and raced around the team, yipping a happy welcome.

The big, silent man ignored the barking dog, wrapped the reins around the brake handle and got down from the wagon without a word to Ana—not that she expected one.

She threw off the coat and eased herself off the high seat. With her feet on solid ground, Ana stood for a moment holding on to the wheel. Her legs were trembly. It had been at least five hours since she had stood on them. She'd had nothing to eat since morning, and her bladder was not the size of a bucket, she thought irritably. It was painfully full. Anxious to see Harriet, Ana held onto the side of the wagon and made her way to the back of it even though her feet and legs still tingled. The tailgate had been let down and her trunk pulled to the end of the wagon.

The man said nothing to her. No words of welcome. He didn't so much as acknowledge her presence. A door slammed and a man came ambling out toward the wagon. A gruff male voice called out. The words caused Ana's hands to freeze momentarily on the rough boards and her mind to doubt her hearing.

"Ya made good time, Owen."

Owen? Harriet's husband's name was Owen Jamison! Ana's disbelieving eyes went to the dark shape of the man lifting her trunk.

"But I wore the horses out doing it." The reply was gruff, surly.

"*You're* . . . Harriet's h-husband?" The words just barely came from Ana's dry mouth. This gruff, hostile, infuriating man was Harriet's *beloved*?

"Who did you expect?"

"Certainly not someone like—"

A scream pierced the air cutting off Ana's words. It was high and shrill and filled with torment.

"Oh! Oh! What's that?" Ana gasped.

"It's the lass, Owen. She's been a yellin' like that off 'n' on for a spell. Esther's plumb put out with her." The man who had come from the house leaned against the side of the wagon with his hands in the bib of his overalls.

"Is he talking about Harriet?" Ana asked, fear making her voice loud. "Is she having the baby?"

"Sounds like it," Owen said and lifted the trunk.

Ana didn't wait for an escort. She hurried toward the light shining from the back door of the house. As she stepped up on the back porch, another scream rent the silent night. This one was cut off abruptly. Terrified, Ana threw open the door and vaulted into the kitchen. A woman with dark, curly hair floating around a plump, pleasant face sat in a rocking chair, resting her head against the back. She was rocking and humming. When she saw Ana, she stopped rocking, sat up straight, and stared at her with large dark eyes.

"Who in thunder are you?"

"Where is Harriet?"

"Upstairs." The woman leaned back and started rocking again.

Ana's glance swept the kitchen while she hurriedly removed her gloves and hat and placed them on the table. The room contained the necessities, but nothing to make it cozy or homelike, not even a curtain on the window. Stark was the only way she could describe it.

"Take me to her, please."

The woman in the chair looked at her and slowly shook her head. Ana gave her a second startled look and realized that although she was not a young girl, she seemed childlike.

"Esther said stay down here."

"Take her upstairs, Hettie." The words came from Owen as he angled himself and Ana's trunk in through the doorway.

"I don't want to." The woman began to rock furiously.

"Do as I tell you," Owen said impatiently.

"No! That city girl's makin' a awful racket 'bout havin' a youngun. Esther said it ain't decent."

"This is Harriet's mother. Take her upstairs."

"'T'aint so. She ain't old enough to be Harriet's ma. She ain't got no gray hair."

"I'm Harriet's stepmother."

Ana was tired, hungry and her patience was wearing thin. She turned to face Harriet's husband. He seemed even bigger and taller than he did when she met him on the street in Lansing. He was looking her up and down in such a way that she fought the urge to cross her arms protectively over her chest. Her hair had come loose from the pins again. She lifted her arms to poke the errant strands in place, not realizing how the movement outlined her firm, high breasts, and not seeing the man's eyes flick down to them.

Owen Jamison also noticed Ana's trim waist, the soft skin of her face and neck, and the resentment in the eyes that stared back at him.

"Did you bring me a pretty, Owen?" The whining voice of the woman in the chair broke the silence. "What's she got in the trunk?"

"Mind me, Hettie. Take her upstairs."

The man in the overalls came in and the door slammed behind him. He stood leaning against the doorjamb, his hands still in the bib. His hair was iron gray, his face lined. His faded eyes, once as blue as Owen's, watched the scene with interest.

"Esther won't like it," Hettie said stubbornly.

"Gowdamighty! Don't you ever do anything you're told to do without arguing about it?"

The trunk hit the floor with a loud thump.

Hettie burst into tears.

Three

Owen took the lamp from the kitchen table and motioned for Ana to follow. She hurried after him, noting that he limped even more than he had in Lansing. They passed down a narrow hallway to a door at the end. Owen flung it open and handed Ana the lamp.

"She's up there." He turned on his heel, and left her.

Ana went up the steep stairway holding her skirt up with one hand and the lamp in the other. The upper hall was as narrow as the lower one. A light shone from beneath a door at the far end. Ana's heels on the wooden floor echoed as she hurried down the hall and pushed open the door.

The room was dimly lit, but what Ana saw caused her eyes to go wide with surprise and horror. Harriet lay writhing on the bed. Her hands were tied to the iron bedstead above her head. A rag was tied over her mouth. The girl's eyes rolled with crazed terror. A woman in a black, high-necked, long-sleeved dress stood beside the bed, her arms folded across her flat bosom. She jerked around to face Ana.

"Who are you? What are you doing here?" The woman's

hair was parted in the middle and slicked back into a knot at the back of her head. Her face was sharp and bony, and her ears large.

"I'm Harriet's mother," Ana said in a no-nonsense voice, setting the lamp on the washstand and hurrying to Harriet's bedside. "Oh, honey—" Her nervous fingers began to work at the knot tied in the rag holding the gag in place.

"Stop that!" The woman's heavy hand came down on Ana's shoulder. "If she can't keep quiet, the gag stays."

Ana reared up in surprise. Her arm went flying out across the woman's chest, shoving her back.

"Get your hands off me! I've never heard of such inhumane treatment in all my life. If you don't want to hear her screams, get out!"

"It's disgraceful the way she's been carrying on."

"You'd carry on, too, if your body was being torn apart. Now stay out of my way." Ana had never been so close to hitting anyone in her life.

The instant Ana pulled the rag from Harriet's mouth a powerful contraction shook her. She let out an agonizing scream as pain took over her body and mind.

"See what I mean? It ain't decent."

"M-ma . . . ma! M-ma . . . ma!" Harriet rolled her head on the pillow while Ana worked to loosen the bonds that held her arms above her head.

"I'm here, honey. I'm here," Ana crooned.

"M-ma . . . ma! M-ma . . . ma!" Harriet's eyes, glazed with pain, looked right through Ana without seeing her. Her face was white and slick with perspiration.

"My word!" Ana gasped when she threw back the covers to lift Harriet's legs and bend them at the knees. The girl lay on an oilcloth in a puddle of blood, water and excrement. A stench arose that almost choked Ana. She looked into the dark, glittering eyes of the woman who stood like a black vulture at the foot of the bed, her arms still folded across her flat chest.

"How dare you let her lie in this . . . filth!"

"What do you mean . . . filth? The oilcloth protects the bed from the mess of birthing."

"I don't give a holy damn about the bed!" Ana shouted in a voice she had never used in her life.

The woman drew in a quick, gasping breath. "Swearing! I'll not have swearing in my house."

"You'll get more than swearing, you mean old witch, if you don't get clean bedding for my daughter."

"Well, I never! You're wicked! Just like her." She jerked her head toward the suffering girl.

"You're a stupid, ignorant woman!"

"It's God's will that all women suffer during childbirth. It's his punishment for Eve tempting Adam in the Garden of Eden," she said with her mouth puckered like a prune.

"Leave God out of this! You're the one who's wicked," Ana shouted, almost beside herself with anger. "You'd let a child be born in this filth?"

"Women have been having babies since the beginning of time. My mother had a child out in the potato patch all by herself and carried it to the house."

"You ignorant clod! You crazy, cruel-hearted woman! I'll not argue with you now." Ana ripped off the sheet covering Harriet and threw it on the floor. "Get me some clean bedding for my daughter, or . . . I swear I'll . . . pull every hair out of your ugly head!"

"My brother will throw you out of this house! You're nothing but an intruder."

"Damn you, and damn your stupid clod of a brother to hell! Harriet needs clean bedclothes, and I'll tear this place apart if she doesn't get them."

The woman stood with her head up and her arms crossed, a defiant gleam in her dark eyes. Ana marched to the door and threw it open.

"Owen!" she yelled at the top of her lungs. "Owen Jamison, get up here."

"No!" the woman screeched and exploded into action.

"He'll not come in here!" She tried to close the door, but Ana shoved her aside.

"Owen!" The yell was accompanied by Harriet's sudden scream. Ana ran to the bed and grabbed her daughter's hands. Minutes passed while the tortuous pain rolled over Harriet.

The woman closed the door and stood against it.

There was a pounding on the door, then Owen pushed it open and came into the room. Ana almost didn't recognize him without his hat. His hair was soft and wavy. He had an aura of hard vitality about him she hadn't noticed before. His size overpowered everything else in the room. For a minute she could only stare at him helplessly. He turned to his sister who had grabbed his arm possessively.

"Esther?"

"Get out, Owen. It's not fitting for you to be here." She tried to push him back out the door.

"Stay!" Ana commanded. "Why shouldn't he be here? He's the one responsible for her condition!" Ana was holding tightly to Harriet's hands as pain rolled over her again. "My daughter needs a doctor."

"The nearest one is in Lansing. He couldn't get here until tomorrow night. Esther and some of the women attend the birthings here in White Oak."

"Then I'm surprised if any of the women live! Look at this bed," Ana demanded. "This stupid woman had her hands tied above her head and a gag in her mouth. If you're any man at all, Owen Jamison, you'll get clean bedding for your wife. Do you want your child to be born in this filth?"

"What's going on here, Esther?"

Ana heard the puzzled tone in Owen's voice. She looked up to see the look of dismay on his face as his eyes fastened on Harriet and the condition of the bed.

"Don't let her interfere. It's God's will that women suffer during childbirth."

"What is the matter with that crazy woman?" Ana demanded of Owen. "Your wife and your baby will die of fever if she delivers in this mess. I need clean pads to put under her. There isn't even warm water here to wash her, or the baby either, for that matter. What did she plan to wrap the baby in?'' Ana demanded, her voice quivering with rage. ''Or did she plan to let it lie here and die?''

''Get what she needs, Esther.''

''Owen! No! The stain will be forever on our mother's bedsheets!'' Esther's voice was a horrified screech, her thin mouth worked even after she had finished speaking.

''Who in hell cares about the stains on the sheets?'' Ana's voice was even louder than Esther's. ''This woman is crazy. Can't you see that?''

Ana stood, drew off her suit jacket, rolled the sleeves of her blouse up above her elbows, and unfastened two buttons at the neck of her blouse. She looked pleadingly at the big man with the puzzled look on his face.

''Well, I never!'' Esther gasped. ''Flaunting yourself in front of my brother in the very room where his wife is giving birth! That shows what kind of a loose, ungodly woman you are. A woman who swears is a disciple of Satan. It says so right in the Bible.''

The last of her words were drowned out by Harriet's bellow. When the pain rolled away, the girl opened her eyes and stared at Ana.

''M-mama? Is it you? Am I . . . dreamin'?''

''No, darling. You're not dreaming.''

''Don't go!''

''I'm staying right here with you. You'll have your baby soon now.''

''Mama, I'm so . . . sorry—''

''Shhh . . . It's all right—'' Ana placed her hand on the girl's swollen abdomen. ''How long has she been in labor?'' she demanded of Esther.

''How do I know? Ask her.''

''M-mama . . . don't go. Don't let Esther run you off,'' Harriet said frantically, holding tightly to Ana's hands. Tears rolled from the corners of her fearful eyes. She rocked on the bed and moaned like a wounded animal.

"Don't worry, honey. That old black crow doesn't scare me at all."

Ana's words seemed to comfort Harriet as she closed her eyes against the pain. Ana lifted her head and glared at Owen, surprised to see the look of concern on his face. Their eyes met. Ana made no attempt to hide her contempt for a man who would abandon his wife and allow her to be treated in such a manner by a woman who was obviously demented.

"Mr. Jamison," she said bitingly, "do you put clean straw in the stalls when your animals give birth? How many of those born in the manure live?"

His eyes searched Ana's face. He was having difficulty thinking of her as Harriet's stepmother, and he was shocked by Esther's treatment of the girl. He knew his sister didn't like Harriet, thinking she had enticed him to marry her on the day he met her in Lansing. She had told him again and again the girl was lazy, shiftless and ungodly. He knew that Esther would resent any woman coming into this house, but to treat her like this—

"Get the sheets, Esther. Plenty of them," he said briskly. "I'll fire up the stove and put on the water."

"I'll not stay and see our mother's things desecrated," Esther said heatedly, her dark eyes flashing hatred at Ana. The two spots of red on her cheekbones were the only color in her face.

"The child is a Jamison, Esther," Owen said on his way to the door.

"If you insist that I do this, I'll leave, never to return," she threatened.

"Do what you have to do," he answered with a bite in his voice, "but get the sheets or whatever else she needs. The damn sheets will wash!"

"See what you've done," Esther said as Owen's footsteps faded down the hallway. "See what you and that *slut* have done!"

Ana didn't know what she meant and didn't care. She

ignored her, and the woman went out, slamming the door behind her. Ana eased the filthy nightdress up and over Harriet's head. Her arms were painfully thin, but her feet and legs were so swollen it looked as if the skin would break. What was the most frightening for Ana was that Harriet's stomach was oddly shaped. The bulge was low, but high and lumpy on one side. Ana had been present at more than a dozen births and had never seen anything like it. She wished with all her heart for the doctor in Dubuque who had taught her all she knew about childbirth.

She covered Harriet and jerked open the drawers of a bureau looking for a clean nightdress. What she found were the few things Harriet had brought with her and two crudely made baby dresses and two neatly hemmed blankets. Ana wanted to cry, but there was not time.

Owen came into the room, his arms filled with sheets and pieces of pieced quilts.

"I'm looking for a clean nightdress." Ana opened and closed the drawers in the chest. "Do you know where I can find one?"

"As far as I know, her things are there."

"There's nothing here." Ana closed the drawer and took a deep trembling breath. "Well, never mind that now. Will the woman downstairs help me?"

"Hettie went home with Esther."

"Esther doesn't live here?"

He shook his head.

"Thank heavens for that!" she said, boldly looking him right in the eyes. "You'll have to help me. I can't do it alone." Ana made no attempt to disguise the contempt in her voice or in her eyes before she turned her gaze on her stepdaughter.

The pain seemed to have left Harriet for the moment. She was breathing deeply through her mouth and appeared to be asleep. Quickly Ana whipped off the sheet covering her and sopped up the water and blood on the oilcloth. She tried not to think of the man standing at the end of the bed or her daughter's naked body lying on it. She gently eased the girl's heavy body over onto her side and rolled up the soiled bedding. After spreading a clean sheet on half of the bed, she rolled the girl over the soiled bedclothes and onto the clean one. Then, she hurried to the opposite side of the bed, pulled away the soggy mess and smoothed out the clean sheet. Ana quickly folded two pieces of tattered but clean quilts into pads, slipped them under the girl's hips and covered her. She glanced at Owen. He stood with his face averted, the muscle working in his tight jaw.

When Ana finished, she straightened and looked at the big, silent man when he turned to her. Her amber eyes were rock-hard and as cold as a stormy sea.

"Have you ever seen a woman give birth, Mr. Jamison?" Ana asked, tight-lipped.

"No. But I've tended my animals."

"Evidently you take better care of them than you do your wife."

The cobalt eyes watching her revealed nothing. She might as well have been talking about the weather. When he spoke, it was to ask, "What else do you need?"

"Right now I need soap and warm water to wash Harriet. Later I'll need linen string to tie the cord and a sharp, clean knife to cut it."

"I'll get it."

"Wait. Stay with her while I get her a clean nightdress out of my trunk."

"It's in the room across the hall."

Ana picked up the lamp and went out. The room she entered was as sparse as the rest of the house, furnished with a bed, a four-drawer chest, and a washstand, but they were beautifully made and looked as though they had never been used. Her trunk sat at the end of the bed. She opened it and took out a nightdress. Then she delved deeper for two baby gowns, two flannel blankets and the diapers she had brought as gifts for her step-grandchild.

"I need the water now," she said briskly to Owen when she returned to the room. She walked past him without looking at him, placed the baby clothes on the bureau and moved both lamps closer to the bed. After he left the room, she slipped the gown over Harriet's head, pulled her arms through the sleeves and tugged it down to her waist.

Ana's brows puckered in a frown. The pains had stopped and Harriet, worn out, was sleeping fitfully. Ana pulled the chamber pot from beneath the bed. It had been used and stank. Repelled as she was, she was forced to use it. When she finished, she replaced the lid and carefully pushed the chamber pot back out of sight.

"M-ma . . . ma!" Harriet screeched suddenly.

"I'm here, honey. Hold onto my hands." Fear constricted Ana's stomach. She would never forget the wild, terrified look on her stepdaughter's face as long as she lived. Sweat drenched the girl's brow, and she panted with the force of her contractions. "Take deep breaths, honey. It'll be over soon."

"The baby . . . won't come—"

"It will, in time. Hold on to me."

"I . . . want Owen."

"He went to get water. He'll be back." How could she want that beast of a man after what he'd done to her? Ana thought angrily.

Owen came as the pain rolled away. Harriet's dull eyes turned to him.

"Owen! Come here. I want Mama to raise my baby."

"You'll raise your own baby," Ana said quickly.

"No, I won't," Harriet panted. "But it's all right."

Ana looked up at the man holding the steaming kettle and saw the wholly tender look cross his face before he turned away to set the kettle down on the washstand. Pain took Harriet again. Ana threw off the covering and lifted Harriet's legs, placing her feet on the bed.

Harriet's eyes opened wide. "Owen!" she screamed and reached for him. "Help me!"

"I'll try, girl. Let it come. It will only make it worse if you hold back—" He knelt beside the bed and took her hands.

Harriet stared into Owen's face, not seeing him, but using him as a point on which to focus her mind while her muscles knotted and pulled. Ana placed the palm of her hand on the hardened mound and waited for another contraction.

"Promise . . . Owen. Mama will love . . . him."

"You're going to be all right, girl."

"No. I don't want Esther to have—" Pain took her and she was lost to the world. After several minutes, her cries became weaker. "M-mama, I can't . . . stand it."

"It'll be over soon, honey. Push as hard as you can."

"You don't blame him, do you, Mama?" Harriet gasped when the pain ebbed.

Ana glanced at the man's set profile. "Of course not, honey," she crooned the comforting words that were not true.

"He made me happy and he . . . loved me—"

"No doubt he made himself happy too," Ana hissed, then gasped at the amount of blood that suddenly poured from the girl.

Harriet reared and grabbed her abdomen as pain took her again. She let out a piercing scream, quivered in her agony, then lay limp as the world retreated.

"It's coming, but it's turned around," Ana cried in anguish. She looked helplessly into Owen's eyes. "I don't know what to do."

Four

O_{wen} moved quickly to the end of the bed.

"We'll have to take it or it will strangle."

"It'll kill her!" Ana looked at the pale face of the unconscious girl and back at the man.

"She'll bleed to death if it hangs there, and the baby will choke. The cord will be around its neck." He picked up a cloth and grasped the protruding feet.

"She's fainted! She can't help."

"Can you feel the head?"

"Yes."

"Push on the top of it," he ordered.

Gently, Owen pulled the tiny being from its mother's body. With bloody fingers he unwrapped the cord from around its neck and sliced through it with his knife. It was all done in a matter of seconds. The baby was dark and still.

"Is it alive?"

Owen didn't answer. He lifted the child by its heels. Ana held her breath thinking he was going to bash its head against the wall. He swung it back and forth, then laid it on its back and wiped its mouth and nose with a cloth. Still it did not move.

"Breathe," he commanded roughly. "Breathe."

Owen dug a finger into the baby's mouth to clear it of mucus. He then turned it over and whacked its tiny buttocks with the palm of his hand. The tiny chest heaved, the little mouth opened and drew air into its lungs. It made a mewing sound like that of a newborn kitten, then opened its mouth and let out a screech of indignation and rage.

Ana massaged Harriet's stomach with strong, knowing hands. This was something she knew how to do. After a short time, the afterbirth came and with it a fresh flow of blood. Scarcely aware of the crying baby, she quickly rolled up the soiled bedding and packed fresh cloth between the thighs of the pale girl who lay limp and drained.

With this done, Ana turned to Owen and the baby he was holding in his two big hands. Together they looked at it in awed silence; Ana fighting tears. It was a beautiful baby with a plump little belly with its cord cut and tied, its dark hair plastered against its head, its little face blood-stained.

"God Almighty! A boy—" Owen said in a shaky whisper.

When Owen raised his eyes to Ana's, he was smiling. The change in his face stunned her. He looked years younger. He was actually handsome, handsome enough to turn the head of any young girl.

"He needs to be washed."

"You'll have to do it. I'm afraid I'll hurt him." He held the newborn out to Ana. She shook her head and turned away.

"He's your son. Wash him," Ana said crossly, remembering his seduction of a young and naive girl.

Ana poured water from the teakettle into the washdish and cooled it with water from the pitcher. She dipped her elbow into it to test the temperature, then wet a cloth with the cold water and laid it on Harriet's head.

Owen placed the naked infant in the washdish and carefully washed the blood and mucus from its tiny body.

Fear made Ana weak and sick to her stomach when she checked the pads between Harriet's legs. She had lost so much blood and it was still flowing much too fast. Suddenly Harriet's eyes opened and she looked directly into Ana's.

"Mama?" Her lashes fluttered and fell.

"Yes, honey."

"Is it . . . over?"

"It's over and you have a boy."

"Is he all right?"

"He's perfect. Mr. Jamison is washing him."

"I want to see him—" Her voice, a low painful whisper, trailed.

Owen lifted the baby from the washdish, wrapped him in a blanket and brought him to the bed. His big hands held the baby carefully. The boy's head, nestled in the big rough palm, was covered with dark wet hair, his face was red and wrinkled. A tiny fist was seeking his mouth. Harriet smiled as she looked down at her son. She stroked the fuzz of dark hair with her fingertips, then moved them down to the velvet softness of the baby's cheek.

"He's beautiful, isn't he, Owen?" With tear-filled eyes, she looked at the man who knelt beside the bed. "What shall we name him?"

"Do you have something in mind?"

"You name him."

"Then I'll call him Harry after his mother. Harry Jamison. How's that?"

"Harry O. Jamison. You've been good to me, Owen."

Ana had to choke back the snort of disgust. The lump that thickened her throat prevented her from making the caustic remark that came to her mind.

"I did what I could, girl. I'm sorry you were so miserable most of your time here."

"Promise you'll let Mama have him."

"Ah, girl—I can't just give the boy away. He's a Jamison," Owen said in strangled voice.

"I wish he'd died!" Harriet cried. "With all my heart, I wish he'd died!" She hugged the baby as sobs shook her.

"Oh, no! Honey, you don't know what you're saying," Ana gasped and reached over to make sure the baby was not pressed so close that he couldn't breathe.

"Yes, I do, Mama. Esther has no love in her. She'll take over my baby like she has Owen, and Hettie, and Lily, and like she—" A sob clogged her throat. Her strength gave out and her arms dropped from around the child.

"We'll not talk about it now. It just gets you upset." Ana picked up the baby and cradled it in her arms. "You'll feel better after you rest and eat something."

"Promise, Owen," Harriet insisted. Her anguished brown eyes were fastened on his face. She had not heard a word Ana had said. "Please promise me that if I . . . if I die you'll let Mama have my baby."

Ana wanted to smash her fist into the face of the big, silent man. Why didn't he say the words that would bring comfort to the girl whose life he had ruined? Why was he sitting there like a big stump? Damn him! Holding the child in her arms, Ana bent over her stepdaughter.

"Don't worry, honey. You're going to be all right, but if not, I'll move heaven and earth before I leave your baby here. You know how stubborn your mama can be when she sets her mind. I promise that your baby will have all the love my heart has to give. Now you've got to rest. Sleep is what you need. Your son will be hungry soon."

Ana forced her voice to stay firm until she finished, but she never felt more like crying in her life. A desperate feeling of loneliness possessed her—a loneliness that would be her future without Harriet.

Harriet's eyes, glazed with tears and exhaustion, went from Ana's face to Owen's. It was all she could do to keep her eyelids from drooping over them.

"Owen? You know how it is here. I'd rather my child be dead than to have the spirit crushed out of him. Promise you'll let Mama have him or I'll pray with my last breath that God takes him.'' Her voice had lowered to a painful whisper and her eyes were dull and staring.

"Rest easy, little girl." Owen was holding one of Harriet's hands in both of his. "Mrs. Fairfax and I will work out something so she can look after the boy."

"Thank you," she whispered. "Mama, I love . . . you—"

"I love you too, honey. Can you rest now?"

Ana turned away lest Harriet see the tears in her own eyes and the worry on her face.

"I don't want to go to sleep. Soon I'll be sleeping for a long, long . . . time." Her voice faded, then came back stronger. "Owen! Tell him . . . I love him—" Her lids drooped over her eyes as if they were too heavy to hold up.

Owen lifted her hand to his lips. "I'll tell him," he whispered huskily.

Harriet was dying.

Owen knew it. Ana knew it. She had never felt so helpless in all her life. She sat in a chair beside the bed as the lifeblood slowly drained from the girl. Ana thought of the first time she had seen her—a toddler taking her first steps. A child herself, Ana had knelt on the floor and held out her arms. The trusting, chubby little cherub had staggered into them, confident that Ana wouldn't let her fall. In the joy of her accomplishment she had placed wet kisses on Ana's cheek. From that moment on she had been Ana's child. Ana slept with her, fed her, tended to her while her grandmother did the work.

Her anguish too deep for tears, Ana held Harriet's hand throughout the long night hours. She was losing the dearest thing she had in the world. She wanted to rage at the injustice of it and at the man responsible. If he had needed a woman, why hadn't he gone to one of the establishments up and down the river and paid his money for his pleasure. Instead he had seduced a young, innocent girl and brought her to this.

The baby lay in a bureau drawer that had been lined with blankets. Ana had dressed it in one of the gowns she brought with her and wrapped it in a soft blanket. She picked it up, brought it to the bed and laid it in the crook of Harriet's arm. He was a big baby. Ana guessed that he weighed well over eight pounds. It's no wonder the baby was so big, Ana thought bitterly. The father was a big, powerfully-built man. It took all of Ana's self-control to keep her anger at bay and to be civil to Owen Jamison.

He came in, set a cup of coffee on the table within Ana's reach, and took his place on the other side of the bed. He hadn't said anything for hours. Occasionally Ana caught him massaging his thigh when he thought she wasn't watching him. She would have rather kept the vigil alone, but the man was Harriet's husband and he had just as much right to be here as she did. Owen rested his forearms on his thighs, his hands hanging between his knees, his head down, as if he wished he were anywhere but where he was. The lamplight shone on the top of his head where a few silver threads were mixed with the brown.

"She's going to die," Ana said tersely. "I've done everything I know to do to stop the bleeding, but it isn't enough."

Owen's eyes moved over Harriet's quiet face. "Poor little thing," he whispered sadly.

The words so shocked and angered Ana that she was up and out of the chair before she realized it.

"It's too late for that now. You should have thought of it when you came to Dubuque. Harriet said she had met a *man*. A real man would have never taken his pleasure of an innocent fifteen-year-old girl and left her to face the consequences. I bet you were surprised when she showed up here." Ana drew a quick hurtful breath. "If she'd only have told me, I would have taken her away somewhere and taken care of her. She was wrong to give in to you, but she shouldn't have to die for it." Angry tears streamed down Ana's cheeks. "Were you so angry that she found you that you worked her to death?''

Owen looked up as if startled, his heavy brows drawn together in a deep frown. He held her angry gaze with his for a long while. The silence between them seemed to crackle.

''You're not entirely without blame, madam. You should have kept her off the street.''

He got to his feet and left the room without giving Ana a chance to reply. She sank back down in the chair, tears blurring her eyes. She picked up Harriet's hand and held it between her own. A rooster crowed in the barnyard below, announcing the coming of dawn. Time passed and a faint light came in through the east window.

Owen came silently into the room. ''I've sent Uncle Gus for the minister. They should be here anytime now.''

''Did you and Harriet go to the church in White Oak?''

''She did once or twice.''

''But you didn't.''

''No.'' He stood looking down at the baby. ''He'll have to be fed. The minister's wife will bring a bottle and nipple if she has one to spare.''

''Aren't you asking a lot of them if you don't even go to their church?'' Ana asked.

''Maybe.'' He sat down and ran an agitated hand through his hair, disturbing the lock that had fallen over his forehead. ''How old are you?'' he asked suddenly.

''Twenty-six,'' she answered before she thought. ''Twenty-six, not fifteen. How old are you?''

''Twenty-nine.''

The cold hostility on her face discouraged Owen from asking anything more. He knew she was worn out. There were deep shadows beneath her eyes and lines of fatigue around her mouth. Her eyes were on her daughter's face, her expression bleak. Owen thought he had never seen a sadder face, or a lovelier one.

Time passed slowly. The house was so quiet that Owen

could hear the timbers creak and the mice scamper around in the attic.

Ana held Harriet's hand and gazed at her face. She continued to look at her while seconds turned into minutes, minutes into timeless silence. Her brain knew that Harriet was no longer with her, but her mind refused to accept it. When it did, a keening groan escaped her, and she fell to her knees beside the bed.

Silent tears rolled from her amber eyes and fell on the hand she held clasped in hers. She wept for the young girl taken before she could really taste life; she wept for a baby who would never look on its mother's face, and she wept for herself, now alone except for the small mite who lay beside his lifeless mother.

Ana felt a hand on her shoulder. She had not been aware that Owen had left his chair and had come to stand beside her. Feeling empty and a little mad with grief, she leaned over and kissed Harriet on the cheek.

"Good-bye, honey," she whispered. "I'll take care of your baby. I swear it." She picked up the child and moved away from the bed.

The minister and his wife arrived shortly after Harriet had breathed her last. He said a prayer over Harriet and then went to the kitchen with Owen. Mrs. Larson, short, plump and motherly, had brought a glass bottle and nipple. She sized up the situation immediately and took charge of the baby. She rubbed the little body with oil, put a soft pad over the child's navel and wrapped a flannel cloth around his middle to hold it in place. After diapering him, she put him back in the bureau drawer to sleep.

With Mrs. Larson's help, Ana bathed and dressed Harriet and arranged her hair in the style she liked best. It was comforting to have the little woman with her. She knew when

to talk and when not to. She asked no questions, nor did she
mention any of the Jamisons by name. When they finished,
they laid Harriet out on the clean bed, and Ana went to the
room across the hall.

A kettle of hot water, a pitcher of cold water, and a washdish sat on the washstand. In a daze of fatigue and grief, Ana
stripped off the clothes she had worn since she left Dubuque,
washed herself, and dressed again in her good black dress
from which she had removed the white collar.

From the window she could see several buggies and wagons
parked in the yard below. News of Harriet's death had reached
the neighbors quickly, and they came with somber faces and
gifts of food. A group of men stood at the end of one of the
wagons. Owen was not among them. Had it been less than
twenty-four hours since he met her in Lansing? So much had
happened. So very much.

Ana stood at the bureau and brushed her hair. Her arms
felt like dead weights. She was coiling and pinning it when
Mrs. Larson came in, a worried look on her plump face.

"Why don't you lie down and rest for a while? I'll sit with
Mrs. Jamison and keep my eye on the baby."

"I'd rather not."

"You'll want to sit with her tonight, dear. The burial will
be tomorrow."

"Is that what Mr. Jamison said?"

"Yes. He and some of the men are building the coffin."

"If you're sure you don't mind sitting with Harriet, I'll
lie down."

"Would you like something to eat first?"

"No, thank you. If I fall asleep, wake me in a couple of
hours. Did you plan to stay that long?"

"Yes, dear. I'll stay as long as you need me."

"Thank you."

Ana removed her dress and hung it over the end of the
bedstead. She eased her tired body down on a bed bare of
sheets or pillows. The upper part of her body was covered
with her shawl, and using her bent arm to pillow her head,

she fell into an exhausted sleep that seemed to last only minutes.

A hand on her shoulder awakened her, and she looked into the face of a young girl with dark auburn hair. Her swollen eyes tried to focus on the person bending over her.

"Uncle Owen wants to know if you want to come down and eat dinner."

Ana sat up on the edge of the bed. At first she had thought the girl was Harriet. Slumping forward, she braced her elbows on her knees and held her face in her hands until the heavy pounding in her head ceased.

"What time is it?"

"Past noontime. Everybody else has done eat."

"Who do you mean? The family?" Ana got up, went to the washdish and splashed water on her face. The cold water cleared her head.

"Everybody."

"Who?" Ana asked tiredly while she patted her face with the towel.

"Mama, Grandpa, Grandma, Uncle Gus, the Hansons, the Ericsons, the Kephardts and" —the girl frowned— "I don't know if the Neishems are here or not."

"Is Mrs. Larson still here?"

"Yes, but the preacher went home."

Ana hung the towel on the bar at the side of the washstand. "What's your name?"

"Lily."

The girl was tall, thin and very pretty. She wore a loosely fitted dress with a round collar and two pockets on the shirt. Her hair was in braids, the ends looped up to just above her ears and tied there with a ribbon. She kept her eyes on the floor but darted quick glances at Ana when she spoke.

"Were you and Harriet friends?"

"I didn't see her much."

"Why not? You're about her age."

"I got to go now. I got to do dishes." The girl hurried out and closed the door.

Ana dressed. Her eyes felt dry and scratchy as if filled with sand. While brushing her hair, she looked once again around the room at the dark polished furniture. The beautifully crafted pieces seemed out of place in a room without floor covering or curtains. The carved headboard of the bed was decorated with insets of a lighter color wood. The same matching design decorated the drawers of the chest and the washstand. Ana opened one of the drawers. It was empty and obviously had never been used.

After she coiled and pinned her hair, Ana braced herself to leave the room and cross the hall. She felt emotion begin to infiltrate the barrier she had erected to protect herself from the crushing grief of losing Harriet. At the door she waited for the sickening, spinning feeling to leave her. It had been more than twenty-four hours since she'd had anything in her stomach but two cups of coffee, and she realized she had put off eating for as long as she could.

The door opposite hers was open. She stood in the doorway for a moment, her eyes on Harriet. She looked so young, so peaceful, as if she were sleeping. *I'll be sleeping for a long, long time.* The words would haunt Ana forever. Harriet couldn't be gone! She couldn't be!

Mrs. Larson sat beside the bed. The baby lay in a cradle of polished dark wood. It had a high headboard, slanting, spindled sides and was beautifully made.

"Where did that come from?"

"Isn't it beautiful?" Mrs. Larson asked in hushed tones. She gave the rocker a little nudge with her foot and it rocked gently. "I've never seen one so well balanced."

"Yes, it's beautifully made."

"Mr. Jamison brought it up while you were sleeping. I took the liberty of using the new little blanket to cover the pillow he brought to go in it."

"How is the baby?"

"Sleeping like an angel. I heated some bricks and packed them around him to keep him warm. He took almost an ounce of milk. It's three parts water and one part milk. He'll need to be fed about every two hours for a while.''

"Thank you, Mrs. Larson. I don't know what I'd have done without you.''

"You'd better go eat, dear. I'll have to head for home soon and take care of my brood. Reverend Larson is not the most patient man when it comes to taking care of little ones. And they've closed the school so the older children can help with the planting.''

"I'll hurry then. I appreciate your staying.''

"It's all right, my dear. I'm glad to do what I can. I'm only sorry I didn't know young Mrs. Jamison better.''

"You'll have to tell me what you've been feeding the baby. He seems content.''

"I'll do that before I go. He's hardly cried at all. Poor little mite. Unless you're able to find a wet nurse, dear, you may want to speak to Mr. Jamison about getting a goat. Goat milk is often more agreeable to a newborn than cow's milk.''

"I'll do that.''

The door at the bottom of the stairs was open. Ana didn't remember that there was a landing where she turned and went down several more steps to reach the hallway that ran through to the front door. It was open and sunlight streamed in across the bare floor. Ana had been in houses built similarly. They were built for large families. The parlor was in the front with a bedroom opposite that was usually used by the head of the house. Adjoining it would be another bedroom and four more upstairs. Only the front of the house was two-storied. A long single-story kitchen-dining room fanned out from the back with a side porch attached.

Ana could hear voices coming from the kitchen. Feeling like an intruder, she went toward the sound. As she neared she could hear the rattle of pans and dishes and a voice that could only be Esther's giving orders.

Five

Ana paused in the doorway leading to the kitchen. The aroma of food assailed her nostrils, making her acutely aware of her hunger. The table, with an extension added, was laden with food; pies, cakes, loaves of bread, ham and other meat dishes. On a side board were glass jars of fruits, vegetables, jams and jellies—all of which Ana was sure had been brought in by the neighbors.

Hettie was up to her elbows in dishwater at the dry sink. Lily, drying dishes, glanced at Ana and then quickly away as if not wanting to be caught looking at her. Two women wearing dark dresses and bib aprons worked at the end of the table. One peeled potatoes, the other peeled boiled eggs. At the back door Esther was accepting a cloth-covered dish from a man in overalls and a wide brimmed, sweat-stained straw hat.

"Helga she be down in the back, Mrs. Knutson." He spoke with a heavy Norwegian accent. "She can no be come this day but tomorrow we come. Ja, we be but sad 'bout young Mrs. Jamison, but glad Owen has son."

"Thank you, Sophus. If there's anything I can do for

Helga, let me know. Tell her we're holding up. Of course, we're heartbroken about losing Harriet, but we know the good Lord had his reasons for taking her and leaving the babe. We trust in him. Who are we to question his wisdom?''

Who indeed! The words came so strongly to Ana's mind that she was not sure whether or not she'd said them aloud. Esther turned. On seeing Ana, the pious look on her thin, bony face dropped away. Her dark eyes narrowed angrily, then passed right over Ana as if she were not there.

"Helga sent gooseberry cobbler. This makes three cobblers and six pies.'' She spoke to the women at the table as she unwrapped the cloth-covered granite pan. The woman peeling eggs looked up and saw Ana.

"Esther, someone's here.'' She smiled and started to get to her feet, but sank back down when Esther's hand landed on her shoulder.

"As soon as you finish peeling the eggs, Elsie, slice them lengthwise and take out the yolk. Oh, my! I don't know what I'd do without my neighbors. Owen said just this morning that the neighbors might not come knowing so little about Harriet, her being unfriendly and all, but they've gathered around the Jamisons as they've always done during troubled times.'' Esther positioned herself with her back to Ana and began to rearrange the dishes on the table.

A puzzled look came over the face of the woman peeling eggs. She glanced at Ana, then back at Esther. Ana felt a blush of embarrassment creeping up no matter how hard she tried to stop it. Never in her life had she known such crude, rude people. Even working as a servant she had been treated with more consideration.

What to do now? Owen had invited her to eat. Would it cause a scene if she took a plate, filled it and carried it back upstairs? Or should she retreat like a puppy with its tail between its legs? Tired and steeped in grief, she had neither the strength or the patience to confront Esther now. She would ask Mrs. Larson to bring her something, because if she didn't eat soon she would be sick.

As Ana turned away, wondering how she was going to handle the huge lump that lodged in her throat, Owen came in the back door. She looked over her shoulder and their eyes met across the room. His alert eyes read the situation immediately.

"Mrs. Fairfax—"

Godamighty! he fumed silently. Esther had promised she would be polite to Harriet's mother. He didn't care if she liked the woman or not. Mrs. Fairfax was a guest in their home and should be treated accordingly. His eyes stayed on Ana's white face. Her cheeks were hollow, her skin so pale it seemed to be transparent. And her amber eyes, almost the color of her hair, were swollen and rimmed with dark circles.

"Come in, Mrs. Fairfax, and meet Mrs. Fields and Mrs. Schmulker. This is Harriet's mother from Dubuque."

"How do you do?" Ana said, full-voiced, determined now not to let Esther's actions intimidate her.

Both women smiled and nodded, then looked at Esther who had gone to the cookstove and was busily stirring something in a black-iron kettle.

"She swears." Hettie announced in the quiet that followed. "Esther said so."

Ana colored rapidly. She took a quick intake of breath, her eyes going to Owen of their own accord. He didn't appear to have heard what Hettie said.

"Esther, get a plate for Mrs. Fairfax." Owen's voice was low and firm.

"I can't leave this now or it will stick to the bottom."

"I'll get it," Ana said. "I don't expect to be waited on."

"She ain't Harriet's mother, either." Hettie dropped a cup in the rinse water making a splash. "She's just a stepmother. It means she married Harriet's pa."

Ana was aware that Hettie was a child in a grownup woman's body. She waited for someone to say something to her. No one did.

"Like Esther married my pa," Hettie continued. "Esther don't like her none atall."

Small fires of anger began to build in Ana. What kind of man was Owen Jamison to allow his wife's mother to be treated so rudely? She faced him squarely, her eyes a mirror of her feelings. An odd look of strain tightened his features.

"She was going to pull all Esther's hair out—"

"Hush, Mama!" Lily's strangled whisper was heard by everyone.

"I ain't goin' to hush up and don't you be a tellin' me to hush up 'cause you ain't nothing but a snot-nosed kid and I'm a grownup woman," Hettie said all in one breath.

Shame-faced, Lily handed Ana a plate still warm from the rinse water.

"Fill your plate," Owen said. "I'll get you a cup of coffee and you can eat out on the porch."

Ana took a helping of ham, a slice of bread and a spoonful of cabbage slaw. The woman named Elsie smiled and silently offered an egg. Ana held out her plate and nodded her thanks. With two cups of coffee in his hands, Owen led the way to the door, held it open with his back and waited for Ana to pass through.

The sun was warm on her face and the air smelled of freshly turned earth. Owen led her to the end of the porch where a table was pushed against the wall. It was much too nice a table to be used on a porch and Ana guessed it had been put there this morning. He set the coffee on the table, went back into the kitchen and returned with a chair. Ana sat down and he sat opposite her on a keg.

"You can see how it is with Hettie. She tells everything she hears and sees."

"She's Lily's mother?"

He nodded. "Don't mind Esther. She's upset."

Taking a sip of her coffee, Ana almost choked. She looked directly into his eyes. "Over Harriet?"

"And other things."

"You mean me being here. She'll not have to put up with me for long." Ana looked into his calm face and something coiled painfully in her chest. "Harriet may have lived if she'd had decent care," she said tightly. "Your sister is a cruel, hateful woman."

He was silent for a while, then he said with a sigh, "She doesn't mean to be. She's had a hard life."

Their eyes held. In his she saw intelligence and patience. She wondered what it would take to cause him to lose that patience and put his sister in her place.

In the golden depths of her eyes he saw contempt and anger. He forced himself to observe her with objectivity. Her hair was the stunning color of pale honey. It was coiled and pinned loosely to the back of her head. Wisps like silken threads floated about her face. Her eyes, golden, but just a shade darker than her hair, reflected her every mood. Now they were bright with anger. Her skin was unmarked. It was a delicate pink because she was outraged. She possessed an uncanny beauty of which she seemed to be totally unaware.

"Are you making excuses for your sister's bad manners, or for her cruelty to Harriet?"

It took Owen a moment to bring his mind back to their conversation. "Both, I guess. Life has made Esther what she is."

"Life has made me what I am too, Mr. Jamison; but I'd never be rude to a guest in my home or neglect a girl because I didn't approve of her. I've been so hungry that when I did eat, it made me sick. I've slept in an open shed when it was below freezing, put paper in my shoes to keep my feet off the hot, paving bricks. When I was eight years old, I was washing rivermen's clothes to earn enough money so my grandmother and I could eat. Don't tell me about a hard life. I've lived it."

"Is that why you married Harriet's father?"

"That is none of your business. I've done what I've had to do, but it hasn't made me bitter. Harriet has been in my care since she took her first steps. She was the dearest—" Ana choked and couldn't go on.

"I'm sorry I asked. Eat your dinner."

Owen picked up his cup and went to stand at the edge of

the porch. Ana placed her fork on her plate and massaged her temples with her fingers. A few days. She would have to stay a few more days. Then she would take little Harry and go back to Dubuque. Somehow she would manage. Her throbbing head reminded her that she had to eat. She would need her strength to get through today and tomorrow. She took a bite of food, chewed slowly, and forced herself to swallow.

When she finished, Owen came back to the table. "Would you like more coffee?"

"I can get it."

"Sit still."

She watched him until he reached the door and went in. He was not wearing work clothes today. His dark britches were held up with wide, white suspenders and his white, gray-striped shirt appeared to be freshly ironed. His limp was even more noticeable than it was the day before, causing Ana to wonder if he'd had any rest at all.

She found it harder and harder to believe that Owen was Harriet's *laughing, dancing* man. But yet it was true. He had readily accepted his responsibility and married her. Counting back nine months, Ana figured Harriet had conceived in September. The baby was full term, there was no doubt about that.

Ana watched the smoke drift from the fire beneath a huge washpot in the yard. Esther was washing her mother's *precious* sheets. Steam rose from the boiling water; the strong smell of lye soap was in the air. Lily came from the house and poked at the cloth with a large paddle.

Owen returned with the coffee and sat down on the keg.

"Don't you have chores to do?"

"A couple of the neighbors sent their boys over to help."

"It's too bad this is keeping you from your planting," she said with a touch of sarcasm.

"It'll get done."

Ana looked up at the clear blue sky that Harriet would never see again, then toward a pasture at the side of the house where two milch cows were grazing contentedly. The cowbell fastened around the neck of one of them tinkled softly. The windmill creaked, the hogs rooted in the pen beside the barn, a chicken wandered up to the edge of the porch, flapped its wings and pecked at something on the ground. Lily carried a bucket of water from the tank beside the windmill and filled a wooden tub.

Life went on.

"The . . . burial box is ready. I'll set it up in the parlor."

Ana raised stricken eyes to his. *Burial box.* The words brought reality crushing down on her. She stood as if to run away from the words. The floor porch began to roll and pitch crazily beneath her feet. She sat down quickly and gripped the edge of the table.

"Are you all right?"

"Of course I am," she said sharply.

"The box is made of good, seasoned walnut. It needs to be lined with something."

"I have nothing here of my own to . . . line it."

"You'll have whatever you want. I'll ask one of the women to help you."

"Mrs. Larson has to go home. She's the only one I know."

"There are others." After a few minutes, he asked, "Do you want a church service or a graveside service?"

"Why are you asking me? You're her husband." Ana held her back erect and looked him in the eye.

"I want what . . . Harriet would want, and I don't know what that is." The agonized look in her eyes tore at him. It was a mixture of loneliness, grief and desperation.

"What is customary here?"

"The Jamison's have always had a service here at the house and a short one at the cemetery."

"Your marriage to Harriet was legal, wasn't it?"

"It was."

"Then Harriet was a Jamison whether your sister considers her one or not."

"All right. That's what we'll do. I'll tell Esther."

"Do you need her approval?"

"No. But arrangements will have to be made to accommodate the number of people."

A huge sigh shook Ana's entire body. Her hand shook as she picked up her coffee cup. The last twenty-four hours had been the most unbearable of her life. The pain and the pressure seemed endless. She desperately wanted to despise this man that Harriet had loved, but he was trying to be kind. Ana studied his face while he looked toward the open fields. He was sorrowful, but he was not grieving as she was. His was not the gut-wrenching grief of a man who had just lost the woman he loved—his bride of less than a year.

For that she could hate him!

"I'll have to stay here until it is reasonably safe for the baby to travel. Mrs. Larson seems to have found the right formula to feed him."

He tensed and stood. "We'll not speak of that until this is over and things have settled down."

"I've no intention of breaking my promise to Harriet," Ana said firmly, getting to her feet. She still had to tilt her head back to see his face.

"Nor do I. I promised her that we'd work something out, and we will if you're reasonable."

"There is nothing to *work* out except transportation for me and the baby back to Lansing."

For a long moment, Ana held his gaze with amber eyes as hard as agates. His mouth tightened and an unreadable look came over his face. When it appeared he would say nothing more, Ana stepped off the porch and went down the path toward the outhouse.

The eulogy was brief. Not much had happened in Harriet's short life. Reverend Larson had come to the farm the night before and spoken at length with Ana. She stood beside Owen at the gravesite and wept silently while the gathering of the

Jamison's neighbors and relatives sang, "Shall We Gather At The River." The coffin was lowered while they sang "Nearer My God to Thee." The faces of the people gathered around the grave were sorrowful, and a few of the women squeezed a tear or two from their eyes; but Ana knew that she was the only true mourner. She felt as if her heart had gone down with the coffin and remained there when the grave was filled in.

After the service, the mourners filed by to shake Owen's hand and then Ana's. He had introduced Ana to some of them when, quietly and solemnly, they had arrived at the house in the forenoon. Because there were so many guests, dinner had taken a long time. They ate in the kitchen and on the porch—the men first, then the women and children. After eating, the diners stood and clasped hands while the minister said a prayer. The table was then cleared quickly and set for the next group. Before and after her turn at the table, Ana had sat in the parlor alongside Harriet's coffin so numb with grief that she neither saw nor heard much that went on around her.

It was early evening by the time they got back to the farm. Ana had ridden in a buggy with Owen to the cemetery behind the wagon carrying Harriet's coffin. He offered his hand to help her down and she accepted. He looked and acted like a different man from the one who had met her in Lansing. His dark serge suit was old-fashioned, but well cut and fit his large frame perfectly. His black, square-crowned hat was much newer than his suit. Ana had to admit that he was far more mannerly than any of the other family members she had met.

Esther and her family pulled into the yard behind them. Owen went to the buggy to speak to them and Ana went to the house. Mrs. Hanson from a neighboring farm had stayed with the baby; she was in the kitchen putting food on the table. Ana looked at the laden table with dismay. Heavens! Didn't these people do anything but eat?

"The baby is sleeping like a lamb."

Ana nodded. The woman was kind, but Ana felt a desperate need to be alone. The cradle had been brought down to the room across from the parlor so that the mourners could see the baby. Ana went there, picked the sleeping child up in her arms, and went up the stairs to her room. After changing from her funeral clothes to a washdress of striped calico, she sat in the rocking chair beside the window and rocked the infant.

Harriet was gone. She had to accept that. Mama, Papa, Granny, Mr. Fairfax, and now Harriet. She was alone except for this precious mite she held in her arms—so tiny, so dependent. Harriet's son. Somehow Ana couldn't think of him as being Owen's son.

She wished with all her heart that she and the baby could leave this place tomorrow. It was an impossible wish. She would have to stay here for at least two weeks, she thought now, trying to think sensibly. The long ride to Lansing would be risky for the baby even two weeks from now. The infant needed clothes. He had practically nothing at all to wear. It occurred to Ana that she could spend this time crocheting booties, a cap and a long warm cloak.

The yarn she had brought with her was the dark yarn she used to knit heavy stockings and caps for the merchant in Dubuque. Besides being dark, it was too coarse and heavy for baby things. If the merchant in White Oak didn't have yarn, she would unravel and use the white yarn in her shoulder cape. On second thought, she'd not wait. She needed something to keep her hands busy.

Ana placed the infant on the bed and took the cape from her trunk. After carefully untying the end, she pulled on the yarn, wrapping it first around two fingers, then rolling it into a ball.

The house was full of people again. They were laughing and talking. Ana understood that weddings and funerals were a time for families to get together. It had been the same in

Dubuque. This group wouldn't lack for something to eat, Ana thought drily, her own stomach rebelling against the thought of food. There was enough down there to feed an army.

Owen had introduced her to aunts and uncles and cousins on his mother's side. Most of which, Ana was sure, hadn't even met Harriet. Ana had paid little attention to any of them. Why were they here now? Why hadn't they come when Harriet needed them?

Undoubtedly Esther was in her glory. Everyone conferred with her before they did anything. She was a tyrant who ruled the family with an iron hand. Her husband was old and spoke very little English. Of course Hettie needed supervision. But Lily, poor girl, was totally dominated by Esther.

Ana thought back to the night she arrived. Had it been only two days ago? Esther had threatened to leave and never come back if Owen used her mother's sheets on Harriet's bed. That hadn't lasted long. She had been back the next morning acting as if she lived here, enjoying the attention as the neighbors came to call.

Of all the family Ana had met, Gus Halvorson was the most likeable. She had been surprised to learn that he was the brother of Owen's mother and that he lived here with him. Had Esther, Hettie and Lily taken care of the women's work here as well as in their own home before Harriet came? Harriet would have been capable of taking care of the house if Esther had allowed it. Had Owen allowed his sister to run roughshod over his wife?

No sound prepared her for Owen's appearance in the doorway. She looked up and he was there. Their eyes caught and held before hers traveled down the length of him and saw that he wore no shoes. He was still dressed in his dark trousers, but his shirt was open at the neck. The high stiff collar was gone and his hair looked as if he had run his fingers through it. He looked tired.

"We've getting ready to sit down to supper."

"I couldn't eat a thing."

"You ate hardly anything at noon."

Ana shrugged and pulled on the yarn she was wrapping into a ball.

"What are you doing?" Owen took a few steps into the room, his eyes on the fluffy white bundle in Ana's lap.

"I'm unraveling this cape so I can make booties, a cap and a cloak for Harry."

"We can buy yarn. You needn't destroy something you've put hours of work into."

"It's mine, Mr. Jamison. I don't need your permission to unravel it." Ana clenched her jaws to keep from crying.

"Suit yourself." He looked about the stark room. Her towel was on the rack above the washstand, her shoes sat on the bare wooden floor beside her trunk. The windows were bare of curtains.

"Would you rather use the downstairs bedroom?"

"Whatever for? For the time I'm here, this room will do. I've never seen lovelier furniture than this."

"I suppose you've seen plenty."

"I have. I've worked in some of the finest homes in Dubuque."

The baby awakened and began to cry. Ana put the shawl down on the end of the bed and picked him up. Making a cradle of her arms she clucked to him softly. He continued to cry.

"I'll bring up the cradle," Owen said.

"He's hungry. It's time for his bottle. I'll have to fix it."

"I can do it if you tell me how."

Ana looked at Owen gratefully for she had dreaded going down to the kitchen.

"All right. The bottle is there on the bureau. Fill it with one third milk and two thirds water from the jar in the warming oven."

"Is that all there is to it?"

"Be sure the bottle and nipple are clean. Is Mrs. Hanson still here?"

"Yes, she and Lars are staying for supper."

"I'm sure she won't mind fixing the bottle."

"I can do it."

When he added nothing to that stark reply, Ana turned her back. He picked up the bottle and went out.

Six

"There's no reason for you to spend the night here, Esther."

Owen sat at the kitchen table, one hand clutching his coffee cup, the other rubbing his thigh.

"It's not proper for you to be here alone with that woman."

"I don't give a damn about what's proper. Take Hettie and Lily and go on home while it's still light."

"She don't want to go off and leave you with that fast, city woman." Hettie wiped the dishpan with a rag and hung it on the side of the cupboard.

"Hush up!" Esther said sharply. "Go on out and get in the buggy. Lily, leave the eggs here until morning. Tomorrow we'll put them in the cellar and bring out the older ones."

"Yes, ma'am."

"Esther's 'fraid you'll get in bed with that blond hussy and get a baby on her like you did Harriet." Hettie came to the table and leaned against Owen's shoulder.

"Christ Almighty," Owen muttered and looked down into his cup.

"We didn't have to use a single egg," Esther said, ignoring

Hettie. "That shows you how we stand with our neighbors. Everything was brought in, including eggs, coffee, sugar— What are you waiting for, Hettie?"

"Owen ain't married no more. He could marry me and Lily. We could live here with him."

"Lily, take her out to the buggy," Esther said impatiently.

"Come on, Mama."

"I'll swan to goodness," Esther said when she was alone with her brother. "There are days when she drives me wild. Now, Owen, it isn't fitting for you and Uncle Gus to be here alone with that woman."

"*That* woman's name is Mrs. Fairfax. She's my mother-in-law for Christ's sake!"

"What in the world has gotten into you? You never used to swear."

"Yes, I did. I just didn't do it in front of you."

"Well! I declare." Esther folded her arms across her flat chest and glared at him.

Owen raised the cup to his mouth and took a big gulp, almost scalding his tongue. "Don't push me, Esther. I have a splitting headache. Go on home and take some of that food with you. It'll spoil before we use it up."

"Oh! The whole family has been in a hubbub since you married that—"

"Enough!" Owen slammed his hand down on the table. "Go on home. I'm tired and want to get to bed. I'm behind with my work. Tomorrow I've got to harrow that field behind the barn."

"Why didn't you have Uncle Gus do that? Land sakes, Jens has our field planted. Gus don't do enough around here to earn his eats."

"Don't tell me how to farm."

"You lost two days work going to Lansing to get that woman. I suppose you'll lose two more days taking her back. As far as I'm concerned—the sooner *she* leaves the better."

"Drop it. I have enough on my mind without butting heads with you."

Esther was undaunted by her brother's angry scowl.

"Don't worry about the baby. With my help, Lily will make a good mother."

"I'm not going to marry Lily. Good Lord! Can't you get that through your head?"

"Why not? You married that . . . girl, and she was but sixteen. Lily's almost eighteen."

"Leave it be and go on home."

"If Paul hadn't run off—"

"He didn't want to marry Lily, either. He has a right to decide for himself what he wants to do with his life."

"Then who is going to marry a girl who was born out of wedlock to a mother like Hettie?"

"If you'd stop bringing it up that she was born out of wedlock, people would forget it. If you'd give her some freedom, she might meet someone." Owen's hand went to his thigh and massaged the sore muscles.

"The neighbors know anyway."

"I am tired, I don't want to talk about Lily, Hettie, or Mrs. Fairfax."

"All right, I'll go. When is she leaving?"

"I haven't asked her."

"I'll be back in the morning."

"You needn't bother. I'll be in the fields at first light."

"All the more reason for me to be here."

"Do you think she's going to steal something?"

"You can never tell about women like *her*."

"Thank you for what you've done."

Esther sniffed. "What's a sister for if not to pitch in in times of need." She covered her shoulders with a shawl and picked up a basket. At the door she paused and looked back. "After Mama died, I was all that stood between you and Papa when he got in one of his mean moods. Do you remember that, Owen?"

"I remember."

"I've always wanted what was best for you. You're very dear to me, Owen."

"I know that," he said gently.

"We'll take care of the boy—Lily and I."

"Goodnight, Esther."

The house was as quiet as a tomb after Esther left. For a man who liked peace and quiet, the last few days had been a nightmare for Owen. He leaned back in his chair, his arms raised, his hands laced together behind his head. He was twenty-nine years old and had lived half his life. Would he spend the last half alone? At times he longed for the companionship of a sweet, soft woman; one who would be waiting for him when he came in from the fields. He wanted to hold her at night and talk about the events of the day, plan with her, work for her, cherish her.

The lass he had married was but a child—the poor little thing. She had given him the boy, a tiny little human being to love and who, he hoped, would love him in return. Little Harry might have a yen to see the world and would turn away from the farm as Paul had done. Maybe someday he'd go to the university. Maybe he'd take to the river boats. Maybe—

Owen didn't understand why his thoughts had taken that direction. The immediate problem was how to care for the boy now, not what he'd do twenty years from now. The child needed a mother. It wouldn't be hard to find a woman to take care of him, but if he wanted a mother for the boy and a wife for himself he didn't have much to choose from. Half the women between here and Lansing were related to him; the other half married or older widows.

Esther had pushed Lily at him for the past two or three years. It was one of the reasons he had married Harriet. Esther just couldn't understand why he refused to court Lily, and he was determined not to tell her.

A heavy step on the porch broke into Owen's thoughts.

"What ya sittin' in the dark for?" Gus's voice boomed in the quiet as he came into the kitchen. "Looky here who's come."

Owen squinted at the tall man following his uncle, then got up from the chair.

"Soren? Soren, you ornery cuss!" Owen held out his hand. "I'll be damned. I didn't expect you until time to cut the winter wheat."

"Howdy, cousin." The tall man clasped Owen's hand. "I guess I got homesick."

"Mighty glad to see you. Mighty glad." Owen continued to pump Soren's hand, his stern features softened by the broad smile on his face.

"Pa's been telling me you got yourself a wife and lost her since I was here last. Sorry to hear it."

"Thanks, Soren." Owen lit the lamp. He turned to look at his cousin, then clapped him on the shoulder affectionately.

Soren had the blue eyes and the blond hair of his Swedish mother. Two years younger than Owen, he had grown up with him, and the two had left home together to see what was down the big river. One Christmas, Owen came home for a visit. While he was here, his father was gored by a bull. Owen's thigh was pierced by a horn as he tried to rescue him. The elder Jamison died, and it took the rest of the winter for Owen to recover. He stayed to work the farm and Soren had continued to roam, coming home once a year at harvest time to help Owen and to see his father.

"Welcome home." A broad smile washed the gloom from Owen's face. "Are you hungry, Soren? There's plenty here."

"Pa told me the neighbors had dragged in something to eat. I'd sure like to have a go at it."

Owen laughed and glanced at his uncle. Gus stood with his hands in the bib of his overalls watching his son and his nephew greet each other. They were both fine men and he was proud of them.

A broom-maker by trade, Gus had moved out to the farm when Owen took it over. He lived in the small log house Owen's father and grandfather had built when they settled here in 1840. He had a patch where he grew his broom corn and a shed Owen had built for him to dry his crop. Twice a year he took a wagonload of brooms to Lansing. A merchant there resold them to the merchants down river.

"I saw one of your brooms in New Orleans, Pa," Soren said. "The name Halverson burned in the handle just jumped right out and grabbed my attention."

"'Twas more than likely the pretty lass sweepin' with it that caught your eye," Gus snorted.

Soren laughed. "It was standing in the corner of the toughest saloon on the river front."

"Humph!" Gus turned his back to hide his smile, took a plate from the kitchen cabinet and began to fill it for his son.

"How's all the folks, Owen?"

"Folks are fine. Most of them came today."

"Heard anything from Paul?"

"Not for a while. Paul always hated the farm."

"I saw Esther leaving. Has she mellowed any?"

Owen looked away from his cousin. Esther was a topic they usually avoided. Soren had no patience with Esther, but then he didn't know the hell Esther had to live with.

"I think you've put on some muscle," Owen said, changing the subject. "But that doesn't make you a damn bit smarter."

Soren smiled. "I'm working on the day I can take you down and sit on you—" He turned his head to listen. "What's that?"

"That's Harry," Owen said, his eyes suddenly shining.

"Harry?"

"The boy. He'll soon be three days old."

"Pa told me. It's hard for me to think of you as a papa."

"It's hard for me to think of it, too."

"Who've you got taking care of him?"

"My mother-in-law is here."

Soren raised his brows. "Mother-in-law! Lordy mercy!" He made a sour face. "Then it's best we go out to Pa's for what I got in mind."

"What's that?"

"Getting rid of a jug of good Irish whiskey."

"Sounds like a good idea, but eat first."

* * *

In her room upstairs, Ana listened to the sounds from below. She had seen Esther's buggy leave the yard and was grateful that Esther was in it. Shortly afterward Uncle Gus came from the old house with a tall blond man dressed in the clothes of a riverman. When they entered the house, Ana heard Owen give the man a boisterous welcome. Had another relative come to pay his condolences? Would he be leaving soon?

Ana lit the lamp and listened to ascertain when the men left the kitchen. She needed to make a trip to the outhouse and she had to fix a jar of the baby's milk to bring up to the bedroom so that she'd not have to go down in the night.

A half-hour passed and Harry began to fuss. He was wet and hungry. She changed his diaper, rinsed the wet one in the wash dish, and hung it on the towel bar. When Harry began to cry in earnest, Ana knew she could wait no longer.

The sound of the baby crying preceded her. When she reached the doorway leading to the kitchen, three pairs of male eyes greeted her. Owen and the handsome blond giant at the table got to their feet.

"I'm sorry to interrupt," Ana said.

To Owen she looked even younger with her blond hair hanging loosely around her shoulders, framing her delicate features. It highlighted the golden brown eyes made more vivid by the dark smudges beneath them. She seemed different to him in a way. The soft material of her dress hugged her rounded breasts and small waist. Although she stood only an inch or two over five feet, the proud and erect manner with which she carried herself made her look taller, even statuesque.

Owen glanced at his cousin and saw the look of open-mouthed admiration on his face.

"Mrs. Fairfax, my cousin, Soren Halverson. You've met my Uncle Gus."

Ana nodded to both men.

"I'm pleased to meet you, ma'am," Soren said softly. His eyes lingered on her face and a soft smile curled his lips.

Ana met his glance with a pretense of calm.

"Please sit down. Don't let me keep you from your meal."

"Noisy little rascal, isn't he?" Soren nodded toward the crying infant she was holding, and his smile spread over beautiful white teeth.

"Right now, he is. Mr. Jamison, if you'll hold Harry, I'll fix the milk and leave you to visit with your cousin." Without waiting for a reply, Ana placed the squalling infant in Owen's arms. Holding him as if he were butter that would melt and run all over the floor, Owen backed up to a chair and sat down.

"Let me have a look at your boy, Owen." Soren moved his chair closer and leaned over to peer into the red, wrinkled little face. "Hell! He's no bigger than a picked chicken!"

"What did you expect? He's only three days old." Owen supported the little head in his palm and held the infant close to Soren.

"He's not much to look at." Soren looked over Owen's head and winked at Gus. "What do ya think, Pa? Do you reckon the poor little bugger will grow up to be as ugly as Owen?"

Ana saw the look exchanged between Soren and his father. Both of the men were very fond of Owen. She opened the door of the warming oven to get the jar of boiled water. It was not there. The crock that held the morning milk was no where in sight. Puzzled, Ana turned to Owen.

"Mr. Jamison, did you use all the boiled water when you fixed the bottle at suppertime?"

Owen's eyes met Ana's. "No. It was half empty. I asked Esther to finish filling it when the teakettle boiled."

"The jar isn't here, and neither is the stone jar the milk was in."

Ana wasn't sure, but when Owen's lips moved she thought he swore under his breath.

"Watch his head," he said gruffly and passed the infant to Soren.

"Hellfire, cousin. I've caught fish in the creek that weighed more than this little scrap." Soren's friendly blue eyes met Ana's briefly, then he was smiling down at the infant and lifting him up and down. "Hush your bawling, little scrap. Your cousin Soren's got you." Unexpectedly, the baby stopped crying, found his mouth with his tiny fist, and began to suck. "Whatta you know!" Soren said with a delighted smile. "He likes me! His eyes are wide open. Look, Pa. They're blue, like mine!"

Gus shook his head and chuckled. "He ain't got no more sense than he had when he left, Owen."

While Ana ladled water into the teakettle from the water pail, Owen shook down the ashes, opened the firebox and poked in kindling from the woodbox. Then he lifted a trap door in the floor at the far end of the room, went down into the cellar, and came up with a covered stone jar.

"Is this what you're looking for?" Owen asked, setting the crock on the work table.

"Yes. We've used out of it all day. Mrs. Larson said to let the milk age for twenty-four hours and skim off the cream before feeding it to the baby."

Ana removed a lid from the stove and set the kettle over the flame. She searched the cupboard and beneath the work counter for the glass jar. Finally she looked in the pie safe and found it back in a corner.

"It'll be a while before the water cools after it boils. Hettie probably threw the other out." While Owen was speaking he studied her face with his intense blue gaze; starting at the top of her head, he took in every feature.

Ana shifted, uncomfortable under his intense perusal. She breathed easier when he went to the stove to add another stick of firewood, determined to swallow her resentment of the man—for the time being. How convenient to blame Hettie, Ana thought. She hadn't been here long, but she knew Hettie and Lily didn't make a move without Esther's permission. This was Esther's doing. The woman was going to do her best to make her stay here as unpleasant as possible. Now Ana knew what Harriet had meant when she said, "Don't let her run you off."

Ana was embarrassed at leaving the men and going directly to the outhouse, but it had to be done. Owen had sat back down and was watching Soren bounce the baby. When they began to talk about putting in the crops, Ana opened the screen door, went out onto the porch, and started across the yard to the small building that sat among the honeysuckle bushes.

"Miss . . . ah . . . ma'am—" Gus called, holding the lantern that hung on the nail inside the kitchen door. "You should take the lantern—" He was lighting it by the time Ana got back to the porch. The light shone on his kindly face.

"Thank you."

"You're welcome, lassie."

Gus watched the bobbing light until it disappeared inside the outhouse before he went back inside. Esther was up to her mean tricks again. One of these days she would meet her match. With her bossy ways and possessiveness of Owen and the farm, she had made Owen's wife miserable. Esther was sly. He and Soren had talked about the hold Esther had on Owen many times. Would the man ever see his sister for what she was—a miserable woman who was determined to dominate all of those around her? Mrs. Fairfax was a nice woman. Owen should get down on his knees and beg her to stay and take care of his son. She would certainly be a better influence on the lad than Esther.

"She's not like any mother-in-law I ever saw," Soren was saying when Gus went back inside the house. "Hell's bells! She's pretty as a speckled pup."

Owen grinned. "A speckled wolf cub is nearer the truth. She can get her back up quicker than scat. Then watch out. She was Harriet's stepmother," he said as an afterthought.

"That's more like it. How about Harriet's father?"

"Mrs. Fairfax has been a widow for five years."

"She's a damn handsome woman." Soren looked hungrily at the pie his father brought to the table. "I bet Esther went up like a puff of smoke as soon as she set her eyes on her."

"I'll take the boy so you can finish eating. Uncle Gus, cut this hungry gut a big hunk of that pie."

The water had boiled and the teakettle had been moved to a cooler part of the stove when Ana came in. She washed her hands, then the baby's bottle and nipple. Now there was nothing to do until the water cooled. Owen was holding the baby, his blond cousin was eating, and Gus was listening to the conversation between the two men.

"That's the God's truth, Owen. It's called the Maxim machine gun. It's got a single barrel and will shoot six hundred rounds a minute. It's being built in England, but it was a man here in America that invented it."

"People are getting too smart. A crazy man could wipe out a whole town with one of those."

"That's the price you pay for progress. Say, this is good pie. I'd marry a woman that made pie this good."

"I think Widow Larkin is looking for a man," Owen said seriously. "I know she's got at least two head of hogs, one cow, about twenty chickens and a goose or two. She'd make you a good wife, Soren."

"*Old* Widow Larkin? Christ! She'd be older than my grandma if I had one."

"Many things get better with age," Owen said with a straight face. "Wine, whiskey, cheese—"

"But not women!" Soren said with a snort of disgust.

Ana saw a twinkle in Owen's eyes when they met hers. He had a sense of humor after all. She refused to allow her heart to soften toward him. If not for him, she and Harriet would be at home in Dubuque. Instead, she was an unwanted guest and Harriet was in a cold . . . grave. Desperate to keep her mind from dwelling on her loss, Ana took a plate from the cupboard.

"If the pie is so good, maybe I'd better have some."

"I highly recommend it," Soren said pleasantly. "It's pumpkin with raisins. It's good, but my favorite is rhubarb."

Ana helped herself to the pie and sat down at the far end of the table. She caught Owen looking at her and thought once again that he had the bluest eyes she'd ever seen. Was it his eyes that attracted Harriet to him? How different he was from his cousin. Soren seemed to have a permanent smile on his handsome face. Ana had seen Owen smile only one time and that was when he first looked at his newborn son. He held him now cradled in the crook of his arm. He didn't appear to be in the least uncomfortable holding the child.

Uncle Gus, quietly listening, took his pipe from his pocket and filled the bowl with tobacco from a tin can. The aroma was very pleasant.

"The country's changed from the day you and I went down the river, Owen. Telephone poles all over Chicago. Can you believe you can talk on the wire all the way from Chicago to New York City? By the way, I brought you a couple of books. A fellow by the name of Mark Twain wrote a book called *Huckleberry Finn*. It's the damnedest thing you ever read. Have you read it, Mrs. Fairfax?"

"No, but I've heard about it."

"You might not like the other book, Owen. A lady friend gave it to me. It's about a white woman and her Indian lover. It's full of love and tears—the type of stuff usually written by a female."

"Are you talking about *Ramona* by Helen Hunt Jackson?" Ana asked smoothly. She loved reading above all else. Her leisure time was limited, but when her employer offered to lend her a book, she made the time to read it.

"That's the one. It's a mushy tale of love and sacrifice."

"*Ramona* is a beautiful story. It's not only about the love of a woman for her husband, but it tells of the unjust treatment of the American Indian. It should arouse public sentiment for improving the conditions described in that book. Mrs. Jackson also wrote *A Century of Dishonor*, critical of government Indian policy. She's a great lady and a talented author."

"Bless my soul, Owen," he said with mock horror. "We've got one of those free-thinking women in our midst."

Soren winked at Owen, then smiled directly into Ana's eyes. It was impossible for her to be irritated with a man who had such a lilting voice and beautiful smile.

"Mr. Halverson—"

"Call me Soren."

"All right . . . Soren. Why shouldn't women have a say in matters that affect their lives as well as the lives of their husbands and children? Women in government would be far more practical than men. If women were running things there would be a smaller national debt and no more wars. You can be sure of that."

"But, my dear Mrs. Fairfax, if women were running things, the country would be in even more of a mess than it is. There wouldn't be a decent saloon in the country where a man could drown his sorrow."

"Why should they *drown* their sorrow and disappointments? Why don't they face up to them like women do? Furthermore, I didn't know there was such a thing as a *decent* saloon."

"By all that's holy, Owen! She's a member of the Temperance Union too!"

"Not yet, but I'm thinking about it!" Ana retorted. "But I'll tell you this. You and I may not live to see it, but someday every woman in this country will be able to vote and hold public office. One might even be president. Heaven knows, a woman would be better than what we've got."

Soren leaned on his elbows, his smiling blue eyes locked with her amber ones. Soren loved nothing more than a good debate, whatever the subject.

"You're a female Republican!" he accused in a horrified tone. "You'll have to admit that old Grover Cleveland isn't doing too bad a job for the short time he's been in office."

"Everyone in the country has heard about his . . . his admission that he fathered a child out of wedlock. That's not an example to be setting for the young people."

"Come on, Mrs. Fairfax. The slogan, 'Ma, Ma, where's my Pa?' got the old boy elected."

"For shame!"

Soren laughed, delighted with her wit and quick comeback. She was not only beautiful, but charming and intelligent.

In spite of herself, Ana's lips tilted in a smile. She was well aware that he had been leading her on, trying to get a rise out of her. She had enjoyed the discussion too. She glanced at Owen. His face was as somber as it was when they rode in the wagon from Lansing. His electrifying eyes went from his cousin's face to hers, caught her eyes and held them.

Ana wondered if he disapproved of the banter between her and his cousin. She didn't care if he did. The talk with Soren was stimulating. For one nice long moment she had not thought of the long, lonely years ahead without Harriet.

Seven

"I t was a pleasure meeting you, Mrs. Fairfax. But I'm sorry that the reason for your being here is a sad one."

"Thank you, Soren. And call me Ana."

"All right, Ana. We'll see you in the morning. Owen will be kicking me out of bed at dawn and putting me behind a plow to earn my keep."

Soren glanced at Owen and saw him looking at Ana as if he were looking at a blank wall. What the hell was the matter with the man? Something was going on between Owen and his wife's stepmother that Soren didn't understand. Ana seemed to avoid looking at him, and at times Owen was barely cordial to her.

"You're so mule-headed, I should hitch you to the plow." Owen scowled and picked up the lamp.

"I'll go on out to Pa's." Soren gave a snorting laugh. "Will you be out later?"

"In a bit. I'll see Mrs. Fairfax and the boy upstairs."

Ana couldn't help wondering about the differences between the cousins as Owen went ahead with the lamp to light the way. As soon as she left the warmth of the kitchen, she noticed the cooler air and knew that it would be colder yet upstairs. She paused.

"Mr. Jamison . . . wait. I just now realized that it may be too cold for the baby in the unheated room upstairs. It wasn't this cold last night."

Owen turned and looked down at her. The lamp between them threw a wavering light on his face.

"This is only the first week in May. The nights will be cool for another month."

"Harry and I will not be here a month from now."

"The bedroom across from the parlor has a stove."

"Would you mind if we used it?"

"Of course not. You said the room upstairs was fine."

"It was if it was just me. But I'm afraid it'll be too cold for Harry."

Owen moved the lamp to the side and bent his head to look down at the child. The scent of Ana's hair came at him in a fragrant rush. His eyes moved from where she cradled the sleeping infant against her breast up and over her face. He lost himself in the golden depths of her eyes for one moment. Then resentment rushed through him—resentment of the tender feeling that came over him. He tightened his jaw ominously, and for an instant Ana thought that he was going to refuse to allow them to use the downstairs room; but he nodded as if in agreement.

"You can wait in the kitchen while I build a fire in the stove. It'll take a while for the room to warm up."

"I can do it. You were going out to visit with Soren and his father."

"They can wait."

"I'll leave Harry here and bring down what he'll need for the night," Ana said placing the baby carefully in the middle of the kitchen table.

"As soon as I get the fire going, I'll bring down the cradle." Owen filled his arms with wood and kindling from the woodbox.

"It's a beautiful cradle. Did you send to Dubuque for it?"

Ana tucked the blanket about the baby. When he didn't answer, she looked up. He was leaving the room, and if he did answer, she didn't hear it.

A half-hour later, Ana carried the baby to the bedroom, where Owen had built a fire in a round iron stove sitting on an embossed tin platform. She placed Harry in the cradle and covered him with a warm quilt. The air in the room was stale as if the room had been closed up for a long time. The furniture, dating back fifty years or more, had been well cared for. A metal drawer-pull had been replaced by a wooden one. The lace-edged dresser scarf covering the top of the bureau had yellowed, as had the crocheted doily on the square pedestal lamp table beside the bed. A faded rag-carpet covered the floor, and a beautifully pieced sunflower-patterned quilt was spread over the bed. White fishnet curtains hung at the windows.

Owen appeared in the doorway with Ana's trunk. She had brought down a nightdress, wrapper, her towels, and brushes.

"You needn't have brought that down now."

"You might as well settle in here. Where do you want it?"

"Next to the washstand."

"You liked the furniture up there?" he asked while still bending over the trunk.

The words caught Ana by surprise. "Yes, I do. It's lovely. Why are you hiding it away in a room that's not used?"

He shrugged his massive shoulders and placed a box of sulfur matches beside the lamp. "This room hasn't been used for years either. The bed's clean. I saw Esther putting fresh sheets on it this morning."

Owen turned at the doorway, lifted his hand in a gesture of farewell and went out. Ana stood looking at the closed door for a long while. He was a strange man. For the life of her, she couldn't reconcile him with the picture of the man Harriet had said she had fallen in love with. Soren was the type of man Harriet had described. Ana could easily picture him as the laughing, dancing man who had captured Harriet's heart, but not Owen Jamison. As far as she could see, the only thing the cousins had in common was their size, yet there was a strong bond of affection between them.

The soft featherbed was made up with fresh-smelling sheets. Ana fell asleep almost as soon as her head hit the pillow, but not before she had time to wonder if Esther had not prepared the bed for herself. If so, why hadn't she stayed?

Ana was awakened twice in the night by the baby. Each time, he went back to sleep after she fed him and changed his diaper. The third time she was awakened, the roosters were crowing in the barnyard. It was not yet light. She put on her wrapper, belted it tightly at the waist, and made her way to the kitchen in her bare feet. Light shone from the kitchen door.

Owen was standing at the cookstove in a faded, blue flannel shirt, unbuttoned and hanging down over his britches. The instant he was aware of her, he dropped the cloth he was using to lift the coffeepot from the hot stove and began buttoning his shirt, covering the generous growth of dark hair on his chest. His hair was rumpled, his cheeks and chin coated with a night's growth of beard.

"Morning."

"The cloth is burning."

"Gawdamighty!" He grabbed the lid lifter from one of the round iron stove plates and raked the burning cloth into the hold. "Phew! It stinks!"

"Not for long. Is the water hot? I need to wash the bottle."

"It's hot. How'd the boy do?"

"I fed him twice in the night. Will there be anyone going into White Oak today? I need cloth to make diapers and a couple of bottles so we can return this one to Mrs. Larson."

"Make out a list of what you need and Uncle Gus will get it. They've got yarn too."

"No need for that. I have plenty to make what he'll need until we get home. Is this what you're having for breakfast?" Ana asked when he uncovered the left-over pie.

"It's enough."

"If you'll get Harry and hold his bottle, I'll fix a plate of ham and eggs. You have plenty of eggs and I'll slice off the ham left over from yesterday." Ana was not sure why she offered to cook his breakfast. He seemed to be perfectly capable of cooking for himself, but she was hungry too. This would give her a chance to eat without Esther's tryannical presence hovering over her.

"It's a trade-off I can't refuse." Ana thought he was going to smile, but he didn't.

When he returned a few minutes later, his shirt was tucked into his britches and the wide suspenders were in place. The infant was tucked into the crook of his arm. He dropped Ana's slippers on the floor at her feet.

"Better put those on."

"Thank you." Ana sat down and pulled on the soft slippers. The man was full of surprises! Kind and thoughtful one minute, gruff and completely unlikeable the next. She watched him fold the blanket back from the baby's face.

"His eyes are open," he said with something like awe in his voice. His big forefinger gently nudged the tiny chin and the baby opened his mouth. Owen chuckled. His cobalt-blue eyes glinted, and smile lines bracketed his wide mouth. "He isn't so red today."

"He will be if he doesn't get his bottle. Didn't you hear him cry last night? His face was red as a beet before I could get the bottle to his mouth."

"Yeah?" He looked up at her and smiled again. Ana couldn't look away. The smile transformed his face completely, making him almost as handsome as Soren. "He's got a temper," he said proudly.

"He's got a big appetite," she said dryly, and handed him the bottle. "Let him have about a third of it, then he'll have to be burped.

"Burped? What's that?"

"He has to get rid of the air in his stomach. Hold him up against you and pat his back."

"Oh, no. I can't do that. I might hurt him."

"Then you'll have to cook the eggs."

"Ah . . . shoot! I guess I'd better learn how to burp him."

"I guess you had."

Ana took the big iron spider from the nail behind the stove and set it over the flame. While slabs of ham were sizzling in the hot grease, she cut slices of bread, buttered them and slid them into the oven. After she had set the table, she brought out a jar of applebutter from the pie safe.

Owen had lifted the infant to his shoulder and was barely tapping the child on the back.

"Pat him a little harder than that or the air bubble will never come up."

"I'm afraid I'll hurt his back."

"No, you won't." Ana moved over to stand beside him and thumped the baby on the back. Immediately the puff of air came from the tiny lips. "Now he can have more milk."

"That wasn't so bad, was it?" Owen said to his son in a soft, whispering tone as he carefully shifted him back into the crook of his arm. When he put the nipple to the baby's mouth Harry grasped it eagerly.

Ana stood beside Owen for several seconds looking down on thick, dark hair that curled at the nape of his neck, and on top sprang rebelliously toward his forehead. A sprinkling of silver threads gleamed in the lamp light. He was big and solid as an oak, hard and stubborn and proud. Yet she had caught glimpses of a softer man inside. There were so many things about this man that were puzzling. He seemed to be genuinely fond of his son, and yet she was sure he had not loved Harriet as Harriet had loved him.

"How do you like your eggs?" She spoke so impatiently that his head jerked up and he stared at her for a moment.

"I can eat them any way."

"Raw?"

"Except raw. I prefer them scrambled."

Ana went back to the stove. The long braid of hair that

hung down her back to her waist swished back and forth across her shoulders. She could feel Owen's eyes on her and was stirred by feelings she couldn't control. The warm kitchen had wrapped them in privacy, giving Ana a glimpse of how it would be to have the companionship of a man and a child for them to share. She worked nervously under his watchful eyes, searching about in her mind for something to say to end the gripping awareness that had suddenly sprang up between them.

"Are we invited for breakfast?"

Soren came into the kitchen followed by his father. The men hung their hats on the peg beside the door.

"Morning," Ana said cheerfully.

"Morning." Both men answered in unison.

"Sit down," Ana invited, forgetting that it wasn't her place to issue the invitation. "I'm about to scramble eggs."

"Hear that, Pa? Scrambled eggs! We were thinking we'd have to eat cold potato salad and cabbage slaw. How's the son and heir, Owen?"

"Sleeping if you don't wake him up," he growled. "Shall I take the boy back to the cradle?"

Ana turned to look at him. "It may not be warm enough in there."

"It is by now. I added a stick or two to the stove when I went to fetch him."

"Cover him well, but keep the cover away from his face."

Ana broke a dozen eggs in the bowl, feeling terribly extravagant. She whipped them into a froth, added milk and poured them into the skillet where she had cooked the ham. Moving swiftly, she took the buttered bread from the oven and put in another batch. When the eggs were ready she scraped them into a bowl and set them on the table alongside the platter of ham. Soren had poured coffee for himself and his father. Now he poured some for Ana and Owen.

Owen returned and stood beside the table waiting for Ana to sit down. It suddenly occurred to her that she was still in her wrapper, her hair hanging down her back. She looked down at herself and shrugged. She was as fully covered as she would be in a washdress. She sat down and passed the eggs to Owen.

It was a pleasant meal. Soren complimented the cook, his blue eyes warm and friendly. Uncle Gus was quiet as usual, but on several occasions Ana caught him looking at her. Their eyes would meet for only a second before he looked shyly away. Ana decided that Soren and his father were the only members of the family she had found likeable.

"We'll plant corn as soon as the field is ready," Owen said. "The time is right. The leaves on the oak trees are the size of squirrel's ears."

"If it's dry enough, one of us can ride the harrow and the other one plant," Soren said after mopping his plate with his bread and poking it into his mouth. "Pa says he's putting in the potatoes today come hell or high-water."

"It's the dark of the moon. They'll make less vine and more potatoes," Uncle Gus said in way of explanation. "I've used the signs for as long as I can remember, and I always have a good crop."

"Pa really believes in that nonsense." Soren looked at Ana and winked.

"It's not nonsense," Uncle Gus said. "Dig a hole on the new of the moon and you'll have dirt to throw away; but if you dig it on the old of the moon, you'll not have enough to fill it back again."

"Ana, do you believe in all this moon-sign bunkum?" Soren asked trying to keep a serious look on his face.

"Of course." Her smile at Uncle Gus brought a flush of pleasure to his faded eyes.

"Try it, you young scutter, you. If it doesn't work, I'll give you a twenty-dollar gold piece."

"Why, Pa. I didn't know you threw your money away on foolishness!"

"My granny used to believe in the moon signs," Ana picked up her coffee cup and blew on the steaming brew. "She said the blooms would fall off bean and cucumber vines if not planted in the light of the moon. She said they planted corn so that it would flower on the bright nights of the moon. My granny was from Kentucky, and she said they even butchered''—Ana paused, suddenly realizing how she was rattling on—''by the signs of the moon,'' she finished lamely.

''Your granny sounds like a smart woman,'' Uncle Gus nodded in agreement.

''She was.''

Owen got up and brought the large granite coffee pot to the table and filled the cups. He had just taken his place at the table when he cocked his head to listen. Ana heard a horse snort. Owen's brows were drawn together in a familiar frown. He left his chair to go to the door. It opened before he reached it, and Esther stood there surveying the scene at the table with a scowl of disapproval on her face.

Soren was the first to speak. He got to his feet and reached her in two giant steps. He pulled her stiffened body into his arms and gave her a hug.

''As I live and breathe. Cousin Esther!''

''Hello, Soren,'' she said pushing herself away from him. ''What are you doing here? You usually show up in July.''

''I got homesick to see that smiling face of yours, Cousin Esther.'' Soren captured her chin with his thumb and forefinger, not in the least put out by her cold response to his greeting. ''Don't you have a smile for your favorite cousin?''

She jerked her chin loose from his grasp. ''Stop acting the fool, Soren,'' she snapped. ''I came to fix breakfast.''

''We've had breakfast. Mrs. Fairfax cooked us up a bait of ham and eggs.'' Soren said pleasantly. ''Mmmm . . . it was good.'' He patted his midsection.

Esther's icy glance swept over Ana, over the table, and into the empty egg basket sitting on the work counter.

''I see she used the eggs I was saving for a custard. Well, I hope you enjoyed them.''

''There's more in the cellar, so don't fuss about it.'' Owen's voice held only a slight rebuke.

"But not enough," Esther snapped. "I suppose she used the cream too."

"Esther! Don't fuss." The tick flashed in Owen's jaw again.

"Don't fuss? I got up an hour early to come over here and make you a custard. I find the eggs have been used and the kitchen in a mess."

"I told you that you needn't come today," Owen said in the way of an answer.

"I always come on Mondays, Wednesdays and Fridays. I have for years and years. Why should my routine be disrupted just because *she's* here?"

Ana looked up into Uncle Gus's shy eyes. What she saw there was a brief glimmer of sympathy before he got up from the table and took the milk buckets from beneath the workbench. Soren went to the door and stood looking down at his feet. Ana didn't know if he was embarrassed for himself or for her. She did know that she had never been subjected to such rude treatment and that she was not going to tolerate it any longer.

"What's she doing in here in her nightclothes?" Esther continued scathingly. "She's a disgrace, is what she is! I hope the neighbors don't get wind of it. The Jamison's have a good name in this county and I don't intend to stand by and see it smirched by the likes of her!"

Ana stood. "Mrs. Knutson! Don't talk about me as if I were not here." Self-respect was all that kept Ana from saying several swear words that came to her mind. "How dare you stand there and tell me so piously that I'm a disgrace!"

Esther's eyes raked over her. "I've got eyes. I can see what you are."

"That's enough, Esther!" Owen's voiced thundered.

The silence after Owen's shout only added to Ana's mortification. Blood surged to her face. She clamped her lips together and willed the tears to stay behind her eyes. With her head high, she met Esther's accusing eyes head-on before she transferred her contemptuous gaze to Owen. His tolerance of his sister's dictatorial behavior was disgusting.

"Poor Harriet. Her life here must have been . . . hell! It's too bad her *husband* didn't have the guts to run his own household. In my opinion there is nothing more disgusting than a weak-kneed, henpecked man! If you'll excuse me"— she looked at Uncle Gus and Soren—"I'll take my leave and *she* can clean up this . . . mess. I doubt that I could do it to suit her." Ana waved her arm toward the table and walked out of the room.

"I'm not cleaning up *her* mess."

Esther's voice reached Ana before she reached the bedroom. The sleeping baby was all that kept Ana from slamming the door so hard it would shake the house. Her anger was directed more at Owen than at his sister. She'd like to pound him to a pulp. A grown man who would allow himself to be so firmly under his sister's thumb was beneath contempt.

Ana paced the room. How could she survive in this place until the baby was strong enough to make the trip to Dubuque? What could she do? She had actually begun to like Owen Jamison, not that she forgave him for what he had done to Harriet. *Don't let her run you off!* Harriet's pleading words played over and over in Ana's mind.

"Don't worry, honey," Ana muttered. "When I leave here, little Harry will be with me."

In the kitchen, Owen closed the door leading into the hall.

"Go on ahead, Soren. I'll be out . . . shortly."

"I'll fill the water tanks, then hitch up."

"Why'd he come back now?" Esther asked as soon as the door closed behind Soren. "Land sakes! He's turned out to be nothing but a wanderer, floating from pillar to post turning up here to fill his stomach when he runs out of money."

"This is Soren's home. He's welcome to come back anytime he wants to."

"This *isn't* his home. It's yours and mine and Paul's when he chooses to remember it."

"Sit down, Esther. It's time we came to an understanding about a few things."

"What do you mean? I can't sit down. I've got this mess to clean up." She waved her arms, forgetting she had just said she wasn't going to.

"No one asked you to clean the kitchen. Sit down," Owen said quietly, but there was a tone in his voice that sent a chill of apprehension down Esther's spine. She plunked herself down on a chair in an irritable manner.

"All right. I can see you've got something in your craw. You've not been the same since you brought that girl here last October."

"There was no call for you to be insulting to Mrs. Fairfax."

"I say there was. The idea! There she sat as brazen as a hussy in her nightclothes with you, and Soren, and even Uncle Gus fawning over her."

"She was wearing a perfectly decent wrapper."

"Decent? Pshaw!" Esther puckered her lips and sniffed.

Owen was quiet for a moment, then said firmly, "You've got to turn loose here, Esther. Your home is with Jens and Hettie and Lily. You should be putting your time and energy into a home for them. Instead you're here three, four, and sometimes five days a week. It's got to come to an end."

"This is my home," she cried, "not that rundown place up the road." Owen tried to ignore the stricken, hurt look on her face.

"It wouldn't be so rundown if you spent more time there and took an interest in it," he said kindly.

"I was born here. Mama died here."

"You married Jens—"

"I had too. What else could I have done?"

"I don't know. The decision was yours."

"Don't drag up that muck again!"

Owen covered her clasped hands with one of his. "I won't bring it up. I'm just trying to make you understand that the time has come for you to let go here. Esther, I want a home and a family."

"Well, for goodness sake! You've got a home and now a son to carry on after you're gone. What more do you want?"

"I want peace. I hate to say this, but I think Mrs. Fairfax may be right. You made life hell for Harriet. The girl could do nothing to please you."

"That stupid girl didn't know the first thing about running a house or anything else. I washed and ironed and cooked and cleaned while she lolled around upstairs in the bed. I can see now why she was the way she was. A fine example that woman set for her!"

"You disliked Harriet from the first."

"Yes! A girl like that had no business here. Why did you get tangled up with her in the first place? You didn't have to marry her to . . . sleep with her."

"I don't have to justify my actions to you." Owen's eyes searched every feature of his sister's face and found nothing but bitterness. "You'll always be welcome in my home, Esther, but it is my home."

"And mine," Esther said stubbornly. "My garden is here and the chickens that I raised in a box behind that stove." Her voice rose as she pointed her finger to the cookstove, then softened. "Oh, Owen, things will settle down once that woman leaves. Lily would make you a good wife. She's biddable and does what she's told. With my help she'll soon learn how to take care of little James."

"The baby's name is Harry."

"Harry? No one in our family is named Harry."

"There is now. I named the child Harry after his mother. I'll tell you another thing. I promised Harriet that I'd make arrangements for Mrs. Fairfax to raise the boy."

Esther gasped. "Why in the world would you do such a thing? He belongs here . . . on the farm. Your son should be here to take over the farm some day. We can't depend on Paul. He's just like Soren. Now if you and Lily—"

"Gawddammit! I will never, never marry Lily."

"Well, I never! You've gotten to where you swear like . . . a drunken sailor. At least Lily isn't a slut like the one you married. She's never been with a . . . man. I've seen to that. She's pure as the driven snow."

"I have nothing against Lily. She'll make some man a fine wife, but not me."

"All right, Owen. I never thought you'd forget all we've been through together and turn your back on me. I remember standing over you and taking the lash when you left the gate open and the hogs got out. Have you forgotten the times Pa would have killed or maimed you for life if not for me? His temper was a terrible thing. I know that more than anyone. I've still got scars on my back."

"I remember all those things too. I doubt if Paul and I would be alive if not for your taking care of us after Mama died. It doesn't change the way things are now. I'm grown up, Esther. I don't need you to protect me anymore."

There was a long silence between the brother and sister. Owen sat with his head down, staring at his clasped hands. He didn't want to hurt her. Poor Esther had had no girlhood. He shuddered when he thought of what she'd had to endure those years before and after he'd gone away. Oh, hell! If only he'd known what was going on, he would have never left her here alone. Esther's scathing voice broke into his thoughts.

"When is she leaving?"

"I haven't discussed it with her."

"The sooner she leaves, the sooner things will get back to normal."

"Go on home, Esther," Owen said tiredly. "I've got a field to plant."

"Then go plant it. I've a few things to do."

"I don't want trouble between you and Mrs. Fairfax."

"There'll not be any if she stays out of my way. My land, Owen. I can't imagine what's come over you. Things will work out. We Jamison's have always looked out for one another.''

Esther emptied the teakettle in the dishpan, ladled in cold water from the bucket and set the kettle back on the stove. She hummed softly to herself as she worked, confident that things would work out just as she wanted.

Eight

O wen stood on the porch, uneasy about leaving Ana alone in the house with Esther.

The breakfast he had eaten so enjoyably a few minutes ago suddenly turned on him. His stomach churned. Pain on the top of his head knifed down between his eyes. His life had been anything but peaceable since he'd brought Harriet home from Lansing last fall. To say that Esther had been unpleasant about an addition to the family would be putting it mildly. Since that time he'd had the feeling that he was on a runaway train headed for disaster. The premonition had become a reality the night Harriet died. She was so young and appeared to be healthy. He hadn't given a thought that she might die in childbirth. He had protected her against Esther's bad temper as much as he could, but he couldn't be in the house all the time.

Until now he had been content here on this farm, planting his crops, tending his animals and doing the thing he loved to do above all else, working in the shop he'd built beside the barn. The two trips a year downriver to Dubuque, and an occasional trip to the races at Prairie Du Chien, had added variety to his life. But this morning, before Esther arrived, he'd had a glimpse of family life that had always eluded him.

Poor Esther. For the past year, a hint of something Owen had not wanted to think about had lurked in the back of his mind. Several incidents had surfaced that forced him to believe that what he suspected was more than just a hint. Esther was becoming more radical, more possessive, more unreasonable, more bitter. She still went to church; she was still friendly and helpful to the neighbors, but while she was here at the farm she was a harsh tyrant. Hettie, in her child's world, was occasionally hurt by Esther's sharp tongue, while Lily and Harriet had taken the brunt of it.

Owen had been shocked to the core of his being when he returned from Lansing with Mrs. Fairfax and learned that Esther had tied Harriet to a filthy bed and gagged her. And he was even more shocked by Esther's steadfast refusal to allow the bed to be changed. Two questions had pounded in Owen's brain since that time. Would the girl have lived if she'd had better care? Was Esther responsible for her death?

Ana's accusing eyes, staring at him from across the bed, still haunted him. This morning, her scornful words had scorched him like no others had ever done. *Weak-kneed. Henpecked. Not enough guts to run his own household.* Was that the impression he gave outsiders? Over the years he had gradually given in to Esther because it was easier than constantly butting heads with her.

Owen's thoughts switched to Paul. Paul had resented their sister's dictatorial manner. He was young, his sap was rising, and Esther's constant criticism rankled. She had been after Paul to marry Lily since the girl was fourteen. Both Owen and Paul were fond of Lily, and someday Paul might have given in to Esther's demands. When it seemed that he might be leaning in that direction, Owen had been forced to talk to him to prevent a disaster and Paul had left home.

Thinking about it now, Owen thought that Esther didn't believe that he'd ever marry. Paul would have been the one to bring a strange woman to the farm. With Paul safely married to Lily, whom she could manage, there would be no challenge to her authority here.

Soren came out of the barn leading the team. Owen left the porch and crossed the yard. Ordinarily he would have unhitched the horse from Esther's buggy and let it into a fenced enclosure beside the barn. This morning he went on by, leaving the horse tied to the fence.

"Owen," Soren said as soon as he reached him. "You may think this is none of my business and that I'm speaking out of line, but I've got to say what's on my mind."

"Say it."

"There was no call for Esther to treat Ana the way she did this morning. It was mean and humiliating to Ana."

"I know." Owen pressed his fingers to his temples. *Ana.* She had not asked *him* to call her Ana.

"Esther doesn't bother me . . . much," Soren was saying. "I know how she is, and I know that she doesn't want me here. But as long as Pa is here, I'm coming back."

"Good Lord, Soren!" Owen looked at him with worry on his face and alarm in his eyes. "This is your home, and it will be, as long as there's a stick of it standing." He grabbed his cousin's shoulder and squeezed. "Gawdamighty! Don't ever think about *not* coming back."

"Pa said there's a sow down." Soren turned his face away and hunkered down to work on a kink in the chain attached to the drag. "He expects her to farrow before noon. He said to tell you that he'd keep an eye on her."

"This is birthing time. I'm expecting litters from two more sows, calves from two cows, and the sorrel mare should foal any time now."

"That black and white cat that hangs around the barn has a mess of kittens in the loft." Soren's old grin was back.

"It's a good thing she had them in the loft. Old Digger will kill them if he gets a chance."

"He knows they're there. He had a barking fit till Pa threw some cobs at him." While they were talking, Owen helped

Soren attach the iron drag to the chains. "Pa says that field down by the stream is ready to plant. The Watson boys harrowed and dragged it for you."

"Good of them. I didn't know they had worked down there. If you'll drag the north field, I'll get the bag of seed corn and the planters. We'll finish that field today. I meant to ask you, Soren, if you saw anything of Foster when you came through Lansing."

"I saw him. He was drunker than a hoot owl, and the barkeep told me he had been that way for a week. He'll not be here until his money runs out."

Owen shook his head. "He'll kill himself."

"It's his life."

"I hate to see it wasted. He's smart as a whip. Always has been."

"It was tough enough getting shot up during the last week of the war, but to come home and find your wife's belly swollen with another man's child was tougher."

"He worshiped that woman," Owen said hooking the chain to the doubletree. "Watch that mule's hind legs," he cautioned when Soren bent to hook the chain to the other side. "He's a mean son-of-a-bitch."

"Pa told me." When Soren straightened and picked up the reins, he looked at Owen from across the backs of the mules. "You've not said much about your wife."

"There's not much to say. She was young and . . . foolish."

Soren looked at him with a puzzled frown. "Did you love her?"

"No."

"What are you going to do about your boy—turn him over to Esther?"

"No."

"Have you decided what you'll do?"

"I'm thinking on it."

"You're not giving out anything, are you? You haven't changed a bit."

Owen grinned. "Did you expect me to?"

"No." Soren said in the same curt tone Owen had used.

Ana tidied up the bedroom.

Later she stood beside the window looking out at the apple orchard she had not noticed before. The suckers had been pruned from the limbs and the brush cleared away from beneath the branches. The trees, planted in neat rows, were budding. In a few weeks they would be in full bloom. It was as neat and as clean an orchard as she had ever seen.

Overhead, the sky was blue with an occasional white cloud, the air was warm, and robins were building nests in the lilac bushes. The honeysuckle and bridal wreath were in bud. Evidence of spring was everywhere except in her heart.

She turned from the window and took a dark gray washskirt and a waist of white lawn out of her trunk. Dainty tucks down the front and embroidered flowers decorated the shirtwaist. Ana had decided that she was not going to let Esther intimidate her into keeping to her room, and when she went out she was going to look her best if only to boost her own confidence.

She washed, cleansed her teeth with *Pearl* toothpowder, then dressed. The wide band on the skirt emphasized her small waist and soft full breasts. After brushing her hair vigorously, she swept it straight back from her forehead, puffed it, then twisted the long honey-blond tresses loosely and pinned the coil to the back of her head. Curls at her temples escaped from the pins, but there was no help for that. After she tied a black ribbon, a symbol of mourning, around her upper arm, she picked up the soiled diapers and left the room.

In the kitchen Esther was scrubbing on a black iron kettle; her sleeves were rolled up to her elbows. The front of her apron was wet. Strands of gray-streaked dark hair had come loose from the tight knot on the back of her head and were plastered to her sweat-dampened forehead and cheeks. Her eyes glittered in her bony, gaunt face.

"Where can I find a bucket and some soap?"

Esther bent her head lower over the pot and ignored her.

"Mrs. Knutson, I'm trying to get along with you. Tell me where I can find a bucket so I can wash the baby's diapers, and I'll get out of your way." Ana waited a full minute for an answer. When none was forthcoming, she said, "Very well, I'll use the wash basin."

Esther dropped the tool she was using to scrape the pot and moved quickly between Ana and the end of the shelf where the wash basin sat beside the water-bucket. Her eyes were so full of hatred that Ana took a step back.

"You'll not use *my* wash pan to wash that brat's shitty drawers."

"Then tell me what to use," Ana said patiently.

"Use the horse trough. It's good enough for that slut's brat!" Esther spat, her thin lips drawn back from her teeth in a snarl.

Pure fury propelled Ana forward as a blinding rage possessed her. Her hand flew out on its own accord, and before she knew it she had slapped the woman's cheek so hard it sent her head sideways.

"You hateful, miserable excuse for a woman! Don't ever call my daughter a slut again! Do you understand me?" Angry words spewed from Ana's mouth. "I fully intend to leave here as soon as I can, but while I'm here, I'll take no more of your abuse, and I'll hear no more of your slurs about Harriet or her child!"

With eyes as bright as polished agates, she stared into Esther's face as the print of her hand reddened it. Ana had never slapped anyone in her life, but she was not one bit sorry for what she had done. She faced the woman with her jaw set and her fists clenched.

"You . . . hussy! Owen will . . . throw you out!"

"Throw me out? My foot! Your brother doesn't have enough guts to step on an ant. And I'll certainly not leave on *your* say-so." Ana's finger jabbed at Esther's flat chest.

A sound at the door caused Ana to turn. Uncle Gus, with his hand on the screen door, stood looking from one woman to the other with a stunned look on his face. Pride and anger refused to allow Ana to feel embarrassment.

"I meant every damn word, Mrs. Knutson. Open your nasty mouth about Harriet again and I'll scratch your eyes out!" Ana's anger was laced with contempt and confidence. She turned back to the man who was backing out the door. "I'm sorry you had to witness that. But Mrs. Knutson and I had to come to an understanding. Can you tell me where I can find a bucket to wash the baby's diapers?"

"There's a small wash tub and rub-board hanging here on the porch," Gus said through the screen door.

"If she had told me, it would have saved all that," Ana said when she set the small tub on the washbench and put the diapers in it. Reaction set in and her voice trembled when she spoke again. "I don't know what came over me."

"Esther can . . . try a body's patience."

"Do I dare go back in for warm water and soap?"

"I'll get the soap outta the cellar. If ya ain't in no yank, ya can draw the water and set the tub out in the sun. In a little while the chill will be off."

Ana carried the tub out to the pump, worked the handle until the water came and covered the diapers. Then she pulled the tub out into the sun. Gus lifted the slanting cellar door and went into the cave beneath the kitchen. He returned with a bar of yellow soap.

"It's a lovely day." Ana had calmed until her heartbeat was almost normal. "Did you get your potatoes planted?"

"Not all of them." Gus took this pipe out of the bib of his overalls, struck a sulphur match on the iron pump handle, and lit it. "We got a sow down 'n' I'm keepin' a eye on her."

"Is she sick?"

"She's 'bout to farrow."

"Have little ones?"

"She'll have 'em sometime today. We got a fresh batch of kittens the other day. The mama's white and black. The papa must've been Wilson's old gray tomcat. They're the sorriest lookin' little beggars I ever did see."

Ana laughed. "Little kittens couldn't be ugly. May I see them?"

The sights and smells of the farm were new to Ana. She'd been on a farm only one other time and that was when she had gone with her employer to visit a relative. They had gone directly into the house. Now she realized that there was so much of farm life she had not experienced—new kittens, a sow having a litter of little ones, a big white goose waddling across the yard, and the acres of freshly-turned earth that would nourish the seeds. Ana had enjoyed her small garden plot and her window box of flowers; but this was growing things on a much larger scale, and she was afraid that she could come to love it.

The sound of a sassy bluejay, the squawk of a noisy crow, a cowbell tinkling softly, combined with the rhythmic creak of the windmill as the huge blades were turned in the wind, were the melody of Spring, she thought as she followed Gus to the barn. Inside it was dim and cool and smelled of manure, hay and animals.

"They're in the loft. I'll climb up and bring one down."

"Will the mother let you have one of her babies?"

"We're on pretty good terms. She manages to be around at milkin' time."

When Gus backed down the ladder, Ana thought he had been unable to get one of the kittens, then he took the small, furry bundle from the bib of his overalls and placed it in her hands.

"It's so little and it doesn't have its eyes open." She held the black, white and gray-splotched kitten in one hand and stroked its furry head with her fingertips. "Isn't it sweet? How many does she have?"

"She had six, but one died." Gus tucked the kitten back into the front of his overalls before he climbed back up the ladder to the loft.

Ana moved down the dim corridor looking into the stalls. A sorrel horse nickered softly. She caressed its velvety nose. At the far end of the barn a pen housed a huge sow that lay on her side. The back door of the barn was open and a wire fence stretched across it.

"We have to keep her in the pen or the other hogs would eat her younguns as soon as they're born." Gus had come to lean on the rail beside Ana.

"How terrible! I didn't know they would do that."

"It's the nature of the beast. That sorrel mare back there should foal before long."

"She isn't a work horse, is she?"

Gus grinned around the pipe stem in his mouth. "Far from it. Owen hopes to get a champion trotter out of her. He went to the harness races a time or two down at Prairie Du Chien and got the bug."

"He wants to race?"

"I don't think he's got it in mind to race himself, but to breed and sell the horses."

"She's a beautiful horse." Ana paused at the stall on the way back and patted the horse again.

"He took her to a stud in Wisconsin last summer and went back for her in the fall. He paid a pretty penny to get her bred."

"Mr. Jamison was quite busy last fall," Ana said coolly when they came out into the sunlight again. She looked straight into Gus's eyes so that there would be no mistaking her meaning.

"I don't know nothin' 'bout that. Didn't figure it none of my business. But I do be knowin' that Owen's as good a man as there is."

Ana blinked her eyes rapidly to hold back tears. "You're his kin and you've a right to your opinion. But I'll never forgive him for seducing a young, innocent girl and destroying her life.''

Harriet had been the only person she could claim as kin and now she was gone. Ana moved away from Gus before he could see the tears in her eyes. When the big white goose came to peck at her shoe, she impatiently shooed her away.

On the way back to the house, Ana paused at the tub and jabbed at the diapers with the legs on the washboard, then went across the porch and into the kitchen. Esther was not there. At first Ana felt nothing but blessed relief. She took a long drink of water and hung the dipper back on the nail above the waterbucket. The house was as quiet as a tomb.

Suddenly, out of nowhere, a chill of apprehension quivered along her spine.

''Oh, dear God! The baby!''

Near-panic moved Ana's feet swiftly through the kitchen and down the hall to the bedroom at the front of the house. By the time she reached it and burst into the room, her heart was beating like a hammer in her chest, strangling the cry that rose in her throat.

Esther was bent over the cradle!

''Get away from him!'' Ana cried and darted across the room.

Esther straightened. The eyes that turned to Ana were mocking, her lips drawn back over her teeth in a malicious smile. The expression on her face sent a quiver of fear to Ana's heart. In anguish, she snatched the baby up in her arms, noting with relief that his eyes were open and he was sucking contentedly on his fist.

''Get out!''

Esther's dark eyes held hers. She looked like a silent black vulture ready to swoop down upon her.

''I said . . . get out!'' Ana shouted so loud the babe in her arms was startled and began to whimper.

Esther stared unblinkingly at her for a moment longer, then turned and walked from the room.

Ana placed the baby on the bed, quickly unwrapped him and lifted the gown. She had no idea what she was looking for. The belly-band was still in place. He was wet, but otherwise he appeared to be all right. Ana changed him, coating his little bottom with the oil Mrs. Larson had given her. Her mind was in a turmoil. Was Esther's hatred of her and Harriet so deep that she would hurt this tiny baby? Fright kept Ana's heart thumping painfully.

Holding the baby, she sat on the bed and let tears roll down her cheeks. When Harry became restless, she gave him some of the milk in the bottle, burped him, and carried him back to the cradle. She bent to lay the child down, then froze. Her breath caught and held. Snug against the side of the crib was a small pillow that hadn't been there before! A horrifying thought sprang into her mind.

Esther was going to smother the baby with the pillow!

"Dear Lord!" The words burst from Ana as the breath went out of her. She grabbed the soft feather pillow, threw it across the room and carried the infant back to the bed. With her hands cupping her cold cheeks, she stood looking down at him for a long time while the silence pounded in her ears.

Owen Jamison would never believe that his sister meant to kill his son, but Ana knew beyond a doubt that that was exactly what Esther had in mind to do. The baby was not safe here in his own father's house. The woman was mad! She had to be to even consider snuffing out the life of this tiny being. Ana tried to shove her terrible suspicion to the back of her mind while she planned, but over and over again it rolled like the turning of a wheel in her brain.

Whom did she know who would help her? Desperation brought Ana to a quick decision. She would go to Mrs. Larson in White Oak and ask to stay there until she could arrange for someone to take her and Harry to Lansing where they could board a boat back to Dubuque.

The decision made, Ana packed her small traveling bag with the baby's belongings, a nightdress, stockings, and a shawl for herself. She was already wearing her most comfortable walking shoes. After putting everything that was hers in the trunk, she locked it and put the key and her money in the travel bag. Within fifteen minutes she was ready to leave.

Carrying the baby and the bag, Ana passed swiftly through the kitchen where Esther was peeling potatoes at the table, and out into the May sunlight. A flock of blackbirds rose in flight and fanned out across the sky as she hurried down the lane toward the road. By the time she reached it, she realized she had to slow down or she would wear herself out. It couldn't be more than two or three miles to White Oak, she reasoned. She had walked such a distance many times, but never carrying so heavy a load.

Relieved to be away from the Jamison house, Ana trudged on down the two-lane track, confident that if the Larson's didn't have room for her and Harry, they would know someone in the village who did. She stopped beneath a giant walnut tree and switched the baby to her other arm. Before she picked up the bag to go on, she took one of the blankets from around the infant, wiped the moisture from his face with the end of it and looped it through the handles of the bag.

A half-mile down the road Ana began to pant. She stopped again and sat for a while on a downed log.

"I never thought it would be easy," she said to the sleeping babe. "But we'll make it. We couldn't spend one more day in that house."

The baby seemed to weigh a ton by the time Ana came to another place to sit down. Her face was covered with moisture, her shirtwaist clung to her back, and her feet hurt, but she could see the top of the church steeple over the hill.

His booted feet spread to keep his balance as he rode on the iron drag, Soren pulled the mules to a halt and jumped off. He loped across the plowed field to where Owen worked with the corn planter, shoving the end into the ground, squeezing the two handles to release three seeds, taking a measured step and repeating the process.

"Hey, Owen!"

Owen pushed the planter into the ground to mark his place before he looked up. He wiped the sweat from his brow with the sleeve of his shirt and waited for his cousin to reach him.

"What's wrong now? Did that damned chain break again?"

"It's all right. While I was at the top of that hill yonder,"—he indicated a crest covered with oak trees,—"I stopped for a breather and saw a woman walking down the road toward White Oak."

"There's nothing strange about that. Lily walks to town sometimes. By Jupiter! It's hot for this time a year. I'd give a nickel for a drink of cold well water."

"It wasn't Lily unless she got light-haired all of a sudden," Soren said irritably. "This woman had blond hair—real blond. She was carrying a bundle in her arms and a bag. I'd bet my bottom dollar it was Ana."

"Ana?"

"Unless I miss my guess."

"What in the world would she be walking to town for? I told her to make out a list of what she needed and Uncle Gus would get it for her."

"Shitfire, Owen! She's not going to the store." Soren took off his straw hat and wiped the sweat from his face with his shirt sleeve. "She's leavin' as sure as shootin'. She was loaded with a bundle and a travel bag."

"She'd not leave the boy with Esther! She's determined to have that boy." Owen dropped the corn planter. "Gaw-damighty, Soren! Do you think she's taking the boy and leaving for good?"

"Esther is enough to try the patience of an angel. I think you'd better go find out. Leave the planter and the seed corn. I'll bring them in when—"

Owen had already taken off across the field. Soren watched him run, limp, and stumble over the broken ground as he hurried toward the farm buildings. Wasn't anything ever going to turn out right for Owen? He was stuck here on this farm with that crazy sister. He needed someone. Someone of his own.

Soren went back to the team. Owen had always seemed more like a brother than a cousin. For years Soren had hated the hold Esther had on him. He had asked himself a hundred times why Owen let her run roughshod over him. When he asked his Pa why Owen put up with his sister, he had said that he believed something had happened to Esther a long time ago that had warped her mind, something that was making Owen's life miserable too.

Soren climbed back upon the iron drag and slapped the mule's rumps with the end of the reins. He hadn't been surprised when Owen had said he hadn't loved his wife. Last night and again this morning he had caught his cousin looking at Ana with an expression of hunger and longing on his face.

"Be careful, cousin," he muttered. "It wouldn't take much for you to fall in love with that pretty woman."

Nine

O wen was breathing as hard as if an iron band were squeezing his chest. Why had Ana left without a word to him? Had she waited until he was in the field to sneak away? He found it a bleak and frightening thought, leaving him with a feeling of . . . emptiness.

Esther's horse and buggy had been moved to the shade beneath the oak tree—Uncle Gus's doing, no doubt. The animal stood there patiently swishing its tail. Owen hurried across the yard, stomped upon the porch and threw back the screen door so hard the spring broke and the door hit the side of the house and flopped back.

Esther was seated at the end of the table working the dasher up and down in the churn.

"Where's Ana?"

"You mean Mrs. Fairfax?" she asked calmly.

"You know damn well who I mean?"

She shrugged. "How do I know?"

Owen went through the house to the front bedroom, his boots trailing mud on the clean floor. He needed only one glance into the room to tell him that Ana and the baby were gone. Nothing of hers was in sight except her trunk.

"Esther!" he roared on his way back to the kitchen. "What did you do to make her leave?"

"I didn't tell her to leave. Land sakes! It's not my fault if she ran back to the city. Good riddance, I say! She ain't fit for this life no better than the other one."

Owen looked down at his sister as if seeing her for the first time.

"I'm going to bring her back. I want you to be gone by the time I get here. Dammit to hell, Esther! I'm tired of living in this bedlam."

"Let her go! Let her take that slut's brat and go back where she belongs!"

"I meant what I said," Owen shouted.

"I'm your sister and this is our house."

"This is not your house, it's *my* house, and I intend to live here in peace! Go home to your husband."

"It's my mama's house! These are my mama's things! You'll not give them to some prissy-tailed, sweet-smelling, blond-headed whore!" Esther screeched, her face rigid with anger.

"My God! Can't you see what you're doing? You're making life hell for all of us!"

"She's worse than that slut you married! She knows this is a rich farm, and she's set out to turn you against me. All my life I've sacrificed for you, Owen. I went down into hell for you and Paul!"

"I know what you've done for me. It's like a millstone around my neck! Go home and leave me in peace!" Owen slammed out of the house.

Esther followed him to the door. "Dinner will be ready at noon, Owen," she called as if nothing unusual had happened. "Will you be back in time?"

Gus was hitching the horse to the buggy when Owen entered the shed. One glance told Gus that Owen was in a state of rage.

"Have a breakdown?" Gus asked calmly. With his fists clenched tightly at his sides, Owen turned his back and didn't answer. "I'm thinkin' that sow ain't goin' to farrow 'til night," Gus continued. "I might just as well go to town and get that chore over with. Did Mrs. Fairfax make up a list a what she wants?"

"She's gone!" Owen blurted as he turned to face his uncle. "She took the boy with her. Soren saw her walking to town. I'm going to get her."

"Good grief!" Gus muttered and shook his gray head. "She and Esther had a awful set-to after you went to the field this mornin'."

"What about?" Owen buckled the shaft to the harness.

"It was a piddling thin' to fuss over. Mrs. Fairfax asked for a bucket to wash the youngun's drawers." Gus came to the side of the buggy as Owen climbed in and took the reins. "That house ain't never goin' to be big enough for Esther and another woman."

"I swear, Uncle Gus, I don't know what I'm going to do about Esther."

"I don't know either, son." Gus stepped back from the buggy. "Go fetch the lass and your boy."

Ana sat on the log beside the road with the baby on her lap. She dug into her travel bag for something to wipe the sweat from her face. Why hadn't she thought to wear her hat? She'd have a face full of freckles before the day was over. But what did that matter? she chided herself. Thank heavens for the breeze. It cooled her face, but she didn't dare let the wind blow on the baby; he would be sure to have colic. She looked at the puckered little face of the sleeping child and wiped the dribble of spit from his cheek with a corner of the blanket. They should be at Mrs. Larson's before time for another feeding, but if not, she still had a few ounces of milk left in the bottle.

"You're safe for now, little man," she murmured.

The silence was full of lazy sounds: a dog barking in the far distance, a bee buzzing in the sunshine, the cheerful song of a meadowlark and the sad call of the mourning dove. Another sound reached Ana's ears—the hoof beats of a running horse. A buggy was coming down the road at a fast clip, dust trailing behind it like a big, bushy tail.

Instinctively Ana knew who was in the buggy. She didn't care. It made not one whit of difference if Owen found her now or later. But how did he know she had gone? Esther wouldn't have told him—she was happy to be rid of her. Ana had not seen Gus when she came out of the house, but perhaps he had seen her and had gone to tell Owen. As Ana watched the buggy approach, she wished that Owen had been more like Soren and his father.

Owen didn't slow the horse until he had almost reached her, then he pulled up on the reins so tightly that the animal squealed and fought the bit.

"What the hell are you doing out here?" He was angry, his face set and hard.

Ana studied him, taking her time answering. He was hatless, his shaggy brown hair windblown. He wasn't as handsome as Soren; his features, covered with a film of dust, were rough-hewn, as if carved from a piece of oak by an unskilled artist. The sleeves of his shirt were rolled up above his elbows, showing thick forearms sprinkled with dark hair. She could see angry lights in the deep blue eyes that stared at her. At least he was capable of showing some emotion. When Ana finally spoke, it was in a softly comtemptuous tone.

"It should be obvious even to you."

Owen climbed down out of the buggy, picked up her travel bag and flung it upon the seat. "Get in."

"Not unless you agree to take me to Mrs. Larson's."

"Preacher Larson's? What for?"

"I'm going to stay there until I can find someone to take me to Lansing," she said calmly, but there was a militant light in her eyes that told Owen she was burning inside with anger.

Owen stared down at her, not believing she had actually said that. Wide, golden eyes stared back up at him. The breeze blew a strand of her hair against her mouth that she didn't bother to brush away. His throat worked, and he swallowed repeatedly while trying to gather his splintered thoughts. Finally the words came in a frustrated shout.

"You're . . . not going to the Larson's or anywhere else! You'll not make me the talk of the whole damned county. You're coming home with me!" He reached to take the baby from her arms. She stood and walked away from him.

"It isn't necessary to shout to make me hear you." Her voice was even and smooth. It grated on his already-raw nerves. "It matters not a whit to me if you're the talk of the whole damned state of Iowa. I'm taking Harry and going home to Dubuque!"

"Go where you please, but that boy stays here!" He put his hand on her shoulder and turned her around.

"I'll die before I leave this baby in that house for your crazy sister to murder! And . . . get your hands off me, you blind, stupid dolt!" she hissed like a spitting cat.

"Don't talk foolish. Get in the buggy." His hand slid down to the small of her back to push her forward.

Instead it pushed Ana to the limit of her control. Holding the baby tightly against her with one arm, she drew back the other and swung. Her balled fist connected solidly with the side of his face. A stunned look dropped over his features like a curtain.

"You . . . stinking polecat! I'll fight you every step of the way if you try to give this baby to your demented sister to raise."

"What'n hell's the matter with you?"

"You . . . you pea-brained lunkhead! What in hell's the matter with you?" she shouted, now that she had worked up a full head of steam. "Are you so stupid that you can't see what's best for this child?"

"I've got more rights to that boy than you have." The sound that came out of Owen was something between a snarl and a jeering laugh.

"You blind toad . . . wart . . . fool! You're *rights* be damned!" Words spewed from Ana's mouth like a fountain. "You're nothing but a weak-kneed, yellow-bellied, gutless . . . b bastard!" The last was the worst thing that came to Ana's mind. "I don't care if you *are* Harry's father, he's not going to grow up to be a spineless worm like you and crazy like that old crow of a sister of yours. In fact, he'd not get a chance to grow up at all . . . if I leave him h-here with y-you and . . . her. I w-won't. Do you hear? I w-won't!"

Ana swallowed to clear the lump from her throat and blinked hard to clear her eyes, but it was no use. Tears like dewdrops shone there and slowly rolled down her cheeks.

"Gawdamighty!" For a long moment Owen watched the silent tears streak her dusty cheeks. Then he moved over to the log and sat down. He rested his forearms on his thighs and stared at the ground between his knees. Her contemptuous words had hit him like stones. What hurt the most was that she was right . . . about some of it.

The silence between them went on and on. The baby began to fret. Ana walked up and down, crooning softly to him. No doubt the little thing was hot, and tired of being held for so long. She wanted to lay him on the buggy seat to rest her arms, but she couldn't bring herself to let go of him.

She glanced at Owen sitting on the log with his head down. She felt no regret for what she had said to him even though she had never torn into anyone that way before. What was this family doing to her? They had brought out traits in her she had never known were there. Twice in one day she had struck another person in anger. It was unbelievable.

Owen raised his head and watched her swing her arms in a rocking motion in an effort to comfort the child. She was slim and straight—he was sure he could span her waist with his two hands. He studied her face, unable to pull his eyes away from her delicate features and the huge golden eyes that refused to look at him. On the outside she was as delicate as a flower, yet on the inside she was as sturdy as a rock. The cruelties of life hadn't made her bitter; they had made her stronger.

Ana knew the minute he lifted his head to watch her and wondered what was going on in that head of his. She wished he could make up his mind if he was going to take her to the Larson's or not. If not, she had a long walk ahead of her.

"You're tired." He had come up behind her. "You've walked a long way."

"I'm not too tired to walk on to White Oak if you're not going to take me." She turned to look up at him. He was big—he was still angry—she was alone with him in this vast emptiness. Why wasn't she afraid?

"Would you like a cool drink of water? There's a little stream over by those willows. We could talk."

"I'm not going to change my mind."

"I don't want to lose the boy, Ana." *I don't want to lose you, either*, he admitted to himself. *Ana*. The name slipped from his lips, but she didn't seem to notice.

Ana realized when she looked at him that the anguish was as much in him as it was in her. His eyes were bleak. His mouth looked as if it had never smiled.

"You could come see him," she offered gently.

"Let's go get that drink of water and decide what to do. You look as if you're ready to wilt."

It was the gentlest tone he'd ever used with her. Ana let him take the baby from her arms to hold while she climbed into the buggy. He placed the infant in her lap, went around and climbed in beside her. Neither spoke as he guided the horse off the road and across a grassy field toward the willows.

It was cool and quiet in the shade. He stopped beside a small, clear stream of water that traveled southeast over a rocky bed. Owen tied the horse where he could crop the new green grass and extended his hand to help Ana down. Leaving the baby sleeping peacefully on the buggy seat, she went to kneel beside the water. She wet her handkerchief and dabbed at her face and neck. After drinking from her cupped hands, she went back to the buggy and waited for Owen to join her.

"Do you want to sit down?" His face was wet. Water rolled down his cheeks.

Ana shook her head. "I'll stay near the baby. I saw a bee buzzing around."

"Well, sit here on the floor of the buggy. I know you're tired."

With his hands at her waist he lifted her the few feet off the ground as easily as if she were a child and set her down on the floor next to the seat. It happened so quickly that Ana had no time to protest, no time to feel his hands on her. When she looked up, he was standing with his back to her. He had slid his hands in his hip pockets. The thought went through her mind that he was as strong as an ox. *And as dumb*, whispered an inner voice.

"I know you despise me because of Harriet," he said abruptly as he turned to look at her. "I can only say that at the time I thought I was doing the right thing."

His words shocked and angered Ana. "The right thing? Is ruining a young girl's life your idea of the *right thing*? You're right about one thing, Mr. Jamison. I do despise—"

"It's over!" He held up his hands. "It's over, and there's nothing we can do to change it." His brows were drawn together, and his big hands looked as if they were going to grab her, but they didn't. "It's the boy we've got to think about."

"Yes, it's over for Harriet. It's her son I'm thinking about. I promised her I'd give her baby love and a good home. I intend to keep my promise."

"How?" he asked bluntly.

"I have a house that Mr. Fairfax left to me and Harriet. I work for people on the bluff, and I knit caps and stockings for the merchants in Dubuque. I'm also a dressmaker." Ana suddenly snapped her teeth shut so hard they clicked. Why was she telling this cold man her life story? It was none of his business.

"Who will look after him while you work?"

"Most of my work is done at home. When I have to go out, I'll find someone. A neighbor—"

"The boy stays here," Owen said flatly. "His roots are here. Someday the farm will be his."

"If he lives to grow up!" Ana snapped, anger washing over her again. "You've got to be out of your mind if you think I'll leave him here with Hettie and that warped sister of yours." Ana put her hands on his chest to push him away so that she could get down. He didn't budge—he stepped closer. "Get out of my way, or I'll hit you again," she said rashly.

"You hit me once today. Don't try it again." His voice was low and firm. Their eyes did combat. "Calm down. I'm not asking you to *leave* the boy here. I'm . . . suggesting that you stay here and take care of him."

"You're . . . suggesting that—" she sputtered. "I wouldn't stay in that house a day with that woman if you gave me the whole damn farm on a silver platter!"

"You wouldn't have to go out and work," he continued as if she hadn't spoken. "You and the boy would have a home, and I could watch him grow up."

"A home? You have a house, not a home, Mr. Jamison. Your house is the coldest, most un-homelike house I've ever been in, and I've been in plenty."

"You could make it a home. It would be different if it was . . . yours."

"Your sister treated me like dirt and I was a guest. How do you think she'd treat a paid servant? No! Absolutely not! Do you think I want security so badly that I'd live in a place where I was afraid to leave my baby alone in a room? I'd rather work my fingers to the bone in a cold attic and eat cornbread three times a day."

"I'll handle Esther—"

"The way you handled her when you brought Harriet home as your wife?"

"Harriet was unable to cope with the work and—she didn't

want to. I didn't know things between her and Esther had gotten so bad until that . . . night. I'll regret it for the rest of my life.'' Something in his voice made Ana believe him, but still she couldn't resist a jab.

''Go out to the cemetery and tell that to Harriet, Mr. Jamison,'' she said quietly.

Owen turned from her accusing eyes and stood with his back to her for long seconds. When he looked at her again, his gaze took note of the circles under her eyes and the weariness in her face. The past week had been difficult for her.

''I made Harriet a promise, too. I told her that you and I would work out an arrangement so that you can raise the boy. I want you to live with him in my house, make it a home.''

Ana answered quickly. ''I can't do that. Life is too short to live it in a constant turmoil. I'd rather have less, work harder, be less secure, and have peace of mind.''

''The house and all I have will be yours. Esther will have to come to terms with it.''

''No, Mr. Jamison. In the first place, I don't think your sister is of sound mind. She will not come to terms with it. In the second place, I have a house in Dubuque. If I stay here, I'll have to sell it. And where would I go if things didn't work out here? Third, and most important, I'll not put myself in the position of being gossiped about by your neighbors and friends because I'm living in your house, even though you are my son-in-law.''

The quiet was absolute as they looked at each other. And then, from far away, came the soft, melodious call of a mourning dove breaking the silence. Owen took a step back. Ana took a quick breath.

''I don't think you understand, Mrs. Fairfax. I'm offering you . . . my name.''

She gaped at him as the import of his words sank into her mind. ''Your . . . name? You and I . . . you're asking me to marry you?'' she asked in a brittle voice.

''It's the only solution.''

"It's no solution at all! How can you even suggest such a thing? It's not decent. I'm your mother-in-law!"

"What's that got to do with it?"

Ana didn't answer right away. She stared fixedly at him, then slowly shook her head. "I can't do it. I'd be betraying Harriet."

"Harriet would want what was best for you and the boy. I'm not a poor man if that's what you think. The farm is clear. I have money in the bank—"

"You also have Esther."

"Yes. I have Esther. Esther is my problem, not yours."

There was another little silence while Ana looked into his face. She had married once in order to have a home. She couldn't do it again. When she was young, like all other young girls, she had dreamed of love. As the years went by, she had come to realize that would never be. She wasn't looking for a man to sweep her off her feet as this man had done with Harriet. But it would be nice if she could look forward to companionship in her old age.

"As my wife you'd have the duties and the authority to run the house any way you pleased, answerable only to me," Owen said, bringing Ana's mind back to the present.

Ana shook her head again. "Esther won't let anyone take charge of the house . . . or you. She—" Ana bit off the words. Should she tell him that she was sure his sister had meant to smother this baby with a pillow? Would he believe her? Probably not, she decided.

Owen raked his fingers through his tousled hair. "You said you needed some things from the store. It's just over the hill. Let's go get them."

Huge hands beneath her armpits lifted her down from the buggy platform. A hand at her elbow helped her back up to the seat. Ana cuddled the baby in her arms as they left the glade as silently as they had entered it.

"You're a good little man," Ana whispered to the baby as she loosened the blanket and held up one corner to shield his face from the sun. She glanced at Owen and found him watching her. "He is good," she said defensively. "He seldom cries. I'm going to get a goat. Mrs. Larson said that goat's milk is better for a newborn than cow's milk."

Owen turned his face away, but he could still see floating before his eyes the blond head bent over the child, the smooth cheek, the soft mouth and . . . the big amber eyes that looked so defiantly into his. She was like a wildcat protecting her young. He knew without a doubt that the boy would be better off with her. Her love for the child would be as deep as the hate she felt for him. Even so, she could brighten his life, chase away all the dark shadows that haunted him . . . if only—

Ana's thoughts were spiraling too. She wondered what it would be like to be married to this big, brooding, silent man. He had been such a grouch on the way from Lansing. Would he be a good father to this child? He seldom looked at Harry unless she shoved him into his arms. It was clear that he and Harriet were unsuited to each other. Why had he chosen her when he came to Dubuque to sow his wild oats?

Don't think about the past, Ana cautioned herself. Think about now and what is the best thing to do not only for the child but also for yourself. If she married Owen she would be committed to him for life. If she didn't, would he allow her to take his son home with her? She understood his reluctance to part with his own flesh and blood even if he didn't love the child's mother.

One thing was certain, she was not going to leave this helpless baby at the mercy of a woman with an unbalanced mind. But on the other hand, if she took Owen up on his offer—she would have Esther to contend with.

Ten

Owen stopped the buggy in front of a long, two-storied building. In the space between the roof peaks, a sign read: WHITE OAK STORE—NEW AND EXTENSIVE STOCK OF STAPLE AND FANCY GOODS.

"I'll hold the boy while you go in. Get what you want and tell McCalister to put it on my bill."

"That won't be necessary."

Ana surrendered the bundle in her arms, combed her hair back with her fingertips, and reached into her traveling case for the handkerchief where she had tied her money. She backed carefully out of the buggy and went up the steps to the porch and into the store.

"Howdy." A male voice greeted her as her eyes were adjusting from the bright sunlight. A man with a white apron tied about his middle, sparse hair on his head, but with a big welcoming smile beneath his waxed mustache, came from behind the counter. "Vi-o-let!" he bellowed up the stairs as he came around to greet Ana. "Violet's my wife. I know she'd be plumb put out if I didn't call her down. You're Owen's mother-in-law, ain't ya? I saw ya at the buryin'."

"Yes. I'm sorry, but there were so many people I can't remember all the names."

"It ain't no wonder. Name's McCalister." He held out his hand and Ana put hers in it. "Sure hated it 'bout Owen's wife. My, my, that man waited long enough to wed. It's a pure shame to have something like that happen. Violet hated it, too. Hated it real bad." He turned, cupped his hands around his mouth, and yelled, "Vi-o-let!"

"Don't bother your wife. I'll not be here long. I just need a few things." Ana took quick stock of the store. It was arranged like most all general stores—groceries on the right, dry goods on the left, hardware in the back. She went to the left and took a bolt of white cloth from the shelf. "Six yards, please."

While he measured the cloth, she chose a piece of fabric for baby gowns and carried it to the counter. A short, plump, pleasant looking woman came down the stairs, poking stray strands of dark auburn hair into the knot on the top of her head.

"Goodness, Hershel. You yelled so loud you woke Hanna."

"Sorry, love. I knew you'd be put out if you didn't meet Owen's mother-in-law."

"Ana Fairfax." Ana extended her hand.

"Laws! Ain't you just as pretty as a button! You don't look old enough to be a mother-in-law, much less Owen's. Betcha he's older'n you are."

Ana, grateful for the warm welcome, smiled faintly. "Maybe a few years."

"I'm sure glad to make your acquaintance, Ana. Call me Violet."

"Thank you. You have a nice stock of goods." Ana fingered the embroidery floss.

"We try to meet the needs of our customers. The floss comes a dozen skeins—any color—for thirty cents."

The price was much more than Ana paid for it in Dubuque, but there competition brought the price down. As she visualized little blue flowers around the neck of Harry's little gowns and over the ears of the cap she would knit for him, she threw caution to the wind. After picking out a dozen skeins, she took them to the counter.

"I also need safety pins."

"Small and medium size are two cents each. The big blanket pins are three cents each." Violet pulled out a divided drawer and showed her the pins.

"Give me four small, four medium and three blanket pins. Also a spool of white thread, two infant bottles with nipples, a box of starch and a bottle of olive oil. Oh, I see you have yarn. What pretty colors!"

"I picked out the colors myself when the drummer came through." Violet delved into the pile and brought out a hank of soft pink yarn. "I made a cap and scarf out of this for Hanna."

"That's pretty for a girl, but I'll take the blue for Harry. Add one hank to the bill, Mr. McCalister, and tally it up please."

"Put it on my bill, Hershel." Owen's voice came from behind her.

Ana turned to see him push himself away from the wall just inside the door and come toward the counter. His eyes were narrowed, but she saw enough of them to know that he dared her to contradict him. Of course, she wouldn't embarrass him. She would settle with him later. With his wind-blown hair and his huge frame, he looked as big and as fierce as a gladiator, but he held the baby gently in the crook of his arm.

"Oh, let me see him," Violet squealed. She stood beside Owen, her head coming to about the third button on his shirt. "He's just beautiful, Owen. My, look at all that dark hair. Ain't it a pity that dear girl will never see this blessed child?" Violet sniffed back sudden tears.

Owen looked over her head to Ana. "Is there anything else you want?"

Ana shook her head.

"Got your plantin' done, Owen?"

"No. I'm working on it. We'll have four cans of peaches, Hershel. A box of cinnamon, a half-dozen cans of sardines"—his eyes scanned the goods on the row of shelves—"a bag of coffee beans, a scoop of raisins and one of apricots."

"I got in that tobacco you like—that Kentucky in the round can."

"Give me a can. We'll take a dozen sticks of peppermint and a lead pencil too."

Ana had heard him use the term *we*, but had kept her eyes straight ahead, determined that she would pay for what she had bought when they left the store.

"Anything else, Owen?" Mr. McCalister sacked the raisins, the coffee beans, and set the last of the cans on the counter. "I got lemons in yesterday," he said while he counted out the peppermint sticks. "They came all the way upriver from New Orleans."

"There's nothing I like better than lemonade on a hot day."

"Did you put up much ice last winter?"

"Enough for a while. We've got it bedded down in sawdust and straw. I'll take a half a bushel of lemons. They'll keep in the cellar. Add on a fifty-pound bag of sugar, Hershel. I don't know what we've got at home, but if we don't need it now, we will later on when the fruit comes on."

"Tell Gus to bring me a dozen brooms when he comes to town. I've got only two left outta that last batch."

"I'll tell him."

Ana turned and Owen wordlessly put the babe in her arms. She moved away from him and edged toward the door. Irresistibly drawn to a table of books, she caressed the covers with her fingertips, surprised to find in this country store a five-volume set of the *Leather-Stocking Tales* of James F. Cooper and a six-volume set of Alexander Dumas's romances. She had read Cooper's *Deerslayer*, and Dumas's *The Man in the Iron Mask*. In her mind she totaled the cost of the books—one set sixty-nine cents, the other seventy-eight cents. Ah . . . she caught her breath—almost a dollar-and-a-half. They were too dear for her now—but someday.

She pulled from the stack a book that was a good two inches thick. *Common Sense Medical Advisor*. She opened it and thumbed through it with one hand. A large portion of the book was on the care and feeding of infants—what to do for colic, fever, running off at the bowels. The price was one dollar and twenty-five cents. She closed it and put it back on the stack. She couldn't afford to spend so much money until she decided what she was going to do.

She looked around for Owen. He had taken the lemons to the buggy, returned and hoisted the bag of sugar onto his shoulder. Now he stood beside the pickle barrel watching her. It made her nervous. Ana hurriedly said her goodbyes to the McCalisters and went out to the buggy. Owen, coming back for the rest of the load, stood aside and allowed her to pass. She could feel his eyes on her face, but she didn't look up.

Harry let out a loud angry cry as soon as Ana settled into the buggy seat. He was hungry and was letting her know in the only way he knew how. She dug into her travel bag, found the bottle of milk, and was feeding him, crooning to him, when Owen climbed in beside her.

"I've decided to go home with you for now, Mr. Jamison. I'll tell you tomorrow what I decide to do about the . . . other. But I wish to make one thing clear. If I leave here, I'm taking this baby with me."

"We'll see." He turned the horse around in the middle of the street and headed out of town.

The short, stark words made Ana angry, made her want to cry, too. They also made her speak more sharply than she would have otherwise.

"I'll pay you for what I bought. I didn't want to make a fuss in the store."

"What you bought was for the boy. I can pay for what he needs. I'll hear no more about it."

"We'll see," she said making her voice just as curt as his had been when he had said the same words.

When the road smoothed out, Owen put the horse into a trot. Once again he had retreated into the deep recesses of his own reserve.

Ana squinted against the bright sunlight and listened to the sound of hooves striking the hard-packed road, and to the jingle of the harness. They covered the distance to the farm quickly—too quickly for Ana. She was much too tired to face the confrontation with Esther that she was sure awaited her.

It was an hour past noon when Owen turned into the lane leading to the house. Beyond the apple orchard, a cloud of dust trailed the heavy iron drag Soren was using to smooth the field for planting. The blade on the windmill spun lazily. The air was warm and scented with the blossoms of flowering trees and vines. It was a glorious spring day, Ana thought, or would be if not for Esther's dust-covered buggy, unhitched now, sitting in the yard like a black omen.

With all her heart, Ana wished she had insisted on going to Mrs. Larson's. The tension of the last few days, the scene with Esther this morning, the long walk and the talk with Owen, all had combined to give her a splitting headache. She shut her eyes tightly. When she opened them, Owen had stopped the buggy near the barn and was looking at her.

"Are you sick?"

Their eyes met and held. The eyes looking so intently into hers were full of concern. For her? How could that be? She wondered what went on in that head of his. He was kind one minute and so remote the next. A strong, unidentifiable emotion held her eyes to his. For just an instant they were enclosed in a timeless world, seeming to come close to each other, spirit moving effortlessly toward spirit.

"I'm all right," she murmured. "Just tired."

"It's no wonder. You walked more than four miles carrying that babe." His eyes searched her face. Then he shook his head, as though denying his thoughts.

"I've walked much farther than that many times, and carrying just as heavy a load." Ana shook herself out of what seemed to be a trance. Glory! What was the matter with her? She didn't have to explain anything to him.

He seemed to sense her return to reality. His eyes moved past her to the house, then back to hers. A stern look covered a face that needed a shave and was streaked with dirt and sweat.

"Stay here." A sigh shuddered through him.

Ana nodded, her eyes questioning, his giving no answer.

Esther was still there. He could hear her in the kitchen—singing. Good Lord! When was the last time he had heard his sister sing? If he was going to change the pattern of his life he had to do it now, and she was not going to make it easy for him.

*"Thine eyes hath seen the glory of the coming
of the Lord; He is trampling out the vintage where the
grapes of wrath are stored; He hath loosed the fateful
lightning of His terrible swift sword;
His truth is marching on."*

When he opened the screen door and came into the house, Esther turned from the stove.

"Your dinner's ready," she called out with a bright smile on her face. "I had to hold back on the custard or Uncle Gus and Soren would have eaten it all. Laws! I don't know where that Soren puts all those vittles. He'll eat us out of house and home before the summer is over. Wash up and sit down, Owen. I'll pour your coffee."

"Esther?"

*"John Brown's body lies a-mouldrin' in the grave,
John Brown's body lies a-mouldrin' in the grave.
John Brown's body—"*

"Stop it, Esther. I want to talk to you."

"Yes, Owen."

"I told you to go home."

"Oh, that!" She laughed—it came out a high cackling sound. "I knew you didn't mean it. It'll take us a while to get back to normal, but—"

"I meant it, Esther. You can't go on like this, dividing your time between my house and yours."

"Well, for heaven's sake! Is that what's bothering you? I've been doing it for . . . years. Hettie and Lily can do the work over there. Now sit down and eat. I made ham gravy to go on potatoes and cornbread. I fried hominy in bacon fat the way you like it. In a week or two I'll pick you a nice mess of fresh greens." She turned back to the stove and hummed while she prepared to dish up the food.

"Esther, please hush and listen! We've got to settle this once and for all. Go on home. I'll come over tonight and we'll talk."

"There's nothing to talk about except the farm. You're behind with the planting. Why don't you hire the Watson boys to come over and help? They'll work for twenty-five cents a day. If you don't want to do that, Lily will help." She let out a snort of disgust. "I've planted many a field." With her back to him, she lifted a cloth from a huge round bowl. "This bread dough needs to be punched down a couple more times before I can bake it. I made it with potato water this time."

Owen followed his sister to the counter. With his hands on her shoulders he turned her gently toward him.

"I don't want to hurt your feelings, sister. But I want you to go home and stay there. You should be doing all these things for Jens, Hettie and Lily." He shook her shoulders gently. "Do you understand?"

Esther's eyes filled with tears and Owen's heart filled with pity as he looked at her homely face and large, floppy ears. He felt anger, but he also felt frustrated and guilty. He had selfishly allowed her to do for him since he'd come back to the farm to stay, and now she felt that he was being unforgivably cruel. She was suffering, too, or she would never have given way to the tears.

"I'll go, if you're so bound and determined. I'll be back tomorrow to do the washing. But first I'll clean up and lay out something for your supper."

"No," he said gently. "You don't have to clean up or cook for me or do my washing."

"Why are you keeping on like this?" she screeched suddenly. "You don't want me here because . . . of *her*!"

"I'll always want you. You're my sister and you're very dear to me. But the way things are now, it isn't fair to you and it isn't fair to me." He spoke in a quiet tone with a tense note of urgency running through it. "If you won't turn loose here, I'll have to take the boy and go live somewhere else."

"Go live somewhere else?" she echoed, her voice strangled. "I'm not good enough now! Is that it? I was good enough after Mama died—good enough for Papa . . . good enough to keep him from beating you senseless! I worked like a dog to keep you and Paul alive! Do you think *he* would have cared if you died? Ha! *He* cared only about how much work you could do and—"

"I know all that. I'm grateful, Esther. But that was then; this is now."

She jerked her shoulders from his hands and stepped back, anger in every line of her thin body and bony face.

"You don't want me near that prissy, sweet-smelling city whore. I'm not blind; I saw her parading around in her wrapper in front of you and Soren. I saw you looking at her with lust in your eyes and Soren panting after her like she was a bitch in heat—which she is!"

"Now stop it," he said sternly. "You've no right to talk about Mrs. Fairfax that way."

Esther was so worked up that his words fell on deaf ears.

"She'll not plant and tend the garden with those lily-white hands of hers. Nor will the cellar be full for winter. Do you think she'll help you slaughter a hog and scrape its hide? Who will cook for the thrashers and help you pick corn when there's snow on the ground? I did all that. I worked in the field from sunup to sundown and if I didn't do enough, I got a whipping."

"So did I. That's all in the past."

"I'll not let Hettie and Lily come help her. You could have Lily if you're so anxious to have a woman in your bed."

"Enough!" Owen was rapidly loosing his patience.

"Enough!" she mimicked. "It was never enough for Papa, and you know it!" Eyes hard and bright glared at him with hatred. "Take the bitch! You and Pa are just alike! He'd've had her on her back before she got her hat off. At least you waited till you buried that slut you married."

"Hush that kind of talk!"

"You don't like to hear the truth. You're just like Paul. He couldn't stand it either." She took a deep breath and let it out through quivering lips. "Do you think I don't know what you're up to? You want to get between her legs, and your sister is in the way."

Owen looked at his sister's hate-twisted face in numbed silence. Her accusations hurt. He knew that she had a sharp tongue and was terribly protective of this house and what she considered "Mama's things." Owen also knew she resented Harriet, resented Ana and the baby. But during the past week, she had shown a vicious side of her nature he'd not seen before. Was she demented as Ana had thought she was? He had to get Esther out of here so that he could think.

"I'll go hitch up your buggy. You go on home and think about the things you've said; and if you don't realize how wrong you are, I'm sorry for you."

Owen left the house, went directly to the pen beside the barn, and brought out the horse. While he harnessed the animal, a dull ache spread throughout his body. He had been ten years old and Esther fourteen when their mother died giving birth to Paul. Only three of her eight children had survived. The other five were buried in the church cemetery in White Oak. Esther had stepped into her mother's place. Oh, God! He didn't want to think of the cold-hearted, bestial instincts that were passed down to his father by his grandfather. He and Paul had escaped the curse, but was it just now coming out in Esther? And what of little Harry?

Owen finished hitching the animal to the buggy and led him toward the house. Esther came out of the house and walked across the yard, her back ramrod straight. She climbed into the buggy, refusing Owen's offered hand.

"I'll be over tonight after supper. I didn't want to do this, Esther. But after a while you'll come to realize it's better for both of us." Owen handed her the reins.

She snatched them from his hands without looking at him and jerked cruelly on the left rein, turning the animal around in the yard. Owen stood for a moment, watching the buggy proceed down the lane, then went to where Ana and the baby waited.

It had seemed to Ana that Owen was in the house for a long time. She had heard Esther singing, then only snatches of voices. The longer she waited the more convinced she became that she couldn't stay here, even married to Owen. He hadn't protected Harriet from his sister. Why would he protect her? A vision of Harriet's hands tied to the bed and a gag in her mouth floated before Ana's eyes.

"Oh, honey—" Ana groaned, her grief rising as if to smother her.

Ana had to believe that Owen wasn't aware of Esther's treatment of Harriet. He had been as shocked as she was when he saw the condition of Harriet's bed. And Harriet had clung to Owen, had not said one word against him. He'd been good to her. But still he hadn't loved her as she had loved him.

Esther didn't come out of the house until Owen had finished

hitching the horse. Ana tried to feel pity for the woman but couldn't find even a spark of it in her heart. She was just grateful that she didn't have to face her.

When Owen came to the buggy and held out his arms for the child, his face was lined with worry. He held the child in the crook of his arm and extended his hand to help her down. Ana put hers into it. His hand, large, strong and rough, held hers gently as if he feared he would crush it. Her eyes rose to meet his and in them she saw flickering shadows of anxiety and something else that caused her heart to flutter. Was it tender regard for her?

"She didn't want to go," Ana said almost breathlessly as she took the infant from him.

"No," he said softly, regretfully. "She didn't want to go."

"I'm sorry. It will only be for a few days."

He frowned slightly. "Go on in. I'll bring your bag and the rest of the things after I unhitch."

Ana went to the house feeling a little light-headed. For the life of her she couldn't understand this man who had married Harriet. One minute she despised him, the next she pitied him, admired him, or she was terribly aware of him as a man.

Holding the child in one arm, she opened the screen door and stepped into the kitchen. Out of the bright sunlight, her eyes took a few seconds to focus, and when they did, she stood stock still, her mouth forming a silent O.

The kitchen looked as if it had been stuck by a tornado. Ana shook her head in silent denial of what she was seeing. Food from the pots on the stove, as well as the plates, had been dumped on the floor along with coffee beans, sugar, milk, and butter. The flour barrel was rolled on its side, spilling a white path from the counter to the table. A big glob of bread dough, apparently beaten with a stick of stove-wood, lay on the floor in front of the range. Gravy, hominy and boiled potatoes were splattered on the table, the stove, and

the floor. A pan of custard sat in the middle of the table with
the smoke-blackened coffee pot smashed down into the middle of it.

A dark smoke rose from molasses burning on the range
top. The thick syrup had also been dribbled over the eating
table and the chairs. Now the jug lay on the floor, the syrup
oozing out and spreading into a path of cornmeal. Amid this
frenzied destruction, dozens of broken eggs splattered the
walls and the floor.

Silent with shock, Ana stood, her feet glued to the floor
by the muck Esther had left behind her, and stared at the
devastation.

Eleven

⸉⸉

It seemed to Ana that she had stood there forever before she heard Owen's step on the porch. Unwilling to walk through the mess to reach the bedroom, she waited just inside the door. As he stepped into the kitchen, her travel bag in one hand, packages in the other, his foot slipped in the slimy mess on the floor.

"What the hell!" he snarled as he regained his balance. Then he sucked in his breath and stared in disbelief at the havoc. "Godamighty! What in the world happened here?"

There was a long moment's silence while he tried to cope with the reality that his sister, in the short time it had taken him to hitch her horse to the buggy, had created this mess.

"I'm sorry," Ana said very quietly. Then with an odd little movement that surprised even Ana, she placed a comforting hand on his arm.

"Why . . . would she do this?" He stammered a little. "And in so short a time—" He looked at Ana with pure torment in his eyes. "Why?" he asked again.

"She must feel that you have rejected her, and it's her way of getting back at me."

"At you?"

"Yes. Because I'll be the one to clean up the mess. She thinks of me as a threat to her position here."

"Godamighty! I never thought she'd go this far."

"Maybe you don't know your sister as well as you think you do," Ana offered.

Owen felt a sudden rush of anger. "Hellfire! I've a right to a home of my own! Damn her! Damn all the Jamison's!"

"Damning everyone isn't going to clean up this mess or keep that syrup from burning on the stove and smoking up the house." Ana managed to keep the agitation out of her voice.

Owen swore quietly, battling to control his frustration. He took a deep breath and let it out slowly, his anger leaving as quickly as it had arrived.

"You're right."

"How am I going to get to the bedroom to put Harry down without tracking this all through the house?"

"We'll go around to the front door and go in that way." He backed out the door and held it open for her. "Be careful and don't slip."

Ana scraped the soles of her shoes on the grass when she reached it and followed Owen around to the front door. The first thing she noticed when she entered the bedroom was that her trunk was not where she had left it. As soon as that fact registered, she became aware that the cradle was not there either. Every trace of her and the baby had been removed from the room. Owen didn't seem to notice. He placed her traveling bag and the packages from the store on the bed and turned to leave.

"I left my trunk here. It's gone. So is the cradle."

"She may have taken them upstairs—"

"How could she?" Ana interrupted. "It's so heavy I could hardly move it. Well, never mind. It's got to be here someplace. I'll change Harry, then I'll start cleaning up that mess in the kitchen. He'll be wanting to eat in a couple of hours. I hope there's more milk in the cellar."

"Last night's milk should be there."

"It's a good thing you have plenty of brooms," Ana said trying to lighten the mood.

"It'll take hot water to get that syrup off the floor. I'll build a fire under the washpot."

"As soon as you can get in the kitchen, rake the fire out of the firebox so the range top can cool off. Phew! I smell that syrup burning." While she talked, she took a dry cloth from her travel bag and pinned it on the baby. "I'll be in to help you as soon as I get Harry settled."

"You'll ruin your dress."

"I have work dresses in my trunk."

She flicked a glance at him as he went out of the room. All at once she wondered if she had been wrong about him. Cold and uncaring? Not today. She couldn't blame him for wanting to keep his son close. A son was a son even if he hadn't loved the boy's mother. Although he was hurt and embarrassed by what his sister had done, she could feel compassion in him too. But, she chided herself sternly, that doesn't excuse him for what he did to Harriet. In a small way he was being paid back. Being here, she was making his sister's life miserable just as he had made hers by being in Dubuque last fall.

Ana had settled Harry and was rolling up the sleeves of her shirtwaist when she heard Owen coming back into the front hall. He came to the doorway and stood hesitantly, holding her trunk in front of him.

"You found it. Did you find the cradle?"

"Not yet." He set the trunk down as he answered. "I could see where the trunk had been dragged across the porch." He straightened and they faced each other, seeing grim awareness of Esther's mental state mirrored in each other's eyes. Finally Owen took a deep breath, letting it out slowly. "For the life of me, I can't understand what's got into her. She's always been abrupt and outspoken, but this—"

"—It may have been there for a long time and is just now coming out."

"I'll look for the cradle later. It's got to be here somewhere."

"Where was the trunk?"

"In the lilac bushes at the end of the porch." He didn't leave as she expected him to. Instead he stood in the doorway, somberly regarding her until she began to feel uncomfortable. "I suppose this will make you more determined than ever to go back to Dubuque."

"No," she said firmly, shaking her head. "But it will make me more determined than ever to take Harriet's baby with me if I go."

He nodded slowly as if in agreement, his eyes holding hers for a long moment before he turned away.

After he left, Ana closed the door and fished around in her travel bag for the key to her trunk.

She hurriedly dressed in a workdress and tied a faded apron around her waist. She sat on the edge of the bed and took off her shoes, reasoning that her feet would be easier to wash than the shoes. After she propped the door open so that she could hear the baby if he cried, she went down the hall to the kitchen.

Ana had taken only a few steps into the room when Owen's voice stopped her in her tracks.

"Wait! Don't move! There's a broken fruit jar here."

He had a scoop-shovel in one hand and a broom in the other. He leaned the two of them against the table and came to her. Before she knew what happened, one arm was beneath her knees, the other at her waist. He swung her up in his arms as if she were a child. Her arms went around his neck and she held on to him tightly. She had never been lifted and held like this. It was frightening, yet exciting.

"Oh! Put me down! I'm too heavy—"

"Too heavy? Good lord! You don't weigh as much as a sack of grain."

He stood holding her, looking for a clean place to set her down. He decided on the end of the counter. His heavy boots smashed the broken glass on the floor as he carried her there.

As he eased her down, she held onto his shoulders to keep her balance. She thought he would move away, but he grasped her bare ankle in his big hand and lifted her foot.

"Did you cut your feet?" He peered at the bottom of first one foot and then the other.

"I don't think so." She wiggled her toes. "But that syrup sure is sticky."

"Sit here until I get the floor cleaned up."

Wondering why her stupid heart was acting like a runaway train, Ana watched him sweep the broken glass and globs of food into the scoop shovel and dump them in a bucket. He pried the bread-dough from the floor, righted the tin flour barrel and set it on the porch until they could wash the syrup from the side. He worked swiftly and efficiently with no awkward pauses. It made Ana uneasy to sit and watch him.

"If I had my shoes I could help."

"No need. There'll be plenty for you to do."

He swept and scooped until he cleaned up everything he could attack with the broom. Flour, cornmeal and sugar glued to the floor with syrup had to be scooped up with the shovel. After he set the bucket and shovel on the porch, he carried out the kitchen chairs.

Ana had braced herself to slide off the counter and take her chances on the floor when Owen came in with a wet cloth in his hand. To her utter amazement he began to clean the muck from her feet. She stared at him with panic running just below the calm image she presented to him. Every nerve in her body jumped to attention. The warm fingers curled around her bare ankle sent blood surging to her cheeks. She was forced to disguise the raggedness of her breathing.

"You . . . don't need to do that—"

"I know it, but I want to," he murmured and reached for her other foot.

Ana tried not to look at him, but this was the most intimate she had ever been with another person. He seemed to surround her. His physical nearness paralyzed her thought process, but not so much that she didn't realize that she wasn't indifferent to him. Far from it. She was tingling. Although her expression was calm, her nerves were quivering.

Owen concentrated on his task. Her feet were narrow, her arch high, her ankle so slim he could span it with his thumb and middle finger. When he finished, he looked into her face and saw a breath quiver her parted lips. As a blush began to stain her cheeks, he became fascinated by the sight of her clear, white skin turning rosy pink and the startled questioning expression in her amber eyes. Vaguely he noticed that her hair had come loose from the knot, framing her face with golden wisps. Over the lingering odor of the burnt syrup, he could smell the sweetness of her.

Owen was acutely aware that this was a woman as a woman was meant to be. Her beauty was so subtle that he really had to look at each of her features to see how pure and classic her face and figure were. Why couldn't he have met her long ago? Although there was a good chance that she would stay here, there was an even better chance that she would never be whole-heartedly his even if she did marry him. Because the thought was so depressing, he clamped his teeth against the hurt, and the tell-tale muscle jumped in his jaw.

"I'll take you to the hall and you can get your shoes," he said gruffly and picked her up.

The distance to the doorway took only a few steps, but it was long enough for Ana to feel the pounding of his heart against her ribcage and his warm breath on the side of her face. He let her down slowly, removing his arm from beneath her knees, but holding her tightly to him with the other until her feet reached the floor. She could feel his eyes on her face as he loosed his arm and straightened, towering over her.

"Thank you. I'll get my shoes and be in to help."

Ana was surprised that her voice was so normal because she certainly didn't feel normal. By golly damn! What was the matter with her? She wasn't an adolescent school girl but a mature twenty-six-year-old woman, for heaven's sake! Feeling absurdly nervous, Ana went quickly to the bedroom, and even though it wasn't necessary just to put on her shoes, she firmly closed the door.

It was late afternoon before the work was finished. Ana was so tired that she felt as if her arms would fall off. The only time she had rested was when she stopped to feed the baby. The diapers she had put to soaking that morning were found in the horse tank; the small washtub and the rub board were hanging on the porch. Ana set them soaking again with the day's accumulation. She had to cut a length of the new material from the store in order to keep the infant dry.

Owen brought meat from the smoke house. As soon as the stove was clean, Ana cubed the meat and put it on to boil. Later she would add dough to make dumplings. It would have to do for the night meal. Owen went back to the field, saying that he and Soren would be in at dusk.

When Uncle Gus came to tell her the sow had farrowed and all the piglets had lived except two, Ana made a hasty trip to the barn to see the new arrivals. She looked with delight at the eight tiny piglets already sucking lustily at their mother's teats.

"I didn't think they would be so strong," she said with laughter in her eyes. "Look at the greedy little things tumbling over each other."

"Wait 'till you see the new calves. They'll stand within a few minutes of birth and follow their mamas. It's more'n humans can do."

"And the mare's foal? Will it stand right away too?"

"If it comes out all right. Owen's going to be sorely put if it don't."

"Oh, I can hardly wait to see it."

Suddenly she sobered. What was she saying? She hadn't decided to stay here. She hadn't even had time to think about Owen Jamison's offer. She glanced at the old man leaning

on the rail smoking his pipe. On a sudden impulse she put
her hand on his arm.

"Oh, Lord. I don't know what to do," she whispered as
if to herself.

A wrinkled, rough hand slid over hers and squeezed gently.

"Ya, lass. 'Tis a hard choice. This ain't a happy place."

"But . . . could it be?" she asked with desperate eagerness.

"I'd not be knowin' that. Owen's grandpappy come from
Norway and built this place. He handed it down to Owen's
pa along with a mean streak a yard wide and a temper to go
with it. They loosed it on man, woman or beast alike. This
ain't never been a happy place," he said with a sigh.

"I can feel it—in the house." Her voice held a queerly
resigned note. "Mr. Jamison asked me to stay as his wife
and take care of his son."

"I figured he would."

"But . . . I'm his mother-in-law! It doesn't seem right."

"You ain't blood kin."

"I wasn't blood kin to Harriet, but I loved her as if she
were my own. I can't leave her baby here, and he won't let
me take him with me." She felt the damnable lump come
up in her throat and tears sting her eyes.

"It'd go hard to give up a son." The old man smoked
quietly for a moment, then he said, "Owen ain't got a mean
bone in his body, lass. He shies from quarrels. That's the
reason Esther's got such a foothold here."

"Will he take my side against his sister if I marry him?
He didn't take Harriet's. He let Esther run roughshod over
her," she added bitterly.

"Ya. But the lassie made no effort to be lady of the house.
'Twas easy for Esther to keep on a doin' as she'd always
done—takin' charge."

"If I stay, it'll mean that I've burned my bridges behind
me. This will be my home, and I'll not stand aside for Esther
or anyone else to take over. But, oh, it will be grief if I go
and grief if I stay."

"Ya."

Ana went out into the sunshine. She stopped in the middle of the yard, and turning slowly, she looked at everything in sight. If she stayed, this would be her home for the rest of her life. She looked toward the field where Owen worked. The dust no longer trailed the drag. Soren and he were walking the rows side by side, planting the corn they would harvest in the fall. This earthy man would be no Ezra Fairfax, allowing a marriage in name only. He would expect to be welcomed to her bed. The thought was not repulsive to her, but it brought her no joy to think of a loveless marriage.

The big fat goose waddled up and picked at the laces on her shoe. Her ears were tuned to the sound of the hens clucking in the hen house and the robins singing happily in the tight grove on the north side of the farm. A strutting rooster with a high, proud comb pranced across the yard in search of a tidbit. Pigeons resting on the barn roof disregarded the iron cow on the weathervane that turned gently in the breeze, and cooed softly to each other.

Over it all, the sturdy metal windmill stood a silent sentinel—the watertanks were filled.

Could she be a part of this? Could she sink her roots in the fertile black soil and call this home? Her family would be Owen, little Harry, Uncle Gus and Soren. She would have to accept Esther for what she was, and Hettie and Lily as well.

While she was thinking these thoughts, Uncle Gus came out of the barn with a long staff in his hands. He let himself out the gate and started across the pasture to drive the milch cows home for the night. *This is not a happy place*, the old man had said. What a pity, Ana thought as she walked to the house. The setting is so perfect for a happy home.

The shades of night had fallen by the time the men came to supper. The lamp in the middle of the table cast a glow over the room that smelled not only of lye soap and wet wood, but also of fresh coffee, meat with fluffy sage dumplings, and hot buttered cornbread.

"Something smells larrupin'." A smile creased Soren's handsome face. The men had washed the dirt from their upper bodies at the washbench on the porch and put on clean shirts before they came to the table.

"I don't know how good it is, but there's plenty of it," Ana retorted with an answering smile as she carried a bowl of the dumplings to the table.

After she took the bread from the oven, she slipped into her chair at the table so the men would sit down. They filled their plates and began to eat with intensified interest. Eating was a serious business to these men who had worked hard since sunup. Ana kept the dumpling bowl, the bread plate, and their coffee cups, filled. She discovered that she enjoyed doing for these big, kind, hard-working men.

Nothing was said about her trip to town, Owen going after her, or the mess Esther had left in the kitchen. The talk was about the piglets, the planting, and the possibility of the mare giving birth within the next few days. They also talked of someone named Foster who would show up any day and stay a month or two and even into harvest time if they could persuade him. It was evident that they looked forward to his arrival.

"If I thought Foster would show up in a day or two, I'd not ask the Wilson boys to work," Owen said serving himself a second helping of dumplings.

Ana realized that he must be hungry. They'd had only a handful of raisins and a peppermint stick while they cleaned the kitchen. Not much food for a man his size.

"He might not be in any shape to work for a couple days after he gets here," Soren said, taking a sip of his coffee. "If you want to get the corn in before it rains, the best bet is to hire the Wilson boys."

"You may be right. I'll stop by there tonight. I hear they've got their corn in already."

When the meal was over, Soren leaned back in the chair and stretched his arms over his head.

"I'm frazzled to the bone. I used muscles today I haven't used since this time last year."

"He's getting soft, Uncle Gus," Owen said. "I was going to ask him to ride over to the Knutson's with me, but maybe he's not up to it."

"I've been looking at the back end of those mules all day. I'm not going to spend my evening looking at the back end of a horse when I can sit here and look at a pretty woman." Soren's blue eyes smiled into Ana's, expecting to see a blush creep up to her cheeks. He was disappointed.

"If you stay here, you'll work," she said primly. "The milk has to be strained and put in the cellar, the woodbox filled for morning, the dishes washed and put away. And—"she added with smile lines crinkling her eyes—"the diapers washed and hung on the line."

"Well . . . on second thought, I just may amble on off to bed." He pressed his hand to the small of his back. "I'm kind of down in the back—"

A bubble of laughter burst unknowingly from Ana's lips. She got to her feet and began to clear the table. She didn't see the look that passed between Soren and his father when they saw Owen's smiling eyes following her. Nor did she know how rare it was to hear a woman's laughter in this house.

After the Halversons left to go back to the small cabin in the grove, Ana strained the night's milking and Owen carried it to the cellar.

"I'll be gone for an hour or two," he said when he returned. "Do you mind staying here alone?"

"Of course not. When I finish here, I'll cut the cloth we got at the store today so Harry will have clean napkins for tomorrow."

"If you need the ones in the tub, I'll hang them up before I go."

Ana looked at him sharply. Was he offering to wash diapers?

"There's no need. I was just teasing Soren."

"You like Soren and my uncle?" It seemed to Ana that he had asked her that before.

"Of course. Is this Foster you speak of a relative too?"

"No blood kin, but I've known him for a long time and think of him as kin. Soren, Uncle Gus and I are about the only family he has, and he spends a month or two here in the summer. He sleeps in the barn or at the little house with Uncle Gus and Soren."

"Why not here? There are four bedrooms upstairs that aren't in use."

Owen shrugged. "Foster does as he pleases."

Esther is the reason his friend Foster sleeps in the barn, Ana thought with disgust after Owen left her. He knows it, and still allows it.

When the kitchen was orderly once again, she carried the hot teakettle and a bucket of cold water to the bedroom. She was glad for the opportunity to be alone so that she could take a washrag bath. After stripping to the waist, she washed the upper part of her body, then the lower part. It felt so good to be clean.

Tomorrow or the next day she would get water from the rain barrel and wash her hair. She stopped in the act of pulling her nightdress over her head. She hadn't fully decided that she would stay here—or had she?

Twelve

*O*wen put a bridle on the horse and opened the gate. Ordinarily he would have walked the mile across the back pasture to the Knutson farm, but tonight he had to take the road so that he could stop at the Wilson place to talk about hiring the boys.

The sky had darkened and the stars were out when he rode away from the homestead. He looked back over his shoulder to the ray of light marking a window of the farm house. He had been reluctant to leave. That in itself was a startling discovery. Usually he spent only as much time in the house as was necessary to eat and sleep. Early this morning and again tonight, because Ana was there, the house had been a warm and welcoming place, the home he yearned for when he was a boy.

Mixed and troubled emotions raked him. Would his marriage to Ana, if she accepted him, cause a permanent break between him and the sister who had done so much for him when he was unable to do for himself? Was he abandoning Esther now when she needed him the most? Looking back, he could see that Esther's behavior had gradually become strange. And what she had done today was the act of a person totally out of control. Another worrisome question rose up in his thoughts. What could be done for a person with a sick mind?

Owen continued ahead, urging the horse to greater speed as he came closer to the Wilson farm. The family, lingering in the kitchen after the meal, welcomed him warmly. It took only a single look to sense the closeness between the parents and the children. When Owen asked if he could hire the boys for a few days, Wilson looked proudly at his sons and bragged that there were no better boys in the state of Iowa and none that would give him a better day's work.

The boys hung their heads and murmured, "Ah . . . Pa—"

Wilson clapped each fondly on the back and told Owen they would be at the Jamison farm by sunup.

Owen rode away from the Wilson farm trying to remember a time when his pa had bragged about him. He could only remember hearing him say what a lazy and worthless boy he was.

"Good Lord, man," Owen murmured aloud. "The old bastard's dead. Stop thinking about him!"

Jens Knutson took better care of his animals than he did his family. The barn was large and tight and kept in good repair. The house was small, the roof leaked, and the wind blew in the cracks around the windows. Jens was tightfisted. The neighbors were fond of saying he had ninety-nine cents out of every dollar he had made. He had been a widower whose simple-minded daughter Hettie had already given birth to a "woods-colt" when Esther was offered to him by her father. There had been much speculation as to the father of Hettie's child, but she either didn't know or was too frightened to tell. Jens saw in Esther a good worker and someone to keep an eye on Hettie.

Owen rode up to the back of the house and tied his horse to a rail. Lily came out onto the porch.

"Is that you, Uncle Owen?"

"It's me. How's things here?"

"Why do you ask? Things are never good here."

"I came to talk to Esther."

"Esther's in an awful state. She slapped Mama and made her cry." Lily wrapped her arm about a porch post and rested her forehead against it.

"Where's Jens?"

"Gone to bed. Esther went to bed right after she got home this afternoon, and she wouldn't even come down for supper."

"She's upset with me. I asked her to go home and stop making trouble for Mrs. Fairfax and she . . . well, she's not pleased about it."

"She was fairly foaming at the mouth when she got here. I've never seen her so mad. She flew into me and Mama and said she hated us and wished we would die. Mama got upset and—oh, Uncle Owen, sometimes I wouldn't care much if I did die."

"I've told you before, Lily, that if you want to leave here and go to Lansing or Dubuque, I'll put you up until you can find a way of earning your keep."

"I can't leave Mama. I know she's simple-minded and people make fun of her, but she wouldn't hurt anything for the world. Grandpa hates her; Esther hates her. If I left her, I don't know what she'd do. I'm all she has."

"I understand and think the more of you for it."

"Esther thinks you're going to marry Mrs. Fairfax."

"I asked her. She hasn't accepted me yet."

"Esther says it wouldn't be decent for you to marry your mother-in-law."

"I don't know why not. Mrs. Fairfax is not kin."

Lily shrugged. "You know how Esther is when she makes up her mind. The devil couldn't change it."

"Then she'll just have to live with it."

"What will you do with the baby if Mrs. Fairfax leaves?"

"I haven't thought that far ahead."

"She could take him with her."

"I can't let someone else take over a responsibility that's mine."

"Mama and I could take care of him."

"It would be the talk of the county, Lily. I can't let that happen. You'd never have a chance to marry a decent man."

"I don't anyway. Everybody knows about Mama and that I don't have a pa."

"They don't blame you, Lily."

"Ha! If a boy even spoke to me, his ma would have a conniption fit."

"You know that Esther wanted Paul, and then me, to marry you. It's not that you're not a nice, sweet, pretty girl—"

"—Is that why Paul went away?"

"Partly, I guess. But he wanted to see the world before he settled down. I can't blame him for that."

"Nothing would be changed if we married, would it, Uncle Owen? Esther would still have control over both of us. I thank you for refusing. I hope and pray I can choose my own man when I marry."

Owen lifted a hand and stroked the auburn hair back from the earnest young face. Lily had grown up. No, Lily had never been a child. She had been burdened with taking care of her mother all her life. Owen felt a pang of guilt. He hadn't done much to help Lily. It must be hell for the girl to live with Esther and Hettie.

"I'll see to it that you don't have to take a man you don't want," he said gently. "It would be good for you to get to know Mrs. Fairfax, Lily. She's a real lady. I think you would like her."

"Esther wouldn't stand for it. She wouldn't even let me get near Harriet or look at the baby. Now I wish I had done it anyway."

"There are things that I regret too. But what's done is

done and in the past. What I want to do is change things so the future will be more pleasant for all of us.''

"I don't see much hope of that," she said with a slump of her shoulders.

"Maybe not, but I'm going to try."

"Esther said Soren is back and that we are to stay away from over there. She said she doesn't want any more 'woods-colts.' Oh, I hate it when she calls me that.''

"You have nothing to fear from Soren, Lily. He would never take advantage of you or Hettie."

"I know it, but Esther don't. Will you talk to her and see if she'll let me come over and see the baby?''

"How old are you now?"

"I'll soon be eighteen."

"You're old enough to come over without asking her."

Lily snorted. "She'd have a fit and fall in it. She treats me like she treats Mama.''

"Then it's up to you to put a stop to it. I want to talk to Esther. Will you tell her to come down?''

Lily led the way into the kitchen, then went on up the stairs. Hettie pushed aside a curtain and came from the small room she and Lily shared. She had a bright smile on her pleasant face. At times it was hard to remember she had the mind of a child.

"Hello, Owen. I didn't know you were here. Did you come courtin' me and Lily?''

"Hello, Hettie. I came to talk to Esther."

Hettie's face turn sulky. "Esther hit me and said I ain't got the sense of a pissant. Lily said I did too have sense and to pay Esther no mind. Lily's smart, ain't she, Owen?''

"Yes, she's smart and so are you. Didn't you grow the biggest pumpkin in the county last fall?''

The smiles returned. "Mrs. McCalister said mine was the biggest brought to the store. Is the slut still here?" Hettie asked, her mind jumping to another subject lightning fast.

"Don't talk about Mrs. Fairfax like that, Hettie," he said firmly.

"Ain't she a slut? Esther said she was. Is a slut a whore, Owen? Sometimes she says slut; sometimes she says whore." Hettie sighed as if the problem was too weighty for her to understand.

"She isn't like that. She's a nice woman. Why don't you call her Mrs. Fairfax or Ana?"

"Esther's awful mad. She says we can't come over while that slut's there. She said Soren's there loafin' and eatin' everything in sight, and he'd get Lily on her back if he could. Would he do that, Owen?"

"No, he wouldn't. He's fond of Lily, and of you too."

"I like Soren. He makes me laugh. But Esther said he'd pull up my skirt and pull down my drawers if I come over."

Owen ground his teeth in frustration. He heard voices in the rooms above.

"Shut up that jawin'," Jens bellowed. "A man can't sleep in his own house!"

Lily came back down the stairs. "She won't come down. She said that she don't want to see you again until you come to your senses. Then she began to rant and rave about Mrs. Fairfax. That's when Grandpa yelled."

Owen's irritation blossomed into anger. "Gawdamighty! Tell her I'll be back tomorrow night and she'd better be down here."

"She'll not pay us no mind," Lily said.

"Tell her anyway," he said gruffly. "And tell her I said she was not to come back over to the farm until I talk to her." Owen swore softly as he turned to leave.

"Are you mad?" Hettie's distressed voice turned into a wail. She grabbed his arm. "Don't be mad at me 'n' Lily."

"I'm not mad at you and Lily," he said gently and patted her hand. "I'm angry because Esther is being stubborn. It has nothing to do with you and Lily. Try and be good and stay out of her way until she cools off."

"I will, Owen. I try to be good."

"I know you do. Mind Lily, and she'll keep you out of trouble."

"I wish we could live with you—"

"Mama, Owen's got to go."

"Yes, I've got to get back. I'll be back over tomorrow night."

Owen rode across the pasture toward home. The horse knew the way even on the darkest night, but tonight there was a half moon. Owen absently watched the clouds scud across it and tried to combat the hot waves of frustration that kept surging over him.

Suddenly he thought that if this was difficult for him, what must it be like for Ana. She had come to this strange, unfriendly place, buried her stepdaughter, taken over the care of an infant, been the brunt of Esther's hostility and witnessed her bizarre behavior. Now she must decide if she should join her life to his and spend the rest of her life here.

He asked himself in slight bewilderment how things had ever come down to this. The image of Ana's face rose before him. Instead of being almost a stranger who had touched the fringe of his life, she had suddenly become the most important person in it and he was determined not to lose her.

Ana fried smoked side-pork and made a kettle of hot mush with raisins for breakfast. Owen was in the kitchen when she got there at first light, grinding coffee beans at the wall grinder. He said good-morning but nothing more. After he had stoked up the fire and carried in a bucket of fresh water, he went out to do chores. She wondered if the man had slept. She had been so tired the night before that she was asleep as soon as her head hit the pillow, and she hadn't heard him come in.

Soren, friendly as a puppy, kept the conversation rolling during the meal. Owen was quiet, and Ana thought it could be because of something that had happened when he went to the Knutson farm. She half expected to see Esther come in the door and loom over them like a black shadow. Uncle Gus announced that he was going to plant the garden, and Ana wondered about his willingness to do it. Gardening was usually women's work, but he seemed to be taking an unusual interest as if he hadn't had free rein before. Esther again? Ana wondered.

Owen lingered at the door after his cousin and uncle had left.

"Uncle Gus will be close by if you need anything."

"I'll be fine."

"The Wilson boys will be helping out for a few days. They'll be here for dinner and supper. I could come in early and fix it—" He left his words hanging.

"I'll have a meal ready at noon."

"You don't mind?"

"Of course, I don't mind." Their eyes caught and held. Both of them were thinking that she was still a guest here and under no obligation to cook for his work crew. Both were also aware that things would have to be settled between them soon. "I don't mind," she repeated and somehow summoned a conventional smile to her lips.

"Thank you." His voice had a hoarseness she hadn't heard before.

After he went out, Ana went to the door to watch him cross the yard. There was power in his every movement. Even as he walked to the barn with his slight limp, it was purposeful. He appeared to be a gentle man, tender and strong—yet he had not cherished his wife. The thought provoked the doubt that was always in the back of her mind.

Was it his raw physical strength that had attracted Harriet to him? The more Ana got to know him the more difficult it was for her to picture him and Harriet in the relationship Harriet had described.

Ana wrapped her hands in her apron and stepped out onto the porch to look at the morning. The sky was blue and cloudless, the grass green. White and pink blossoms were sprouting on the fruit trees. In the sky a sparrow chased a blackbird, and in a crosspiece joint of the windmill a robin with a beak full of dried grass was building a nest. The air here smelled pure and clean, unlike the smoky air that hung over Dubuque. She filled her lungs with it and let it out slowly.

This morning she looked around, seeing everything through different eyes. If she lived here, she would prune out about half of the wild rose bushes that grew in profusion along the sides of the lane, so that there would be more blossoms. She would plant morning glories at the end of the porch, fill that old hollow stump with rich black soil and plant it full of tulip bulbs.

Water could be piped into the house and an iron hand-pump put on the dry sink. She would open up all the rooms, and they would all be lived in. She would install a fancy heater in the parlor where they could sit on long winter evenings. A carpet runner in the hall, curtains at the kitchen windows, a fringed scarf on the library table and a wall clock that struck the hour would do wonders toward making this house a warmer, more welcoming place.

Lost in her daydream, Ana imagined sitting in a porch swing after her work was done. On a warm afternoon she would go to the orchard and pick the biggest, reddest apple she could find, sit under the tree, read or compose a poem. When her husband would come looking for her, she would run into his arms, and he would lift her and whirl her around before he passionately kissed her lips.

She halted her daydreams and scolded herself. "Oh, Ana, you are such a dreamer. You're twenty-six years old, for heaven's sake. Love and romance are for the young." Saying the words aloud made her see the bleakness of her future. She swallowed the lump that rose in her throat on a surge of self-pity, straightened her spine, and pushed the pleasant daydreams to the back of her mind.

The morning passed swiftly. Ana bathed Harry in the wash-dish, oiled his little body, and settled him in the middle of the bed. He was such a good baby. Some of the red was leaving his face, and his eyes, blue as the sky, were staying open for longer periods of time.

With the noon meal well started, she began her search for the cradle. The downstairs was laid out with two rooms on one side with a connecting door and doors leading into the central hall. On the other side was the parlor and the long kitchen-dining area.

Ana opened the door directly across the hall from the kitchen and looked into the room that connected with hers. This was Owen's room. It smelled of tobacco, leather and shoe polish. The furniture was polished oak and as beautifully made as the walnut set in the room upstairs. There was a bureau, a washstand, a bedside table, a wardrobe against one wall, a handsome combination bookcase and writing desk against another. Behind the glass door on one side of the desk were six shelves filled with books. On the stand beside the neatly made bed was the book she had seen at the store in White Oak—*Common Sense Medical Advisor*. Had he bought the book for Harriet or had he bought it after she left the store?

Ana couldn't bring herself to go more than a few steps into the room. One glance told her the cradle wasn't there. She backed out into the hallway and closed the door, deciding that there was a lot more to Owen Jamison than she had at first believed. With her lower lip caught firmly between her teeth and a puzzled frown puckering her forehead, she went upstairs.

The cradle was not in the room she had used or in the one where Harriet had died. Neither was it in a small room with two bunks nailed to the wall. The remaining room was filled with pieces of broken furniture. While searching through the discards, Ana lifted an old moth-eaten blanket in the corner of the storage room and discovered the cradle. Ana managed to get it to the top of the steps and set it down, wondering how in the world Esther had been able to carry it up the stairs.

Winded from the exertion, she decided to leave it until Owen came in for dinner.

While the meal was simmering on the stove, she sat down at the table with a pencil and tablet. She had already decided that she didn't have any choice but to stay here if she were to keep her promise to raise Harriet's son. But that didn't mean she would go blindly into marriage with Owen Jamison. She moistened the pencil lead in her mouth and began to write, listing the conditions he would have to agree to before she would consign her future to him and his son.

Ana sliced the pork Uncle Gus had brought in from the smoke house, floured it, pounded it with the back side of a heavy butcher knife, and cooked it in rich brown gravy flavored with sage. Potatoes, sauerkraut and cornbread rounded out the meal along with a cobbler pie she made from a can of the peaches Owen had bought at the store. She seasoned the pie with butter and cinnamon, dampened the top crust with cream and sprinkled it with sugar to make a golden, sugary crust. Then she set a pitcher of milk on the table with a crock of butter and a bowl of thick blackberry jam she had found in the pantry.

The men came in from the fields at high noon. Ana heard Soren's shouts of laughter as he teased the Wilson boys and splashed one of them with a dipper of water. The horseplay between Soren and the boys went on during the time they were washing up. When they stepped into the kitchen, the boys bashfully hung their heads after nodding a greeting to Ana.

The boys, Soren, and Gus were already in the kitchen when Owen came in. His eyes scanned the cloth-covered table laden with a tempting meal, then sought Ana's face. As far as he could tell, she wasn't even aware he was there. She was smiling at Soren and urging them to sit down and eat while it was hot. As Owen took his place at the head of the table, Ana slipped into the chair nearest the stove so that she could refill the bowls and coffee cups.

"Are you sure you won't marry me, darlin'?" Soren's smile spread charm all over his handsome face. He looked across the table at Ana as he continued to heap the food on his plate.

"I've given it some thought," Ana retorted seriously. "But I decided that there's more to life than being chained to a cookstove twenty-four hours a day, and that's what it would take to keep you filled up."

"Woe! Oh, woe is me!" Soren groaned dramatically. "Pa, tell her what a fine chap I am."

Owen's serious eyes studied both Ana and Soren covertly as he made a big to-do about filling his plate. Uncle Gus read the expression on Owen's face. It was hard for the serious, hard-working man to understand how Soren could tease a pretty woman such as Ana, and how she could engage in light-hearted banter with him. Why shouldn't Owen be puzzled? Unnecessary talk, much less tomfoolery, had not been tolerated in this house while he was growing up.

"I'll have the root crops in today—potatoes, carrots, turnips and rutabagas," Uncle Gus said, thinking it time to put Owen at ease. He helped himself to a square of cornbread, split it, and covered it with gravy.

"I have a hill of rhubarb in Dubuque. It's probably ready to cut by now," Ana said, passing the bowl of potatoes to one of the Wilson boys.

"We have more here than we ever use."

"I usually make a few jars of rhubarb-and-wild strawberry jam. During the long winter months it's nice to have a taste of spring."

"We got wild strawberries aplenty too. But it takes a heap a pickin' to get enough."

When the bowls and platters were empty, Ana removed them and set the cobbler on the table. The pie was golden brown, and juice bubbled in the slits she had cut in the crust.

She set a pitcher of rich cream beside it, conscious of Owen's eyes on her face. She was careful not to look at him. Was he disapproving of her extravagance? The cream could be churned into butter and sold at the store.

The Wilson boys ate heartily with their heads down and their eyes on their plates. One of them didn't speak at all during the meal. The other only asked for the potatoes, then meat. Both ate large helpings of the cobbler, then thanked Ana for the meal and hurried out.

"You've got those boys buffaloed, Ana," Soren said, his mouth looking as if it would never smile again.

"What do you mean?"

"They talked a blue streak on the way in from the field. They come in here and you scare the talk right out of them. What's their pa going to think when they get home?" His eyes began to sparkle and his mouth twitched in a grin he couldn't hold back.

"If I'm so scary, how come I can't scare the sass out of you, Soren Halverson? I'll thank you to get out of this kitchen and get back to work," she retorted spiritedly.

"She's throwing me out, Owen. She's mean and cruel—"

"I can be meaner. Now scat!"

Good-natured laughter burst from Soren as he headed for the door.

Ana turned and caught Owen watching them with a grave and brooding darkness to his features, and his eyes, when they met hers, looked as if they were seeking something. Abruptly he turned, reached for the half-empty water bucket, and followed Soren out.

What's the matter with the man? Was he turning back into the *grump* he was on the way here from Lansing? Surely he knows his cousin well enough to understand his teasing. Did he think it unlady-like for her to respond to Soren's banter?

Now was the time to get a few things straight and clear the air. Owen would ask her for her decision when he returned. Rather than wait for him to ask, she would bring up the subject herself and perhaps it would give her a small advantage when she presented her list of conditions he must agree to before she would stay.

Owen returned and set the waterbucket on the shelf beside the door.

"Mr. Jamison, I've decided what I will do," Ana said before her nerve deserted her. "I'd like to discuss it with you if you can take the time."

He stood stone-still for a moment, then nodded, stepped around her and went to the door.

"Soren," he called, "go on out and start on the east field. I'll be there in a while."

Ana cleared away some of the dishes to make room at the table while Owen poured himself a cup of coffee, silently cursing the nervous trembling in his hands.

Thirteen

"*I found* the cradle in the storage room, Mr. Jamison. I managed to get it as far as the top of the stairs. If you will bring it down here to the kitchen, I'll get Harry. I don't like leaving him alone for such long periods of time."

Mr. Jamison. She could laugh and tease with Soren, but she couldn't even call *him* by his given name. To her he was a degenerate, a seducer of young girls.

A cold knot of dread began to form in the pit of Owen's stomach as he left the room and went up the steps. *She was going to leave!* That was what she wanted to discuss. She would insist on taking the boy, and, of course, he would let her take him. It would be selfish of him to keep the child here, board him out with a family like the Larsons or the McCalisters, and see him only occasionally while he was growing up.

Owen tried to gather his scattered thoughts. Ana had said that he could come to Dubuque to visit. It would be a way of keeping in touch with her and maybe someday—. He dropped that painful train of thought and went on to another. The one thing he could do for her was to see to it that she didn't have to go outside her home to work. He would insist that she agree to at least that much.

"It's a beautiful cradle," Ana said as she followed him into the kitchen.

"Is this where you want it?" He set the cradle in the corner out of the draft and backed out of the way.

"This is fine." Ana cuddled the infant to her shoulder, her eyes tender. "He's such a good baby. I've never known one like him. Do you think I might be prejudiced?" She laughed lightly, her eyes seeking his. "It seems so funny to think of myself as a grandma, even a step-grandma."

Because he was looking at her so intently, the smile froze on her face and the laughter died from her eyes. *Ana Fairfax, get a hold on yourself, you're rattling on like a featherhead.* She wanted to appear composed, confident. But her heart was throbbing in her throat. Her future would be decided during the next few minutes, so why shouldn't she be nervous? She tucked the blanket in place around the baby and looped a strand of her hair behind her ear before she turned to look up at the big man standing beside the table.

"Sit down, Mr. Jamison. I'm nervous enough without having to stand here and look up at you."

The chair legs scraped on the floor as he pulled out the chair. Ana took two sheets of paper from the top of the pie safe and sat down across from him.

"I've given your . . . suggestion serious thought. Harriet was near and dear to me. She was the only family I had. And although I probably will never be able to forgive you for seducing a young and innocent girl, I have no choice but to marry you if I am going to keep my promise to raise her son. But—" she held up her hand when he opened his mouth to speak—"I will insist that you agree to certain conditions. I'm not so desperate, Mr. Jamison, that I will compromise myself. For instance, I will not become a mere servant in this house. I want that understood from the beginning. I have written some of my concerns down so that you may read

them over, and then we will discuss them.'' Breathless from
the long speech, she moved the papers across the table.

Owen moved his chair back, leaned forward with elbows
braced on knees spread wide, and slowly read what Ana had
written. Her tightly clasped hands rested on the table as she
watched him. Not a muscle twitched in his face, nor did a
line appear to indicate his approval or disapproval of the
conditions stated. His lashes covered his brilliant blue eyes,
preventing her from reading his reaction there.

He was more rugged than any of the men she had known.
His face was not as handsome as Soren's, she decided, while
giving it careful scrutiny. But it had character. The brows
above his thick lashes were well shaped. His cheeks were
smooth, his mouth firm, his hair soft and clean, his hard-
columned neck sturdy as an oak tree.

He was clean in spite of working in the fields since sunup.
The collar of his shirt was frayed and needed to be turned,
but it was clean. His fingers were long and tapered, his nails
cut close. The ground-in dirt usually found in a working man's
hands was not there, yet she knew he worked hard.

Would he be like Mr. Fairfax and ignore his right to her
bed, or would he insist on sharing it? If so, those hands, so
generously sprinkled with silky dark hair, would touch her
in her most intimate places. She went rigid with shock. Oh,
God—the blood rushed to her face—was she ready for this?

Owen was looking at her. His head was still bent over the
papers, but he had raised his lids, and his eyes, as deep and
blue as the sky, were staring into hers. They made her a bit
giddy.

''What you want sounds reasonable to me.''

''I don't want blanket approval,'' she said quickly and
sharper than she intended. ''I want to know what you think
of each condition. I'm trying to be honest with you. My
future is at stake here.''

''I realize that.''

''If I stay, this will be my home . . . our home. I'll not

stand for any interference from your sister." Ana's golden eyes looked earnestly into his. "Esther will be welcome to come here as a *guest*, but that is all. Do you agree to that?"

"I'll speak with Esther and try to make her understand." She heard the unsteadiness in his voice. Why, he was just as nervous as she was!

"If there's anything inside or outside the house that is hers or that you want her to have, I want her to take it. What will be left will be mine . . . rather ours. Do you agree?"

"Sounds reasonable."

"About the farm. Are you the sole owner, or do your brother and sister own a share?"

"It is mine. I paid Paul, my younger brother, for his share, and our Pa gave Esther her share when she married Jens."

"You may think I'm mercenary, Mr. Jamison, but I vowed a long time ago that I would never again be put in the position where I had to scrounge for something to eat. I'm more than willing to shoulder my part of the work here, but I need assurance that in the future I won't be put out to shift on my own."

"I'll have your name put on the deed."

"No. You misunderstand me. That won't be necessary. As your wife and the guardian of your child, I would have rights if the farm were yours."

"It's mine—every stick and stone."

"Another thing. I'll sell my house in Dubuque and use part of the money to make this a more comfortable home. You must admit it has been . . . neglected. The rest of the money, Harriet's half, will be saved for Harry's education."

"I have money to fix up the house any way you wish. Keep your money to use as you want."

"No. By sharing the expense I'll feel as if part of this is mine." She gestured with a wave of her arm.

"Good God, woman." Owen showed the first sign of impatience. "It will be anyway."

"I'll not budge on that point," she said firmly.

He shrugged. "If that's the way you want it."

"I go to church," she continued in the same firm tone of voice. "I'll expect my . . . husband to accompany me."

"Every Sunday? That's the day I . . . dally around in the shed."

"You'll not have to go every Sunday, but enough so that the community thinks of us as a family. Sunday is a day of rest. I don't understand why you choose to work."

"Some men like a ball game on Sunday afternoon. I like fooling around with my tools."

"Oh. I see," she said, but it was evident that she didn't. Ana was busy looking at his lips that twitched in the corners as if they wanted to smile but were afraid to.

"I enjoy building furniture out of native wood. To me it isn't work."

"I see," she said again, her eyes locked with his. "Working with wood? You made the cradle," she blurted accusingly. "And that beautiful furniture upstairs."

"Why does that surprise you?" His face had turned serious again.

"I don't know. Did Harriet know you were making the cradle?"

"She saw it while I was working on it."

"You made the furniture upstairs and what's in your room, didn't you?"

"It's something I like to do," he said defensively.

"You must be proud of it. It's as fine a quality as any I've seen in the big houses on the bluff in Dubuque. You're a gifted craftsman."

He shrugged. His eyes were lighter now, his face not so serious. Ana was sure he was pleased by her praise.

"Does that cover everything?"

"No. What about . . . children?" she asked.

"I'd like some."

"You have one," she said sharply and turned her eyes away from him to look out the door. Her breath came in and out of her parted lips rapidly.

"I'll not pounce on you and demand my rights, if that's

what you're concerned about. But if in the course of time we
. . . become better acquainted—if we agree mutually—'' He
let the suggestion hang.

Her eyes, brilliant in her crimson face, came back to his.
"Thank you," she whispered.

"Is there anything else?"

"I guess not. But . . . I feel so guilty because of . . .
Harriet. She loved you!" she said accusingly. "I hope she
knows that I'm not trying to take her place in your . . . in
your affections."

"Mrs. Fairfax . . . Ana—"

"—I'm not ready to talk about that now," she said and
thought that she would strangle on the words. "I want to
assure you that this will not be a one-sided bargain. I'll give
Harriet's and your son loving care, I'll tend your house, and
I will never shame you in the community."

"I'll ask for nothing more."

"Do you want to talk this over with your sister?"

Owen's eyes were drawn to her. She looked steadily into
them. Did she think him so spineless that he had to consult
his sister? Self-consciously he shifted his attention toward the
door, fumbled in the pocket of his shirt, withdrew a watch,
checked the time, and moved his eyes back to her.

"I'll not talk it over with Esther, but I will tell her."

"Then the only thing to settle is . . . when."

"When I talk to Esther?"

"No. When will we . . . ah . . . make a legal commit-
ment?"

"Get married? Well, anytime is all right with me. We can
go see the preacher this afternoon."

"I thought you were in a hurry to finish the planting?"

"We'll be at that for a week or more. We should be wed
before the tongues start to wag. I can spare a couple of
hours." He stood looking down at the top of her head. "Do
you want me to sign the papers agreeing to what we've discussed?"

"No. Your word is good enough." Ana gathered up plates and carried them to the counter. "Give me some time to put these to soak, and I'll change my dress."

"Uncle Gus will stay with Harry."

"I'd rather take him." The picture of Esther bending over the cradle floated though her mind. "He'll not be any trouble. I'll take along a bottle and dry napkins."

Owen shrugged. "I'll hitch up the buggy before I change out of my overalls."

In a white shirtwaist and blue skirt, and with her hand held firmly in his, Ana stood beside Owen and spoke her vows. It seemed unreal to her that for the second time she was marrying for security and respectability. Owen stood coatless before the preacher in his dark pants and white shirt. It was not a fancy wedding by any means, but it was just as binding.

On the way to town it had occurred to Ana that Preacher Larson and his wife might be uncomfortable about marrying her son-in-law. But her fears were groundless. Not a word was said. Mrs. Larson greeted her warmly. They discussed the baby, then Owen explained that Ana was going to stay in his home and take care of his son, and that rather than create gossip about their relationship, they wished to be united in marriage. Preacher Larson nodded his approval and sent one of the children scurrying down to the store to fetch Violet McCalister to act as one of the witnesses.

Mrs. Larson held the baby during the brief ceremony that united Ana and Owen as man and wife for as long as they both lived. When the minister said that Owen could kiss the bride, his lips grazed her cheek in a symbolic gesture, and it was over. All present understood that this was not a love match. It was a practical matter, one that required no gushy congratulatory remarks, so none were forthcoming. It was

not unusual in this sparsely settled land for a man to take a
new wife within days of burying his spouse in order to have
a woman to tend his house, take care of his children, and
share his bed.

After the ceremony, Violet and Mrs. Larson welcomed
Ana to the community and invited her to join the Busy Bee
Quilting Circle that met on the second Wednesday each month
in the church basement.

"At our next meeting we'll plan the Fourth of July celebration," Mrs. Larson said. "It'll be an all-day affair with
dinner on the ground, races, fireworks and the like."

"We'll have a pie booth and a cakewalk," Violet added
enthusiastically. "In the evening there'll be a street dance.
Two of the best fiddlers in the state live right here in Alla-
makee county."

"It sounds like quite a celebration."

"Oh, it is! We put a tent up here in front of the church
and sell everything from canned goods to crocheted doilies.
It's our biggest fund-raiser. People come to White Oak from
miles around. Some even come a couple of days early and
camp out if they don't have folks living near by."

"Let me know if there's anything I can do." Ana climbed
into the buggy and held her arms out for the sleeping infant.

Violet laughed. "Everyone donates and everyone works."

"You can plan on me to work and to donate knit stockings
and caps to sell."

Ana was eager to leave, to have a little time to herself to
adjust to this drastic turn her life had taken so suddenly.
Owen evidently felt the same. He shook the preacher's hand,
took his place beside Ana in the buggy, and slapped the reins
against the horse's back. The two women and the preacher
stood in front of the church and waved goodbye as Owen
turned the horse around, and they drove away.

"They'll have plenty to talk about for the rest of the day,"
Owen said and glanced at Ana briefly.

"They didn't seem to be shocked."

"Shocked? Why should they be shocked?"

"I doubt that Preacher Larson has ever married a man to his mother-in-law before," she retorted drily.

"He knew you were Harriet's step-mother. Even if you were her real mother, what difference would it make?" When she didn't answer he asked, "Are you ashamed of marrying me?"

"Of course not! I can't help it if I feel I've somehow been disloyal to Harriet. But I'll not hang my head if that's what you mean," she added crisply. "I've done what I had to do to keep my promise."

He was quiet for a moment, then asked, "Is there anything you want from the store?"

"No."

"Anything for the boy?"

"No."

Nothing else was said until they passed the place where Owen had caught up with Ana when she walked to town.

"It looks like rain." He had been watching the south-western sky darken.

"I suppose you'd rather it held off till your crops were in."

"No. A good shower will soften the ground."

"I don't know anything about farming, but I like growing things. I'll miss my garden patch and my flowers in Dubuque." A wistful tone she was unaware of entered her voice. It caused him to turn and look at her.

"You can have a garden here and all the flowers you want," he said slowly.

When she didn't answer or look at him, he studied the perfectly etched lines of her profile. For the first time he noticed the faintest dusting of gold freckles across the bridge of her nose. He tried to hold down the elation he felt as he gazed at her. This golden-haired, golden-eyed woman beside him was his *wife*. She was not an impetuous, flighty girl like Harriet but a woman, a mature woman. Could he live up to her expectations? The thought of having her as his own both thrilled and frightened him. He felt a masculine stirring inside him and hastily looked away.

To have and to hold until death you do part. It was enough for now that she was his to protect and provide for. Perhaps in time she would be more than his in name only. He wanted to talk to her, keep the lines of communication open, and racked his brain to think of something to say. Finally it was Ana who broke the silence.

"Will your sister allow Lily to come over and visit with me and Harry?"

It took Owen a minute to pull his thoughts together before he could answer.

"Esther will forbid her to come, but I think Lily will find a way. She's no longer a child. She's starting to think for herself."

"Has Hettie always been the way she is?"

"I think so. I've never heard anyone say differently. She's harmless though. You needn't worry about her hurting you or the baby. I've seen her dig worms for a bird with a broken wing. She's soft-hearted and will tend anything that's sick and helpless."

"Did she ever go to school?" Ana knew she was asking a lot of questions, but he wasn't going to tell her anything unless she asked.

"Not that I know of. Old Mrs. Knutson doted on her. Then after Lily was born, she doted on both of them. When she died, Hettie was turned loose. By then Lily was seven or eight years old. She tried to keep track of her mother, but Hettie wandered all over the county. Jens was afraid some man would take advantage of her again."

"He married Esther and turned the responsibility over to her. I suppose Lily is the result of someone taking advantage of Hettie."

"That's about the size of it."

"Poor Lily."

By the time they turned into the lane leading to the farm, lightning quivered in the dark clouds, and the wind, cooler now, had switched to the southwest. As they approached the white farmhouse silhouetted against the dark clouds, Ana wondered if arriving at her new home in a storm was symbolic of things to come. Regardless of what the future held, she was married to this man for better or worse. This was her home now. She would live here for the rest of her life, locked into a loveless marriage with this big, sometimes snarling grump of a man.

She wanted to cry.

A loud crack of thunder interrupted her thoughts. The horse shied, and only Owen's strong hands on the reins held the animal in check. He maneuvered the buggy as close as possible to the back porch and stopped the horse. Above them a brisk wind turned the blades on the windmill. On the shed a loose board rattled rhythmically.

"Damn. I forgot to shut down the windmill. The tanks will be running over." Owen helped Ana down from the buggy. "Hurry on inside. Those clouds will open up any minute."

And they did. Ana had no more than stepped inside the kitchen when a solid sheet of rain hit the side of the house. Seconds later there was another, and then a steady downpour hammered on the roof. She put Harry in the cradle, closed the kitchen windows, and hurried to check those in the other parts of the house. By the time she returned, the baby was letting her know it was time to eat, and she spent the next half hour cuddling and feeding him in the old chair that Hettie had sat in the night she arrived.

This was her wedding day! Her second wedding day. Ana thought of the first one. It had not been much different from today—it had rained that day too. She had met Mr. Fairfax at the tailor shop, and they had gone to Judge Henderson's office. After the brief ceremony Ezra had gone back to his shop. Ana had hurried home to tend Harriet who was sick with a cold and to get the wash off the line before it rained. Mr. Jamison was using her in the same way Mr. Fairfax had used her. Neither man cared for her personally. Each needed her as a nursemaid for his child.

Ana allowed herself a moment of regret. She would never hear the sweet, intimate words a man whispered to the woman he loved or know the joy of being held and cherished. The deep and abiding love between a man and a woman she had read of in novels had turned her fanciful, she thought after her brief lapse of self-pity. She had to stop day-dreaming. Marrying Owen Jamison had been the practical thing to do.

Deep in her thoughts, Ana was unaware that the rain had let up until she heard shouts of laughter and the sound of heavy boots on the porch.

"Get on home, little sugar teats, afore you melt!"

"Ah . . . shut up, Soren!"

"Yore ma'll be lookin' for her baby boys."

"Ya ain't nothin' but a loose-mouthed lunkhead, Soren Halverson!"

"I'll get a piece of your hide for that, sissy-britches! You can count on it."

"Ya got ta catch me first, 'n' yore the sissy-britches. Ya can't even plow a straight row."

"Soren's a lunk . . . head! Lunk . . . head!" the twins chanted. "Soren's an old lunk . . . h-head and a piss-ant!"

"Watch your mouths, sissy boys!"

"You're the sissy! Sis . . . sy, sis . . . sy, sis—" The young voices faded as the Wilson boys headed their mule across the pasture toward home.

"Just you wait 'til this rain lets up," Soren shouted. "I'm going to stuff your butts down the hole in the outhouse."

Ana had put the baby in the cradle and moved it back away from the draft by the time the men removed their boots and came into the kitchen.

"Shame on you for teasing those boys," Ana said while smiling into Soren's laughing face.

"Who says I'm teasing?" he retorted, wiping his wet head with the towel she handed to him.

"I do," she replied handing another towel to Owen who crowded in the door behind his cousin. "Is Mr. Halverson coming in?" she asked Owen, but Soren answered.

"Later. He's fixing a place in the barn for the goat Nils Brandt brought over while you were in town tying the knot with this big, ugly cousin of mine."

"A goat? Oh, that's grand. Harry can have goat's milk. Mrs. Larson said that goat's milk is better for a baby than cow's milk."

"Did she say that?" he exclaimed, dramatically. "I always wondered about why Noah let them cantankerous creatures on the boat."

"Oh, Soren. Can't you be serious?"

"I'm trying to, darlin'. But you've gone and busted my heart right in two."

Ana's eyes flicked to Owen. His face was covered with the towel, and his fingers were burrowed in his ears. She looked back at Soren.

"Oh, poor you! I can see that you're cut to the quick."

"How come you picked this big, old ugly cousin of mine over me? I'm much better looking than he is."

"Because I didn't want to be responsible for all the desperate women who would have thrown themselves in the river when they learned you were lost to them," she said lightly and glanced at Owen again. His back was to them.

"That was mighty considerate, darlin'."

"But then again, when they gave it serious thought, I'm sure that they'd appreciate my sacrifice."

Soren laughed, then playfully pinched her chin.

"Dammed if you didn't get a prize, cousin Owen."

"Stop horsing around, Soren, and let me get to work," Ana scolded.

"Not till I kiss my new cousin." Soren grabbed Ana by the shoulders. His kiss landed somewhere between her eye and her ear. "Welcome to the Halverson side of the family, cousin Ana. Owen's ma was a Halverson. So there's a little bit of good in him if you can find it.''

"I'm terribly relieved to know that. You men sit down out of my way and I'll heat up the coffee. I've got the noon dishes to do.''

Fourteen

The rain turned into a steady drizzle and continued for the remainder of the afternoon. Owen, Soren and Gus sat at the table after the night meal and talked while Ana washed the dishes and put the kitchen in order.

"I'm thinking about putting in an acre-and-a-half of sorghum," Owen said. "What do you think, Uncle Gus?"

"Good idey. Tops make good feed; so do the stalks after the juice is pressed out." Gus packed tobacco in the bowl of his pipe and lit it with a sulfur match.

"You can ship all the syrup you can't use down river," Soren added.

The conversation went on to broom corn, the harvesting of the winter wheat, the new litter of piglets, and the foal they expected most any time. Nothing more was said about the wedding that had taken place that afternoon. Soren had stopped teasing Owen after a quelling glare from his father.

Ana dreaded the time when she would be alone in the house with her new husband. She glanced at him as she hung the dishpan on the nail at the end of the counter. His big muscular forearms rested on the table; his powerful hands wrapped around his coffee cup. The lamplight shone on the rich brown hair that lay in curls low on his neck. Suddenly he looked up. Their gazes met and locked while she slowly folded the dish towel, and he wiped the back of his hand across his mouth. Ana's eyes moved down to the indentation in his chin below his wide, firm lips, then back up to his eyes. Only seconds went by as they stared at each other, but to Ana it seemed more like an hour. Owen Jamison was a goodlooking man in his rough-hewn, masculine way that any love-hungry woman would adore. It was no wonder that Harriet had fallen so deeply in love with him.

When Harry began to whimper, drawing Owen's attention to the baby, Ana took a long breath and released it slowly. Soren's voice came to her ears as from a great distance. She caught only words and phrases as he talked about visiting the Martin Flynn farm, the largest and most completely appointed farm in Polk county, where Flynn was breeding a strain of short-horn cattle.

Glad for an excuse to leave the kitchen, Ana went to the bedroom with a stack of clean napkins for the baby. As soon as she lit the lamp she saw the copy of *Common Sense Medical Advisor* on the bedside table. When had he put it there? Did he plan to move in here with her? Tonight?

The spring rain had brought a chill to the rest of the house. When she returned to the kitchen, she filled the hod with small clumps of coal for the small round stove in the bedroom. Owen stood and took it from her hand as she started to leave the room.

"I'll start a fire. I forgot that it will be too cold in there for the boy."

"Thank you."

Gus pushed himself away from the table and stood. "Looks like the rain's set in for the night."

"Mr. Halverson—"

"What's this Mr. Halverson stuff? Pa's your Uncle Gus now," Soren said teasingly.

"Leave the lassie be, son. She can call me whatever she wants."

"I've never had an uncle. At least not one that I knew," Ana said somberly.

"You got one now, and a cousin too." Soren drained his coffee cup and stood.

Ana's eyes swung from Soren to his father. "There's no need for you to go out in the rain. There are beds upstairs."

"Thanks, lass. But these old bones are used to their own bed." The old man took a slicker from the peg beside the door and went out.

Ana glanced at Soren, unaware of the panic in her eyes. He came to her, slipped an arm about her shoulders and gave her a brief hug.

"Good night, Cousin Ana," he said to the top of her head. "See you in the morning."

Ana stood looking at the screen door after it slammed shut behind Soren. She had a home, an uncle, a cousin and a *husband*. By and by, perhaps she and Owen would have a child to be brother or sister to Harry. It was strange, she thought painfully, Harriet's passing had left her standing on the threshold of a new life that included everything she had ever dreamed of having except for one thing—love.

The baby had almost finished the bottle when Owen came into the room. He set the coal hod beside the stove and took a drink from the water bucket before he spoke to her.

"I'll take the cradle to the bedroom. A carriage would be more useful than this heavy thing," he said picking it up. "I never thought of that when I was making it."

"It's a beautiful cradle," Ana said when Owen came back into the room.

"We'll get a carriage so you won't have to carry him all the time."

"There's one in the house in Dubuque. It was Harriet's."

"What do you want to do about the things you have there? Will they be all right for a while? It will be three or four weeks before I'll be free to go fetch them for you." He leaned against the work counter, his booted feet crossed at the ankles, his arms crossed over his chest.

"There isn't an awful lot there that I want other than my personal things and a few of Harriet's to keep for Harry. I'll sell the furniture with the house. My neighbor, Mr. Leonard, is looking after it for me."

"I know a banker in Dubuque who will take care of it for you. Would you like for me to write him and ask him to sell your house? If you make a list of what you want, he'll pack it and send it up on a freight wagon."

"Well—" She avoided his eyes, and lifted a hand to tuck stray strands of hair into the bun on the back of her neck.

"Would you rather go down there and do it yourself? I'll take you in a few weeks."

"No. I don't think I want to go back there. I'd just as soon your friend took care of it for me. I'll make a list, but I'd like a few days to think about it."

He nodded but said nothing. Ana looked down at the sleeping child in her arms. She could feel Owen's eyes on her face, and the tightness in her chest increased with alarming intensity.

"I'll go take a look at my mare. She could foal any time. Her bag is already full of milk." Owen felt suffocated, there wasn't enough air in the room. His restricted lungs struggled in an effort to drag enough air into his body. He took his slicker from the peg beside the door. "I hope she doesn't decide to have it tonight."

Ana got to her feet as soon as Owen went out the door. What did he mean by that? He didn't want the mare to foal tonight because it was raining or because it was his wedding night? She hurried across the hall to the front bedroom where the lamp cast a soft glow on the already warm room. In a small part of her mind she was sure Owen would not come to her room tonight even though it was his right, and she had admitted to him her willingness to have children. In a larger part of her mind she was not absolutely sure.

After settling Harry in the cradle, she quickly undressed, washed her face and arms with a wet cloth, and slipped into her nightdress. The absolute necessity was to use the chamber pot before Owen returned. The tinkling sound of letting water could easily be heard through the thin walls. Ana let down her hair, placed her precious supply of hairpins on the bureau and crawled into bed.

She lay with her hands tucked beneath her cheeks, her eyes fastened to the darkened door. Her new husband was not a man like Ezra Fairfax who ignored all women including his daughter and herself. All Ezra had cared about was his tailor shop. He gave far more attention to his young male apprentice than he did to his daughter and his wife.

Owen Jamison was a young, strong, earthy man. Sooner or later he would be possessed with the unresistable biological urge that God gave to all males to assure the continuation of their species. He would come to her with *that* and only *that* on his mind. It would have nothing to do with his feelings for her—she would be merely a convenience, a means to slake his lust. He would no longer have to go to Dubuque or Prairie du Chien to seek out a young girl.

Oh, how could she bear his touch knowing he had been so intimate with Harriet? This was the price she was paying for security, for having the privilege of raising Harriet's son.

After what seemed an eternity, she heard the back door close. The house was quiet except for the splattering sound of rain against the window panes. Ana curled herself in a tight ball, her ears straining for the sound of footsteps approaching the bedroom door. Long silent minutes passed.

Finally, Ana flopped over on her stomach and buried her face in the pillow, but she couldn't block from her mind the image of deep blue eyes, soft wavy hair and a dimple in the middle of a square chin. Nor could she stop thinking about large, work-roughened hands that had held her bare feet so gently as he washed the molasses from between her toes.

* * *

Owen was up and building a fire in the cookstove when the rooster flew up onto the fence post and announced the new day. After putting the coffeepot on to boil, he had gone to the barn to check on the mare and the nanny goat. The mare whinnied softly as soon as the light from the lantern reached her. She seemed no nearer to coming to foal than she had the night before. Owen spoke to her, caressed her velvety nose and put a measure of oats in her feedbox.

The goat had rubbed her neck raw trying to get loose from the rope holding her. She was resentful and tried to butt him with her head. He scowled at her and swore. She needed milking, but he would leave that to Gus. The less he had to do with that creature the better.

The rain had stopped sometime during the night, and a warm gentle breeze blew from the south. Owen leaned against the porch post and looked toward the east where a rosy glow was lighting a cloudless sky. The promise of a fine day was in the making. As the ground was too wet for field work, he arranged in his mind the work for the day: fix the hog house, move the sow and her litter out of the barn and make it ready for another sow, build a pen for the goat, grease the windmill, go to the Knutson's and talk with Esther. The last was a must. He had been relieved of the chore last night because of the rain.

Slipping out of his muddy boots and leaving them on the porch, Owen went silently into the kitchen and paused just inside the door. By the light of the lamp he had left on the kitchen table, he saw Ana the same instant that she saw him. Startled, she stared at him, her mouth forming a silent O. Barefoot, her loose hair hanging down to her hips like a golden waterfall, she stood beside the cookstove in her night-dress, her face flaming.

"I . . . need a bottle for . . . Harry," she mumbled in confusion.

It was the first time Owen had heard her stammer. She was usually so pale and composed and sure of herself.

"I didn't mean to startle you. I had to see about the mare."

"Is the mare all right?" Ana poured water into the milk from the teakettle, snapped the rubber nipple in place, and headed for the door.

"So far."

"I'll feed Harry and be back to fix your breakfast."

Owen sank down on a chair and propped his elbows on the table. Big stupid lummox, he chided himself. Why hadn't he looked before he came barging in. Catching her in her night clothes had embarrassed the hell out of her. Worst of all he had not been able to look away. His eyes had feasted on the slender form beneath the gown, the glorious hair hanging down her back, and her soft, quivering mouth. She was becoming an obsession with him, depriving him of common sense. Ana was the only woman he had ever met that he wanted so violently that he couldn't even think straight when he was around her.

And she *despised* him.

The sky was lit with the eerie light of dawn when Owen cocked his ear toward the door. He had heard the jingle of harness and the snorting of a trotting horse. Getting to his feet, he went to the door and looked out. He said something violent under his breath when he saw Esther's buggy pull to a stop in the yard. He went out the door and slipped his feet back into his muddied boots.

"Morning, Owen," Esther called cheerfully and climbed down out of the buggy. "It's a fine day for washing. You usually have the fire built under my washpot by now," she scolded good-naturedly.

Owen cursed again under his breath and went out to meet her.

"I was coming over to see you this morning, Esther."

"Whatever for? You know I always come here on Monday to do the wash."

"It isn't Monday. It's Saturday."

"Saturday? Ah . . . go on! You're funnin' me. It's Monday and you know it." She reached into the buggy and brought out a wicker basket. "I brought a few of our things to wash. I can't depend on Lily and Hettie to do it. Lily is moonin' around and Hettie's so addle-brained she can't do doodle-d-squat unless someone's standing over her to tell her every move to make."

Owen went to his sister, took the basket out of her hands and set it back in the buggy. My God! Didn't she even know what day it was? And had she forgotten the mess she made here the other day? She was as bright and cheerful as a brand-new penny, acting as if nothing at all had happened.

"I told you that there was no need for you to come back over here. You don't have to do my wash or cook or keep house for me any more."

"Are you out of your mind? Of course, I do. Get on now and draw water for the washpot."

"No, Esther. Go home and do your own work."

"That's sweet of you, brother. But I'll take care of you as I've always done. Is that crock of hog grease still in the cellar? We're going to need a batch of lye soap—"

"—Esther! I don't need you to do my wash or make soap!"

"Well for crying out loud! Mama's gone, brother. If I don't do it, who will?"

"Ana will do it."

"Ana? Who's Ana?"

"Ana Fairfax. Harriet's mother."

"Oh, her. She's gone, Owen. She left days ago."

"No, she hasn't gone. She's here."

Esther's dark, feverish eyes darted toward the house then returned to his face.

"That slut's not still here!"

"Ana is still here and she's staying here. You must come to terms with that. She'll keep house for me. You don't need to come—"

"No! She'll not keep house for you!"

"She's staying," Owen said firmly. "We were married

yesterday by Reverend Larson. She's my wife now and I don't want to hear you call her a slut ever again. Do you understand me?'' The only way Owen was able to control his anger was to admit to himself that Esther was not in her right mind.

Esther sucked in her breath, staring at him. ''You . . . you married *her*!''

''Yes. The boy needs a mother—''

''—Owen! Brother! Did you say you . . . m-married t-that—'' Esther's screech trailed.

''Ana and I were married,'' he said firmly. ''She and the boy will live here with me, and she'll take care of the house now.''

Esther bared her teeth and let out a howl of pure fury. She balled her fist and swung at his head. Owen caught her wrist and held it while she struggled.

''You'd . . . do that to me after . . . after all I've done for you? You'd throw me out of my Mama's house and take in that city whore?''

''Calm down and be reasonable. You're my sister. It isn't a case of throwing you out!'' Esther was too violently angry to listen. Her eyes flashed, her lips were drawn back in a vicious snarl, and she tried her best to rake his face with her fingernails.

''You . . . bastard! Son-of-a-bitch! Fornicator! You're a Jamison all right. Just like Pa . . . and Grandpa. You . . . ruttin' boar!'' she shouted.

Owen grabbed her by the shoulders and shook her. ''Hush that talk,'' he demanded, but Esther was wild with anger.

''Swine! He-goat! Tomcat!'' Her eyes blazed furiously into his, and she struggled with a strength he didn't know she possessed.

''Stop that! For God's sake, get a hold of yourself,'' he demanded gruffly, holding her away from him so that she couldn't kick his shins.

''Let go of me! Shithead! Horny rooster! Filthy bounder! Dirty rotten son-of-a-bastard! Go plow your whore—''

Unsure of what to do, Owen held onto her upper arms while she called him and Ana every filthy name she had ever heard. Shocked by her savage attack with fists and feet, and the rough language, he could only stare into her hate-twisted face. It was heart-rending for him to hear the nastiness that poured from his sister's mouth.

Suddenly Soren and Gus were there. Each took one of her arms and pulled her back away from Owen.

"I don't know what to do," Owen said over Esther's hissing voice that continued to spit out filthy accusations. "She's not herself."

"Calm down, Esther," Gus said gently. "We'll take you home."

Esther turned on him. "You'll not get me off by myself, you dirty, ruttin' bastard. I know what you want! You think I'll spread my legs for you. I'll not do it for you or any other horny old goat. Work off your lust on that city slut—"

"Stop it!" Owen shouted. "Shut your filthy mouth or I'll backhand you." He reached for her and shook her viciously. "Don't say such things to Uncle Gus. Hear me?"

"It's all right," Gus said calmly. "She doesn't know what she's saying."

"Let's get her in the buggy and take her home." Soren picked Esther up bodily, locking her in his arms, and plunked her down on the buggy seat. He climbed in and threw his leg across her thighs to keep her from jumping out while Owen went around to the other side.

"I'm sorry, Uncle Gus. I . . . just don't know what to say." Owen was so shaken by the scene that had taken place that his voice was raspy.

"There's no need for you to say anythin', son. For quite a while now, I've been ponderin' if Esther was quite right in the head."

"I kind of thought something was wrong but didn't want to believe it."

"She's been actin' queer for 'bout a year."

"Will you see to Ana, Uncle Gus? If she heard any of this

commotion, she'll be wondering what's going on. Explain to her that Esther just went out of her head.''

''Don't worry about Ana. Take Esther home and try to calm her down. If they've got any laudanum over there, give her a bit to make her sleep.''

Owen squeezed into the seat, picked up the reins and headed down the lane. Esther was sandwiched between him and Soren. She had stopped struggling, but she was still babbling.

''Wash clothes . . . wash the dirty goddamn clothes. Mend, cook, feed chickens, hoe the corn . . . rotten, stinkin' old bastard—Clean the spittoon, Esther. Damn you to hell, you ugly bitch! No, Papa, I won't, I won't! I'll . . . bite you,'' she shouted, then broke into sobs.

By the time they reached the Knutson farm, Esther was silent and limp. She seemed to have retreated into herself.

Fifteen

J ens Knutson cast an uninterested glance at his wife's buggy returning to the farm and went about the chore of slopping his hogs. He continued at a leisurely pace even after Owen stopped the buggy and called to him. When he finished, he shut the gate and sloshed through the mud to where Owen waited.

"Mornin'." The old man's eyes went to his wife sitting in the buggy beside Soren, then back to Owen.

"Morning, Jens. Esther's not well. Soren and I brought her home."

"Ja. She busted down again from the looks a her." Jens shrugged indifferently. "Damn woman be more trouble than what she be worth."

"What the hell are you talking about?"

"Spells is what she gets. Flies off the handle 'n' acts like she ain't got no sense a'tall. Then gets the sulks like she be now. Lily 'n' Hettie get plumb 'fraid of her 'n' I get plumb put out."

"How long has this been going on?"

"She ain't been right since the day she come here," he

snorted, then added when Owen scowled, "Started actin' queerer after ya brought that gal back last fall. Ranted 'n' raved, she did, till I be sick a hearin' it. Warn't natural, her bein' so worked up 'cause her brother took a woman."

The way the old man uttered the words rather than the words themselves, and the sly look in his eyes, caused Owen's back to stiffen and his hands to form fists.

"Watch what you're saying, Jens," he warned.

"Ain't no more'n what's been talked of by other folks. Take her back. I got no use for her no more. 'Sides I done Eustace a favor takin' her. Ya know that. What she done here was shipshod anyhow. Lily does for me 'n' looks after Hettie."

"She's your wife, man!" Owen said, knowing what the man said was true, but refusing to acknowledge it.

"I don't give a hoot if'n she is. She ain't never been no real *wife*. Not from the first. I ain't ort a wed up with her nohow."

By looking away from him Owen was able to keep his temper under control.

"She brought you a pretty good chunk of money and she took care of Hettie and Lily. You seemed happy with the arrangement at the time."

"'Twas more a bargain fer Eustace than 'twas fer me," Jens said. His hard old eyes never wavered from Owen's.

Owen opened his mouth, closed it. There was no point in arguing with this stubborn old Norwegian. He turned his head to look at his sister. Esther was sitting as still as a stone, looking straight ahead. Her eyes were vacant, her dark hair straggling down over her big ears. The pity Owen felt for her was like a pain in his chest. He looked back and fixed Jens with a cold stare.

"Regardless of whether you want her or not, this is her home and here she stays."

Jens lifted his shoulders in resignation.

"Owen's here." Hettie's voice came from the porch. "Lily, Owen's here." She stepped off the porch and came toward them with a huge smile on her pleasant face. "Hello, Owen. What did Esther come back for? Did she get the washin' done already?"

"Esther's . . . not well. We brought her home."

"She wasn't sick this morning. What's she sick of? Is that slut still there? Esther's mad as a hornet over that slut being there. Is that what she's sick of?"

"Don't talk like that about Ana!" Owen's jaw was clenched so tightly that the words were hissed through his teeth. "Goddammit to hell!" he muttered under his breath.

"Why ain't Esther sayin' somethin'? Why ain't she scoldin' me for comin' out here? Why'd ya bring her back for if the washin' ain't done?"

"Hush up, dangbustit!" Jens snapped. "You ain't got no business out here. Get back in the house."

"I don't want to." Hettie tossed the words over her shoulder, then ignored her father. She went around the buggy and smiled up at Soren. "Hello, Soren. Me and Lily can't come over to Owen's 'cause of you. Esther said you'd get under our skirts, and she didn't want no more woods-colts like Lily. Esther said you'd get in our drawers. Would you do that, Soren?"

Soren reached out and patted the top of Hettie's head as if she were a small child. His smile was gentle, understanding.

"Of course not. How are you, Hettie?"

"Esther said you was randy as a billy-goat. She said for me and Lily to stay clear of you."

"You don't need to worry about me, Hettie. I wouldn't hurt you for the world," Soren said patiently.

The screen door slammed. Lily stepped off the porch and came toward them.

"Lily! Guess what?" Hettie called cheerfully. "Soren ain't goin' to get under our skirts like Esther said. He said he won't hurt us none a'tall."

Lily spun around and barged back into the house.

"Lily's mad." Hettie cocked her head to one side, a puzzled frown on her pleasant face. "Somebody did something mean to Lily."

Soren watched the young girl dash for the house. Poor Lily. The humiliation she faced each day must be like a fist in the gut. Living with Esther and Hettie must be hell for a young girl. He had known Hettie all his life and was used to her frank, childish ways. He wasn't the least bit shocked by her frankness. Like everyone else in the community, he also knew the circumstances of Lily's birth.

A strange feeling of protectiveness swept over him. He'd caught just a glimpse of Lily's white face before she had lifted her skirt, showing slim ankles and legs, and run for the house. She had grown into a beautiful young woman in the year since he'd seen her last.

Esther allowed Owen to lift her down from the buggy and guide her into the house. She stumbled along beside him until they entered the kitchen. Then she pulled away from him and headed for the stairs. Standing at the cookstove, turning potato pancakes, Lily caught Owen's eye and sent a silent message that his sister would be all right.

Jens came into the kitchen followed by a man in dirty tattered overalls. His cheeks and chin were covered with a stubble of beard, and tobacco stained the corners of his mouth. The brows over his deep-set eyes came together over his nose, giving him the look of a timberwolf. Procter Himmel was a shirttail relation of Jens from near Decorah and had worked at the farm off and on for several years. Jens seated himself at the table without as much as a glance at Owen and began forking meat onto his plate.

"Ya make them tator pancakes fer me, sweetie?" Procter gave Lily a sly grin, smirked at Owen and sat down.

Lily ignored him. "Have some breakfast, Uncle Owen."

"No, thanks. Breakfast will be ready when Soren and I get back to the farm."

"Coffee, then?"

"No, thanks. I'll go unhitch Esther's horse." He looked

at Lily over her grandfather's head and jerked his toward the door.

Lily glanced quickly to see if her grandpa or Procter had intercepted the message. Their eyes were on their plates, and they were forking food into their mouths as if they expected a famine.

"Tell Mama to come in and watch the table," Lily called as Owen went out. "I've got to gather the eggs."

"Hettie can gather eggs," Jens growled.

"I want to see about my setting hen. Mama don't know where she is."

Lily turned back to the stove. She could feel Procter's beady eyes on her back and wanted to hide. Why was he here now? The fields were planted and it wasn't time to hoe. Lily had a feeling Procter was working to get his hands on the farm, and the only way he could do it was by marrying her or Hettie. Come to think of it, her grandpa had been mighty nice to Procter since he arrived two days ago. A sickening realization caused Lily to pause and close her eyes tightly. *Her grandpa was going to try to match her up with Procter!* Lily's stomach almost heaved at the thought.

When Hettie came in, Lily picked up the egg basket and hurried to the door, certain that if she stayed a minute longer she would be sick.

"Yore grandpa said Hettie could do it." Procter spoke with his mouth full.

"I'm going to see about my setting hen," Lily said defiantly.

"Yore wantin' to switch yore tail 'round in front of them fellers out there is what yore wantin' to do."

"What's he mean, Lily?" Hettie's large brown eyes were puzzled as she looked at her daughter. "Why is he saying that? You don't switch your tail."

Procter let loose with a loud guffaw.

"Pay no attention to him, Mama. Just keep the coffee poured and fry more potato cakes. *He'll* eat anything that don't bite him first."

Procter laughed again, spewing food from his mouth.

"I don't like him," Hettie said and set her chin stubbornly. "His face is ugly."

"Shut up yore mouth! A woman don't say such to her men folk." When Jens roared, Hettie cringed. "Procter's kin. Ya treat him with respect, hear?"

Owen and Soren were waiting beside the gate leading to the pasture they would cross on the walk back to the farm. Lily came toward them. Her hair, caught at the back of her neck with a ribbon, hung to her hips. To Soren she seemed so small, so young to have such a burden of responsibility.

"Hello, Lily." He tried to catch her eyes, but she looked down at her feet.

"Hello, Soren."

"If I'd known the prettiest girl this side of the river was here, I'd have come home sooner," he teased, trying to make her look at him.

Lily's white face turned beet-red. Her lips parted slightly as though to speak, but she didn't. Instead, she tilted her head to one side and scrutinized the pasture behind her uncle's head. A strained silence went by during which Soren was exceedingly sorry he had teased her.

"You wanted to talk to me, Uncle Owen?" Owen looked at her as if his mind was a thousand miles away when she turned pleading eyes to him.

"I wanted to tell you that Mrs. Fairfax and I were married yesterday. This morning I told Esther and she just went out of her head."

"Yes, I suspect she'd do that." Her voice was low and husky, a throaty whisper. Soren felt a tingling go down his spine. "I thought you'd marry her."

"She'll be a good mother to Harriet's boy, Lily."

"I've been thinking that, too."

"But she'll not put up with Esther coming over and running things like she's been doing. Esther has got to stay here. Not that she won't be welcome to come visit," he added hurriedly.

"I don't know how she'll take to that," Lily said softly. "She's not been . . . acting right."

"How long has this been going on? I couldn't get Jens to tell me anything."

"For a while. She has a spell when things don't go to suit her. Like about . . . Harriet. Now it's the baby or Mrs. Fairfax. We don't dare mention them. When she came home the other day, she went to bed and wouldn't talk to anyone."

"Has she tried to hurt you or Hettie?"

"No. But she slapped Mama and she talks . . . nasty to us."

Lily glanced at Soren as she spoke. Her look seemed as tangible as a touch, her throaty voice a cry for help. His throat felt suddenly dry, parched.

"I hate leaving her here with you." Owen took off his straw hat and combed his hair with his fingers. "But I don't know what else to do. Do you think you can get her to take a little laudanum in some water? It would calm her down."

"I think I can. When she's like this, she stays in the room upstairs. This morning she was up bright and early and seemed so cheerful—" Lily's words trailed and she shot another glance at Soren. His intense gaze made her short of breath.

"Do you think she's going out of her mind, Lily?" Owen finally voiced the question that had bothered him for days.

"Sometimes, I do. One day she talked about going home because her mama needed her. Another time she said she'd let Paul eat worms and her pa had whipped her. She tried to show me the switch marks on her back."

A sharp expletive cleared Owen's lips.

"It'll be all right, Uncle Owen. I'll look after her." Lily placed a comforting hand on his arm.

"I can't bring her home just now."

"She hates Mrs. Fairf . . . ah . . . Ana and she hates Harriet's baby."

"I wish I could get you away from here, Lily." Owen

covered her hand with his. "Slip off and come over to my place as often as you can. Ana would like for you to come visit."

"I'll try. Maybe at night. But Procter and grandpa stay up with a jug—"

"What's Procter doing here?"

"Grandpa said he needed him to hoe corn."

"Good Lord! It'll be a month before he has a field to hoe. It isn't even time to hoe thistle. Look out for him. Don't let him get you or Hettie alone away from the house. Stay together. I don't trust him."

"I don't . . . like him none atall." Lily's voice betrayed her fear.

"Has he bothered you?" Soren asked and Lily's eyes turned to him for a fleeting instant.

"No."

Owen placed his arm across Lily's shoulder. "If Esther gets out of hand, let me know."

"And if Procter gets out of hand, let *me* know," Soren said his voice low and grating.

"I will," Lily whispered.

She looked up at the handsome blond man looking down at her. She remembered a laughing Soren, a teasing Soren. This Soren's face was hard and impatient. His impatience was not directed at her. Instinctively she knew that. Their eyes caught and held. Uncertainty had darkened the brown eyes that stared into blue.

Suddenly Soren smiled the smile she remembered and nudged her chin with his knuckles. Lily thought she had never seen anything as beautiful as Soren's smile. Soren thought her eyes were incredibly lovely, the soft brown of a young fawn's eyes. Lily had never before been aware of a man in relation to herself as a woman. A soft morning breeze carried his earthy masculine scent to her, and she felt for an instant how it must feel to be cherished by a strong, good man. Wavering beneath the intensity of Soren's blue eyes, Lily realized her skin was becoming uncomfortably warm. Reluctantly she dragged her eyes away, swallowed hard and gathered her scattered senses.

"I'd better get the eggs. Grandpa—"

"Will you come over soon?" Soren asked.

"I'll try." The words were said as she walked away.

Soren watched her hurry toward the chicken house. His eyes went hard as unfamiliar feelings assailed him. He ran an agitated hand through his light hair, disturbing the lock that usually fell over his forehead.

"Hell," he burst out as he followed Owen across the pasture. "It's a crying shame is what it is. That's too much to put on that girl!"

"Lily has been looking after her mother for a long time,"

"Damnation! That's not what I mean. Now she's got to watch Esther and guard against that Procter who's dumb as a stump and horny as a rutting bull—and there's the work. Old Jens will work her to death. It's not fair, Owen. Hell! It's the drizzlin' shits is what it is!"

Owen listened to Soren's outburst, and a thought tripped in his mind. Seldom had he heard Soren speak so passionately about anything or anybody. He decided to goad him a bit to find out if what he suspected was true—that his devil-may-care, flirting cousin was attracted to shy little Lily.

"Lily will be all right."

"How do you know?"

"I don't."

"Then why did you say so?"

"Lily can take care of herself."

"Goddammit, Owen. That's the dumbest thing you've ever said. She don't know the first thing about taking care of herself and you know it. The girl don't stand a chance against that kraut-eating German. My God! I thought you liked her."

"I do like her. Procter won't do anything to turn Jens against him. If he tumbled Lily, Jens would be frothing at the mouth even if he is a cantankerous old goat. Procter's got it in mind to marry Lily so he can have the farm. Jens may be all for it.''

"Do you think he would marry Lily off to that . . . dirty bastard?''

"Why not? Procter's distant kin. He'll get a little something from home. Jens might look on him as the son he never had.''

"From what I hear, the Himmels are a bunch of lazy, no-good beer-guzzling slobs. There's not a sound fence on their farm, and the hogs root under the porch. Procter wouldn't get much if it was sold tomorrow.'' Soren's mouth twisted in a sneer.

"Most Germans like their beer. But it's seldom you see a lazy one,'' Owen said calmly. "The Himmels are the exception.''

"Lily wouldn't marry that suck-egged mule, would she?'' Agitation quickened Soren's stride until Owen had to lengthen his to keep up, and his lame leg began to ache. "The dumb bastard don't know his ass from a hole in the ground.''

"Lily might not have anything to say about it. Her grandpa is as stubborn a Norwegian as I've ever known. If he decides to wed Lily to Procter, he'll call out the preacher and get it done before you can drop your hat.'' Owen gave his cousin a sidelong glance and saw his jaw tighten as he clenched his teeth.

"She'll not wed that pig-ugly jackass unless she wants him, by God! I'll see to that.'' Soren bellowed the words into the quiet morning.

"Maybe you'd better keep an eye on her, seeing as how I've got my hands full at the moment.''

"Maybe I had.''

Owen had to swallow the chuckles that rumbled in his chest and rolled up in his throat. He'd bet his last dollar his world-traveled cousin was having an attack of the heart. Lord! Wouldn't it be grand? It was more than he'd ever hoped for—Lily and Soren together.

As Soren strode along, his hands deep in his pockets, he was aware of two things. Lily, always shy as a mouse, had grown into a beautiful young woman, and something new and strange was making his heart pick up speed, sending a tingling sensation racing over his skin. In all the time he had known Lily, she had not said over a dozen words to him. He had teased her; she had run. He had tugged on her braid; she had shyly looked at the floor.

Now softly rounded with smooth sun-browned skin, straight dark brows and curling eyelashes, Lily was lovely in a quiet, innocent way. Her thick, wavy hair had darkened to a rich brown. The dress she had worn, Soren remembered now, had patches on top of patches. He clamped his lower lip between his teeth, and his brows drew together in a deep frown. What was the matter with him? In less than a hour his mind had been thrown completely out of circuit.

Sixteen

The day was well on its way when they reached the farm. Ana was hanging diapers on the line that stretched from the windmill to the corner of the porch. With her arms raised Owen could see the rounded outline of her breasts pushing against the bodice of her dress. The wind whipped her skirt against her legs and thighs and billowed it out behind her. She finished and disappeared into the house just as they came into the yard.

"I couldn't get near that damn goat." Gus came from the barn with the milk pails in his hands. "Ana milked her."

"How come she let Ana milk her?" Owen took one of the pails from his uncle.

"Beats me. Ana said she was not used to being tied up and was scared."

"We'll make a pen today there beside the hog lot. I'm sure we have enough extra wire." Owen held the screen door open for Gus and followed him into the kitchen.

Ana was removing a pan of biscuits from the oven. Her eyes caught Owen's for a mere instant before he lifted the milk pail to the counter and bent over the washdish. He scooped up water to slosh on his face. Then he dried it on the fresh towel that hung on the towel bar.

"Breakfast is ready. Uncle Gus and I went ahead and ate." She turned hot puffy biscuits onto a platter, carried it to the table, and went back to the stove to stir the mixture in the skillet. The potatoes left from the night before had been diced, eggs added and fried in meat grease. She turned them into a bowl and set the spider on the back of the stove.

"Mornin', Sunshine." Soren had washed at the bench on the porch. He greeted Ana with his customary grin.

"Morning."

As Owen took his place at the table, he noticed the clean tablecloth, the places set with the fork on the left, the knife on the right, the spoon holder beside the caster set, the cups on *saucers* beside each plate. Butter had been scooped from the crock into the cut-glass butter dish with the dome cover. Such niceties had been absent before.

Although Ana's brown work dress was faded from many washings, she was neat as a pin. The sleeves were rolled up to her elbows, the bodice fit snugly over her firm breasts, her snowy-white apron was tied securely around her small waist. While her back was to him, Owen could feast his eyes on the coils of honey-colored hair pinned to the top of her head. When she turned, he could see that her cheeks were flushed from the heat of the stove. She had scarcely looked at *him*, but she was smiling at Soren.

"Cousin Ana, you're as pretty as a speckled pup this morning." Soren's drawl was thick and teasing.

"Why, thank you, Soren. I don't know when I've been so pleased by a compliment." Her smiling face abruptly turned sour. She lifted her brows haughtily and looked down her nose at the man grinning at her. "Speckled pup indeed! I think I saw some old turnips down in the cellar that I can boil with moldy sauerkraut for your dinner."

"Turnips and sauerkraut? I take back every last word, Cousin Ana. Have pity! I've had to eat a ton of turnips while on-board ship."

"Is that so? Well, you'd better watch your mouth from now on, Cousin Soren, or you'll be eating more." A girlish giggle escaped her as she ladled water into the dishpan from the reservoir.

Silence fell as the men ate. Owen willed away the jealousy that washed over him, telling himself that his cousin was a natural-born flirt. Nonsensical talk came as easy as breathing to Soren, while unnecessary talk of any kind was an effort for Owen. Compared to Soren, he must seem like a dull clod to Ana.

The men ate with lusty appetites. The biscuits were light and hot. One after the other they disappeared from the platter. Finally Soren placed his knife and fork on his empty plate, pushed back his chair and stood. Now was the time to make himself scarce so that Owen could explain to his new wife about the rumpus with Esther this morning.

"I'll get that roll of fence out of the loft and see how much we have before we start digging fence posts for the goat pen." Soren said, and walked out of the kitchen, leaving Ana to study an empty doorway.

Now that he was alone with her, Owen was unable to summon up his voice. He needed to know how she felt about the scene Esther had pulled this morning. She would have to be deaf not to have heard it. Somehow all he could think of was how fetching she looked and how her golden eyes matched her hair. He was almost startled when she sat down at the table across from him.

"I heard the commotion with Esther this morning. It was because of me, wasn't it?"

He hadn't expected her to come right to the heart of the matter so quickly. But he should have known; it was her way.

"Partly, I guess. She thought it was Monday and came to do the wash. Right now she's sick and confused. It could be that she'll straighten up and come to terms with you being here."

"If you believe that, you're hiding your head in the sand. It's plain to me that she's having a breakdown. She's not going to accept my being here. I think it would be better if I took Harry and went back to Dubuque.''

Owen felt as if someone had pinched his nose shut, and he couldn't breathe. "But you can't . . . leave. We're . . . married.''

"Can't you see that it would make matters here much easier for you?''

"No. I want you . . . and the boy to stay. We'll work things out.''

"Mr. Jamison, I've not told you the main reason I left that day to walk to town. I was out of the house for just a moment or two, and when I returned, your sister was bending over the cradle. I'm sure she intended to harm the baby.''

"How can you be sure? Maybe she was just looking at him.''

"With a small, soft pillow in her hands?'' Ana's voice hardened.

"Good Lord!''

"She had a mad look in her eyes, Mr. Jamison. I believe that she's dangerous.''

"Good Lord!'' he said again. "I don't know what to do about her!'' He planted his elbows on the table and massaged his temples with long blunt fingers. When he looked across at Ana, he didn't attempt to hide the pleading look in his eyes. "Don't go. I'll do everything I can to keep Esther away.''

The look on his face tugged at Ana's heartstrings. She reached across the table and placed her hand on his warm naked forearm. It was the first time she had voluntarily touched him. He thought the walls of his chest would collapse.

"Are you sure this is what you want? Esther is your sister. I'm almost a complete stranger to you. I'm not asking you to choose between us. If I take Harry to Dubuque, you'd be welcome to come see him anytime.''

"You're not a *stranger*!'' he said hoarsely. "You're my wife. Don't go. Say you'll stay.''

In all his life, Owen Jamison had never begged anyone for anything. He had not even pleaded with his father when he thrashed him so unmercifully with the buggy whip. But he saw his life stretched out before him, bleak and lonely. The words had boiled up out of that imagined eternal purgatory. His heart was a hard ache beneath his ribs as he struggled to bring air into his lungs.

Surprised by his passionate plea, Ana stared into his beseeching and ferocious eyes while something strange, unfamiliar and hot jabbed at the core of her femininity.

"All right. I'll stay."

The softly spoken words were like water to a thirst-crazed man. The relief was so great that he could only look at her and nod his head.

"But maybe I should put off selling the house in Dubuque for a while."

"You think to leave later?" His hand moved and held hers in a tight grip.

"If it should become necessary that Harry and I leave here, Mr. Jamison, we'd need a place to go," she said kindly.

"It will not be necessary for you to leave. Ever!" he said emphatically. "Make a list of what you want out of the house, and I'll write to the banker. He'll send your things. This is your home now."

"There's no hurry about that." Ana pulled her hand out from under his and stood. "Now that that's settled, I have something to ask you."

"And I have something to ask you."

Her back was to him. His eyes feasted on the sight of her sunny hair, like a golden halo around her head, the contours of her curving back, and the soft roundness of her hips undisguised in the narrow skirt. Even without the tight band of her apron, her figure was like an hourglass.

Ana turned and stared into Owen's blue eyes. Once again they were clouded with worry. She should be making plans to leave, to get as far away from his crazy sister as possible. Why was she staying? The earth seemed to be standing still

as she looked into the cobalt blue eyes looking up at her. She
felt suddenly that she and Owen deeply knew each other, that
there was a bond between them that seldom existed between
a man and a woman. The bond was Harry, of course, her
common sense told her.

"What do you want to know, Mr. Jamison?"

"Why do you call me Mr. Jamison?"

"Well . . . it's your name."

"My mother always called my father Mr. Jamison as if
she were a servant instead of the lady of the house. You're
not a servant here, Ana."

"Would you rather I called you Owen?"

"Only when you're comfortable doing so. Now what did
you want to ask me?" he asked with a tremor in his voice
as if he expected to hear something he didn't want to hear.

"Do I have your permission to bring the furniture from
upstairs down to the front bedroom? If I take my things out
of my trunk, there is no place to put them."

"You can arrange the house any way you like." His shoulders relaxed. "I told you that it was yours."

"I understand the front room was your mother's. I thought
maybe you wished her things to stay in it."

"My mother has been dead for twenty years. If you wish
to use the furniture upstairs, Soren and I will exchange it for
you."

"Thank you. It will give me more drawer space for my
things and Harry's."

"We'll do it when we come in for dinner."

Owen pulled his eyes reluctantly from hers and went out,
his heart dancing to a strange exciting beat.

Warm spring winds dried the fields quickly and the planting
continued. The men worked from dawn to dusk, even on
Sunday. One more week of good weather, Owen told Ana
one evening, and the crops would be in. As the days passed,

they fell into an easy, comfortable routine. Owen and Ana rarely talked, though Soren and Uncle Gus gave them plenty of time alone. Work and caring for Harry was a good way for Ana to avoid Owen, Ana decided almost immediately after their talk about Esther.

While the men toiled in the fields, Ana worked in the house. She cooked tempting, filling meals, washed the clothes, and cleaned, even to washing the windows with a mixture of warm soapy water. The shiny-clean result was well worth the back-breaking work. For the first time in years the windows in the parlor were opened to let in the fresh air.

Carpets were hung on the line, beaten with a wire rugbeater and the floors scrubbed before the carpets were put down again. The furniture from upstairs had fit wonderfully well in the front bedroom. Ana put her things in the lower bureau drawers, Harry's in the top. Owen carried the empty trunk to the storage room upstairs. A clean white sheet served as a spread for the bed, Ana's shawl became a scarf for the table.

In the evenings after the supper dishes were done, Ana lit the lamp in the parlor and knitted on the cap and coat she was making for Harry. The first few evenings she sat alone while Soren and Owen sat at the kitchen table. Then one evening, shortly after she heard the screen door slam telling her Soren had left the house, Owen came to the parlor. He sat on the faded upholstered loveseat and thumbed through a well-used mail order catalog.

Terribly conscious of the big, silent man, Ana tried to concentrate on her knitting, tried so hard that she tilted her head toward the light and her brows furrowed.

"You're frowning."

His softly spoken words broke the silence. As Ana lifted her eyes, they slammed into brilliant blue ones. Her stomach quivered and her heart picked up speed.

"I wasn't aware of it."

"You should do that in the daylight."

"I've knitted for so long that I could do it blindfolded. I

want to finish this for Harry. Then I can make something for the church to sell at the celebration.'' She had difficulty filling her lungs and talking at the same time. Her heart seemed to expand and her head felt light.

''What will you make?''

''Stockings and mittens and caps.''

''All of that in such a short time.''

''I can make a stocking in an evening.''

''Do you have the yarn?''

''Yes, I brought it with me thinking I'd have time to work on an order for a store in Dubuque.''

He studied her face. ''You're working too hard.''

''Pshaw! I'm used to housework. I still haven't worked in the garden.''

''Uncle Gus will take care of it. Soren and I will help him hoe weeds.''

''But you have so much to do.''

''Soren, Uncle Gus and I can do in an hour what it would take you a couple of days to do. We'll take care of the garden.''

''I want to do my share of the work,'' she said stubbornly and glanced at him. He was looking at her so intently that she almost forgot to breathe.

''Taking care of the house and the baby is enough.'' He spoke in a voice that brooked no argument.

''I'd like to plant some flowers in that hollow stump by the cellar door and a climbing rose vine at the end of the porch.''

Bowing her head over her knitting, she tried to analyze the look in his eyes. It could only be described as a *hungry* look! Was this the night he would come to her bed? She hoped not. Oh, God, she hoped not. It wasn't time. She wasn't ready to accept her stepdaughter's lover . . . yet.

It was a cozy scene, the two of them sitting in their parlor. The thought came to Ana as if she were clinging to the ceiling looking down at them. They could be a happy, loving couple who chose to be together because it was unbearable to be apart. Instead they had been bound together out of necessity, out of her obligation to Harriet, and out of his desire to raise his son.

"When will you cut the wheat?" Ana asked after frantically searching her mind for a safe topic.

"In another two weeks. I'm hoping Foster will be here by then."

"Foster? Is he the one who helps you during the harvest and sleeps in the barn?"

"Foster Reed. I've known him all my life. His folks had a farm north of here."

"Isn't he sort of a . . . vagabond?"

"Yes. I guess you could call him that. Some call him a bum, a worthless drunk."

"Tell me about him."

Owen glanced up as if he wasn't sure he'd heard correctly. There was no sign of condemnation on her calm, beautiful face. When Foster's name was mentioned, the usual reaction was blatant disgust.

"He's one of the smartest people I've ever known. He can fix anything from a steam locomotive to a windmill. When he's sober, which isn't often—" he glanced up to see how she reacted to that "—he can read something one time and recite it back word for word. Or he used to be able to. Soren thinks drink has befuddled his brain."

"So he's drunk most of the time?"

"As long as he has money. He works in the iron foundries until he has enough money to stay drunk for a few months."

"What a terrible waste."

"You don't have to worry. While he's here, we keep all the spirits locked up."

"Oh, I'm not worried. Has he always been this way?"

"No. It's all because of a woman."

"Women. The root of all evil," Ana said softly, teasingly, but Owen didn't smile.

"In this case—yes. Foster had loved her all his life. Just before he left for the war, he married her. He was only eighteen. He was gone for a year and came home with an ear shot off and blind in one eye. His wife was big with another man's child."

"Oh, the poor man. What did he do?"

"He almost went out of his mind. He knocked her down the stairs. She lost the child and almost died. When she recovered, she ran off with her lover, a whiskey drummer. They were on a steamer that blew up and sank in the river. All aboard were lost."

"Poetic justice." Ana said softly, tilting her golden head to the light.

"It's what I thought. It all happened twenty years ago. Foster is only thirty-nine but looks sixty. He has spent half of his life grieving over that woman, and she wasn't worth the tip of his little finger."

"Poor man," Ana said again. "I'll fix up one of the rooms upstairs for him."

"Are you sure you want him in the house?" Owen asked, his compelling eyes on Ana's face.

"Is he dangerous?"

"Gawdamighty no! He's one of the gentlest men I know and pleasant company when he's sober."

"I'll fix a room for him upstairs," she repeated, then added. "There's plenty of room up there for Soren and Uncle Gus too."

He looked at her for so long that she turned her eyes back down to her knitting and waited for him to say something. When he did, it had nothing to do with what they had been talking about.

"I was wondering if you'd like to have a porch swing."

She sent him a pleased smile. "Oh, yes. I've always wanted a porch swing."

"I can make one. I'll cut oak slats from some of the pieces I had left over from the kitchen cabinet I'm making."

"You're making a cabinet for . . . our kitchen?"

He smiled and years dropped from his face. Her heart raced.

"If you want it. If not, I can sell it down river."

"Owen Jamison! What do you mean . . . if I want it? One of the ladies I worked for in Dubuque had a kitchen cabinet with a flour bin, a pull-out breadboard and even a place for the rolling pin. It was as handy as a button on a shirt. Everything I needed to make anything at all was within easy reach. Of course, I want it. I never thought I'd have one."

"I haven't put the legs on it yet—"

"—When can I see it?"

He laughed. It was a low sound of pure pleasure.

"I need to know how high you want the table top. There's no need for you to break your back bending over it."

"Oh. That's one thing about Mrs. Fitzgerald's—the table top was too low."

"I'll need to know if you want a row of brass hooks along under the top shelf, or if you'd rather have small drawers—" His voice trailed. Because she was looking at him squarely, he lost his train of thought in the golden depth of her smiling eyes.

"I've always wanted a kitchen cabinet with a flour bin."

"It has one. It'll have a salt box on the side and a pull-out breadboard."

"A tilt-out flour bin?" she asked as if the prospect of one was overwhelmingly wonderful.

"Yes," he said, feeling incredibly happy. "I lined it with tin so it would be mouse-proof."

"Well . . . forevermore. Imagine that!" A trill of pleased laughter burst from her as she gazed at him in a breathless hush of appreciation.

He wasn't prepared for her enthusiasm or the pleasure he saw on her perfectly beautiful face. Her eyes were warm and full of smiles, her lips laughing. *All because of a kitchen cabinet.*

He had offered to make one for Esther. She had not wanted one in the kitchen. He remembered her saying that "what was good enough for Mama was good enough for her." This wonderful laughing creature was beaming because of the cabinet. He still hadn't quite grasped the fact that she was his wife.

It was incredible. How had this miracle happened? *I now pronounce you man and wife.* How binding were the words? Yet they were only words. Ana was still as far from him as the day she arrived. A pain of regret pierced his heart. He longed to go to her, hold her, take comfort from her and give comfort in return. Not yet. The time wasn't right. He didn't want to merely slake his thirst on her body. He wanted more, much more. He wanted her to want him, confide in him her thoughts, dreams, to come to him with love in her heart. He wanted to hold her all through the night, her slender naked body against his. He wanted to love her, protect her, cherish her.

She would be horrified if she knew what he was thinking. Good Lord, man! You don't want much—only the moon and the sun. Owen held himself rigid, struggling to retain control over his suddenly trembling limbs and swollen, throbbing sex. *Thank God for the catalog!*

A thick silence fell between them, this one heavy with emotions only Owen understood. Ana bowed her head over her knitting. The only sound in the room was the swish of pages as Owen absently turned the pages of the catalog. From time to time Ana glanced at the dark head bent over the book and he took furtive glances at the slender hands working the knitting needles. It finally occured to Ana that he was probably waiting for her to go to bed. She carefully folded her knitting, secured it with the needles and placed it on the table.

"Goodnight, Owen."

"Goodnight, Ana," he murmured.

They avoided each other's eyes as she passed him. In the bedroom Ana lit the lamp and closed the door. She leaned against it, not sure if it was relief or disappointment she was feeling.

He had said *goodnight*.

Seventeen

After Soren left the kitchen, he stood on the porch and waited for Owen to blow out the lamp. Soren wondered if his cousin would go to his room or join his wife in the parlor. There was no doubt in his mind that Owen was thoroughly smitten with this fair-haired woman he had married. Hell! Imagine falling in love with your mother-in-law! But sure as sin, that's what Owen had done. His eyes were drawn to her constantly—that is, when he was sure she was unaware of it. Soren sighed in exasperation.

Owen was the most decent man Soren knew. But was he so boring that he bored his new wife to distraction? He was as tongue-tied around her as a youth who had just discovered girls. Soren chuckled. Maybe when they were alone he was different. God, he hoped so. He sure as hell deserved some happiness after living all those years with old Eustace Jamison, the meanest old son-of-a-bitch in the county, not to mention having to put up with Esther.

Soren was sure that Ana was not indifferent to his cousin. Now there was a woman—not for him, but perfect for Owen.

It was still a mystery to him why Owen had married Ana's stepdaughter, a girl not even as old as Lily.

Lily. Just thinking her name caused his heart to beat faster. Soren's eyes turned toward the Knutson farm. He stepped down from the porch, but instead of heading for the small house he shared with his father, his steps took him out the gate and across the moonlit field. He was acting like a love-sick calf, he admitted to himself. But the thought didn't cause him to turn back.

This was the third night in a row he had walked to the Knutson farm, stood in the shadows beneath the trees, and watched the house. The first night he had heard old Jens yell for Lily to bring him and Procter another jug of whiskey. She had come out from the kitchen, lifted the slanting door, and gone down into the cellar to draw the whiskey from the barrel Jens kept there. Why he hadn't stepped out and spoken to her he didn't know. The second night he hadn't caught sight of her, but tonight he was determined not to let the opportunity pass if she came outside the house.

Since the morning he and Owen had brought Esther home, he had been unable to get the vision of Lily's white face and fearful brown eyes out of his mind. She was so small and so alone with so much responsibility resting on her thin shoulders. Being the bastard daughter of a woman like Hettie was more than any young girl should have to endure. Now she had to watch over Esther, who was acting as crazy as a loon, and endure old Jen's pushing that slob of a Procter at her. It might be enough to push her over the line and cause her to give in to Procter. The thought of his beefy hands pawing her young body was gut-wrenching.

Something moved in the kitchen, and Soren straightened from his leaning position against the tree trunk. The screen door opened and Lily came out onto the back porch. She stood for a moment looking at the moon while Soren waited, holding his breath for fear she would go back into the house. To his utter relief, she stepped off the porch and walked slowly down the path toward the outhouse. Soren's heart began to gallop like a runaway horse as he moved out from under the tree and hurried across the garden to the board fence where he could intercept her when she came back up the path.

How in the world was he going to let her know he was there without scaring the life out of her?

The screen door slammed again. Soren froze alongside the fence. Procter's large frame was silhouetted against the light. He went to the end of the porch and stood there fumbling with the front of his overalls. Soren heard the unmistakable sound of water hitting the ground as Procter relieved himself. The crude bastard! He knew Lily was outside and didn't even bother to go around the house. If he followed her to the outhouse, Soren swore he'd brain him with a stick of stove wood!

With his eyes on the man on the porch, Soren waited, tense and ready to do what he swore he would do. Procter came back to the middle of the porch and leaned his shoulder against a post. He was facing the path to the outhouse. Just when Soren had decided that he would risk being seen and dart around the corner so he could call to Lily, Jen's loud slurred voice came from inside the house.

"Procter! Ain't ya done pissin' yet? C'mon, let's finish up this hand."

Procter shaded his eyes with his palm as he peered into the darkness. "Ya, ya," he called, but made no move to go back inside.

A long minute passed. Procter stepped down off the porch.

"Air ya comin' or ain't ya?" Jens yelled.

"Ya, I'm comin'." A vicious snarl graveled Procter's voice. He turned, grabbed the porch post, pulled himself up, and stomped into the house.

Soren let out a sigh of relief. As he moved swiftly around the corner, he saw Lily's slender form beside the outhouse. She was standing as still as a stone amid the hollyhocks that grew beside the building. She had been waiting for Procter to go inside. Now she started up the path toward the house. Soren called to her softly.

"Pssst! Lily. Don't be scared. It's me, Soren." At the sound of his voice the young girl froze like a frightened doe. "I'm over here by the board fence."

For an instant he thought she would run. Then she moved toward him.

"Soren?" she whispered.

"Yes. Don't be scared."

"What are you doing here?"

"Waiting for you. I knew I'd not be welcomed at the house."

"No, you wouldn't. Grandpa wouldn't like it. Is something wrong? Has something happened to Uncle Owen?"

"Nothing's wrong. I wanted to see you, talk to you."

"Talk to me? Why?"

"I just wanted to."

The moonlight shone on her face. He took her hand and pulled her into the shadow of the board fence. The fear, the vulnerability in her eyes went straight to his heart. She could be so easily broken, so easily hurt. But he wasn't going to hurt her, and, by God, he'd see to it that that rutting son-of-a-bitch didn't hurt her either.

"Can you stay out for a while?"

"Not very long. Procter knows I'm out here."

"I saw him. Has that slimy bastard been pestering you?" Soren drew in a sharp breath and his hand tightened on hers.

"I'm careful not to let him catch me by myself."

"You don't have to be careful with me. I'll not do any of the things Esther said. You believe that, don't you?"

"Y-yes. Esther likes to talk nasty sometimes."

"Esther is sick in the head. Real sick. Has she tried to hurt you?"

"No. Sometimes she acts all right. But she can fly off the handle at the drop of a hat—and over nothing. Today Grandpa had Procter carry her upstairs and lock her in. He wouldn't let me or Mama take her any supper."

"Is she getting worse, Lily?"

"I think so. Her good times are getting shorter and her

bad times longer. A lot of the time she don't make sense atall.''

"You poor little thing." He placed her hand on his chest. The frenzied beating of his heart was almost painful. He cupped her face in his hands, his fingers sliding into the curls behind her ears. "I wish you didn't have to stay here," he muttered. His voice was raw with emotion when he spoke. The need to protect her spiraled up and out, spreading throughout his body. The desire in him had nothing to do with sex, nothing at all.

"Soren—"

"Will you meet me tomorrow night?" When she didn't reply, he whispered harshly, "You're afraid I'll take advantage of you! Esther has drummed that into your head, hasn't she?"

"B-but I know you won't."

"I swear to God, I won't. Please, Lily. I've thought about you since that day Owen and I brought Esther home. I'm not like Procter, or . . . whoever it was that took advantage of Hettie."

Lily moved her face away from his hands, stepped back, and looked down at the ground. Soren knew immediately that he had embarrassed her. He hated himself for being so thoughtless as to mention her parentage.

"Let's get something straight right now." He placed his hands on her shoulders and pulled her gently toward him. "It doesn't mean a damn to me that . . . that Hettie is more like your . . . little girl than your mama. I don't give a damn about your pa either, or who he was. I'm sorry as hell that some man took advantage of Hettie, but to tell the truth, I'm glad too. Look what they made—a sweet, pretty girl with soft, brown eyes and the disposition of an angel. Lily, I want us to get to know each other."

He had gradually pulled her closer until her forehead rested on his shoulder. His heart was thumping wildly and he could feel the trembling in her body as his hands slid across her back.

"Meet me tomorrow night out by the oak at the end of the garden," he whispered urgently into the hair above her ear.

"It might be late."

"I'll wait."

"I'd better go in now."

"Lily, don't ever be afraid of me. I'd die before I'd hurt you."

"I know."

"If you have trouble with Procter, will you tell me?"

"I'll tell you." She was in such a state of bliss that she would have promised him anything.

Soren's hands came to her shoulders. He held her away from him so he could look into her face.

"Go to the house, honey. I'll watch until you're inside."

His hands moved down her arms to her hands. He squeezed them slightly, and reluctantly let them go. Lily moved away from him and out onto the moonlit path. She turned and looked at him, then with head bowed, went up the path toward the house.

Soren wondered at the knot of emotion that twisted his insides as he watched her go.

A month of busy days passed. Ana was puzzled. Her husband was a mystery to her. He still hadn't come to her bed to demand his conjugal rights. For all he knew, she had slept with Mr. Fairfax and was no quaking virgin. Heavens! If he only knew. She was a grown-up woman in the body of an innocent girl. She was as innocent as her sixteen-year-old stepdaughter had been—maybe more so. Young people talked of such things these days. All she knew about the intimacies of marriage she had learned by reading *Dr. Hood's Plain Talk.*

Had Owen Jamison been gentle with Harriet or had he roughly taken her maidenhead, planted the seed of his son in her womb and continued to take his pleasure night after night on her young body? It was something Ana didn't want to think about. Something she tried *not* to think about. One thing she did know and took pleasure in knowing—the man was aware of her. Suddenly, at the oddest times, she would catch him looking at her and a dull red would cover his cheeks.

Late one afternoon, Ana peeked into Owen's workshop. She was surprised to find him there bent over the table of the cabinet he was making. He straightened as she entered, wiped the sweat from his brow with the sleeve of his shirt, and waited for her to speak.

Ana cleared her throat. It felt as dry as dust.

"I didn't know you were here." She purposely kept her eyes on the cabinet.

A questioning look came over his face. "Is something wrong?"

"No. I—" She cleared her throat again and looked around with curiosity. "I wanted to see how much you'd done on the cabinet."

His mouth quirked in a crooked grin that softened his features, made more stern looking by a day's growth of beard.

"I came in from the field early so I could work on the finish in the daylight."

On this second visit to the workshop, Ana was just as awed as she was the first time, by the array of small tools neatly held in place by leather straps nailed to the walls and the larger tools hanging from the rafters. She was equally fascinated by the heavy carpenter's bench with its many holes, clamps and vises, and the rough plank from which he would make a beautiful piece of furniture. Ana was unable to conceal her appreciation of his workmanship as she admired the cabinet. Owen's craggy face creased with smiles as he viewed her pleasure.

"This is something you really like to do, isn't it?" Golden eyes smiled into blue.

"Yes," he admitted, rubbing his fingertips over the satin-smooth table of the cabinet which he had just oiled and rubbed to a smooth luster with fine pumice stone. "I'd much rather work with wood than farm, but—"

"But the land must be used," she finished for him.

"Yes, the land must be used. It's been used by Jamisons for more than seventy years. Someday it will be Harry's."

"Maybe someday you can hire someone to farm so you can spend your time here, making beautiful, lasting things. Would it pay?"

"I don't know."

Suddenly she laughed. The musical sound filled the shop and his heart.

"If I had my say, you'd not sell one single piece. I'd want them all—for Harry," she added quickly and looked away, her cheeks tinged with sudden color. She clasped her hands together in a grip that revealed her nervousness.

He looked at her for a long intense moment as her blush deepened. Tall and slender, with that crown of glorious hair, she was like a goldenrod—fragile, yet strong. Warmth and beauty surrounded her like an aura. Owen longed with all his heart to lean into that aura and be one with her, but he knew for the moment that he had to be satisfied basking in her admiration.

"I've got some things in William's Furniture Store in Dubuque," he said, his mouth and his brain working independently of each other. *You're like a bit of sunshine, a drink of cool water. You're so wonderful to look at.*

"You do? That's the most expensive store in town. Rich people on the bluff buy their furniture there. Oh, shoot! I wish I'd known. Not that I could afford to buy," she added hastily, "but I could have looked."

"You didn't know me then."

She laughed again. "You're right. They wouldn't have been as important—" Her voice trailed into nothing.

"I'll make your porch swing out of this after I finish the cabinet." Owen sensed her embarrassment and pulled a long piece of white oak from crosspieces he had fastened to the walls to keep the lumber off the floor.

"Where did you learn to make such beautiful things?"

"Here and there. I worked for a year with a furniture maker in Davenport."

After a brief silence they spoke, both at the same time. "We're going to have bread pudding for supper," Ana began as he said, "I'll be in as soon as I wash up—"

"No hurry. There's at least another hour of daylight."

As she returned to the house, Owen leaned against the door frame and watched her cross the yard. She moved smoothly, her skirts swishing around her ankles, her head riding proudly on her slender neck. Good God. If not for Harriet, he would have never met her. It had to be fate that first brought Harriet to him and then this wonderful slip of a woman.

Of late, his longing for her knew no bounds.

Soon he would have to tell her about Harriet. What would her reaction be? Would it be easier for her to accept him as her husband, or would she despise him all the more for his deception? He had waited for her to get settled in, to think of this as her home.

"You liar," he murmured aloud. "You're waiting until you've heard that her house is sold. You think she'll stay if she has no place to go back to."

And, dear God, what was he going to do about Esther? Owen felt the raw edges of pain when he thought of his sister. He had to get things settled with Esther before he could even think about finding happiness with Ana. He made almost daily visits to the Knutson farm. At times Esther seemed perfectly rational and at other times she would look right through him and refuse to communicate at all.

Jens was becoming difficult. Owen suspected Procter was urging the old man to get rid of his wife. Lily was spending too much time taking care of her. Esther had slipped away from them one afternoon and crossed the field to her old home. Owen had intercepted her before she reached the house. Lord, how he hated to tell her she couldn't go in. She didn't understand at all. The look on her homely face had ravaged his heart.

* * *

The days that followed Ana's visit to the woodworking shop were peaceful, if not entirely happy. Owen and Ana spent an hour in the parlor each evening. They talked, but tension lay beneath the calm surface. Each night he planned to reach out and take her hand as she passed him on her way to her room after her nightly visit outside. Each night the fear of her rejection caused him to rub his sweating palms against his thighs, growl "goodnight" and head for the porch to sit alone for another hour before he retired to his room.

Saturday night after the supper dishes were washed and put away, Ana brought a washtub into the kitchen and filled it with water for her weekly bath. She looked forward to this hour of privacy behind closed doors and blanket covered windows. She bathed, washed her hair and rolled it in a towel. Dressed in a clean nightgown she went to her room, leaving the tub of water in the kitchen. The first time she had attempted to empty it, but Owen had told her in a tone that brooked no argument to leave it to him.

Sitting on the side of her bed, Ana dried her hair and brushed it until it was a damp, shimmering mass hanging down her back to her hips. The chore didn't keep her from thinking about how she became undone by just knowing Owen's eyes were on her. She could feel them all the way down to the tips of her toes. What irony, she thought painfully, that she would have these feelings for the man who had seduced her young stepdaughter.

The question of what was keeping him from coming to her was constantly in her mind. He had said he wanted more children. He certainly wasn't going to get them by staying out of her bed. Did he think she was too old? She looked down at her breasts. High and firm, the nipples poked against the cotton nightdress like large, hard pebbles. She pushed against them with her palms and yearned with all her heart to be a beloved wife—not just a wife, a wife loved by her husband and family.

The thought that had been in the back of her mind for weeks came forth. *She wanted her husband to come to her and love her with his body as well as his heart the way Alessandro had loved Ramona in Helen Jackson's novel.*

Guilt swept over her like a prairie fire.

Ana put her hands to her cheeks, disgusted with herself for her wanton thoughts. Dear Lord. She was lusting after her son-in-law. But he was her husband too, a voice inside her cried.

Moving swiftly, she blew out the lamp and groped her way to the bed where she lay for a long while listening for the sound of Owen's footsteps crossing the hall to his room. A few short weeks ago she had not known he even existed. And because of his chance meeting with Harriet, she was here. After she got to know the man, she realized he was kind and gentle beneath his gruff facade. It was impossible to hate him and even possible for her to be . . . fond of him. Her practical mind rejected the word *love*. Love was for young, starry-eyed girls. Women her age were lucky to be provided for.

Ana turned over on her side and stared into the darkness. Tears trickled from the corners of her eyes. A small voice in her head whispered, *I'm not bad because I want him. I'll not be taking anything from you, Harriet.*

Ana wasn't aware of falling asleep, but she *was* aware of waking up when the door between her room and Owen's creaked. Her eyes flew open. She saw his darker outline against the night. He stood hesitantly for the space of a dozen heartbeats. Ana forgot to breathe. Finally he moved. Without a sound to break the stillness, he crossed the room and stood beside the bed. His chest was bare, the skin much lighter than that on his face and forearms. Ana was still, all breath suspended in her body. She looked up at him, waiting.

His knees bumped the bed. The hands hanging at his sides clenched and unclenched.

It was the longest moment of Ana's life.

"Ana?" His voice was whisper-soft, but she heard it all the same.

"Is something wrong?"

"No. No. I just . . . I just—"

"Yes?"

Owen pulled back the cover and lay down beside her. It was so sudden she had no time to move to the other side of the bed. His weight caused the mattress to dip and she rolled against him from shoulder to hip. With great suddenness he was holding her against his rock-hard body, his face in the curve of her neck.

"I had to come." The words wrenched out of him were filled with pain and longing. "The nights have been hell!" His voice was choked with the harsh sound of desire. "I just want to hold you. I'll do nothing more . . . I swear it."

His bare skin surprised her with its smoothness and its hardness. His only clothing was something soft that covered him from his waist to his knees. Ana had never been so close to another human being with so little between them. His arms wrapped her to him with unbridled need, crushing her breasts to his chest so tightly that it was difficult for her to breathe. She could feel the virile hardness of the body pressed to hers. Even though there was no question of her rejecting him, shock made her stiff as a board.

As if suddenly aware of his strength, his arms loosened. He moved his lower body away from hers and cradled her to his chest reverently.

"I'm sorry . . . sorry. I didn't mean to hold you so tight."

"It's all right. I'll not break."

A sudden flood of tenderness overwhelmed her and her hands glided over the firm muscles of his shoulders and back and around to the silky down on his chest. She wanted to touch every part of him. His body answered the movement of her hands with a violent trembling.

"Nights are hell!" he growled. "Knowing you're on the other side of that door is . . . driving me . . . crazy."

"You could have come. I'm your wife." Her senses reeled. This was like a sweet dream.

"I want more than a body for sex," he muttered fiercely against her cheek.

She pushed against his chest. His arms dropped away immediately. She moved her head so that their noses were inches apart. His heart thumped angrily against her palm, his warm breath fanned her lips.

"What do you want?" she whispered shakily.

"I don't know if I can put a word to it." His hand rested on her hipbone.

"Try." Her hand moved to cup his cheek, her thumb stroked the dent in his chin that she had longed to touch. He had shaved. His skin smelled of soap and his hair was damp.

"Oh, Ana, I'm not good with words."

"Yes, you are! Yes, you are," she crooned. "You can tell me."

"I want . . . I want to sleep with you, hold you in my arms every night."

"You can. It's your right."

"To rut on your body like a stallion in heat?" His voice was angry. "Oh, God!" His voice lowered to a mere breath. "I want to give you . . . my heart, my s-soul."

"You can. You can—"

"No. No, I can't. There are too many things you don't know."

"Then tell me. I know you were kind to Harriet. Did you give your heart to . . . her?"

"Good Lord, no! Harriet was a child, a pitiful child."

"You didn't love her?"

"I felt sorry for her."

"My word!" Ana moved until no part of her touched him and turned on her back. "You ruined my stepdaughter's life. You got her with child because you felt sorry for her?" Her low-toned voice was heavy with hurt and accusation.

"I didn't get her with child. My brother, Paul, did."

"What?" Ana's head rose up off the pillow as the cry was wrung from her lips.

"Harry is Paul's son." Owen's hand moved onto her arm just above the elbow as if he had to hold her to keep her from flying off the bed.

"Why did *you* marry her?"

"It's a long story." His hand stroked her arm.

"We've got all night."

Eighteen

"*Let* me hold you."

His deep voice was strained. He was tense, his fingers rigid where they lay on her arm. Even in her distressed state, Ana was aware of how very gentle he was being. He slipped his arm beneath her shoulders. With his other hand he turned her toward him. It didn't seem possible that such a giant of a man could be so gentle.

"Why didn't you tell me Harry wasn't your son?"

"Come here. Please—" Unhurriedly he pulled her against his side, ready to release her if she protested. When she came willingly, he settled her head on his shoulder. "I promised Harriet I wouldn't tell. I was going to tell you after the funeral, but then things seemed to . . . get mixed up." Whether by intent or by accident, his hand rested on the side of her breast and he stopped talking.

"Start at the beginning," Ana breathed. Her heart was soaring like a bird on the wing. The rest of her tingled as if she were being pricked by a thousand needles. *He had been Harriet's husband, but not her lover!*

"Paul left home a few years ago. He and Esther got along like a cat and a dog. As I look back on it now, Esther was acting strange even then."

"Hindsight," she murmured.

"I'm not very observant. I see that now."

"Where did Paul go?"

"Chicago, New York, that I know of. He had the money I paid him for his share of the farm."

"He was in Dubuque last fall."

"Yes. I heard he had been there when I went down to collect money that was owed to me. I fear he's taking his pleasure where he can get it and to hell with the consequences." He captured one of her hands, pressed it to his chest and held it there. They lay quietly except for the thump of his heart against her palm.

Ana tilted her head to look at him. He was staring up at the ceiling.

"Harriet fell hard for him. She said her love was a laughing, dancing man."

"That's Paul. Not much like me, I'm afraid."

"She loved him."

"He didn't deserve that love." He sounded irritated. "He should have faced his responsibilities. He wasn't coming back to the farm," he scoffed. "He liked city life too much. Yet he told her she would find him here. He had absolutely no intention of doing right by that girl."

"She came here?"

"She sent a postcard telling him to meet her in Lansing —that it was urgent. I went there. She was a pitiful little wretch—young and scared. After she told me she was carrying Paul's child, I married her and brought her home."

"Why would you do that? She was nothing to you."

"The child was a Jamison—a bastard Jamison. I know how hard life has been for Lily."

"Harriet could have come home. I would have taken care of her."

"She said she'd rather die than go back and face you.

There was nothing to do but wed the girl and let everyone think the child was mine.''

''You could have told me.''

''I was prepared to dislike you. I wanted to blame someone along with Paul. I had forgotten how charming and persuasive he can be and how he would appear to a very young girl.''

''That day in Lansing you accused me of not doing my duty. I tried, Owen. Really I did.''

''I know that now. I was going to tell you the truth of the thing after the funeral. But by then I wanted you to stay. If you knew that I hadn't fathered the child and that you had as much right to the boy as I did, I'd not have had a lever to keep you here.''

His confession stunned her.

She was quiet for such a long time that he asked, ''Does that shock you?''

''Well . . . yes. I didn't think you liked me.''

His arm tightened. Her hand, captured between his and his chest, could feel the pounding of his powerful heart.

''I was scared to death of you. I still am.''

''Why, for goodness sake? You're much bigger than I am.''

Now he laughed silently. She could feel that, too, against her palm. She tilted her face to look at him and her nose rubbed against his chin.

''I'm such a . . . clod. You must have known all sorts of men in Dubuque who wore suits and straw hats and had fine manners.''

''Well, yes I did, but . . . they didn't give me a second look.''

''I'll never believe *that*.''

She wiggled her hand from under his and moved it up to the curve of his neck. Her fingers slipped into his hair.

''Are you angry that I deceived you into marrying me?'' His voice was husky and anxious.

She hesitated for a moment that seemed an eternity to Owen.

"To tell the truth," she whispered against the warm flesh of his shoulder, "I'm glad you did. So glad that I could cry."

"Oh, Lord, Ana! Are you sure?"

"I'm sure. I'm glad, too, that it wasn't you who seduced Harriet."

"Ana, Ana, I never touched that girl. I let Esther think I did, but I didn't. I swear it." He turned, put both arms around her and held her tightly. His lips moved across her forehead.

It was the sweetest moment of her life.

"I believe you—"

"Is there a chance for us, Ana?"

"I'd say there's more than a chance . . . husband."

Owen made a low groaning sound as his mouth slid across her cheek to her mouth. Her lips were soft; his were hard and insistent. Dear Lord, she was sweet. Her reaction to the kiss was instantaneous. Her lips parted, her whole body shivered, her arm crept up around his neck. A naked heat began to build in him. He wanted to be closer to her miraculous softness, to hold her against him so tightly that their flesh would become one. He breathed the fragrance of lilac from her satin-soft skin, her silky hair, and felt himself flame and harden. His legs and arms began to quake like those of a man with chills.

Ana returned his kiss with an innocent hunger. So this was what kissing was like. His mouth was hard, yet wonderfully warm and sweet. His hardness thrilled her. The rough, seeking touch of his calloused fingers, stroking her from her nape to her shoulder to cup her breast in his huge hand, sent delicious quivers throughout her melting flesh. Her body burned with a joyful, alien desire. Her eyes closed in ecstasy.

The long, hard rod pressed to her belly suddenly drew her full attention. He was as aroused as a stallion after a mare in heat! Good grief, she was about to mate with a man, and she didn't know what to do!

"Owen . . . please!" she gasped under his mouth. "I must tell you"—he went as still as if he were frozen in place—

"that I've never . . . that I didn't do . . . anything like this with Mr. Fairfax."

A sigh quivered through him. "Jesus, my Lord! Don't scare me like that."

"What did you think I was going to say?"

"Not *that*. I want to ask why, but I won't. I don't care. I'm so glad!" He laughed a low, happy laugh and hugged her until she thought her spine would crack. "We'll learn together. I've been with a few . . . ah, women, but they don't count." His lips took up the kissing again, covering every inch of her face.

They were totally absorbed in the pleasure of new discovery when Baby Harry let out an earsplitting cry that could only be a cry of intense pain. Within seconds Ana was out of bed and lighting the lamp. She rounded the end of the bed scarcely aware that Owen had swung his feet over the side and was sitting there, a look of confusion on his face.

Ana picked up the screaming child and cuddled him to her.

"Sshhh . . . don't cry," she crooned. "Oh, honey, what's hurting you?"

"What's the matter with him?" Owen asked anxiously, trying to make himself heard over the child's screams.

"He's drawing his legs up and his tummy is hard as a rock. I think he's got colic."

"What's that?"

"Pains in his tummy. He may have sucked air after he emptied his bottle. I try to watch and take it away as soon as he's finished. Sshhh . . . baby. Oh, darling," she cooed, as the little face puckered, and he let out another loud cry of pain. "I know you're hurting." Ana walked back and forth, patting the baby's back. Owen stood. When she turned, she ran up against his bare chest.

"What can we do for him?"

"I've read about colic in the *Common Sense Medical Book*, but I don't think we have any of the things they suggest."

"What do they suggest?" He walked beside her while she paced.

"A little Jamaica ginger in brandy, or opium, which I will not use." she said firmly. "If we had a syringe, we could give him an enema. Do you have castor oil?"

"Not that I know of."

"The only other thing I know to do is to put warm cloths on his tummy and get him to drink warm water with a little salt in it. It should make him vomit." Baby Harry continued his loud, lusty cries even when Ana cradled him in her arms and swung him back and forth.

"Do you want to fix it, or do you want me to?"

"I'd better do it. You take Harry." She transferred the baby to Owen's big hands and watched him lift the child to settle him on his shoulder. "Press his tummy to you and pat him on the back. It's gas that causes the pain. Sometimes the gas will come up with a force that will make him throw up; sometimes it goes the other way."

"There, there, boy." Owen began to walk and to pat. "We'll get you fixed up soon, and you can get back to sleep."

"You can pat harder than that."

"I'm afraid I'll hurt him."

"He's already hurting. The jarring might bring up some of the gas."

Ana went to the doorway and looked back. Her eyes and Owen's met with sweet familiarity. She stood before him in a thin nightgown, her hair loose and hanging down her back. Owen wore only a pair of drawers that rode low on his hips and stopped at his knees. Yet it didn't occur to Ana to be embarrassed. She was thrilled by the deep blue, velvety look absorbing her.

"I'll hurry. You can jiggle him a little, Owen," she said and disappeared into the dark hallway.

The picture of him stayed with her while she lit the lamp on the kitchen table and shook down the ashes in the cookstove to find a few hot coals. She had never seen a man in so few clothes. His arms and legs were as powerful as the limbs of a giant oak. Muscles corded his great shoulders and his chest that narrowed to a sinewy middle without an ounce of superfluous flesh. The soft down on his chest was only a shade lighter than the thick hair that curled down over his forehead. Ana felt the strength leaving her as she thought of how she had lain pressed tightly to him from her head to the soles of her feet.

Owen had not been the one who seduced her stepdaughter.

In a daze of joy and disbelief, Ana added kindling to the coals. With the bellows that hung behind the stove she supplied the air that caused the flame to erupt. After placing the teakettle directly over the fire, she sprinkled a few grains of salt in the baby's bottle. When the water was lukewarm, she filled the bottle and hurried back to the bedroom.

Ana paused in the doorway. Exhausted from crying, the baby was making small mewing sounds as it tried to sleep nestled against Owen's broad muscular chest. Ana felt a sudden, delicious rush of joy. He was magnificent. She was utterly in love with this man, the real man behind the rough exterior. He was good, sweet and kind. He had married Harriet so that he could take care of her.

Owen turned, saw her, and flashed her a shy grin.

"He's trying to sleep."

"Did he throw up?"

"No. He wet a lot and did something else. Phew!" The look of chagrin on his face made her laugh with her eyes as well as her mouth. With his hand on the baby's bottom, he held him out so that she could see his wet chest and the baby's soaked nightgown.

"Maybe we won't have to give him this salt water," Ana said, picking up a blanket and spreading it on the bed. "Lay him down. I'll clean him up."

"Will you clean me up too?" His eyes teased her. His smile was beautiful.

"You're a big boy—"

Baby Harry awakened and let out another ear-splitting scream. He drew his little legs up, then stiffened them out. Ana put the nipple in his mouth. At first he refused the slightly salted water. Then finally he began to suck.

"The water in the teakettle should be hot by now. Put some in a washdish, Owen. We'll lay a warm wet cloth on his tummy after I clean him up."

It was almost dawn when Baby Harry fell into a peaceful sleep. Ana lay down on the bed with the child in her arms and Owen covered her with a sheet. She had rocked the child for hours. Owen had applied the wet packs, kept the teakettle filled, and carried the soiled napkins to the tub of water on the back porch.

When Ana awakened, the sunlight was streaming in the windows.

"Do you want to go to church?" Owen asked as Ana prepared breakfast.

"I don't think we should take Harry out in a crowd for at least another week." She glanced at him and saw the relief that slumped his shoulders. "Why, shame on you! You're relieved you don't have to go."

"Maybe we shouldn't take Harry out for the rest of the summer." Smile lines tilted the corners of his mouth, and a teasing light shone in his eyes.

"Oh, no, you don't. You can't use Harry for an excuse not to go to church all summer."

"Another month?" he asked hopefully and laughed, a genuine laugh that made lights dance in his blue eyes. *He was different this morning.* A tingling sensation rippled down her spine.

"Next Sunday." Her voice was firm, but she was smiling up at him. Her face took on an animation that almost made him forget what they were talking about. "We'll go next Sunday. I'll have a dress ready by then."

"Good Lord, Ana! You're not going to put the boy in a *dress.*"

"Of course, you silly man. Did you think I'd take him to church in overalls?"

She turned to dip the butter from milk she had churned the night before. While the water was heating to make mush for breakfast, she worked the milk out of the butter with a wooden paddle. Owen took the fresh buttermilk to the cellar and emptied the milk they hadn't used into the slop bucket for the hogs.

"Violet McCalister sent word by Uncle Gus, when he took brooms to the store, that the Busy Bees will meet next week," Ana said when Owen came back to the kitchen with a fresh bucket of water. "They're going to plan the Fourth of July celebration. Harry and I will go. I don't want the ladies of the town to think I'm a snob."

"There'll be no danger of that after they get to know you."

She watched him lift the bucket and fill the reservoir on the side of the stove. She knew the statement he had made about her had been inadvertent. It was a lovely compliment.

"Will you be entering any of the contests?"

"Why? Are you wanting to see me make a fool of myself?"

Her eyes swept him from head to toes and giggles burst from her lips. "I can hardly wait to see you try to catch the greased pig."

Owen's laughter joined her. "With this bum leg I'm not very swift on my feet, but one year I won the pie-eating contest. Another year I won the watermelon seed-spitting contest and brought home a jar of pickled peaches."

The vision of him toeing the line, spitting watermelon seeds, brought forth spasms of girlish laughter. Their eyes met and held. Ana thought she had given up feeling girlish, but here she was feeling as young and giddy as a school girl. Owen was an enchanting companion now that he had let down his guard. His banter and smiles came as easily as Soren's. He was enjoying himself, too.

He leaned his hip against the washbench, cocked his head to one side, and grinned at her.

"I can see that I'm going to have to prove to you that I'm a real watermelon seed-spitting champion."

"Stop bragging and bring up some of those lemons from the cellar. We'll make a crock of lemonade today."

Ana's heart began to do crazy things—like fluttering, leaping, pounding, racing. She smiled into his eyes, turned and pressed her hand against that thing going wild in her breast. Mercy me! How long had it been since she'd blushed? The world had suddenly become bright and beautiful.

Ana didn't have much time to explore the feeling or get used to the idea. Soren's urgent shout reached the kitchen and sent them both hurrying to the door.

"Owen!"

"Gawdamighty! What's happened now?" Owen muttered and pushed open the screen door.

"Pa said get out here. The mare's going to foal!"

"I checked her an hour ago and she was all right."

"Well, she's havin' it and it's coming out ass-backwards!"

"Good Lord!"

"I'll hold breakfast," Ana called to Owen as he ran toward the barn.

Hours later Ana was still holding breakfast. She had bathed and fed the baby. Exhausted from his sleepless night, he was now sleeping in the drawer she had lined with a quilt and set on two kitchen chairs. The table was set for breakfast and the mush waited on the back of the stove. When all was ready and the men had not come in, she made Indian pudding, poured it into a buttered pan, sprinkled it generously with freshly grated nutmeg, and set it in the oven. In a couple of hours she'd take it out, let it cool, and serve it at the noon meal with thick cream. It was one of Owen's favorites.

Ana looked out the door toward the barn. How long did it take a mare to foal? If anything happened to the mare, Owen would be sick.

Ana's heart gave an odd little lurch at the thought of Owen's disappointment. In the dark of the night she had lain in bed with him, nestled close to his hard-muscled body, her head on his chest, her lips raised for his kiss, her hands free to wander over his shoulders and chest. It had been wonderful.

Suddenly she was fiercely happy that Ezra Fairfax had not come to her bed. She had never wanted to explore the physical mysteries of a man and woman. But now she did . . . with Owen.

Feeling a warm flush on her cheeks, Ana chided herself that she no longer had to feel guilty about wanting Owen. He hadn't shared that special intimacy with Harriet. Harriet had loved his brother, Paul, had lain in Paul's arms; Owen would be hers.

Owen had not actually said he loved her. He had said he wanted to give his heart to her. "*Is there a chance for us?*" he had asked. Ana bowed her head over the dishpan. She hoped and prayed that Owen would come to love her as she yearned to be loved! She sighed deeply as she poured scalding water over the baby's bottles, then wiped her hands on a towel.

Abruptly, a strange, subsconscious instinct caused a cold prickling sensation to start between Ana's shoulders and travel to the nape of her neck.

She turned.

Esther blocked the kitchen doorway leading into the hall.

Nineteen

Ana was so startled at the sight of Esther that momentarily she was thrown off balance mentally. Cold sweat broke out on her forehead. The palms of her hands slid slowly down her apron past the pockets and hung limply at her sides. She opened her mouth to say something, but nothing came out. All she could do was stare at Esther's bony face and fierce, bright eyes.

Dressed in her usual black, her hair slicked back and secured in a tight knot on the back of her head, Esther looked more than ever like a blackbird. Her face was thinner, her eyes brighter, her nose longer than Ana remembered. The picture of a silent vulture waiting for death to provide it with a feast came to Ana's mind.

"Good morning." Ana managed the words calmly even though indescribable panic assailed her.

Silence.

Esther fixed her bright eyes on Ana. Ana could feel the weight of her hatred.

"Owen is in the barn."

More silence. Heavy. Threatening.

"He'll be in for breakfast soon. Sit down and have coffee while you wait."

Only a birdsong and the creak of the windmill broke the silence.

Praying Owen's sister didn't know how frightened she was, she made a supreme effort to make her voice normal.

"The mare is having her foal."

"Shameful hussy!" Esther hissed through thin tight lips.

Ana pretended not to have heard.

"He's hoping for a filly—"

"You trapped him just like that other slut did. Is his seed growing in your belly?"

Now wasn't the time to show anger or weakness, although Ana's patience was wearing thin and her legs felt like jelly. The woman was out of her mind, even dangerous. Ana held herself stiffly, unconsciously braced against an attack. She frantically searched her mind for something calming to say.

"They finished planting Uncle Gus's broom corn yesterday."

"Where's Mama's bed?" Esther demanded shrilly.

Ana's eyes darted to the baby sleeping peacefully in the bureau drawer. Good heavens! She had been prowling around in the house. The hair on Ana's arms raised as goosebumps popped out on her cold flesh.

"Your mother's furniture was moved upstairs. You can go see for yourself."

"Slut! Bitch! You stole Mama's things."

Ana remained calm. "You'll find every single thing that was hers in the room upstairs."

"*He* didn't want her upstairs."

"Owen wanted me to use the downstairs bedroom. I was sure that you wouldn't want me to use your mother's furniture."

Ana swallowed the lump of panic that rose in her when the look of intense hatred came over Esther's face, drawing her lips back in a snarl.

"He wants you in that room so he can crawl on you when

the notion strikes him. He's a horny, ruttin' swine just like
Pa and Grandpa was. He'd poke it in anything that has a
slit.'' Esther was breathless after she spewed out the words.

"Don't talk like that about your brother. Owen is a good,
decent man!''

"Good? Ha! Right away he got a baby on that whey-faced
slut from Dubuque.''

Ana's face turned fiery red. "He . . . he was her husband.''

"Jamison men all got bad blood. Mama said all of old
Grandpa Jamison's brains was in that thing hanging between
his legs. She told me that—''

"Hush that filthy talk!'' Ana said sternly. Then forcing
herself to swallow the lump of fear that rose up in her throat
she spoke again. "Take what you want and go, Esther.''

A dry cackle of laughter burst from Esther's throat. She
placed her fists on her hips and swayed from side to side.

"Go, Esther. Go, Esther,'' she chanted.

"I understand why you want the things that belonged to
your mother.''

"Owen's gone off and left m-me—'' Her voice rose in a
mournful wail. "He not goin' to do anything, just go off.
Why don't he come back?''

"Owen is in the barn—''

"He's gone off and left me here. He don't care, he don't
care.''

"You're mistaken. Owen does care. He thinks the world
of you.''

"You don't know anything,'' Esther screeched.

"I know that Owen is concerned about you.''

"Get out!'' Esther shouted.

"This is my home now, Esther.'' Ana still tried to keep
her voice calm. "I live here . . . with Owen. We're married.''

"No!'' She moaned as if she were in terrible pain. "You
don't live here. *I* live here.''

"I live here, Esther,'' Ana said gently seeing the anguish
on the woman's face. "Go out to the barn and ask Owen.''

"Mama don't want harlots in her house." Her voice rose to an hysterical pitch.

"I'm not a harlot. I'm your brother's wife."

"You're bad! Wicked! Go. Shoo . . . shoo—" She took a menacing step toward Ana, making a motion with her hands as if she were scaring away chickens. "Shoo . . . shoo—"

Ana realized that she had made a mistake in trying to reason with the woman. Owen would have to deal with his sister. The thought that someone out of their mind had been roaming around in the house without her knowing it terrified her.

Ana walked calmly across the room, picked up the baby and his bottle. On not-quite steady legs, she backed out the door leaving Esther standing in the middle of the kitchen, her hands still fluttering in the shoo-ing motion.

Ana hurried across the yard. The double doors of the barn were folded back. Sunlight streamed into the barn brightening the alley between the stalls. The men were in the stall with the mare and the foal. Owen saw her the instant she entered and came out of the mare's stall, wiping his hands on a rag.

"It's a filly," Owen announced proudly with one of his rare smiles that faded quickly when he saw the look of anxiety on Ana's face. "What's wrong?"

"Esther's in the house. She came in the front door." Ana rushed on nervously. "I didn't know she was there until I turned and saw her behind me."

"She probably came over to get something," he said without the least concern in his voice, although his insides immediately turned upside down.

Ana went rigid with anger. She looked at him, stunned, unable to understand why he wasn't concerned about a woman who was of unsound mind, even if she was his sister, sneaking into the house. Couldn't this big, stupid man get it through his head that she was insane and dangerous?

"She didn't come to get *something*," Ana said frostily when she found her voice. "She's crazy as a loon!" It was a cruel thing to say, and she was immediately sorry.

He choked when he started to speak. "Did . . . ah . . . did she try to hurt you?"

"No, but she made it clear that her mama doesn't want a *harlot* in her house."

"I'll go talk to her."

"You do that." She couldn't keep the impatience out of her voice.

Ana turned her back on him and looked into the stall, her mind so confused she barely noticed the foal standing on weak, spindly legs, or Soren on his knees wiping it with a rag. Her mind was in such a turmoil that she was unable to appreciate the miracle of the birth.

"There, there, lass," Gus crooned to the head-tossing mare. "Your little one be in safe hands. Move her up close to the teat, Soren. Once she starts sucking she'll be all right."

Soren straddled the little filly to guide her head beneath her mother's belly. The eager little mouth grabbed a teat and began to suck. The two men grinned happily at each other, backed out of the stall, and closed the door.

Ana walked out of the cool barn and stood hesitantly in the shade beside the big doors. She looked toward the back door of the house, then away. She didn't think she could possibly cope with any more verbal abuse from Owen's sister, even after making allowances for her mental condition. She wanted to cry, to scream that it wasn't fair for Esther to make her so miserable just when she was within reach of all she had dreamed of having. Ana repressed the awful need to give vent to her feelings, lifted the sleeping child to her shoulder, and headed toward the orchard.

"Ana, wait—"

Ana's steps never faltered, nor did she look back.

"Let her go, son. If Esther's in there, Ana needs to get away from the house for a spell." Gus looked past his son to a cloud of dust on the road, but didn't mention it.

"Something is going to have to be done about Esther, Pa. Lily says she's getting more unreasonable and harder to handle all the time."

"You're right," Gus agreed quietly, still watching the traveling dust. "You been seein' Lily, have you?"

"I've been going to talk to you about that, Pa. I've been meeting her at night. That old Jens is as ornery as a mule with his dinger caught in a barb-wire fence. He'd not welcome me as a caller to the house."

"I figured that's where you were headin' when you took off across the field." Gus turned a stern face toward his son, caught his eyes, and held them. The meaning in them was perfectly clear.

"Pa! Don't look at me like that. I'd not dishonor Lily if that's what you're thinking."

Gus's eyes searched his son's face. "I guess I knew that, son, but for a minute—"

"Lily's a sweet girl and she's not had much to be happy about. I've been thinking, Pa, that I'd . . . marry her."

"Because you feel sorry for her?"

Soren's handsome face took on a troubled expression. He chewed on a straw poked into his mouth.

"No. Well, to tell the truth, I'm not sure yet."

"Be sure, son. It'd not be fair to Lily or to you if you wed her for any reason but the right one. You always did have a soft spot for anythin' bein' put upon. Don't get carried away with feelin' sorry for the girl." He put his hand on Soren's shoulder and squeezed. "We'll have to finish this another time. It looks like somebody's comin'."

Soren turned to see a wagon coming up the lane at a fast clip. Lily was on the wagon seat, Hettie's head was visible above the sideboards of the wagon bed.

"What the hell are they in such a hurry for?" Soren trotted toward the wagon as it entered the yard. He caught hold of the bridle to stop the horses.

"Procter hurt Foster," Hettie blurted. "Procter's a dumb ass, is what he is."

Gus came to hold the horses as Soren went back to lift Lily from the wagon seat. Her serious brown eyes clung to his face.

"Are you all right, honey?" he whispered, before he set her on her feet.

"Yes, but Foster's got a big cut on his head."

Soren's hands moved down her arms and squeezed her hands. He held one tightly in his while he looked over the sideboards at the man sprawled in the wagon bed, his head in Hettie's lap. Blood oozed from a cut on his forehead, rolled down over his eye patch and onto his sunken, whiskered cheeks. His clothes were ragged, his body filthy dirty, and through the gap of his torn shirt Soren could count every rib.

"He fell down, Soren. He fell and Procter kicked him." Hettie dabbed at the blood on Foster's head with a rag.

"Is that what caused the cut?"

"He hit his head on the end of the porch." Lily glanced at Gus to see if he had noticed Soren holding her hand, then wiggled it free. "He's awfully drunk, but that wasn't any reason for Procter to kick him."

"I'll take care of that son-of-a-bitch later," Soren promised angrily. "Let's move the wagon over by the barn, Pa, and get him inside."

"Oh, poor Foster," Hettie crooned. "Looky, Soren. He's pee-peein' on hisself."

"I can see that," Soren said, without looking at Lily. "As soon as we see to that cut, we'll dunk him in the horse tank. He smells like he's been wallowing in a manure pile."

Soren and Gus lifted Foster from the wagon bed, carried him inside the barn, and placed him on a bed of fresh straw.

"He stinks." Hettie wrinkled her nose as she looked up at Soren. "Foster's nice to me. I'll wash him with soap."

"Foster's nice to everyone, Mama," Lily said patiently.

"He said to me, 'Well looky here at how pretty Hettie is.' He said that, Soren. And he said I wasn't dumb even when Procter said I was."

"Procter's the dumb one. Lily, Owen's in the house with Esther—"

"Esther's here? I thought she was in her room—"

"She's here. Go to the house and get some clean rags,

soap, vinegar and a tin of salve from the shelf under the washbench.''

"But . . . what'll Ana say?''

"Ana took the baby and went for a walk while Owen talked to Esther.''

"Oh, I hope Esther wasn't mean to her.''

"I don't know about that. Owen will have to handle it. Run along, honey. We have to wash the blood off Foster so we can see how badly he's hurt.''

Soren knelt down and began to strip off Foster's shirt. He ground his teeth in anger when he saw the mean-looking bruise on his side. Foster's lips were chapped, his cheeks gaunt, his dark hair long, gray-streaked, and greasy. He looked worse than Soren had ever seen him.

"He looks like hell, Pa. He's killing himself.''

"Aye, he is.'' Gus said sadly. "I'll get a bucket of water.''

"He ain't going to kill hisself!'' Hettie wailed. "I'll take care of him.''

"I meant he's killing himself by drinking so much. He's just a bag of bones.''

"He thinks I'm pretty.''

Soren tilted his head to look at Hettie. She *was* pretty. Hell, she couldn't be more than a few years older than Owen. She had been only fourteen when she had Lily. Her face was smooth, unlined, and wore a constant smile. Her eyes were as unpretentious as a child's when they looked into Soren's. She was neat and clean. There was a lot more to Hettie than some people thought. Her frank, child-like ways were embarrassing, but she had a heart as big as all outdoors.

"Is he goin' to die, Soren?''

"Naw. We'll take care of him. Take off his shoes. Jesus! He doesn't have on any socks or underwear.''

"I won't look at his . . . thing, Soren.''

Soren bowed his head to hide his grin. "We can't take his britches off. We've got to think of Lily.''

"Lily won't look at it. Lily's nice like that. Do you like Lily, Soren?''

"Of course. I like you, too, Hettie." He rummaged in his pocket for his pocket knife. "His britches are rags. I'll cut them off. We'll cover him with a horse blanket."

When Gus returned with the bucket of water, Hettie dipped into it with the cloth she had used in the wagon and gently wiped the blood from Foster's face.

"It was mean of Procter to kick you," she crooned. "He said you was a worthless bum, but you ain't. You can read better'n Procter." She looked up at Gus. "One time Foster read to me out of a book."

Gus got down on one knee and looked closely at the cut on Foster's forehead. "It isn't bad. Head cuts always bleed a lot. We can put pine tar on it. It's what we do to the mules."

"Foster ain't no mule," Hettie said sternly.

"He's as stubborn as one. What he needs is a good cleanin' up." Gus stood, tipped the bucket and poured a stream of water on Foster's head. Foster wiggled his nose, smiled lazily, but otherwise didn't move. "Here's a bar of lye soap on the washbench. Suds his head, Hettie. If he's got lice, that lye soap will get rid of them."

"He does," Soren said drily. "Take these clothes out and set 'em afire, Pa. We don't want Ana to see what a sorry state he was in. Did he have a suitcase, Hettie?"

"He has a little pack but there's no clothes in it."

"Goddammit, Foster," Soren said to the man in the drunken stupor, "this time you're going to straighten up if I have to whip your butt."

"You'd whip him?" Hettie gasped. "I thought you liked Foster."

"I do. That's why he's going to straighten up."

Lily returned with the rags and salve. "Esther's upstairs rantin' and ravin'. She don't make no sense atall anymore."

"Honey, go with Pa and see if you can find some clothes to put on Foster after Hettie and I get him cleaned up."

Honey. He had said that right out loud. What would Uncle Gus think? Lily's cheeks turned a bright red as she turned her face away from Soren's father.

"C'mon, child." Gus urged Lily out of the barn with his hand on her back. "Soren and Hettie can scrub him down. We'll find him a clean shirt and a pair of overalls. The hard part will be soberin' him up."

Owen found Esther upstairs in the bedroom.

"Where have you been, you naughty boy? Go wash your hands. It's time for supper." Owen gaped at her. "Where's Paul?" Esther demanded. "He'd better clean out that chicken coop or Pa'll have his hide."

"Esther, Paul . . . isn't here."

"Did you lock him in the privy again? Shame on you."

"I d-didn't . . . Paul isn't here."

"You can lie to me but not to Pa." She shook her finger in his face. "You know what'll happen."

Owen frantically searched his mind for something to say. He had been prepared for anything but this. She had regressed to the days when he and Paul were children.

Suddenly she screeched. "What's this doin' here?" She spread her arms over the bureau as if protecting it.

"I brought it up here."

"It's Mama's. Mama don't want to be up here." Tears began to stream from her eyes.

"Yes, it was Mama's. Now it's yours." Owen's heart began to thump painfully.

"It's Mama's. She wants me to polish it and make it pretty." Esther grabbed a cloth from one of the drawers and began to rub it over the front of the bureau.

"I think you'd better go home now, Esther. I'll take you in the wagon."

Esther ignored him and presently began to hum. She moved from one piece of furniture to the other, dusting it carefully. When she reached the rocking chair, she began to sing. "Bye-o, my baby. Bye-o, my baby—"

Owen didn't know what to do. It seemed to him that his

heart was splitting in half. He owed this sister so much, yet a yearning for Ana and the home she was creating for them pulled at his insides.

"Mama would want you to take these things home with you. I'll get the wagon and we can load them up."

"Home with me?" She looked at him strangely. "But I am home, Papa."

Oh, dear Lord! Her mind was completely gone if she thought he was that ornery old son of a bitch.

"Look at me, Esther. I'm Owen," he said desperately.

"Owen's gone. He went off and left me—"

"Oh, sister." Owen had never felt such pain. In his despair he grasped her shoulders to turn her toward him.

"No! No! Please, Papa. I'll be good. I'll be good."

The look of terror on her face caused Owen to drop his hands and reel backward. He stared into her stricken face, then turned and lurched from the room. In the hallway he leaned against the wall, his face buried in the crook of his arm. Tears rolled from his eyes. Silently he cursed the man who sired him. He wished to hell he'd left him in the cow lot for the bull to stomp into the manure from which he came. Instead he had pulled him out, got a horn in his thigh for his trouble, but not a word of thanks from the ungrateful old man.

Owen dried his eyes on his shirt sleeve. He could hear Esther humming and the creak of the chair as she rocked. She had lived a nightmare while he and Paul were growing up. It was no wonder she had lost her mind. A vision of her hovering over him and Paul while their father wielded the buggy whip came to his mind.

And the *other thing*! Goddamn that old man!

Owen owed it to his sister to take care of her.

He would explain to Ana and make arrangements for her to go back to Dubuque if that was what she wanted to do. He wouldn't tell her *all* of it. She would despise him and he couldn't blame her.

Twenty

*T*he first thing Owen saw when he came out onto the side porch was Jens Knutson's wagon beside the barn. Then Gus and Lily came from the house in the grove. When she saw him, Lily moved away from Gus and came to the porch. Gus continued on toward the barn.

"Mama and I brought Foster over, Uncle Owen. He came to our house last night. He said he got a ride to White Oak on a freight wagon. He's in the barn."

"Drunk?"

"And hurt. He was drunk when he got to our place. Procter was awful mean to him. He's got a cut on his head, but Uncle Gus said he'd be all right."

"Have you seen Ana?"

"Soren said she walked off toward the orchard. I didn't know Esther had come here, Uncle Owen. I thought she was at home in her room upstairs. That's where she stays most of the time."

"I moved Ma's furniture upstairs. She's up there now and not making any sense at all."

"Do you want me to go talk to her?"

"Are you afraid of her, Lily?"

"No. She talks mean sometimes, but she's never hit me."

"Do you think you can get her to go back home?"

"I'll try. But Grandpa's getting real ornery. He doesn't have any patience with her anymore."

"Does he mistreat her?" Owen asked.

"Well . . . not exactly. When she gets one of her spells, he has Procter take her upstairs and lock her in. She kicks and fights every step of the way."

"Oh, Lord, Lily. I can't take her to the crazy house. And with Ana and the baby here, I can't bring her here." He groaned a deep sigh of distress.

"Don't worry. Mama and I will look after her."

Owen's arm went around her thin shoulders and he hugged her to him. "Ah, honey. I wish there was some way I could make things easier for you. Is Jens pestering you to take up with Procter?"

"He wants me to, but—"

"But you won't."

"No. I won't."

"Procter wants the farm. He'll do everything he can to get it."

"I worry about Mama."

"Procter doesn't want Hettie. And you don't have to take any man you don't want."

"Soren told me that."

"Do you like Soren, honey? I mean, could you be happy with him?"

Lily hid her face against his shoulder and murmured, "He's not said anything about . . . that."

"Soren's not cut out to spend his life on a farm. He likes to come here for a month or two, but that's all."

"I know. And I couldn't leave Mama even if he wanted me to." She looked at him then and smiled, although there were tears in her eyes. "Soren isn't wanting to *marry* me, Uncle Owen. He comes to see me and tells me about the places he's been. Oh, he's been everywhere."

"It might be that he wants to settle down."

"But not here."

"No, not here. God, Lily, this family is a mess."

"I'll go see about Esther. You'd better go find Ana."

"She won't come back while Esther's here."

"I'll see if I can get Esther to go home. Sometimes if I act like we're both little girls, she'll do what I want her to." Lily opened the screen door, turned and asked, "You like Ana a lot, don't you, Uncle Owen?"

"Yes, I do. I . . . love her."

"I hope she loves you back."

Owen stood for a moment after Lily left him. It was a continuing source of wonder to him how sensible she was. Sweet little Lily could very well be the only sane one in the family.

He stepped off the porch and went to the barn. He arrived just as Gus walked up to the stall where Foster lay. Soren and Hettie backed away and Gus threw the bucket of cold well-water on the naked man.

Foster came up out of the straw like it was on fire.

"Goddammit, Gus! You're killing me. Oh, Lord . . . my head feels like it's been run over by a train." He squeezed his temples between his palms as he stood there shivering.

"Get over here, dry off, and put on these clothes." Soren held up a towel.

Hettie took the towel and began drying Foster's back.

"Get away from me, woman," he snarled, his one good eye glaring at her. "I need a drink. Oh, Lord, I need a drink."

"You're not getting any," Hettie said. "Soren said drink was killing you."

Foster's one blood-shot eye darted to Soren, then back to Hettie. "It's no business of yours."

"It is, too. You ain't goin' to kill yourself 'til you read to me some more."

"Oh, Jesus! Oh, my Lord! You've not got the brains of a tree stump. Give me that towel."

"I do too have brains of a tree stump! I'm pretty. You said I was. So there, Foster Reed."

"Owen! Owen, friend," Foster said with a grimace, as he took a step forward that jarred his head. He held out his hand and Owen grasped it. "Soren and this feather-headed woman are trying to kill me."

"Hello, Foster. You look like you've been dragged behind a wagon for five miles."

"You'd look like hell, too, if you'd had your clothes stolen while you were helpless and attacked with lye soap and a horse brush." Naked as a young jaybird, Foster glared first at Soren and then at Hettie.

"You pee-peed on yourself and had doo-doo in your britches," Hettie said scathingly, and stared unblinking into the one eye glaring into hers. "That ain't being very nice, Foster."

Foster raised his eyes to the roof of the barn. "Gawda-mighty! What have I done to deserve this? I thought you were my friends. Where's my clothes?"

"We burned them."

"But . . . I'm naked and I'm freezing to death, and by damn, I want a drink!"

"A drink of water? I'll get you one—"

"Water? Are you daft, woman?"

"That's not what he means, Hettie." Soren leaned on the stall rails and grinned. "Got a headache, Foster?"

"Shitfire! You lame-brained mule's ass. My head's bustin' right in half. Do somethin', dammit!"

"What do you think we should do, Owen?"

"Damned if I know. We ought to put him in a side show and charge to see him."

"Hell!" Soren laughed. "He'd not win any prizes naked, that's sure."

"You're right about that. He looks more like that bone

skeleton hanging in Doc Shelton's office in Lansing than a live man.''

"You're makin' fun." Hettie's large brown eyes, full of indignation, went from Soren to Owen and back again. She snatched up the clean shirt and overalls and thrust them in Foster's hands. "Put these on. I'll get you a drink of cold buttermilk.''

Foster gagged, then winced.

"Hellfire and brimstone!" He snatched the clothes and looked at Hettie as if he would strike her. With the clothes covering the front of him, he reeled down the alley between the stalls until he found an empty one.

"Why's he mad, Soren? I like cold buttermilk.''

With his hand in the middle of Hettie's back, Soren urged her out of the barn. Owen and Gus followed.

"I don't think his stomach is in the best of shape, Hettie. He'll be all right in a day or two.''

"Nothin'll help his head but a meal in his belly and a good, sound sleep." Gus noticed Owen looking toward the orchard. "The lass was troubled.''

"It's no wonder," Owen said dejectedly.

Hearing the screen door slam, he turned toward the house. Lily and Esther, hands clasped and swinging between them, came toward them.

"We're going," Lily called.

"We're going to get my baby," Esther called cheerfully. "We'll be back.''

"Oh, Lord. What am I going to do, Uncle Gus?" Owen asked.

"She ain't got no baby," Hettie said, a puzzled look on her pleasant face. "What's she mean, Owen? She ain't got no baby.''

"I'll tell you what, Hettie." Soren took Hettie's arm and they went toward the wagon. "Let's play like it's true. What do you say?''

"Play like Esther's got a baby?''

"It'll make her happy."

"All right. I like for Esther to be happy."

"Good girl. I'll drive them home, Owen," Soren said over his shoulder to his cousin.

Gus moved out to the wagon where Lily and Esther were climbing up on the seat. Soren helped Hettie into the back.

"Don't get into any trouble with Procter, son."

"I won't, unless I'm pushed."

Gus and Owen watched the wagon leave the yard. Esther waved gaily and Owen waved back.

"I don't understand it, Uncle Gus. How could she have gone downhill so fast?"

"It hasn't been as fast as you think," Gus said pulling his pipe out of the bib of his overalls. "I caught on a year or more ago that she was actin' strange and gettin' all up in the air over nothing. It's just got worse is all."

"Just now, upstairs, she thought I was the old man." It hurt Owen to say the words, but if he couldn't say them to the man who had been more like a father to him than his real one, he couldn't say them to anyone.

Gus lit his pipe. He understood Owen's feelings about his father. It wasn't until after Eustace was gored by the bull that young Owen had learned what hell his sister had lived in. Gus was the only one who knew. He was quite sure that Owen had not even told Soren and Paul the shocking Jamison family secret.

"I'm afraid Jens will have Esther committed to the crazy house. Lord, Uncle Gus, that's a terrible place. I'll bring her here before I let that happen. It'll mean that Ana will insist on taking the boy and going back to Dubuque." Just saying the words caused Owen's heart to tremble.

"Maybe it'll not come to that. We'll figure something out."

The little glimmer of hope his uncle held out made his insides hot and shaky.

"Go bring Ana home," Gus said. "I'll keep an eye on Foster. He's probably searching the barn for a drink. He knows he'll not find one, but that won't keep him from lookin'."

Ana heard the wagon arrive and Soren's shouted greeting. Without looking back, she walked steadily on through the trees until she came to the far end of the orchard. She stood for a moment looking at the planted field, and beyond to the clump of green that bordered the creek where she and Owen had their talk the day she walked to town. Above her head the little apples were the size of walnuts, and beneath her feet the yellow dandelions bloomed along with white buttercups, violets and daisies. From a distance she heard the call of a mourning dove. A robin sang nearby and a tiny wren called to his mate. She heard the rat-a-tat-tat of a woodpecker as he bored a hole in a tree trunk and the squeal of an eagle as it soared overhead, its sharp eyes searching for a careless field mouse.

She loved it here.

Ana thought that because she was so attuned to the land, she must have been born in a setting such as this. She would *hate* to leave the peace and tranquility of the country and go back to town, and it would *break her heart* to leave Owen . . . now.

She moved back under the shade of a tree. After searching the ground and the tree trunk for ants, she sat down. Pulling her knees up so that her feet were flat on the ground, she propped baby Harry on her thighs and folded back the light blanket. The baby was sweating. She shielded him from the breeze with a corner of the blanket so that he wouldn't cool off too fast.

"What are we going to do, little man?" she murmured and wiggled her little finger into the baby's tiny fist. "It looks like it's going to be just the two of us."

Ana sat there in the quiet morning, reliving every second of the night before. Each word that Owen had whispered was etched in her memory. He was not the baby's father. He hadn't told her earlier because he wanted her to stay here . . . with him. Now she wondered why she hadn't seen it clearly before. Not by the longest stretch of imagination, could Owen be described as a laughing, dancing man. *Bless him.* He had been a haven in the storm for Harriet. He had tied himself to her for life so that her baby wouldn't be born a bastard.

Ana wanted to think that Owen had strong feelings for *her*, feelings that went beyond wanting to sleep with her and make children with her. She thought of his body, warm, hard and big. She had never felt so safe, so cosseted in her life as when he had held her in his arms. He had held her with a gentleness that even now brought tears to her eyes. His sex had been large, firm and throbbing when pressed to her belly, yet she hadn't felt threatened by it. She had been in awe then, as she was now, that this giant of a man trembled beneath her touch, yet demanded nothing she was not willing to give.

What would happen now? Ana was certain that Esther in her demented state was dangerous. She and the baby were both in danger. Ana wasn't sure that she could live with that fear hanging over her head. It was evident that Owen didn't realize or else didn't want to admit the seriousness of his sister's condition.

Time under the apple tree seemed to stand still, yet it passed, and baby Harry began to fuss. He was wet through and through. He finished what was left in the bottle she had picked up and protested because it wasn't enough. She moved her legs in a swaying movement in an effort to lull him to sleep. She knew she had to go back to the house, but not yet. She needed just a little more time.

Before she realized that he was near, Owen had come quite close to her, his steps deadened by the grass. She turned her head to look up at him. His blue eyes were sad and empty.

"Ana . . . come home—"

"Is Esther still here?"

"No. She's gone."

Owen dropped down on one knee beside her and brushed the baby's cheek with the back of his forefinger. He wanted to fling himself down on the grass beside her, gather her and the babe in his arms, and let the world roll away. His heart was beating high in his throat.

It will kill me to let you go!

"It's peaceful here," Ana murmured.

Baby Harry's eyes, as blue as Owen's, opened wide and looked straight into his. The little face puckered like a prune and he began to cry.

"Has he got colic again?"

"He's wet and hungry." Ana lifted the baby to her shoulder.

"Let me have him." Owen slid one hand beneath the baby's bottom, reached around Ana, cupped his head with the other hand, and lifted him out of her arms. "He's wet all right."

His eyes never left Ana's face. He stood and stepped back. As she got stiffly to her feet, she smoothed out her skirt with its telltale wet spot down the front and poked back the strands of her hair that had been pulled loose by the rough bark of the apple tree.

"Turn his face from the wind, Owen. I hope he hasn't swallowed enough wind to give him another colic."

"We'll get you home, boy." With clumsy tenderness Owen nuzzled the baby's cheek with his nose, while being careful not to scratch the little face with his whiskers. "You'll soon be dry and having your dinner."

"I had Indian pudding in the oven. It's probably ruined by now."

"It was sitting on the table. Lily must have taken it out."

"Then it was Lily who came in the wagon to get Esther."

"Lily and Hettie brought Foster over, not knowing Esther was here." As they walked toward the house he told her how Foster had arrived at the Knutson farm and how Hettie, Soren, and Uncle Gus had worked to sober him up. "Soren thinks the world of Foster and doesn't want him to appear so despicable when you meet him."

"Does Foster appreciate his good friends?"

"He does, but not at the moment. He's sick and got a splitting headache. You'll be a surprise to Foster."

There was no mistaking the note of pride in his voice. Ana drew courage from it.

"We've got to talk about your sister, Owen."

"I want to talk about her . . . today, after you get Harry settled."

Ana had never walked beside a man for any distance. She noticed that Owen matched his stride to her shorter one. How nice it would be if she felt free to slip her hand into the crook of his arm. She studied him covertly, noting the muscle twitch in his jaw, noting the tension keeping his shoulders stiff. She was looking at his mouth when he tilted his head down to look at her. A smile curled his lips. Glory be! It was a sin what a smile did to his face even if it didn't reach his eyes. He said nothing, but his eyes spoke for him. They held the look of a man walking to the gallows.

The noon meal was the breakfast Ana had prepared so happily that morning. Gus came in to say that Foster was asleep in the barn, the new foal was getting stronger by the hour, and Catherine, the nanny goat, had climbed up over the hay wagon and was standing on the roof of Owen's shop.

"She's the most cantankerous female I ever knew," Gus sputtered.

"She'll come down when she gets hungry," Ana said.

Gus, his excuse being that he had to see to the new foal, went back to the barn as soon as he finished eating. Ana suspected he sensed the tension between her and Owen. She left a meal on the back of the stove for Soren and tidied up the kitchen while Owen rocked baby Harry to sleep. After he settled the sleeping baby in the cradle, he stood in the kitchen doorway and waited for Ana to finish. Then, wordlessly, he took her hand and led her to his room. He closed the door leading to the hall and opened the one to the connecting room where the baby lay sleeping.

Ana stood in the middle of the room. She didn't think his insides could possibly be acting like hers. She felt as if her heart was going to jump right out of her chest. He seemed so calm, as if a decision had been reached, and all that was left was to tell her about it.

"Sit down, Ana. I shut the door in case Soren or Uncle Gus came in."

Ana sat down on the edge of the bed and clasped her hands in her lap. Owen walked back and forth. Finally he came to stand in front of her. She had to tilt her head way back to see his face. Without thinking about it, she took his hand and tugged.

"Sit down. If I keep looking up at you, I'll have a crick in my neck." She continued to hold onto his hand after he sat down beside her. "I can imagine how hard this is for you. I never had a brother or a sister. I don't remember my mother or father. My grandmother and Harriet were all the family I've had . . . until now. If something like what's happened to Esther had happened to one of them, I would have been sick to the bottom of my soul." In her golden eyes there was a brilliant glow of compassion.

"I never knew there was a woman in the world like you." It seemed natural to slip his arm around her and draw her head to his shoulder. "I have to tell you about Esther and why I can't let Jens send her to the crazy house."

"And I want to know." Her lips moved against the flesh of his neck. The smell of him was in her nostrils. The arm around her tightened, drawing her closer to his side.

"Eustace was a cruel, selfish man—"

"Your father?"

"He sired me, but I don't like to think of him as my father. He came by his cruelty honestly. Old Grandpa was mean, too. I was ten when Mama died. Paul was a baby. Esther was fourteen. Mama had lost a couple of babies after Esther was born and again after me. The old man expected me to do a man's work. When I didn't do as much as he thought I should do, I didn't eat.''

"Oh, myyy—''

"It was better than getting whipped. Usually Esther was able to sneak me something. As Paul and I got older, Eustace got meaner. He seemed to get satisfaction out of whipping us. It didn't take much to set him off. Often he'd catch us in the barn, but if Esther was around she'd stand over us and defy him. I would hear her scream when the lash cut into her back, but she'd take it and not let him work his fury out on us. He was constantly telling us that he was the man he was because his pa didn't spare the rod. I swore I'd never be a man like him.

"I left home when I was seventeen. I came back once a year to see Esther and Paul. About five years ago at Christmas time, I came back expecting to stay only a few days. Esther had married old Jens Knutson. Eustace had approved of the marriage and had given Jens what he considered Esther's inheritance. She continued to keep house here, spending four or five days a week. She'd bring Hettie and Lily with her.

"There was a lot of ice that year. The old man went into the cow lot, slipped down and was gored by the bull. I ran in to pull him out and got a horn in the leg. He lived about two weeks, then blood poisoning set in and he died. I can't say that I was sorry.''

"Does your leg hurt you much now?''

"It gets stiff and aches some, but that's all.''

Owen turned Ana in his arms. His eyes devoured her face.

"Ana, I can't turn my back on my sister and let Jens send her to the crazy house. She would be put into a small, cell-like room without a bed to sleep on. I've heard that they half-starve them and sometimes they take their clothes and keep them naked. Foster worked in a place like that for a short time. He said the crazy people are treated like mad dogs. He couldn't stand it.''

"Of course, you can't let her go there,'' Ana said, her hand coming up to cup his cheek. "Do you want me to take Harry and go back to Dubuque so you can bring her here?''

"God, no! That's the last thing I want.'' His arms tightened around her, hurting her, clamping her to him. "Ana, Ana, I don't want to lose you!'' His whispered words came against the corner of her mouth.

Not realizing how she got there, Ana found herself on her back with Owen bending over her, his arms around her, his face in the curve of her neck. She slipped her arms around him.

"Do you want me to stay?'' she whispered.

"Of course I want you to stay, but I can't ask you to. You said once that Esther was dangerous. I realize now that she's capable of hurting you or the baby.''

"Do you love me, Owen?''

"I love you more'n you'll ever know. I've never loved anyone before, except maybe Esther, a little. But I'll not ask you to stay,'' he repeated the words in a husky whisper.

"You love me! Oh, Owen! Are you sure?''

"Of course, I'm sure. I tried to tell you last night.''

"And I . . . love you.''

He lifted his head and looked into amber eyes glistening with tears.

"You c-can't—'' The words came out as if some heavy weight had suddenly fallen on his chest.

"Why not?'' Her lips trembled and a tear rolled from the corner of her eye.

"Because . . . because I'm not . . . good enough for you.''

"You are! You are, and . . . I love you!''

"Ana . . . An . . . a, sweetheart—'' The soft, sweet smile that curved his lips was reflected in his eyes. "Someone as beautiful as you can't love *me*.''

"Why is that so strange?'' Her palms moved around to his cheeks and pulled his face toward hers.

"I've got to kiss you—"

"I want you to."

He kissed her trembling mouth with incredible gentleness. He kissed her eyes, tracing the outline with sensual, delicate caresses. He sought her lips again. The pressure of his mouth was hard, seeking, demanding, willing her to respond. His tongue stroked her lips, and she allowed it to enter her mouth. Her breathing became erratic. She was swimming in a haze. Shock waves of desire hardened her nipples and twisted her belly. Her hand had found its way to the back of his neck, and her fingers buried themselves in the unruly, thick hair.

Ana caught her breath on a sob when his mouth left hers. She opened her eyes and looked into his. His eyes were devouring every detail of her face from the trembling, kiss-swollen lips to the dilated pupils of her glistening, golden eyes.

"I love you—" His voice was a ragged whisper. "Three words I've never strung together before, but they seem so right when I say them to you."

She drew in a shaky breath, her voice very low. "I love you. I want to be your wife, share everything with you. We'll work out something for Esther . . . together."

"Love, you may want to think about it."

"I've thought about it. A wife shares her husband's burdens. We'll take care of your sister. I think more of you for wanting to do it."

His hand began to stroke her hair. "I wish it was night so we could go to bed and I could hold you. You're the most wonderful woman in the whole world." He sighed deeply. "I don't understand how you can love a clod like me."

"How can you love an old woman like me?" She echoed his words with a soft laugh.

"You're not old. But . . . I'll love you when you are!" The words came from deep in his heart.

She stroked his cheek with her fingertips. His arms tightened again and his mouth moved hungrily to hers. The kiss was long and deep. His tongue teased its way into her mouth with a loving, tender intimacy. He lifted his head, his blue eyes searching hers when she moved her mouth from his.

"I've never kissed before," she whispered. "Am I doing it right?"

His laugh was light with happiness. "I don't know. It sure feels good to me. I'm glad I'm the only one to know how sweet it is." The tenderness in his voice brought moisture to her eyes.

After hours of kissing and touching, they lay on the bed, her head pillowed on his shoulder, and talked.

"Owen, I've been thinking that if Uncle Gus and Soren moved into the house, we could fix up the little house for Esther. Do you think she would be content if we put her mother's things out there?"

"I don't know. We'd have to lock her in. I'd hate to do it, but I can't risk having her come in here and hurting you or the baby."

"We could take her to Dubuque to the doctor."

"If he declared her crazy, he'd lock her up. I don't think I could stand to have her in one of those places."

"Maybe we can hire someone to come here and stay out there with her."

"Lily seems to be able to handle her. But Jens won't let Lily and Hettie come here to live."

"They're both grown. He can't keep them there if they had rather be here."

"He's Esther's husband. He'll have the law on his side if he decides to put her in the crazy house."

"Then we'll have to convince him that it's to his advantage to let her come here."

"The only thing that carries any weight with Jens is money."

"If he puts her in the institution, he'll have to pay for her keep."

"He'll not want to do that."

"You realize, don't you, that we may have to lock Esther in if she gets violent? We can keep her calm with laudanum, but after a while it takes more and more. One of the ladies I worked for on the bluff had a sister they kept in a room upstairs. It was either that or send her away and they couldn't bring themselves to do that.''

"We'll talk to Uncle Gus about it. Dear Lord, you're sweet. Have I told you that?'' he whispered against the top of her head.

It was while he was in the barn doing the evening chores that the heavy blanket of guilt began to cover Owen like a shroud. The miracle of Ana's love had kept it at bay until now. A voice in his head called him a weak, stupid coward for not telling her the awful Jamison family sin. One voice insisted that he had the right to be happy, another told him that Ana would be revolted if he told her, and that she would think of it each time he touched her.

He honestly didn't think he could endure her rejection.

Oh, God! He was so ashamed.

Twenty-One

"*I swear* that I'm going to bash in that stupid German's head before the summer is over." Soren stabbed a potato with his fork and dropped it on his plate.

Owen's eyes reluctantly left Ana's slightly flushed face and turned to his cousin.

"What's Procter done beside kick Foster?"

"Beside kick Foster?" Soren said incredulously. "Hell! That's enough right there for me to rearrange the part in his hair."

"I've yet to meet Foster." Ana smiled at her husband. "His room upstairs is ready for him."

"Better let him sleep in the barn tonight, Ana. If he follows the regular pattern, he'll be in better shape to meet you tomorrow." Owen's smile was shy, but it was a smile Ana loved.

The lamp wick sputtered and the light between them flickered. Ana's eyes, shining with happiness, sought Owen's face again and again as if she could not bear to look away. She felt as light as a cloud. The joy in her heart caused it to beat erratically. *Owen loved her!* And he had not been the

one who ruined Harriet's life. She was free to love him—
and she did. Oh, she did!

Supper was late because the men had become worried about
the milky white matter in one of the new filly's eyes. Fearing
that she was blind in one eye, they washed it with warm
water and tested it by waving a hand near the eye from behind.
To their relief, she reacted. To test further, Owen brought
the bright light of a lantern close to the foal's eyes, and he
believed both pupils had contracted at an equal rate.

Ana had been at the stove when Owen stepped into the
kitchen to tell her they were sure the filly could see with both
eyes. He had glanced over his shoulder to make sure Gus
and Soren were still at the washbench on the porch, then
dropped a quick kiss on the top of her head and squeezed her
shoulder.

"Do you know what that German son-of-a-bitch—excuse
me, Ana,—said to me?" Soren paused to fork another potato
from the bowl and drop it on his plate.

"We don't have to say a word." Owen grinned at Gus
and winked at Ana. "We couldn't stop him from telling unless
we gag him."

"You're damn right. Procter said, 'What ya doin' with my
gal?' He said that. That bastard—excuse me, Ana,—thinks
he's got a claim on Lily."

"What does Lily think?" Ana asked.

"Hell! She can't stand the sight of him."

Soren fumed about Procter all through the meal. When it
was over, Ana refilled the coffee cups and sat back down at
the table waiting for Owen to speak of their plan for Esther.
He brought up the subject almost as soon as she was seated.

"There is something Ana and I would like to discuss with
you—both of you." He waited until Gus set his cup down
on the table. "Would the two of you be willing to move into
the rooms upstairs so that we could make the old house into
a place for Esther? Uncle Gus, you could still use the lean-
to to make your brooms."

Both men looked at him in stunned silence for several seconds before their eyes swung to Ana.

"Her mother's things are terribly important to her. It would be a place where she could have them, and we could watch over her," Ana said gently.

"Lass . . . ya want to do this?"

"Of course, Uncle Gus. I'm part of this family now. A family takes care of its own."

"But after the way she's . . . the mean things she said '' Soren sputtered.

"Esther wasn't of sound mind when she did and said those things. If she had been, I would be hurt and terribly unforgiving. Poor Esther has not always been aware of what she does and says. If we can provide her with some contentment by surrounding her with her mother's belongings, we must do it. I've got everything I ever dreamed of having—right here. It's not only my duty to help take care of her, I want to do it. She took care of my husband when he couldn't take care of himself. Now it's our turn."

"Think on it, lass. Esther could harm ya, or the babe."

"Not if we are careful, Uncle Gus."

Owen was conscious of nothing but the astonishing fact that this woman with the golden hair, with the bearing of a princess, was looking at *him* with eyes shining with love and offering to share his burden.

Ana's eyes settled lovingly on Owen's face, openly declaring her love for him. Her hands moved out onto the table. His large, calloused fingers met hers in the middle and clasped them tightly. Soren and Gus would have to be blind not to see the tender expressions on their faces and the love-light that shone in their eyes.

"Whoa—" Soren's smiling eyes went from Ana to Owen and down to their clasped hands. "Hell! It's about time. Hey, that's great! I was thinking I'd have to give you some courtin' lessons, cousin."

"We'll fix a room upstairs for you, Uncle Gus. Owen and

I want you to live here in the house with us—and you, too, Soren, for as long as you want. It's big enough so that we'll not be stepping on each other's toes.''

"Well . . . I declare," Gus seemed to be overwhelmed.

"Baby Harry will have a grandpa," Ana exclaimed happily.

"Don't forget a handsome uncle." Soren's devilish smile widened.

"How could I forget anything as important as that?" Ana spoke to Soren but her eyes were on Owen's face.

"The house will need a little fixin' before it's suitable for Esther, but nothing we can't take care of in a few days," Gus said to Owen, then spoke to Ana. "Are you sure, lass, you want to take on the chore?"

"I know it won't be easy. The alternative is an insane asylum, and we can't let her be put there. I've heard that they are terrible places. Owen is going to try to persuade Mr. Knutson to let Lily and Hettie come here to help take care of her. Esther will be with her family."

"He'll not do that." Soren shook his head. "Huh-uh. Who'll do for him and Procter? Owen, you know Jens won't let Lily go, and Hettie can't manage Esther by herself."

"He might let them come here when I tell him it will cost him at least ten dollars a month to put Esther in an asylum."

"That much? When are you going to put it to him?"

"In the morning."

"I want to be there to see Procter's face when we drive away with Lily," Soren said gleefully and stood.

"The house is in good shape for bein' old as it is," Gus said "If Esther don't get any worse than she is, we can put chicken wire 'cross the windows and—

"C'mon, Pa." Soren interrupted. "Let's get out of here and leave Mr. and Mrs. Jamison alone. Oh, Lord. I wish Foster was sober. We'd have us a wingding of a shivaree tonight.''

Owen got to his feet, laughter rumbling up out of his broad chest. It was so unusual to hear him laugh that there was a short unexpected hush in the room. He didn't seem to notice as he went to the door and held it open in invitation.

"Good night, Soren. Good night, Uncle Gus," he said still chuckling. After his cousin and uncle went out, he turned to Ana. "I never thought I'd be thankful for Foster's fondness for drink. When those two get together, they can raise the roof."

Ana lifted the dishes to carry them to the dishpan. Golden eyes smiled into blue with a look that spoke of everlasting love. Owen's heart jumped like a caged beast in his breast. Not knowing what to say or what else to do now that he was alone with his wife, he picked up the half-empty waterbucket and headed for the well.

A brisk wind was blowing from the southwest. As lightning blinked, he heard the distant sound of thunder. He stood beside the windmill and stared unseeingly at the sky, thinking of how Ana had felt in his arms as they lay in her bed. She had felt as if she had been made to fit only him. Good Lord! She was sunshine; he was rain. She was the brightest flower in the garden; he the thistle that grew in the ditch along the road.

He shuddered. No matter how much he loved her, he couldn't forget where he had come from. The seeds of a carnal appetite could be lying somewhere inside him, just waiting to sprout and come out. A picture was clear and sharp in his memory—an ugly, wicked, degrading picture that would be with him for the rest of his life. At times he could feel it burning deep into his soul as if it were alive and eating him.

When he was with Ana, he could almost imagine he was an individual set apart from the past. He loved her with all his heart and soul and, miracle of miracles, she loved him. But she deserved someone who could come to her unblemished.

"It's her choice to make," a voice inside his head insisted. It wouldn't be fair to her to turn away now without telling her why. She expected him to come to her and take her as his wife. The thought set his limbs to trembling. He drew the water and headed back toward the house.

Ana was covering the necessaries in the middle of the table with a clean cloth when Owen came. He made a to-do about getting a drink of water and hanging the dipper back on the nail.

"It's going to rain." He looked around, surprised that the dishes were done. He had stood pondering at the well longer than he thought. *He didn't know if he could bear the look of utter revulsion on her face when he told her.* "We don't need more rain. The ground has got to dry so we can cultivate the fields." *Would she despise him?* "If we get much more rain the melons and cabbage will rot." *Lord, how he hated to wipe that smile from her eyes.*

"I plan to pick beans tomorrow."

"You don't need to do that. You'll be eaten alive with mosquitoes. Soren and I can do it after supper. It'll take no time at all."

"We'll see. I'll change the baby and get him settled."

"I'll . . . ah . . . fill the wood box."

Ana escaped to her room, lit the lamp and softly closed both doors. She held her hands tightly against her heart in an effort to slow its beat. Baby Harry was lying on his stomach, sleeping peacefully. She had dressed him for bed and given him his bottle before the men came in for supper. Hurrying, she removed her clothes and washed in the lukewarm water she poured from the china pitcher, all the while listening for Owen's footsteps in the hall. After she slipped a clean nightdress over her head, she took down her hair and brushed it. Should she let it hang or confine it in one loose plait? She would let it hang—this was her wedding night.

Ana was sprinkling lilac water down the front of her nightgown when she heard Owen's door open. She held her breath for a long moment wondering if he would come to her, or if he expected her to come to him. She couldn't open that connecting door, she just couldn't! After what seemed an eternity, she heard a soft knock. She opened the door. Owen

stood fully dressed except for his shoes. He had washed and
shaved. She could smell the bay rum he had patted on his
face.

"Is the boy asleep?"

"Yes. Did you want to come in?"

"Why don't you come in here? We can leave the door
open so that we can hear him." He reached out and stroked
the golden mass of hair on her shoulder. The look of sadness
in his eyes caused her heart to quiver in apprehension.

"I'll turn the light low."

Ana adjusted the lamp wick until just a faint glow lit the
room. Before she went into Owen's bedroom, she looked
down to be sure the ribbon at the neck of her gown was tied.
Owen was sitting on the bed with his forearms resting on his
thighs. His eyes were on his hands clasped between his knees,
and he didn't look up. She sat down beside him. Time passed.
He didn't move or speak. The unease in her chest began to
expand.

"Owen? Is something wrong?"

The eyes he turned on her were full of torment; his voice
when he spoke was a raspy whisper. "Ana! Ana—"

When he spoke her name it seemed a call of distress, lonely
in the silent night.

"Has something happened that I don't know about?"

"No. It's just hit me that you deserve more, much more
than a man like me."

"What do you mean?" she asked in a quiet voice.

"I'm . . . not very good husband material, Ana." Sadness
sagged the corners of his mouth.

"How can you say that? You're a kind, gentle man who
sacrificed his own happiness to spare Harriet and her child a
life of shame." Tears coursed down her cheeks, and she
begged helplessly, "Owen? Did you mean it when you said
you loved me?"

"God, yes! I love you more than life."

"That's what I wanted to hear." Ana sniffed and managed
a weak smile as she stood and stepped between his knees.

With gentle, loving hands she drew his head to her breast
and smoothed his hair back from his forehead with her fingertips. His arms went around her thighs and he turned his
face into the valley between her breasts. "We love each other.
Nothing is more important then that," she whispered against
the top of his head.

Ana turned out the lamp and moved out of his embrace.
She crawled onto the bed and lay down. Waiting was agony
until she saw him taking off his clothes. The ropes creaked
under his weight when he stretched out beside her. The mattress tilted her toward him. In an instant his arms were around
her and she was pressed tightly to his naked chest.

"God forgive me for being so damn weak! I can't resist
you," he whispered hoarsely, his face buried in her hair.

"I'm glad, so glad," she crooned. "I've waited all my
life for you, Owen Jamison. There's not a problem in the
world big enough to keep me from you."

"You're everything I've—"

What he was about to say was never said. Hungry mouths
searched, found each other, and held with fierce possession.
Oh, her lips were so warm, she gave of herself so freely, the
feel of her was so good! Logic fled his mind. Ana was in his
arms. This was now. He held her mouth with his for a long
moment, trying to memorize the feel of her soft lips, silky
skin, so that he could relive this moment. He broke away
gasping and rained fervent kisses on her face.

"Beloved . . . my beloved wife—" he whispered
hoarsely.

Ana gloried in the feel of him. Her hands couldn't stop
caressing the smooth skin of his back—up and down they
moved, and into the waistband of his low-slung, cotton un-
derdrawers. She caressed his hips, so taut they made deep
hollows in the sides. Tenderly she massaged the dent in his
hair-roughened thigh where the bull had gored him. She was
in a dreamlike state where nothing existed but the warm, hard
body pressed to hers, lips that moved coaxingly over her

mouth, parting her lips, making love to them in a tender, caressing way.

Drugged with sweet strangeness, she felt the wild beating of his heart as his hand began to roam softly over her flesh. Every nerve-ending had come alive, and with eagerness she curled her arm around his neck and gave him access to her breasts. His hand slid upward over the soft curving of her hips and inward to the arc of her waist and up over her rib cage. Strong, tender fingers cupped her breast with the lightest touch as if what he was holding in his hand was so precious and so fragile it would break.

Gently he turned her on her back, leaned over her as if he worshiped her, and put his mouth to her tender breast. Ana felt the wetness of his stroking tongue through the cloth of her gown. Burrowing her hand in between them, she pulled on the ribbon that loosened the neck and bared her breast for him. He grasped her nipple with firm lips, and soon her hips began a slow, undulating motion against him. She urged him to suckle her more fiercely. The fires of eternal passion stirred, starting with the delicious feeling of his mouth on her breasts, to the wild pulsing of her heart, on into her belly, and down to her womb.

Her arms held him closer; her body strained against his. His hand moved up under her gown and between her thighs, stroking her soft, inner skin, moving upward. Her cry was muffled when his fingers found her wetness and probed gently inside. His mouth moved to hers. The kiss was deep and long and trembling with desire.

After a prolonged delicious discovery of each other, they came together. Ana never knew how it happened. The bottom of her gown was about her waist, Owen's strong, rough thighs were between hers. She raised her hips and opened to him. Fully engorged, he moaned his pleasure as he probed her gently. She received him eagerly when he inserted himself into her yielding warmth. Together they breathlessly surrendered to a voracious hunger. For Ana there was only an instant of acute discomfort; then they were one fierce flesh, seeking peaks that could not be found alone.

"I love you, love you—" His voice was a breath in her ear.

"I love you—oh, my dearest one—"

He moved within her with a fevered rhythm, emitting soft, stirring gasps. Soaring, he clutched her to him fiercely, as he ascended swiftly into ecstasy.

"Oh, God—" he cried, clutching her against him.

Her heart racing, her mind whirling, her arms and body deliciously full of him, Ana delighted in the weight of his body on hers. Love for him filled her heart. Now that she knew this pleasure she could give him, she would banish that lonely look from his eyes and fill his life with love.

He turned on his side, bringing her with him, wrapping his powerful arms around her, pulling her thigh up over his so that they could stay united. He was too mindless yet to form words; he could only stroke her and kiss every inch of her face. He had not hoped for or expected her sweet willingness to explore with him this intimacy. The swift honesty with which she had given herself overwhelmed him.

"Ana . . . sweetheart, I . . . finished too soon. I wanted to wait, but I couldn't."

"Did I do something wrong?"

"No, sweetheart, no! It was wonderful. My heart is still racing like a runaway mule. I wanted you to . . . to . . . feel what I felt."

"Glory!" she laughed nervously. "I was afraid you didn't like doing it with me."

He hugged her. "You innocent. You don't know much about men, do you?"

"Not about *this*."

"What I meant was . . . did you have this wonderful kind of let-go feeling, tingling pleasure that made you feel as if you went out of your body for a little while?"

"I liked it. I don't think women are supposed to, but I did. I'll not deny it," she added staunchly.

"You're wonderful! I'm almost afraid that all of this is a dream, that you're a dream, and I'll wake up alone in this bed."

"You're not dreaming," she whispered and nibbled his chin with her teeth. "Have you heard of anyone getting bitten in a dream?"

His hand moved down to her hips and pressed her soft down tightly to his groin. He felt the part of him inside her harden again. He held still for one delicious moment, then with a quick intake of breath, and a hungry, eager, forward motion of his hips, he began moving in that slow, ecstatic rhythm again.

Ana met his thrusts and his eager mouth. His firm tongue caressed her inner lips and entered her mouth with sweet invasion. She could feel a flame kindle in her belly that could only be put out by the driving force inside her. The flickering fire went on and on, leading her to a joyous peak. The pleasure was so profound that the widening circle of ecstasy sucked her into a swirling eddy where she thought she would drown. Her flesh leaped and shuddered with an exquisite splintering. Her blood danced the leaping dance of delight. She sobbed his name over and over as together they let go and moved into another world.

Drained, Ana turned her head toward him when he fell away from her. She reflected with wonder at what had happened. She couldn't get over the tempest of emotion that his body had aroused in hers.

"Oh, Owen, now I know what you meant. This time it was different."

"I've read that women can reach the same peak of pleasure as men. I wanted you to experience it." He spoke in a strained whisper.

She turned on her side and stroked the damp, crisp hairs on his chest and ran her hand down over his hard-muscled belly. He grabbed her hand and held it palm down on his lower stomach. She sensed a tenseness in him that had nothing to do with what they had experienced.

"I never knew such things happened between a man and a woman. Oh, I knew what they did, but I didn't know there was so much pleasure in it." She slid upward in his hold and kissed the corner of his mouth. She lay against him while his fingers traced the shape of her side. Then he encircled her body again with his arms and nuzzled his face against her neck.

"Ana, my love, I have something to tell you." His voice was firm and a little too loud. "I'd rather give up my right arm than to tell you this, but I must. I'll not be able to face myself in the morning if I don't."

The stab of fear that shot through her almost took her breath. She went very still as if her blood was draining away. She felt a moistness on her neck that could be tears, and she felt her happiness slipping away. She held onto him with all her strength, unable to speak.

"I'd made up my mind to tell you before . . . we—before it went this far. But I wanted you. God, how I've wanted you since that day we talked on the back porch!" He burrowed his face deeper in the side of her neck and held her as if his life depended on keeping her close.

"What's bothering you? Does it have anything to do with me?" She tried to pull away so that she could see his face, but he held her to him. "Are you sorry for what we just did?" she asked almost choking on the words.

"Lord, no! I'll cherish forever the gift of your sweet surrender."

"I didn't *surrender*. What we did, we did together out of our love for each other. Please tell me this terrible thing that's tearing you to pieces."

"I've got generations of bad blood in me, Ana!" he blurted. "My father and grandfather, damn them to hell, were . . . rotten to the core."

"That's all?" she breathed in relief.

"I was going to tell you tonight. Then I saw you in that pretty nightgown with your hair hanging down your back—"

She pulled back his head and pressed her trembling mouth to his. "Oh, sweet and gentle man. You think I'll leave you because of something your father and your grandfather did?"

She felt a tremor ripple through his powerful body and it frightened her.

"I don't know, Ana. I honestly don't know."

"I won't! Darling, I won't!"

"Don't say that until you've heard what I've got to tell you." Owen met her questioning eyes directly. The pain of longing marked his face with sadness. She was everything in the world to him. "Don't make a promise you can't keep," he cautioned.

"Don't talk like that, Owen." Her eyes pleaded with him and her chin quivered. "You're scaring me."

Twenty-Two

O_{wen} sat up on the side of the bed, hunched over, his forearms on his thighs. Ana sat behind him, curled against his back with her arms around his waist, her mouth and nose against his tangy flesh. She hated the idea that he was hurting. She wanted to share his pain and unhappiness. She wanted to give him everything he needed to be happy.

"You don't have much faith in me, Owen, if you think I'll be put off now about something your ancestors did. Were they horse thieves, traitors, slavers? Tell me about it. A trouble shared is half the burden."

"It's uglier than that, Ana." His rough hands caressed her forearms locked across his middle.

"I'm not a young girl; I know about ugliness. Tell me what's bothering you," she said, as her lips traveled from shoulder blade to shoulder blade. "Tell me and don't leave anything out."

Owen let out a low miserable moan and began to tell her about his grandfather who came to the new world from Norway and settled in northeastern Iowa along with others from the Scandinavian countries.

* * *

Shortly after the Sac and Fox Indians were compelled to cede to the United States the tract of land about fifty miles wide lying west of the Mississippi, settlers pushed into this strip. Owen's grandfather, Ludvig Jamison, was among the first to stake a claim in the fertile land. With a sod-breaking plow and the three oxen necessary to pull it, he plowed his own land and that of his neighbors, charging the exorbitant price of two dollars an acre for the work.

With the money, he built a barn ten times larger than the house he built for his growing family. He bought a bellows, an anvil, and a slave with blacksmithing skills. Owning the only blacksmith within fifty miles, he soon became a rich man. Ludvig Jamison was tough and he was mean. He respected no man unless he was tougher, meaner and stronger than himself.

As far as Ludvig was concerned, women were put on this earth to work, pleasure their men, and produce sons to work. He fathered four stillborn children, three who died in infancy, four who lived to despise him, and one who was his image in both looks and temperament. It was rumored that he worked the slave to death and buried him someplace on the farm. His wife, worn out at the age of thirty-two, died giving birth to yet another stillborn child and was buried in the church cemetery at White Oak. As soon as his sons were old enough to strike out on their own, they left home. The youngest son, Eustace, more like his father than any of the others, stayed.

Eustace Jamison married Olga Halverson, Gus's sister, and the daughter of a neighboring farmer. He brought her to the farm to keep house for him and his father.

Olga was a quiet, frail woman. By the time she was twenty-five she had given birth to eight children; four were stillborn, one died in infancy. The three children who survived grew up in a house ruled by a father who firmly believed that to spare the rod was to spoil the child. Whippings were almost a daily occurrence.

Eustace also believed, as his father had before him, that he owned his wife body and soul. She was his, as his livestock was his, to work and obey his every command. Owen recalled that when he was a young child he often heard his mother pleading with his father during the night. It terrified him. He would put his pillow over his head to keep from hearing her cries.

Esther, the oldest, was her mother's pride and joy. By the time Esther was ten or eleven, she was able to take over the household duties when her mother took to her bed. Olga and Grandpa Jamison both died the same winter. One morning Esther went in to wake her mother and found her dead. The young girl was devastated with grief. Eustace allowed her to mourn until after the burial. After that he whipped her if so much as a tear showed in her eyes.

By the age of ten, Owen was doing a man's work in the fields, and a hatred for his father seethed in his young heart. Hardly a day went by that Eustace didn't whip one of the children. But when the neighbors came to call, he told a different story. He boasted about how well Esther ran the house and took care of his motherless boys. He bragged that Owen could do a man's work and that little Paul could recite the alphabet. When they went to church on Sunday, Eustace played the role of devoted father to his motherless brood.

When Owen turned seventeen, he had taken all the abuse he was going to take from his father. With the full blessing of Uncle Gus, he and Soren left home. They found jobs on the riverboats and worked their way up and down the Mississippi. A few times they went up the Missouri to Kansas City and a time or two up the Ohio to Pittsburgh. It would have been the happiest time of Owen's life had he not felt so guilty about leaving Esther and Paul at the mercy of their father.

Owen came home as often as he could to see his brother and sister. He dreamed of making enough money so that he could take them away from the farm. But when he mentioned it to Esther, she was shocked that he would even suggest that she leave her mother's house. After that, when he tried to bring it up, she refused to talk about it.

One year, Owen and Soren came home for Christmas to discover that Esther had married Jens Knutson—and with her father's blessing. Eustace had given Jens a sum of money, calling it Esther's inheritance. The wedding was held in the church at White Oak with all the neighbors attending. Owen thought the arrangement was a strange one. Esther came to the farm everyday to do the household chores just as she had always done.

Then came the accident when Eustace was gored by the bull, and Owen had been injured. Eustace had a puncture wound just below his shoulder blade and one in his thigh. Neither of the wounds were considered serious.

It was while Owen and Eustace Jamison were recovering from their encounter with the bull, that Owen discovered a family secret that changed his life forever.

Determined not to let his leg become stiff, Owen was up and about within a week. He walked some each day. One afternoon, after a trip to the barn to see about his horse, he limped into the house to hear Eustace bellowing from where he lay in the bedroom upstairs.

"Esther! Goddammit, get in here!"

After the second roar, and thinking Esther had gone to the cellar, Owen started up the stairs to see what the old man needed. Halfway up, he heard a door open and close softly, followed by footsteps crossing the hall. He started back down the stairs, but stopped when Eustace shouted again.

"Goddammit, Esther, I'd better not call you again."

"What do you want, Papa?"

"Ya ugly bitch. Ya know what I want. Hoist up yore skirt, and come'ere."

"N-nooo, Papa. Owen is outside. He could . . . he could c-come in."

"To hell with that namby-pamby son-of-a-bitch. He ain't

got no man parts atall. Get over here. I need ya to get rid of this here itch.''

"Not now! Please, Papa—''

"Don't give me none of yore sass, girl. Get on 'n' ride me good or I'll slap yore jaws!''

"Shhhh . . . please don't be loud—''

"Straddle me 'n' ride, damn you!''

The shockingly ugly words, uttered by a father to his daughter, burned into Owen's mind and would remain there for as long as he lived. Enraged by what he had heard, he pulled himself the rest of the way up the stairs and staggered down the hall.

"Take it all, ya ugly slut—''

Owen threw open the door with a force that sent it crashing back against the wall. The sight of Esther astride their father, his beefy hands holding her by the ears, her stiffened arms braced against the bed, and the look of anguish on her face, was a nightmare he had lived again and again.

A murderous rage consumed him. Somehow he was able to get across the room. With the strength of a mad man, he snatched Esther from the bed as if she were a bag of grain and dropped her on the floor. With his fist knotted and raised, he stood over the man on the bed.

"You rotten, filthy . . . bastard,'' he whispered hoarsely when he found his voice. "I should kill you!''

"Owen . . . don't! Please . . . please—'' Esther wrapped her arms around her brother's leg.

"He ain't gonna do nothin', sister. He ain't got the guts.'' The feverish eyes looked up at Owen defiantly.

"You think not!'' Owen shouted. "You tried to beat all the guts out of us when we couldn't help ourselves. God, how I hate to think that I've got one ounce of your blood in my veins.''

"Ya didn't get much of my blood. Ya got yours from that whining bitch that whelped ya.''

"You filthy old son-of-a-bitch! I wish to hell I'd left you in that cowpen. You're shit!''

"I may be shit, but I'm a *man*. If ya was, ya'd be gettin' yours same as me." His contemptuous glance settled on Esther who lay crumpled on the floor.

Knowing that if he stayed a minute longer he would kill him. Owen spat full in his father's face and stumbled from the room.

It was the last time he would see him. Blood poisoning set in, and within a few days Eustace Jamison was dead.

Sobbing with humiliation and despair, Esther had crawled from the room. In the hours that followed, she told Owen that their father had used her since the day after their mother was buried. When she had become pregnant with his child, he had made arrangements with Jens Knutson to marry her in order to protect his standing in the community. Shortly after the wedding she had lost the baby and had never become pregnant again.

As bad as it was, there was more. Esther told her brother that since the day she came to the farm as a bride, their mother had been used by both her husband and her father-in-law. It was her duty, her new husband had told her.

The days that followed were the bleakest of Owen's life. He holed up in the little house in the grove and refused to attend the funeral services for Eustace. Without Uncle Gus, he told Ana, he might have killed himself to rid the world of the Jamison shame.

Answers to questions that had niggled his mind for years suddenly became clear. He no longer wondered why Eustace would take Esther by the ear and force her up the stairs, and why sometimes he would shout at him and Paul to get out of the house and stay out until they were called.

Owen recalled seeing his father push Hettie into the barn ahead of him and close the door. Later Hettie came out crying and ran home. It had been his own pa who had taken advantage of Hettie, and Lily was Owen's half-sister. Owen kept this information to himself although he thought Uncle Gus and Soren suspected. He did hint of the possibility to Paul when Esther wanted him to marry Lily.

Paul. God, how he prayed the curse hadn't been handed down to Paul. When Harriet arrived carrying Paul's child, all the old torment came back to haunt him. He decided that the only thing he could do to make right the wrong done to the girl was to marry her and give her child a name.

He swore that when he next saw his younger brother he would beat him to a pulp.

"Then you came, Ana," Owen said with a long sigh, his throat dry from talking so long. "I felt as if I had been hit alongside the head with a brick. Golden hair, golden eyes, sweet and proud, and so pretty I couldn't keep my eyes off you."

"I thought you didn't like me."

"Didn't like you?" he echoed. "By the second day I was so smitten with you, I couldn't think of anything else. Then came the chance to marry you. God, help me, I didn't even consider what I was doing to you."

"What you've told me has nothing to do with us and our wanting to be together." Her mouth moved lovingly over his shoulders and back.

"Dear Lord. Don't you understand? The bad blood has been passed down from my grandpa to my pa, to me, Esther and Paul, and now to baby Harry."

"I don't believe in bad blood."

"How do I know"—Owen went on as if she hadn't spoken—"that sometime in the future the seed of evil that old man planted in me won't sprout and grow? What if it's passed down to our children? Dear God! I'd rather be dead."

"I don't believe in bad blood," Ana repeated firmly. "Owen, look at me." When he refused, she moved around in front of him and eased herself down on his lap. "Am I hurting your leg?"

"No, love—" He shifted her weight to his good thigh and wrapped her in his arms.

With her arms around his neck she pulled his head to her shoulder. "Absolutely nothing you have told me will change the way I feel about you."

"Ana, Ana, for God's sake, think—" His voice caught on a sob.

"I don't need to think, my love. Your father learned that despicable behavior from his father who may have learned it from his father. It can stop."

"But . . . Paul used that girl to satisfy his own lust. He could have gone to a whore—"

"My guess is that Esther shielded Paul the way she shielded you and what happened between Harriet and Paul was a coming together of two people who thought they were in love. Think of this, Owen. There are preacher's sons who go bad. Bloodlines have nothing to do with a person's morals. Esther is the one who has suffered."

"Poor Esther. She's had so little that was good in her life."

"Owen, you couldn't have prevented what happened to Esther. You were just a child. Then, after you grew up, she was too ashamed to tell. As soon as you knew about it, you didn't hesitate. You went storming into that room and faced that ugliness."

"I didn't know what was going on when I went away and left her here. Dear God, I didn't know," he groaned, raising his head so that he could see her face.

"I know that." She hugged his shaggy head to her breast. "Oh, dear man, I know. Owen Jamison, you've been worrying for nothing. But I love you, love you, all the more for your concern and for the courage it took to tell me this. Is there anything else you want to tell me?" She placed the tip of her nose against his.

"Just that I love you, and I'll understand if you think it best to take Harry and go back to Dubuque."

"You're not getting rid of me, Owen Jamison. This thing about bad blood is nonsense. Promise you'll stop worrying about it."

"It doesn't bother you?" He held her face between his palms and looked into her eyes.

"Of course it bothers me, but only because I'm sorry you

had such a miserable childhood, and for what it's done to your sister. Don't worry about little Harry. His papa will love him and teach him all the right things.'' She gently kissed the dent in his chin. ''From now on I'm going to love you so much that that unpleasantness will seem like a bad dream.''

His face was still, but she knew he was crying inside when a tear formed on his lower lid, then slid slowly down his cheek. She put her lips to it and sipped it away.

''Don't you want to kiss your mother-in-law?'' she whispered in a light teasing tone.

''No. I want to kiss my . . . beloved wife.''

The sun was peaking over the horizon when Ana awakened and sat up in bed. Heavens, it was sunup! What would everyone think? Her face became hot. In the wee hours of the morning she had gotten up to feed and change the baby. When she returned to the bed, Owen was awake and waiting. They shared kisses and a few whispered nonsensical phrases before she fell asleep in his arms, feeling warm and small and protected. For Ana it was like coming home after a long journey. Owen was home to her now.

She lay listening to him talking to Baby Harry.

''Phew. You're soaked.'' When Harry began to fuss, Owen's voice came again. ''Be quiet, boy, you'll wake her. C'mon, let's get out of here and find you some dry britches.''

When Ana heard Owen's footsteps going down the hall, she got out of bed. Surprised at the soreness between her thighs, she hurried to the other room, washed, dressed and pinned up her hair.

The memory of the night in Owens arms, sharing with him the intimacy of their bodies, answering his kisses and caresses, and talking quietly with him, brought a deep blush of pleasure to her cheeks. Incredibly, Owen Jamison, the *grouch* who had met her at Lansing, had become the joy of her life, the center of her being. Love for him had rooted itself firmly in her heart, and life was beautiful.

Ana tied a clean apron around her waist and went to the kitchen. When she reached the door, she halted in surprise. Harry lay on the kitchen table, emitting cooing, happy sounds, his arms and legs flailing in the air. Owen was struggling to fold a dry diaper in the correct shape. A soft expression of warmth and gentleness shone on his face when he looked up and saw Ana standing in the doorway.

"Did we wake you?"

Ana moved into the kitchen, leaned over the table and offered her lips for his kiss.

"How could I sleep when this is the happiest morning of my life?" she whispered as if there were ears other than the baby's to overhear.

"Mine, too."

He savored the warm eagerness of her mouth as it molded against his and sighed as her lips moved away. His mind reeled back to her shy but charming boldness of the night before. He could only marvel at the change she had brought to his life.

Ana straightened and smiled into his eyes. "Besides, today is washday."

"I didn't know that beautiful, loving angels washed clothes." His eyes sparkled as he gave her a long, deliciously lecherous perusal that made her heart thud in a wild, frantic rhythm.

"They do, and they cook breakfast for their husbands, too." Her ragged whisper came from smiling lips.

"Ana, I can't believe we're . . . truly man and wife."

She chuckled softly, leaned forward and kissed his lips again. "When I start to nag, you'll believe it."

"Then nag, sweetheart, nag!"

As soon as the words left his mouth, he jumped back and looked down. "Hellfire! You . . . you little d-devil you!"

Ana glanced quickly at the infant lying on the table between them. Water, sprouting up from the baby's stiff, little nubbin, was wetting the front of Owen's shirt. The laughter that bubbled up was a whole chorus of joyful notes soon joined by Owen's deeper tones.

"Harry, darling, it's not your fault. Your papa should know better than to take off your diaper and put you on the eating table!"

Looking at her, Owen felt purged, cleansed of the ugliness he had lived with for so long. He felt as if this was the first day of his life. Ana's smile, a smile of pure enchantment said, *Me, too*.

"I didn't know he was going to do *that*."

"Of course, you didn't. Let this be a lesson. When he has to go, he goes. And to be on the safe side, you keep this end covered up."

"He's like a fountain!" Owen grumbled holding his wet shirt out from his chest.

Ana picked up the cooing, happy baby. "Come to mama, darling. We'll have to teach your papa a thing or two about taking care of you, won't we?" It was the first time she had referred to herself in those terms. It came so naturally that she didn't even notice. "Leave your shirt in the tub on the porch with the rest of the dirty clothes, Owen."

Soren pulled open the screen door as Owen reached it. He stepped aside and Owen went out onto the porch.

"And a good morning to you, too, cousin," Soren said cheerfully. "My, what happened to you? Did Ana have to cool you off with a dipper of water?"

"Say more, cousin, and you'll be eating your breakfast with loose teeth." The happy smile on Owen's face was a contradiction to his words.

"The chores are done. Your mare and the filly are doing fine, so Pa says. He said to tell Ana that Catherine is going to be sausage very, very soon. Owen, that fool goat tried to walk across Pa's buggy and went through the top."

"That's nothing to be mad about. Tell him we'll make a tighter pen. How's Foster?"

"Still sleeping it off. What's the plan for the day?"

"I'm going over to talk to Jens after breakfast and after I draw washwater for Ana."

"I'll set up the boiling pot and fill it. Do you think Jens will let Lily and Hettie come?"

"I don't know. If hitting him in the pocketbook won't convince him, nothing will."

"Good luck. I told Pa we'd better hold off working on the house until we find out how Jens feels about Esther coming here."

"She's coming here," Owen announced firmly. "Jens will be glad to be rid of her. If he won't let Lily and Hettie come take care of her, I'll hire someone."

Soren shrugged. "Sure you don't want me to go with you?"

"You just want to go over there and devil Procter." Owen grinned at his cousin's scowl.

"Devil him? I want to lock horns with the bastard. Remember that big Swede in Saint Louis who thought he was king of the hill and I—"

"—I remember. You'd better stay here and keep an eye on Foster. Remember the time he came out of one of his drunken stupors and ran around the yard naked as a jaybird?"

"No. But I remember the time he got up on top of the barn and crowed like a rooster."

Twenty-Three

O_{wen} walked through the cornfield toward the Knutson farm, his boots sinking into the soft, black, fertile soil. Occasionally, he stooped to pull a pesky sunflower plant from between the evenly spaced knee-high shoots. It had been a good growing season; plenty of rain and sunshine. The field, already cultivated twice, would have to be hoed by hand as soon as the threshing was done. These thoughts floated only vaguely in the back of Owen's mind.

In the forefront was the remembered ecstasy he had shared with Ana—Ana of the golden hair and eyes. Dear Lord, how was it possible that she loved a rough clod like him? He had told her what he had thought he could never tell another living soul—and she still wanted to be his wife. She had brought him through the boundary of common sense and made him realize that what his father and grandfather had done had not been his shame, but theirs. The ugliness and ambiguity were gone when he thought of them now. God help me, he prayed, not to disappoint her.

As he approached the farm, Owen forced his thoughts away

from Ana and to the matter at hand. Jens and Procter were working to shore up the end of the chicken house that had been undermined by the streams of water that came down from the hill behind the farm during heavy downpours.

"Morning, Jens. Morning, Procter," Owen said, wondering if he'd get a chance to speak to his brother-in-law alone.

"Ja," Jens grunted and strained on the pole they were using as a lever to hoist up the corner of the building. Procter ignored him.

"Let me do that, Jens. Procter and I should be able to put enough weight on the pole to lift the corner for you to set a stump in place."

Without waiting for an answer, Owen leaned his considerable weight on the pole and Jens moved to roll the block of wood under the building as soon as it was lifted high enough. Within fifteen minutes the work was done, and in all that time Procter hadn't spoken a word to Owen but had given him a few mean glances.

"I need to talk to you, Jens."

"Ja."

Owen waited for Procter to move away, instead the man leaned against the chicken house and poked a straw in his mouth, his small eyes suddenly bright with interest.

"It's a family matter." Owen looked pointedly at Procter who looked back at him with a smug look on his face.

"Procter's family," Jens said obstinately.

"Not mine," Owen stated in a similar tone.

"Talk if ya've got somethin' to say. If ya ain't, we got work to do."

It took considerable willpower to keep Owen from wiping the smirk off Procter's face. He deliberately turned his back on the man before he spoke to Jens.

"We both know that Esther is sick. We need to decide the best way to take care of her."

"Ja. She sick in the head."

"Sick? Horsecock! She's crazy, is what she is." Procter's crude words drove a spike into Owen's self-control, but he ignored him.

"I think we should take her to the doctor in Lansing, Jens, or to the one down river in Dubuque."

"Ya should take her to the crazy house is what ya should do."

Owen turned and glowered at the big straw-haired man. "This doesn't concern you."

"Doctorin' ain't goin' to do no good." Jens spit a stream of yellow tobacco juice into the mud at his feet.

"We should at least find out if there's something that can be done for her."

"She's crazy. Doctorin' ain't fer crazy folks." Procter thrust out his bullet-shaped head and glared defiantly at Owen.

"You're an outsider here. Damn you! Stay out of this." Owen forced the words out from between chenched teeth. The restraint he had put on his temper was slipping.

"You ain't got no call to be uppity with Procter. He's here 'n' sees how we got to put up with Esther. She's plumb crazy 'n' has been fer a spell." Jens's curt tone stung Owen to even more anger. "Thin's is always in a hubbub here. Ain't no peace round her atall. I ain't a puttin' up with it, I tell ya."

"I'll take her to my place," Owen snapped.

"Ya wantin' the neighbors to know she ain't got no sense no more? Helmer Hansen was by yesterday 'n' she was yellin' 'n' carryin' on. Lily told him she had a splinter in her foot 'n' Procter was gettin' it out."

"Folks will have to know sooner or later, Jens. She's sick. There's no disgrace in that."

"That's a crock a horseshit. She ain't sick sick. She's crazy is what she is. Folks is funny about crazies. They'll look down on Jens fer it."

Owen looked as if he wanted to murder Procter, but when he spoke to Jens he spoke in a reasonable tone.

"We can't be concerned with what folks think. She's sick

and she's got to be taken care of. I'll take her over to my place.''

''Ja! Take 'er then, dangbustit! Glad ta be shed a her.''

''I'll fix up the old house for Esther, Lily and Hettie. They can come stay and take care of her. I'll pay them, of course.''

''W-what?'' Procter almost strangled on the word. ''What'd ya say 'bout Lily?''

''Goddammit! I'm not talking to you!'' Owen shouted. ''And I'm getting damn tired of you sticking your nose in where it doesn't belong.''

''Lily and me got a . . . understandin', don't we, Jens?''

''They ain't leavin' this here place.'' Jens ignored Procter's question. His old face was set in stubborn lines.

''They wouldn't have to stay all the time,'' Owen argued. ''Jens, be reasonable. Lily knows how to handle Esther better than anyone else.''

''They ain't goin' 'n' that's that. Who'd do fer me 'n' Procter?''

''You can hire a woman for a dollar a month and board. It'll cost you a hell of a lot more to put Esther in an asylum.''

''Do what ya want.'' Jens threw up his hands. ''I took her as a favor to Eustace so the Jamison's could hold up their heads 'n' look folks in the eye. This's the thanks I get.''

Owen knew to what the old man was referring. If he mentioned it in front of Procter he would shove that chew of tobacco down his throat.

''You took her along with a hefty dowry. Don't forget that. She's legally your responsibility, but I'm willing to shoulder it if you'll let Hettie and Lily help with her.''

''Put 'er in the crazy house, Jens. It won't cost much.''

Jens looked at Procter, then directed his question to Owen. ''How much?''

''Twelve, fifteen dollars.''

''A year?''

''A month!''

''Jehoshaphat! That be a fortune.''

''Then let Lily and Hettie come—''

"Don't do it, Jens. I know what he's awantin'. Him and that cousin a his'n is wantin' to get them women over there to diddle with—"

Owen hadn't planned to hit Procter, but suddenly his rock-hard fist was planted solidly in the big man's face. Surprised, Procter staggered back, righted himself, and wiped the blood from his mouth with the back of his hand.

"Name of a cow! Stop! You got no call to hit Procter."

"He's got no call to stick his nose in our affairs. He's an ignorant, two-bit leech, hanging around Lily thinking to get this farm."

Procter, roaring like a bull, lowered his head and charged Owen.

Owen was ready. He didn't enjoy a brawl as his cousin, Soren did, but he didn't mind this one at all. He'd had enough from this stupid lout. Owen and Soren had fought their way out of many a river tavern and had engaged in dock fights with crews from rival riverboats. Owen was confident he could handle a clumsy oaf like Procter Himmel with one hand tied behind him. He wasn't even to be compared with some of the toughs Owen had fought.

Quick on his feet in spite of his lame leg, Owen sidestepped the lumbering German as he lunged, and landed a fist in his belly. As the air left Procter's lungs it made a swooshing sound. He reeled, but didn't fall. Rage made Procter mindless. He swung his fists recklessly. Owen threw an arm up to protect himself from the windmilling attack, but a fist broke through, landing a blow to his jaw. With a grunt of pain, he stepped back and landed a smashing right to Procter's temple.

Procter was a grappling type of fighter. He grabbed Owen in a bear hug.

"I'm goin' to bust you up. I'm goin' to stomp your guts out!"

"You'll not do it jawin' about it," Owen panted, his feet stamping for purchase on the wet ground.

His lame leg suddenly gave way. He fell to the ground,

taking Procter with him. Owen arched his back to resist the tremendous strength of Procter's arms as he squeezed him. Failing to break free, he brought his head foreward in short, sharp raps, striking Procter's face. He bloodied his nose and raised livid cuts over his eyes. Just when he felt himself began to drift away from lack of air in his lungs, he freed his arms, drew them apart and slapped Procter smartly over both ears with his cupped hands.

The sudden concussion rendered Procter momentarily helpless. He yelled, dropped his arms to clasp his hands over his ears, and rolled away. Owen drew gulps of air into his tortured lungs. Slowly he pulled himself up to his feet.

Procter came up off the ground with a stout stick in his hand. Owen threw up an arm to deflect the blow. Pain shot through his arm and shoulder. For an instant he thought it was broken. A grunt escaped him. In blind urgency he swung his fist, putting all his strength behind the blow. It caught Procter in the mouth, shearing off a tooth. The big German staggered, but didn't fall. He spit out the tooth. His lips were covered with blood and it rolled down his cheeks from the cuts above his eyes. For an instant he stared unbelievingly at Owen, surprised that a man pounds lighter than he could hit him so hard.

Before Procter could recover, Owen grabbed a piece of stove wood from the pile and swung. The blow caught Procter on the collarbone and he yelled like a wounded bear. Disoriented and blinded by the blood in his eyes, he tried to swing the stick. Owen whacked him sharply on the kneecap.

"Drop the stick," Owen gasped.

"Ye . . . ow!" The stick slipped from Procter's hand, but he lumbered forward to attack with his fists, shaking his head like an angry bull and mumbling through his smashed mouth.

"I'll . . . k-kill . . . ya—"

Owen hit him. The uppercut to the chin sent him backward. His knees buckled slowly and he fell to the ground. Owen stood over him until he was sure the big man wasn't getting up, before he turned to Jens.

"You m-mean old s-son-of-a-bitch!" he gasped. "You were hoping he'd kill me."

"Ja. It woulda be all the same to me. Jamisons is lorded it over folks fer years. Ya ain't gettin' Lily. I aim to wed her up to Procter."

"You'd do that to your own granddaughter to spite me. You're no better than that piece of shit on the ground." Age was all that kept Owen from smashing Jens in the face. "I'll be here first thing in the morning to get Esther. If Lily and Hettie choose to come home with me, I'll take them. If . . . Procter gives me any trouble—well, I know ways to cripple a man so he'll wish to hell I'd killed him."

The old Norwegian's eyes blazed hatred.

Owen staggered out from behind the chickenhouse, praying his lame leg didn't fold up beneath him. Lily and Hettie were on the back porch.

"Uncle Owen—" Lily called and stepped off the porch. She stopped when her grandfather came out from behind the building.

"Get back! Get back," Jens roared and picked up a willow switch.

"I'll be here in the morning to get Esther," Owen called. "If you and Hettie want to come live with me, you're welcome."

"Get off my land!" Jens shouted.

"I'm going, but I'll be back."

Owen went through the break in the fence and headed across the field toward home on not-quite steady legs. His face was bruised and swollen. Blood oozed from several cuts. His knuckles were bleeding and his clothes were muddied and torn. It was a toss up which hurt the most, his leg or his upper arm where Procter had hit him with the stick.

Home. The word had never meant much to him before. Now it did. He wanted to go home to the woman who waited for him—the woman who put her soft arms around him and called him her love—the woman who held him as if he were all the world to her.

What would she think when she saw his clothes, his battered face and swollen hands? He groaned aloud.

She'd think him uncivilized!

Ana was bent over the scrub board when Soren and Foster Reed came out of the old house in the grove. She squeezed the water out of Owen's shirt and dropped it into the tub holding the rinse water. At last she was going to meet Foster. She wiped her wet hands on the end of her apron and waited for the men to reach her.

Heavens! The man was as thin as a scarecrow. Dark hair streaked with gray hung down each side of his face to his jawbones. As he approached, Ana could see a patch over one eye and a puckered scar that ran over his cheekbone and into his hairline. Owen had said he had lost an eye and an ear in the war. Poor man.

"Ana, I want you to meet Foster." Soren's smiling eyes went from Ana to Foster and back again. He was clearly enjoying the surprised look on his friend's face. "Ana is Owen's wife. Can you imagine that ugly son-of-a-gun getting a woman like her? Better watch your step around here. She rules the roost."

"Hello, Foster." Ana held out her hand. "Don't pay any attention to Soren. He only talks to hear his head rattle."

"How do you do, ma'am?" The voice was firm, but the hand that clasped Ana's was shaking. His thin frame seemed to be lost in the over-sized clothing. The ravages of dissipation were evident in his face, particularly around his eyes and mouth. Those deep lines made him appear older than he was. He had crammed a lot of living into his thirty-nine years.

"We're so glad you're here. We have a room ready for you."

"A . . . room?"

"In the house. Upstairs. Soren and Uncle Gus are moving into the house, too."

"Oh . . . no. No. I'll sleep in the barn."

"No friend of Owen's will sleep in the barn when he has a bed in the house," Ana said firmly. "I left your breakfast on the back of the stove."

"Thanks, ma'am, but I'm not hungry."

Ana tilted her head and looked at him. His one green eye looked into hers, then away. He shuffled his feet and began to edge toward the barn.

"Foster?"

"Yes, ma'am."

"Am I going to have trouble with you?"

"Oh, no, ma'am."

"Then come on." She took him firmly by the arm and urged him toward the house.

With his hands on his hips and a grin on his face, Soren watched Ana maneuver his reluctant friend up on the porch.

"If you don't like my biscuits, you can eat cold cornbread," she said as they entered the kitchen. "Although I've not had any complaints about them from Uncle Gus. I didn't expect any from Owen and Soren. They eat anything that doesn't jump off the plate."

"I don't want to be any bother, ma'am."

"My name is Ana, and I hope we can be friends."

Later when Ana went back to the washtub and Foster to the barn, she wondered what his life would have been like had he not gone to war. He was very intelligent, she could tell that from their short conversation while he ate a token amount of the breakfast she had saved for him. The hopelessness she saw in his one good eye tugged at her heartstrings. He reminded her of a boat cut loose from its mooring and drifting aimlessly down stream. He needed to feel loved and wanted and needed.

While she was hanging the sheets on the line she heard the rich, mellow whistle of the oriole and looked up hoping to spy the olive-colored bird with the bright-yellow rump and tail. She loved to hear the male's throaty whistle as it called his mate. The bird flew out of the wild grape vines that grew along the lane and headed for a big oak tree on the east edge of the cornfield. Ana's eyes followed the flight and saw her husband coming back across the field toward home.

Owen walked between the corn rows at a snail's pace gazing at the blue Iowa sky, dreading to have Ana see him in such a sorry state. He saw her at the clothes line as soon as he topped the rise. Her white apron was flapping in the wind, her hair shining in the sunlight. He felt his throat fill when she turned and waved. He loved her more than she would ever know. His woman—his wife—was coming to meet him.

Ana lifted a hand and shaded her eyes. Finally she realized what was different about him. His limp was more pronounced, one arm hung at his side and his face—Lord amercy, his face was cut and swollen.

"Owen! Oh, Owen!" She halted twenty feet away. "You're hurt!"

Owen searched her face for disapproval and found her eyes clouded only with concern. Her fingers were wrapped in a tight fist and pressed to her mouth.

"I'm all right."

"You fought Procter."

"Yes."

"And won."

"I guess so. He didn't get up, I did."

"Good! Oh, good! I bet you taught him a thing or two. Come, let me wash those cuts."

Her hand slipped into his, holding it gently. They walked across the yard past the clothes line and the washtubs. He had expected her to fuss, to condemn him for brawling, to demand that he tell her what happened. Instead she took it for granted that he did what he had to do. He swallowed and thought her name over and over on the way to the house. Ana . . . Ana—

He sat in a kitchen chair while Ana brought towels, warm water and witch hazel to dress his wounds. She moaned softly when he removed his shirt and she saw the huge angry-looking red lump on his arm. She ran her fingers lightly over the place that was starting to turn blue around the edges and gently lifted his arm to the table.

"What happened here?"

"He hit me with a heavy stick."

"Can you move your fingers?" she asked with so much emotion he thought she would cry.

"It isn't broken."

"You'll not be able to use it for a while. I hope you gave that awful man a good thrashing! I don't know him, but from what Soren said, and from what he's done to you, he's a rotten, mean . . . louse!" Ana bit back other words that came to her mind.

Owen sat quietly, his heart filled with love for her. She hovered over him and gently washed the cuts on his face and hands. After she bathed them, she dabbed them with a cloth soaked with witch hazel lotion.

"I hope you knocked his teeth out!" she fumed.

"I did." Owen grinned in spite of his swollen lips.

"I hate him for hurting you like this."

Owen felt his own heart beating against his sore ribs. It had been many years since he had known a woman's tender touch when he was hurt. Having her fuss over him was worth the pain.

When she finished, he pulled her between his legs and eased her down on his good thigh. She wrapped her arms about his neck and leaned her forehead against his.

"I need to kiss you," he whispered.

"I need it, too." She put her lips to the corner of his mouth and kissed him softly. "I'm afraid that's all you're going to get till your poor lips heal."

He groaned. "I need more than that."

"Will a lot of little ones do?" she whispered and kissed him again and again, brushing her mouth with his.

He uttered a throaty approval. "Ah . . . hh—"

She searched his face with eyes shining with love. "You're going to have a black eye."

"I can live with it if you can." He put his face in her hair and they sat quietly. He could feel her all through him, and he wanted to hold her forever. The world fell away, and for a moment there was just the two of them. But it had to end.

She tilted his head to see his battered, rugged, almost primitive face. Her eyes held his while her fingers worried the hair over his ears and gently stroked his cheeks.

"Your poor face."

"It wasn't much to start with."

"Don't talk like that about my husband's face. I happen to like it."

"It doesn't hurt as much as my hands. I'll have to soak them in warm salt water. I'm afraid I'll not be able to handle an axe for a day or two."

"You won't have to. There are others here to cut wood. I met Foster, Owen. My goodness, he's shy. I had to drag every word out of him."

"He's probably as scared of you as I was."

"You scared? You were a grouch, Owen Jamison." She kissed him again . . . lightly.

"I didn't have much to be happy about then." He grinned a lopsided grin. "Now I have you. All I've got to do is train you to jump when I holler." His eyes glittered devilishly.

Ana laughed. "You wouldn't like that. You'd not have anyone to argue with you or call you a stinking polecat, or a pea-brained lunkhead." She stroked the thick springy hair at his temples.

"I haven't forgotten about that," he said and nipped her on the earlobe. "Ah, sweetheart, I wouldn't change but *one* thing about you."

"And what's that, Mister Smarty?" she asked with raised brows.

He rubbed his hand over her flat belly. "You know."

"Oh, that!" Her face reddened, but she gave him a sassy grin. "That's your job. You should be good for something around here."

"Maybe I should start working on that right now." His hand slid up under her skirt. She slapped it away.

"Owen, behave!"

Owen laughed and rested his face against her for a moment. When he stirred, Ana moved off his lap and stood between his spread thighs. He swallowed, and a wary look came over his face. His shoulders stiffened.

"I told Jens that I'd be there first thing in the morning to bring Esther home." He watched Ana's face for her reaction. Her eyes held his while she looped a strand of hair over his ear. The smile she gave him was soft and loving.

"Then we'd better get busy. We have a lot to do today."

His shoulders sagged with relief. His arms encircled her thighs, pulling her to him once again.

Twenty-Four

Aside from the necessary chores that had to be done, every moment of the day was spent on moving Soren and Gus into the upstairs rooms and making the house in the grove ready for Esther. Gus and Soren had kept the house surprisingly clean. Soren and Foster carried the furniture that Esther would use to the small house, and arranged it in the bedroom, while Gus and Owen worked on making the room a place where she would be confined, and safe from herself.

Foster suggested the chicken wire be put on the inside of the windows to prevent Esther from breaking the glass and hurting herself. He also suggested the bedroom door be replaced with a heavy screen door covered with the strong chicken wire that would allow the air to flow through in the summer and the heat from the kitchen stove in the winter. Esther could be seen even though she was locked in the room.

Ana knew Owen was hurting both physically and mentally. He worked mostly with one hand because of his sore arm. And building a *cage* for his sister had to be one of the hardest things he'd ever had to do.

By evening the work was done. Supper had been milk and

mush with bread pudding for dessert. No one seemed to mind because they'd had a hearty stew for dinner. Owen sat on the back porch holding baby Harry while Ana fed the chickens and milked the goat. Uncle Gus steadfastly refused to have anything to do with the animal. He and Catherine didn't get along, especially since she had climbed upon his buggy and gone through the canvas top. He was usually so goodnatured that it was surprising to hear him grumble. "Damn goat ain't nothin' but trouble."

It was twilight when Soren and Foster came from the barn and sat down on the edge of the porch. Soren pulled out his jackknife and began to whittle on the block of wood he was making into a potato masher for Ana. At various times throughout the day, Owen had been forced to repeat to Soren every word that had passed between him and Jens, and every blow exchanged by him and Procter. The subject was still on his mind.

"Owen, do you think Jens will force Lily to marry Procter? That blow-hard bastard ain't worth as much as a fart in a whirlwind."

The question had been hashed and rehashed between the two men so many times that Owen felt there was nothing more to say.

"I don't know."

"You don't sound very concerned about it." Soren's head came up sharply and he spoke testily. "Hell! Lily's just a kid."

"She's eighteen, if I remember right. And I *am* concerned about it. As I said before, I think he'll try. But he can't force Lily to say words she doesn't want to say."

"Yes, he can. He can let that rutting son-of-a-bitch have a go at her and she'd be so ashamed she'd marry him."

"Jens wouldn't do that. She's—" Owen's voice trailed. He was not so sure what Jens would do. The man had changed during the last year. There was evidence of a mean streak down his back a yard wide. Lately there had been pure hatred in his face when he looked at him and at Esther. He just might do something to make sure he kept Lily and Hettie with him.

After Ana took Baby Harry into the house, the men sat for long silent moments, each with his own thoughts. Owen wondered what tomorrow would bring. He thanked God for Ana. She had became all things to him—his wife, his lover, his confidante. She shared his most intimate secret. Now he waited anxiously for a decent amount of time to pass. He wanted to give her some privacy to prepare for bed, before he went to her.

Soren waited for nightfall. He was going across the field to the Knutson's tonight. If Lily didn't come out, he was going to go into the house and get her. The thought of Procter's rough hands pawing her filled him with so much rage that he couldn't sit still.

Foster, too, had thoughts of his own. He was fidgety. He perspired. He trembled. His nerves screamed for a drink of whiskey. *He couldn't go through the night without a drink.* He had bedded down with a bottle every night for fifteen years except for the time he spent here. Now it was too late to try to do without. Hell, he was too old to change. What had possessed him to come back here in the first place? He'd brought his misery to the only people in the world who cared for him. Thank God he'd been sober enough to hide his spare bottle in the bushes at Knutson's before the big German had flattened him. As soon as everyone bedded down, he'd go get it and head back toward the river taverns where he belonged.

"Are you going over to see Lily tonight?" Owen asked as Soren folded his jackknife and put it in his pocket.

"You're damn right I am." He answered belligerently as if he were mad at the world. It was unlike Soren. "If that flop-eared jackass has touched her or Hettie, I'll nail his balls to a stump."

"If he's as sore as I am, you may not need but two or

three fellows to help you." Owen waited for Soren to reply to his teasing; when he didn't he said, "I think I'll call it a day. I want to be over there by first light."

"I'll be with you."

"Tell Lily if she and Hettie want to come here to live, we'll bring them in spite of Jens. You may have to marry Lily yourself, Soren." Owen tried once again to get a rise out of his cousin.

Soren ignored the remark. "If we got rid of Procter, Jens would settle down."

"Don't count on it. He's got a bone to pick with the Jamisons and he's going to pick it clean." Owen thought he knew why, but he didn't voice his suspicion. Jens might know that it was Eustace Jamison who had taken advantage of Hettie, and that Lily was Owen's half-sister.

Owen put his hand on Foster's shoulder. "You know where your room is. It's yours for as long as you want it. Ana and I are glad you're with us."

"Thanks. I think I'll . . . sit a bit." Foster silently cussed Soren up one side and down the other for being a "damn lovesick, stubborn Swede." He'd have to wait until he came back from seeing Lily before he could go over there and retrieve his bottle. Hellfire! Soren would be sure to see him searching the bushes alongside the back porch. There was no one more disgusting than a reformer trying to save someone from himself. Lordy. He wished he'd never come here.

Owen made a trip to the outhouse. When he returned, the porch was empty. A light shone from the upstairs room that was now Uncle Gus's bedroom. He wondered where Foster had gone, then lifted his shoulders in resignation and winced as pain shot through his upper arm. Soren and Foster had their own demons to fight. He just wanted to be with Ana.

As soon as he opened the screen door he noticed the air in the darkened kitchen was heavy with the spice Ana had used in the bread pudding. One more reminder of how she had made this house a home. He paused only long enough ‑ a long drink from the waterbucket, then headed for the bedroom where light spilled out into the hall through the half-opened doorway. He had waited all day for this time alone with her and didn't want to waste a minute of it.

"How's your arm?" Ana asked as soon as he entered the room and closed the door.

"Sore, but all right. The baby asleep?"

"Yes. He's such a good little boy."

"Are you tired? You worked hard today."

"We all did, including Foster. I like him. He looks so sad at times."

"He looks bad. I'm thinking one of these days he'll not come back."

"He's wasting his life."

They talked of everyday things, calm on the surface, but excitement simmered within each of them. Ana, in her modest, high-necked nightdress, brushed her hair while Owen sat down on the edge of the bed and unlaced his shoes. When he stood to take off his shirt, their eyes caught in the small mirror over the writing desk and she saw his sweet, hesitant smile. Color came up in her cheeks and the hand holding the brush paused halfway through a sweep of her hair.

As if unable to delay a minute, Owen came up behind her and lifted her hair. His lips brushed the nape of her neck, moved around to the side beneath her jawbone and stayed there. A delicious shiver sliced through her and the brush slipped from her fingers, clattering to the floor.

"Sweet and beautiful. You're trembling." His voice was soft and lazy, almost a whisper.

"No, I'm not . . . beautiful. I'm not young anymore."

He made a small noise. Powerful forearms crossed under her breasts, drawing her to him while his lips rested on her shoulder.

"You're perfect. I can't get used to the thought that you're mine and that I don't have to spend another night in that bed thinking about you on the other side of the wall." His hands moved up to her breasts, gently kneading. His lips found her neck again where her hair parted, falling forward.

She couldn't speak. Instead her lips shaped his name, "Owen, love—"

While he nuzzled her smooth skin, one palm left her breast to flatten against her lower belly, pulling her buttocks tightly against him, molding her against his hard abdomen, letting her feel the rise as his body sprang to life in response to hers.

"I want you all the time." When he spoke, his breath rushed against her ear. His cheek pressed to hers was rough.

Ana squeezed her eyes shut. It seemed to her that the center of her being lay beneath his hands, and she sagged against him. He backed up to the bed, sat down and pulled her onto his lap. She buried her nose in the curve of his neck, breathed in the scent of his skin, and felt the beat of his heart against her breast.

"Tell me what you told me last night," he demanded in a husky whisper.

"What was that?"

"You know. Say it."

"I love you."

"I'm going to ask you every day." While he spoke he brushed his lips to hers, barely touching.

"You won't have to ask. I love you—love you—love you—"

"Kiss me then—"

She looked up at him, then closed her eyes as he covered her mouth with his.

"How is it possible?" he murmured between kisses.

She knew what he wanted to know.

"It's easy to love you. So easy—" she panted.

He pulled back to see her face. "Let's go to bed, love." They gazed at each other; She at his incredible blue eyes and bruised face, he at her tawny eyes, dreamy with love, and her soft mouth waiting for his kisses. "Can we leave the lamp burning for a while?"

"If you want to."

"You're so pretty. I want to look at you before I kiss you and after I kiss you—" he whispered, and gently pushed her off his lap and pulled her between his legs. Feeling shy and absurdly awkward, she allowed him to unbutton her nightdress to the waist. His large hands gently pulled aside the gaping gown as if he were opening a priceless treasure. Her breasts were round and firm, her nipples dark and taut. He looked at them for a long moment before he moved his head and kissed each of them reverently, repeatedly. When he raised his head to look into her face, his was flushed.

"I'll never hurt you, Ana."

The vow was made so sincerely, Ana wanted to cry. Her fingers slid into the hair at the back of his head and she pressed his face to her breast.

"I know, love. I know."

He clasped her bottom in his two hands, holding her to him. When he released her, he slid the gown from her shoulders and let it fall to the floor.

"Let's have nothing between us."

She nodded and lay down on the bed. It seemed that she was living a dream. She watched him while he shed the rest of his clothes. The hair on his chest narrowed over his stomach. His sex, in a nest of dark hair, was fully erect. She gazed at it before her eyes went to the puckered hole in his thigh where he had been gored by the bull, then back to his groin as if fascinated.

"Do I frighten you?" Owen said, catching her look.

"No. You're . . . magnificent."

"Hardly that."

Saying more would have been impossible. He lay down beside her. The mattress dipped, rolling them toward each other. His arms wrapped her tightly to him, his mouth found hers and, despite his sore lips, tried to convey all the love in his heart in the kiss he gave her.

Ana's arms went up to hold him closer as he leaned over her. His rigid sex nudged her belly. He was as hard and firm and as wonderful as before. Instinctively knowing what would please him, her hand burrowed between them. Her fingers closed around him. Thrilled, she felt the pulsing response.

She was drunk with the freedom to touch him, and her heart thundered in her ears.

Owen came close to crying out when she sought and found him. He covered her face with quick kisses, telling of his love with each touch of his lips. All his life he had longed to belong whole-heartedly to someone and for someone to hold him as if he were precious to her. He wanted to cry out that a miracle had happened.

In these moments of closeness, with his hands beneath her hips, he eased her up and filled her slowly and carefully. From deep in his throat came a groan of pleasure. He lifted his head and watched the emotions cross her face, one after the other. Surprise. Passion. Pleasure.

"I'm not good with pretty words," he whispered shakily after they were fully joined. "I can only say that I love you so much it scares the hell out of me."

"I've never heard prettier words." Her lips nibbled at his. She felt like crying for all the lonely years she'd spent before knowing him.

The full length of him was buried inside her. He wanted to laugh with the pure joy of it. Her hands on his buttocks urged on, begging for more. Conscious thought left him, obliterated by the need to put out the fire that engulfed them. He heard a small animal cry come from Ana, and felt the flood of his seed pour into her. He shuddered, striving to reach into her very soul. His heaving body was bound to hers, heart and mind, in total consummation. Breathless and spent, he collapsed over her. He had been lonely, so lonely, and here it was, all the joy he had thought would never be his.

Despite his weight on her, Ana felt a peace like the calm following a storm. She opened her eyes and looked into deep blue ones soft with love. He moved his face so his lips could reach her mouth. He kissed her tenderly and eased his body off hers.

Ana felt as if she were drunk with happiness. A wave of possessiveness washed over her. She slipped her arms around his neck and pulled his head to her shoulder. With her fingers, she smoothed his hair back from his brow and whispered, "I'll love you for ever and ever, Owen Jamison."

He nuzzled his face against her breast, feeling tears build behind his closed lids. He hadn't known how sweet it would be to love and be loved.

Soren had calmed down by the time he walked across the field to the Knutson farm. His agitation would only bother Lily, he reasoned, and the girl had enough on her plate without worrying that he would get into a fight with Procter.

The only light in the house was in the kitchen. Soren sidled up to the window. Procter and Jens were hunched over the kitchen table talking in low tones. Their heads were so close they were almost touching. Suddenly Procter leaned back and pounded his fist on the table. Jens shook his head in silent warning and jerked it toward the door of the room where Lily and Hettie slept.

"Bastards are cooking up something they don't want Lily to know about," Soren mumbled to himself.

Procter looked as if he had tangled with a bear. The sight brought a smile to Soren's face. The German's lips were cut and almost twice their normal size. One eye was swollen shut. His shoulder was hurting something fierce or else he wouldn't be resting his bent arm in the bib of his overalls and moving so stiffly. Owen must have cracked him a good one on the collarbone, Soren thought gleefully.

Soren was glad to see that Owen hadn't lost his touch. A good crack on the kneecap and one on the collarbone puts a man out of commission for a while. His cousin wasn't as dirty a fighter as he was. He'd a given the bastard a whack on his balls that would have made him walk spraddle-legged for a month or more.

Soren moved around to the darkened window and tapped lightly to let Lily know he was there. She would have to wait until Hettie was asleep and the men had left the kitchen before she could come out. He moved back beneath the oak tree where he could watch the kitchen door.

The upstairs windows were dark and there was no sound. Poor Esther. He wondered if they had drugged her with laudanum to keep her quiet. Lily would do her best to see that no harm came to her, but what could one small girl do against men like Jens and Procter. Esther had always been mean and ill-tempered; but she had also taken care of her brothers, and she didn't deserve what had happened to her.

The moon hung over the treetops like a huge ripe pumpkin. Soren squatted down and rested his back against the tree trunk. After a while Procter limped out onto the back porch, stood on the edge and let his water arc into Lily's flower bed. Soon the ground around the house would smell like an outhouse. Soren ground his teeth and muttered, "Crude bastard!"

Finally the light in the kitchen went out. Soren stood and moved around to get the blood flowing in his legs before he moved up closer to the door. It seemed forever before a slim, black-clad figure moved off the porch and, staying in the shadows, ran toward the tree. A strange emotion churned through Soren as it always did when Lily came to meet him. He opened his arms and she came into them.

Lily's arms went around his middle and she held on as if her life depended on it. "Oh, Soren! Oh, Soren!" she gasped against his chest.

"What is it, honey? Has that bastard touched you?" he demanded.

"No. But he and Grandpa are planning something. They made me and Mama go to bed. And Esther—this morning Procter gave her a dose of laudanum and she's been asleep all day." Lily began to cry. "I can't keep Mama from sassing them, and Procter slapped her. Grandpa didn't say anything."

"Did he hurt Hettie?"

"Not very much, but now she's so scared she won't come

out of our room. They're m-mean to her and they're awful m-mad at Uncle Owen." Lily's lips quivered as she tried to hold back the tears.

"They're all in a sweat because Owen's going to take Esther home and he wants you and Hettie to come over and live in the old house and help take care of her."

"Grandpa won't let me go." Lily shook her head as she spoke. "He'll be glad to get rid of Esther, and I think even . . . Mama. She's started to stand up to him. Sometimes she sasses him awful. He's mad all the time. Today he dropped down in the chair, sweating and gasping for breath, after Procter slapped her. I don't think he liked it, but he didn't do anything."

"Owen and I will be here in the morning to get Esther. You and Hettie want to live with Owen and Ana, don't you?"

"Yes, but Grandpa won't let us. He doesn't want the neighbors to know about Esther. He'd like for her to go away. He'd say she was visiting and died there. Poor Esther. S-somebody's got to take care of h-her."

"I know. Now don't cry, baby, don't cry."

"S-Soren? I'm not a b-baby—"

"I know that, too. You're a pretty, sweet girl with a load of trouble on her shoulders." His lips moved across her forehead as if she were a small child. He rocked her back and forth, his arms cradling her to him.

"Is that why you come to see me? You've never even kissed me . . . proper."

Soren was still for a long moment before he whispered, "If I start kissing you the way I want to, I may never stop."

"I've never been kissed by a man."

"Then I think it's time you were."

Lily watched his mouth move toward hers and instinctively raised her lips. His lips pressed hers gently, then took slow, deliberate possession. As if she had no control, her lips parted invitingly beneath his. She could feel the scrape of his whiskers on her cheeks and feel the pounding of his heart against her palm. A wave of gladness made her pulse leap. Her hands moved beneath his arms to his back and she hugged him tightly to her.

His warmth seeped into her. She luxuriated in his strength. Her acceptance seemed to trigger a deeper need in him and the quality of his kiss exploded into a passionate demand that sent a powerful message to the area below her stomach. When he lifted his head, she closed her eyes against momentary giddiness. The tightness in her chest hurt, and the fullness in her throat prevented her from speaking.

"How did you like your first kiss?"

Fearing that she would do something foolish and irreversible brought Lily back to reality.

"I don't think I'd like it from . . . anyone else." In spite of her thundering heartbeat, she spoke calmly. Didn't he know that her love for him was tearing her apart, that every time he left her she cried herself to sleep because he thought she was still a child?

"Ah . . . innocent little sweetheart."

"Have you kissed many girls, Soren?"

"A few. But none as sweet as you."

"You'll be leaving again." Lily's heart moved uncomfortably.

"Not until fall. Lily, I'm not a . . . staying kind of man. I don't know that I could live in one place for the rest of my life."

"You'll never settle down?"

"I've never had the yen to. I like to see what's beyond the next bend in the river. Someday you'll meet a man who will love you to distraction and will want to live right here. You'll have a bunch of little brown-eyed kids and—"

"I've got to go in." Lily pulled away from him and would have run back to the house if he had not grabbed her arm.

"Oh, Lord! Lily, you didn't think—?"

"Think what? That . . . you might be c-courting me? Don't be silly, Soren."

"You've always been like a little sister to me. I can't stand to think of you being over here and . . . and Procter being here, and that he might get ideas—''

"I understand. I've got to go. Grandpa'd have a fit if he knew I'd been meeting you."

"I wouldn't hurt you for the world. You know that, don't you, honey?"

"I know that. Don't worry."

"But, Lily—"

"Bye, Soren."

She slipped away from him. He watched her run to the house and jump on the porch. The screen door closed behind her with a loud bang.

"What's goin' on down there?" It was Procter's voice that came out of the darkness.

"Get to bed. Hear?" Jens yelled.

"I'm getting a drink of water, Grandpa."

Soren tensed, ready to make a dash for the house if a light appeared. He waited long minutes for something to happen. Nothing did. All was quiet except for his own heartbeat.

Dear Lord, what had he done to Lily? She had fallen in love with him, or thought she had. Hell, didn't she know he came over because he wanted to know if Procter had bothered her? He enjoyed sitting with her in the darkness, telling her about the places he'd been and the sights he'd seen. He had painted pictures for her of far-off places that she had never even heard about. He was sure she enjoyed his company. She had told him that she looked forward to his visits.

Suddenly his heart shook with another apprehension. The kiss he had given her had been a lover's kiss. He had wanted it to go on and on. Had his interest in Lily been purely protective, or was there another reason he made the trip across the field night after night?

God's blood! This was a fine kettle of fish he found himself in!

Twenty-Five

Foster sat, knees bent, his feet flat on the ground, leaning back against the rough boards of the barn. He was so impatient for Soren to return from his visit with Lily he could hardly sit still. Soren had already been gone half the night, he grumbled to himself. It would be just his luck to run into him if he went over there before he come back. What was he doing anyway? Had he fallen for little Lily? Didn't he realize that any man who took Lily had to take Hettie, too?

Foster's sour mood lightened when he thought of Hettie. She had changed some since he'd noticed her last. He hadn't been so drunk that he didn't remember Hettie flying into the German for harassing him. She had hovered protectingly over him, giving him tenderness, something he'd not had for many years. She'd been as stubborn as a mule, too, and so damn innocent it made his flesh crawl.

Hellfire, he knew Hettie was a woman with the mind of a child, but she was loyal and compassionate in her childish way. It was a good thing that she was there on the farm where she wasn't as likely to be taken advantage of. It had happened once and Lily was the result. As pretty as Hettie was, some pimp would get a hold of her and she'd spend her days and nights flat on her back.

His thoughts turned to Owen and his new wife. Hell! She was a prize. Owen was a lucky dog. It had been good of them to offer him a bed in the house, but he'd slept where night overtook him for so long he doubted that he would ever be house-broken again. All he wanted right now was to get help to ease this pain in his gut.

He watched for Soren, cussed him silently, and finally dozed.

When Foster awakened from a nightmare of snakes and horned toads, the birds were fluttering in the trees overhead—a sure sign that dawn was no more than an hour away. The raw craving still ate at his gut. He pulled himself to his feet and stood on unsteady legs holding on to the side of the barn until the dizziness passed. He looked at the heavens and promised the Lord one year of his life in return for just one swallow of whiskey.

A rooster crowed. Shitfire! He had to hurry. It would be daylight soon. After a trip to the outhouse, Foster took off across the field running between the rows of corn. His breath rasped in and out of his open mouth, his chest hurt, his legs were rubbery. God, he was weak! He stopped to rest several times, then plunged on, staggering at times.

Finally the farm came into sight. To his horror there was a light in the kitchen window. Dammit to hell! He didn't care who saw him, he was going to get that bottle! He slipped between the break in the fence and moved alongside the chicken house. *Damn the two-legged idiots*. They set up such a racket Jens would be sure to think there was a fox in the henhouse. Foster hurried along the board-fence surrounding the hog lot, knowing that when he reached the end he would have a full view of the back of the house.

He stopped suddenly and pulled back. Not twenty feet ahead was a span of mules hitched to a wagon. Foster pressed himself against the fence, and strained to see what was going on in the kitchen. Jens was holding the screen door open and the big German was bringing Esther across the room and out onto the porch. One arm had locked her to his side and a hand covered her mouth. Nevertheless, Esther was putting up a fight. Her arms flayed wildly, and feet lashed out at Jens when they passed.

Poor, crazy Esther. They were taking her to Owen.

"Goddammit! Be still." The man lifted Esther off her feet, stepped off the porch and carried her to the wagon. Jens followed.

As Procter attempted to lift Esther to the wagonbed, she bucked violently. The hand covering her mouth slipped. He howled, drew back his hand and slapped her across the face. The blow turned her head around, but she didn't cry out.

"Don't hit her," Jens said.

"I'll knock her teeth out if she bites me again!"

"Don't whip me, Papa! Please, Papa. Mama . . . Ma . . . ma—"

"Hurry up. Lily and Hettie will be out here."

"I locked 'em in. Yeow . . ."

Fighting him with all her strength, Esther had landed a blow on Procter's cracked collarbone. He gave her a smart cuff on the ear.

"Don't hit her!" Jens attempted to help hold the struggling woman, but had to back away when she kicked him.

Foster reared up. He could not stand aside and see a woman mistreated. Esther could be handled without hurting her. Even in his weakened condition, and knowing the man could make mincemeat of him, he shoved himself away from the fence to surge forward. As he did, his foot caught in loose wire. He fell face down in the dirt, his breath knocked out of him. He fumbled to untangle his foot from the wire and got to his feet.

Procter's huge hands were clamped to Esther's shoulders and he was shaking her with such a force her head whipped back and forth like a leaf in a windstorm.

"Ya damn crazy bitch! Ya damn crazy bitch!"

"Stop that! Put her in the wagon 'n' go. If ya ain't, take

her back in the house.'' Jens grabbed at Procter's arm. The German was too angry to hear. He continued to shake Esther viciously.

"Leave her be!" Foster yelled.

Startled by Foster's shout, Procter stopped shaking Esther and stared at him stupidly. Esther hung in his hands like a rag doll.

"You don't have to treat her like that."

"Dammed if it ain't the drunk stickin' his nose in," Procter roared, and shoved Esther with such a force that her head whipped back and cracked against the wagonbed. She slid to the ground. He started for Foster but stopped when Jens spoke sternly.

"I'm not havin' no more fightin'. Ya hear, Procter?"

"Yeah. I hear . . . for now. I ain't forgettin' this, ya pickled-brained good for nothin'. Just ya wait. Ya'll get what's comin' to ya." He gave Foster a threatening look, then turned back to where Jens bent over Esther.

"Get up, Esther, and get in the wagon. You'll be all right with Procter's kin. They'll be good to ya, or I'll not pay for your keep. Now get . . . up—" Jens grabbed her shoulders to lean her against the wagon wheel. Her head flopped crazily to the side. He put his hands on each side of her face to hold her head up. When he let go, it fell sideways and she slumped on her side.

"God help us!" he gasped in horror. "Ya killed her!"

Jens knew immediately what had happened. He'd wrung enough chicken necks to know when one was broken. He stood and backed away.

"What'er you sayin'? *I* didn't kill her! I . . . didn't! I . . . never hurt her! Get up, ya crazy bitch." Procter knelt down, grabbed Esther's hair and lifted her head. His mouth opened and closed, opened and closed in wordless horror. When his hand slipped from her hair, her head sagged like the bloom of a wilted flower.

"I told ya not to hit . . . her!" Jens cried.

"I didn't hurt her!" Procter blurted, still backing away.

"Ya broke her . . . neck, is what ya done—Ah . . . Ah—" The old man gasped, grabbed at his chest with both hands and sat down hard on the ground.

"What's the matter, Jens? What's the—"

"Get . . . Lily—" Jens leaned far to the side, then slowly toppled over.

"Jens! Get up. I didn't mean to—Oh, Lord! Oh, Lord! I didn't mean to—"

Both Foster and Procter stood as if rooted to the ground for several long seconds. Then Foster moved. He hurried past the still-rooted Procter and ran to the house. "Lily!" He pulled open the screen door and yelled again, "Lily!"

"In here! We can't get out!"

Foster yanked away the chair that had been wedged under the doorknob and flung open the door. The women had hurriedly pulled dresses on over their nightclothes when they heard the commotion, but their hair hung down in tumbling masses around their shoulders.

"Foster! What you doing here?" Hettie was never at a loss for words.

"I think Procter killed Esther! Your grandpa has swooned or something," Foster explained breathlessly.

Lily hurried to the door, then hung back. "Where's Procter?"

"Out there." Foster reached for the rifle that hung over the door. "Let's go."

"Mama, bring a lantern."

When they reached the still forms beside the wagon, Procter was nowhere in sight. They went first to Esther who lay crumbled and lifeless. The women watched while Foster laid her flat on the ground and straightened her limbs. Her neck had been broken. Lily let out a sob, then went to see about her grandpa.

Foster sat on his haunches beside Esther, wondering if he couldn't have done something to prevent this accident, and it *was* an accident. He honestly didn't believe the big German brute had intended to kill her—he had not been aware of his strength when he shook her.

"Grandpa? Are you all right? Grandpa! Oh . . . oh . . . mercy!" The light from the lantern shone on the old man's face. The eyes were open and staring.

"What's the matter, Lily? Why is Pa looking like that?"

"Foster!"

Foster knelt down beside the old man. He had seen enough of death to know that he was gone. Yet he tried to find a pulse and put his ear to Jens's chest hoping to hear a heartbeat. He was as still as a stone.

"He's . . . gone. His heart must have given out all at once when he saw what had happened to Esther."

"Oh, goodness me! Poor Grandpa—"

"Pa's dead, ain't he, Lily?"

"Yes, Mama."

"He's gone to heaven to be with Ma and Harriet," Hettie said the words as if to comfort Lily. "But you've still got me, Lily."

"Yes, I've got you, Mama."

Lily stood and put her arms around her mother. While they were holding each other, the barn door opened and Procter rode out on his horse. By the time he left the yard the horse had been kicked into a run. They listened to the hoof beats until they faded into nothingness.

"What happened, Foster?" Lily asked.

"Procter was trying to put Esther in the wagon. At first I thought they were taking her to Owen, then Jens said they were taking her to some of Procter's kin. Esther fought and Procter shook her. I'm sure he didn't mean to kill her."

"They were going to get her away before Uncle Owen came."

"Seems like it."

"How come you're here?"

Hettie answered. "You come to get the bottle you hid in the lilac bushes, didn't you, Foster? It's not there any more.

I broke it on a stump.'' Hettie took hold of his hand and gazed at him. ''I like you, Foster. I'm not going to let you kill yourself with whiskey. Soren said you would.''

For the first time in twenty years Foster saw wide-eyed, open admiration in the face of a woman looking at him. It did something strange to his heartbeat. Hettie was the only person he'd ever known who so openly expressed her feelings.

''You're not, huh?'' It was all he could say.

''Soren said drink would kill you. I don't want you dead, Foster.'' She slipped her arm around him as naturally as she had around Lily. ''I'll help you be good, Foster.''

It seemed natural for him to put his arms around both women. They held each other for a long while.

''What do we do now?'' Lily looked dazed.

''We go tell Owen.'' Foster's voice sounded different to him. How long had it been since he'd taken charge of anything? How long since anyone needed him as these two women needed him? ''You two scoot into the house and get dressed. I'll stay here while you go over and tell what has happened.''

They moved to obey. Lily paused. ''What if Procter comes back?''

''Procter has had the hell scared out of him. He won't stop until he reaches the river and finds a boat to take him across. Go on, now.'' He prodded them gently. ''We'll leave the wagon where it is so Owen can get a true picture of what happened.''

''What'll we do without Pa, Lily?'' Hettie asked.

''We'll get along. You're not to worry about that now. Uncle Owen will know what to do.'' Lily took her mother's hand and led her to the house.

Dawn had lit the eastern sky by the time the women started across the field. Foster found blankets to cover the still bodies on the ground. Death was so final, he thought, as he covered Esther's still face.

Would he die in some river-front tavern with a knife in his

ribs, or would he freeze to death lying drunk in a ditch or under a bridge? If things had been different he might have had a family who loved him. Oh, hell, he'd given fifteen years of his life to whiskey because things *hadn't* been different.

Whiskey! Dear Lord, he needed a drink.

Foster thought of how Lily and Hettie had waited for him to take charge and tell them what to do. *Him*, the tavern drunk! He thought of the years he'd spent in a drunken stupor, not caring if he lived or died as long as he had a jug of whiskey.

There had to be contentment for him someplace. He could no longer blame his wife for his drinking. He seldom thought of her anymore, and when he did, it was to wonder how he could have been such a fool. Owen and his new wife had offered him a home. He'd not be worth much if he let them or Hettie down. Hettie, who couldn't take care of herself, had offered to help him.

A voice, steeped with sincerity, rang in his ears. *I'll help you be good, Foster. I'll help you be good, Foster. I'll help you—*

Foster looked toward the east. A fresh new morning had dawned. He hadn't prayed since the war. He did so now.

"God, help me to make this day a turning point in my life."

He slid off the end of the wagon and began the morning chores.

Ana looked at the clock. Owen and Soren had been gone almost two hours. Hettie sat in the rocking chair, crooning to baby Harry. Occasionally she looked to her daughter, and a lost little-girl look came over her face. Lily tried to help Ana, but her movements were wooden.

Owen and Ana had been in the kitchen when Lily and Hettie arrived. Owen was holding Baby Harry while Ana cooked breakfast. Shocked at hearing the news, Owen had shaken his head as if denying what he had been told. Ana took the baby from his arms and handed him to Lily. Then she put her arms around him and hugged his head to her breast.

"I'm sorry, Owen. So sorry—" Ana held him, stroked his head and tried to still the trembling in his wide shoulders.

When Soren and Uncle Gus came in, Lily told them quietly what had happened. Soren exploded in a rage. He wanted to ride out and hunt Procter down. Uncle Gus placed a restraining hand on his arm and nodded silently toward Owen who had pulled Ana between his legs and wrapped his arms around her thighs. Soren calmed down and they stood awkwardly on first one foot and then the other while waiting for Owen to come to grips with his grief.

"We'll bring her home as we'd planned," Owen said when he released Ana and stood.

"And . . . Grandpa?" Lily asked hesitantly.

"Do you want to bring him here, Lily?" He placed his arm across the girl's shoulders. Lily looked at Ana.

"He's welcome, Lily," Ana said gently. "Just tell us what you want done."

"I don't want to go back over there. Not now."

"You don't have to, honey. You and Hettie stay with Ana. We'll bring both of them here." Owen reached for his hat.

After the men left, Ana took the baby from Lily's arms. "I'll put him in the cradle."

Lily saw the disappointment on Hettie's face and followed Ana into the hall.

"Ana?" she whispered looking back to be sure Hettie was still in the kitchen. "Will you . . . will you let Mama hold him? She won't hurt him," she added quickly. "She's just dying to hold him."

Ana looked into Lily's serious face and suddenly saw the resemblance to Owen. Although her eyes were brown and Owen's blue, there was the same pucker to her brow, the same high cheekbones, the same earnestness in her eyes. Owen's little sister was a lot like him.

"Mama has never hurt anything, not a bird or a chicken or anything. She loves little helpless things. She'd be so proud—"

"Of course she can hold Harry. My goodness. I just didn't think about it." Ana marched back into the kitchen. "I forgot to change the pad in the cradle, Hettie. It's sopping wet. Would you mind holding Baby Harry? He loves to be rocked."

"Oh . . . oh—" Hettie's shining eyes went to Lily. "Did you hear that? She said I could hold him, Lily. I'll be *so* careful, ma'am." She sat down in the rocker and held out her arms.

"I know you will. I'll not worry for a minute if he's with you." She placed the infant in Hettie's lap. "Please call me Ana." Ana turned her back and batted the tears from her eyes. The gentle look on the woman's face when she took the baby in her arms tore at Ana's heart.

"Ah . . . Lily," Hettie exclaimed happily. "Looky at his little hand. He's looking at me! See! His eyes are open—"

"Be careful with him, Mama. He's awful little."

"I'll not let him be hurt. I promise. I'll be so careful."

Lily's eyes misted when she saw the delight on her mother's face.

"That baby will be spoiled rotten if Hettie has her way," Ana said lightly, although she wanted to cry for the young girl with such a heavy burden of responsibility. Her loving protectiveness of her mother immediately endeared her to Ana.

"We're going to stay here with her and Owen and the baby, ain't we, Lily?" Hettie asked hopefully.

"We'll see, Mama." Lily quickly looked at Ana and added, "Is there something I can do?"

"No. Yes, there is." Ana thought of how she had sat alone after Harriet's death and how the time had dragged. "It would be a big help if you'd churn." Ana lifted bread dough out onto a floured board. "Uncle Gus will be in with the morning milk. It'll have to be strained and put in the cellar."

Later in the morning, when Ana heard the wagon coming up the lane, she went out onto the porch, wiping her hands on the end of her apron. Owen drove the team with one foot propped upon the splashboard as he had done when they came from Lansing. She had thought him a grouch then. How mistaken she had been. He was the dearest thing in the world to her now. What a difference a few short weeks made in a person's life.

Owen carried his sister's body into the house and followed Ana to the front bedroom. After Esther was laid out on the bed, he turned and put his arms around his wife.

"We've got things to talk about before the neighbors come."

"Lily and I will take care of Esther, if you and Soren will do for Mr. Knutson."

Owen nodded. "I told Soren to put him in my room. Uncle Gus will go to White Oak and spread the news. But first we must talk."

The family gathered in the kitchen. Ana poured coffee and laid out fresh bread, butter and jam for those who wanted it.

"Foster is absolutely sure that Procter didn't mean to . . . ah, kill Esther. She was out of her mind and fighting as he tried to put her in the wagon to take her to his kinfolks. Jens must take the responsibility for that. He thought to spirit Esther away so that folks wouldn't know she was brainsick. Procter had convinced him that he'd be looked down on. He had pride even if he didn't act like it sometimes.

"I don't think folks have to know that Esther's mind was unsettled. I'd like for them to remember the good things she did during her lifetime. Uncle Gus, Soren, and Foster agree. We have decided to leave Procter to his own conscience. He'll be running for the rest of his life. That will be punishment enough. We think it best to say that Esther climbed on the wagon, fell, and broke her neck. Jens's heart gave out when she died. That much is the truth."

When Owen finished, silence was thick in the room. Lily stood with bowed head. Ana's heart hurt for Owen and for the young girl. Of course she would grieve for her grandpa even if he was ornery most of the time. She seemed sincere in her grief for Esther too. Ana wondered if Lily knew she had a brother who would look after her now.

"Lily said that Esther was sick in the head when she hit me, and didn't know what she was doing." Hettie's voice was loud. When she looked at her daughter, Lily put her finger to her lips. "Is that right, Owen?" Hettie whispered.

"That's right. When Esther was mean, it was because she was sick and scared. But we need to keep it a secret about her being sick in the head. Can you do that, Hettie?"

"I can do that. I'll not tell. Can we stay here with you, Owen?"

"Mama! We'll talk about that later." Lily moved over and placed her hand on her mother's shoulder.

"Owen, I like *her*." Hettie's smiling eyes settled on Ana. "She's nice."

"Yes, she is. Ana likes you and Lily, too."

"I didn't feed my chickens," Hettie blurted. "They'll be hungry—"

"Foster is taking care of the chores. He'll feed your chickens and the runt pig you've been taking care of." Soren spoke from where he leaned against the wall. He hadn't been able to take his eyes off Lily's pale face.

"I like Foster, too. I broke his bottle on a stump, Soren. I don't want Foster to kill hisself with that whiskey."

"Uncle Gus is ready to go to White Oak. He'll spread the word and bring back two burial boxes. Is there anything you need, Ana?" Owen reached for Ana's hand.

"Yes. Uncle Gus, have Violet at the store cut off enough pink satin to line Esther's burial box and tell her we want a pretty bouquet of silk flowers to match—the kind she keeps to trim hats.'' She turned to Lily. ''Does your grandpa have a white shirt?''

''Not a good one.''

''Get a white shirt for Mr. Knutson—''

Owen bent his head close to Ana's. ''Honey, I think you'd better make out a list for Uncle Gus.''

Twenty-Six

By mid-afternoon, the farmyard was full of buggies and wagons. Word of the double tragedy had spread fast. Violet rode back to the farm with Uncle Gus, Reverend and Mrs. Larson followed. There were plenty of willing hands to do what had to be done before the burial took place the following day.

Owen greeted each of the arrivals and introduced them to his wife. Ana had met most of them at Harriet's funeral, but at that time her mind had been so occupied with grief she remembered only a few faces and names. She was accepted wholeheartedly by Owen's neighbors, and her fear that he would be criticized for marrying his mother-in-law faded.

Esther was laid out in the satin-lined box in a white lawn blouse she hadn't worn since her wedding day. One of her mother's white sheets covered her from the waist down. The pink bouquet of silk flowers was fastened to her bosom. With her hair loosened and coiled over each ear, she looked peaceful and almost pretty. Uncle Gus had shaved Jens and dressed him in his burial clothes, and Lily had combed his hair. The coffins were set up in the parlor and the curtains drawn.

When this was done, Ana concentrated on suitable garments for Lily and Hettie to wear to the services. With Lily's help she made over one of Esther's skirts and put it with one of her own dark waists for Hettie. From Harriet's dresses they chose a dark blue cotton for Lily, removed the white collar, and added a flounce to the bottom that they had taken from another dress.

Hettie took over the care of baby Harry. She fed him, diapered him, even washed his soiled napkins and hung them on the line. If he as much as let out a squeak she was there to pick him up. Ana was amazed and pleased at the careful way she handled the baby. She spoke to Lily about it while they searched Ana's trunk for the black mourning ribbon she had worn at the service for Harriet.

"Your mother is taking wonderful care of Harry. She takes to it as if she had done it many times before."

"Mama loves to take care of little helpless critters. She isn't dumb like people think. She can learn to do things."

"Has anyone ever tried to teach her to knit or sew?"

"I showed her how to darn stockings. She could never do anything to suit Esther. She treated her like she had no sense at all."

"Maybe you and I can do something about that. Lily, Owen will want you and Hettie to stay here with us. I heard Hettie say she wants to. How do you feel about it?"

"And you, ma'am? How do you feel?" Tears glistened in Lily's eyes.

"Of course I want you." Ana put her arms around Lily and held her close. "You're Owen's family. He loves you like a. . .a sister."

Lily pulled away and looked into Ana's face. "Am I his sister."

"He thinks you are," Ana said quietly and watched for a surprised reaction on the young girl's face. There was none.

"I think so, too. Mama said something that made me think it was Owen's pa that. . .that did it to her. She was scared of him. When he came to the farm to see Grandpa about marrying Esther she hid in a room upstairs. Later when I was old enough to understand, I remembered that she said his *thing* was big and it hurt her.''

"Don't let that make you scared of men, Lily. Owen or Soren would never force themselves on a woman. Think of what Hettie would have done all these years without you. A terrible experience for her turned out to be a blessing. You're a daughter any woman would be proud of.''

Lily's eyes filled. ''Thank you,'' she murmured and hurried from the room.

It was late before Ana was able to have a private word with Owen. She carried a cup of coffee to the parlor where he was keeping vigil beside the coffins. Later, Soren, then Uncle Gus, would take a turn sitting with the dead.

''I made fresh coffee.'' Ana placed the cup on a table beside him. He took her hand and pulled her down onto his lap.

''It's been a long day,'' he said tiredly.

''You're worn out.'' Ana wrapped her arms about his neck and rested her cheek against his.

''I've missed you. I haven't been alone with you all day.'' He closed his eyes and brushed her lips with his.

''It will be over soon.''

''There's a lot to be done, sweetheart. Someone will have to take over the running of the farm for Lily and Hettie.''

''Soren said Foster is staying over there. Will he be all right?''

''Do you mean will he get drunk and burn the place down? I don't know. He feels bad that he couldn't have prevented what happened. He seems to have gotten a grip on himself for now. I don't know how long it'll last.''

''Owen, sweetheart—Lily knows that she's your sister. You should talk to her about it.''

''How did she find out?''

"From little things her mother has said over the years. Hettie was terribly scared of your father for one thing. She would hide when he came to the farm. That isn't like Hettie. She's usually so friendly."

"The low-down bastard!" Owen glanced at his sister's still face and a moistness came to his eyes that he quickly batted away.

"He's gone, and not worth remembering." Ana framed his face with her hands and turned it toward her. "We've got to look ahead, not back."

"Lily and Hettie can't stay at the farm alone. Every unmarried man in the county would come to call—thinking to get his hands on the farm."

"What do you think about them living in the old house? They could have their own chickens and garden spot. Hettie is good with Baby Harry. If they were near, Lily and I could help her to become more responsible."

"You wouldn't mind?"

"Heavens no! We can offer it to them. But they must decide what they want to do. Could you hire someone to work the farm? Maybe Soren—"

He stopped her words with little, pecking kisses. "Sweetheart, Soren isn't ready to settle down."

"It would be nice if he and Lily fell in love."

This time when he kissed her it was deeply, holding her tightly, almost desperately. When he lifted his head, hers fell back and he kissed the pulse in her throat.

"I love you." he whispered hoarsely. "Don't ever leave me—"

"Nothing could make me do that. . .ever."

Scandinavian dishes such as sandbakkelse, lefse, krausekake and krumkake, as well as hams, cakes, cobblers and a variety of salads filled the tables. Families came from miles around with covered dishes and solemn faces. The women who took over the kitchen began serving dinner an hour before noon because there were so many guest to feed. After everyone had a turn at the table they stood, clasped hands, and a prayer was said. When the meal was over, Reverend Larson held a short service in the parlor. The lids were nailed to the coffins, and they were loaded onto the wagon that would take them to the church cemetery. The mourners followed in their buggies and wagons.

Once again Ana stood beside Owen while the congregation sang, "Shall We Gather At The River." This time she held onto his arm. Lily and Hettie stood beside them. Lily cried softly. Tears rolled down Hettie's cheeks, but she made no sound.

Ana took Baby Harry from Mrs. Larson's arms when the service ended and the handshaking was over. Owen helped her into the buggy and they drove away from the crowd in front of the church. Uncle Gus, driving the Knutson buggy with Lily and Hettie, and Soren on horseback, followed them back to the farm. Ana sat close to Owen and once out of town, placed her hand on his thigh. He covered her hand with his and gripped it tightly. Lines of fatigue etched his eyes and mouth.

"Ana, would you think it terrible of me if I say that I'm not grieving for Esther?" Torment clouded his eyes.

"No. I think I understand. Had her life gone on, she would have been merely existing."

"She was proud. She lived in constant fear people would find out about her and Pa. And she was scared Jens would tell people that she was with child when they married. It would have crushed her to have the neighbors know. They would have found out soon that she was out of her mind. And you know how folks are about someone like that. They would have shunned her."

"She was well thought of. You could tell by the crowd of people at the service."

"That's what I mean. She would have been proud of the number of people who came and had something good to say about her. Perhaps later, she would have been just crazy old Esther.''

"Owen, you're a very thoughtful man. I'm glad you belong to me.''

"Not as glad as I am, love.''

It was late afternoon when they arrived back at the house. The weather was hot and humid without a whisper of a breeze. Ana thought longingly of the big crock of lemonade they had made that morning and hoped that some of it was left. She had covered the crock with a quilt to keep the ice from melting so fast. Owen pulled the horse to a stop near the back porch. As he was helping Ana down, the screen door was flung open and a man came out onto the porch.

"Hey, Owen. What's going on?''

Ana looked at Owen. There was no welcoming smile on his face. She looked back at the man who looked strangely familiar. He stepped off the porch and sauntered toward them. He was of medium build, had beautiful brown, wavy hair, a waxed mustache, and a smile that spread charm all over his face.

"Well, well, well. What do we have here?'' His eyes were blue, but not as blue as Owen's. His clothes were well cut and his shiny black boots were made of fine leather. He smiled at Ana, looked down at the sleeping child in her arms and grinned a lopsided grin at Owen. "What've you been up to while I've been—''

He never finished what he was saying. Owen's fist lashed out. Before the young man could draw a breath he was flat on his back in the dirt. He lay there holding his jaw.

"Goddammit! Why'd you do that?''

"Get up,'' Owen snarled.

"Owen?'' Ana gasped.

The man got slowly to his feet. With his eyes on Owen, he haphazardly wiped the dirt from his clothes.

"Fine welcome,'' he muttered, and glanced at the buggy coming up the lane. "What the hell is going on?''

"I'll talk to you in the barn.'' Owen took Ana's arm.

"After I take my wife and my son to the house. Ana, I'm sorry to say that this is my brother, Paul."

Paul. Ana stared at him. This was Harriet's laughing, dancing man. The one who had taken her innocence and then so cruelly deserted her.

"Well what do you know?" Paul's smile returned and was charming. "I bet Esther blew a cork when you brought home a wife."

"We just buried Esther," Owen said bluntly, coldly. With his hand cupped to Ana's elbow he urged her up the path to the porch.

"Buried Esther? Oh, my God!" Paul grabbed his arm. "Owen, for God's sake, what happened?"

Owen jerked his arm free of his brother's hand and battled the storm of anger that pounded inside him threatening to accelerate out of control.

"Wait for me in the barn. I've things to say to you I don't wish to say in front of my wife."

Ana glanced up at Owen's face and what she saw there was frightening. His eyes were pinched, his jaws clenched, his mouth as hard as stone. Yet the hand beneath her elbow was gentle. He ushered her through the house to their bedroom. A chill of dread settled on Ana. That irresponsible, charming *boy* was the one who had seduced Harriet and caused her death.

While she changed the baby's napkin and settled him in the cradle, she could hear Owen in the other room changing his clothes. A thought struck her and she hurried to the doorway.

"Owen, don't tell him," she said anxiously.

"Don't tell him what?" He pulled the wide suspenders up over his shoulders and buttoned them to the front of his britches.

"Don't tell him about Harry."

"He'll not take him away from you. He'll have to kill me first."

"Why does he have to know?"

"Because he has the right to know why I'm going to beat the daylights out of him. Besides that, he should know because, rotten as he is, Harriet loved him." He came to Ana and put his arms around her. "When Harriet lay dying she asked me to tell him that she loved him. I'll tell him . . . after I give him a thrashing for what he did to her."

"Oh, no! Owen, please. What good will that do?"

"It will make me feel better."

He went through the hallway to the kitchen and out the back door. Ana followed him to the porch and watched him go to the barn where Soren and Uncle Gus stood talking with Paul.

"Why'd Owen hit Paul, Ana?" Hettie asked. "Why'd he tell me and Lily to come to the house?"

"He knew that I needed you and Lily to help me with all the food that was left. It'll soon be supper time. We'll put aside everything that will keep until later. Tonight we'd better have the chicken and dumplings and sage dressing."

Ana followed Lily and Hettie into the kitchen and began removing the clean dishtowels that covered the bowls of food on the table, but her mind was on what was going on out by the barn.

Uncle Gus and Soren had been pulling into the yard when they saw Owen hit his brother. Their curiosity was aroused farther when Paul indicated that he was puzzled by Owen's actions too.

As he approached, Owen's eyes were on his brother. He eyed Paul's polished boots, the fine, vested suit and the gold watch chain stretched across his chest.

"Uncle Gus said Esther fell off a wagon and broke her neck. God, I hate that. Esther was meaner than hell sometimes, but she was my sister." Paul's voice was not quite steady.

"Excuse us," Owen said to his uncle and cousin. "I have some private words for this . . . young dandy who's been out sowing his wild oats."

"What's got you in such a snit?" Paul demanded angrily, a dull flush staining his cheekbones.

"In here." Owen opened the barn door.

"What's this all about?" Paul took a step back.

"You'll find out. Now get in here!"

"Have you gone crazy?"

The word lashed Owen like a whip. *Crazy!* Was the whole damn family crazy? He grabbed Paul by the shoulder, shoved him inside the barn, and slammed the door shut.

"What's this all about?" Paul said again.

"It's about a girl from Dubuque named Harriet Fairfax."

"Harriet Fairfax? What's she got to do with anything. She was just—"

Owen hit him. Paul staggered back down the aisle between the stalls and sat down hard on the packed ground.

"Goddammit! What's got into you? Are you out of your mind?" Paul dabbed at his split lip with the back of his hand.

"Harriet was an innocent little girl. You ruined her, damn you!" Owen stared into his brother's face, an emotion akin to hatred stirring in the pit of his belly.

"Hell! She was willing. I've never forced a woman."

"Not physically. You seduced that girl. She was willing to let you have your way with her because you promised to marry her and bring her here to the farm to live. She fell in love with you."

"Well, so what!" Paul got to his feet. "A lot of women have fallen in love with me. I'm a charming fellow."

Owen drew back his fist. "Let's see how charming you are with your nose spread all over your face." This time the blow put Paul flat on his back. Blood spurted from his broken nose and ran down on his fancy vest. "Get up, you sorry excuse for a man. You made that girl pregnant and ran off and left her."

Paul lay on the ground holding a handkerchief to his nose. Finally he sat up. His eyes, gleaming with defiance, reminded Owen of their father the last time he saw him.

"You're wondering how I found out," Owen snarled. "She came here looking for you."

"Shit! I knew I shouldn't've told her where I was from."

"The baby you saw in my wife's arms is the result of what you did to that girl." Owen's fists clenched.

"I suppose you think I should marry the little twit."

"Say one more thing about her and I'll stomp you into the ground."

"Well, goddammit, Owen, how was I to know she'd catch the first time?" Paul sat in the dirt and dabbed at the blood running from his nose. "You broke my nose and ruined my suit!"

"I should break off that whacker you're so proud of, so you'll not ruin another young girl."

"Ruin? Shit! Why didn't she find some sucker to marry her?"

"She did. Me."

"You? Good God! No wonder you're pissed. But . . . but you said the blond was your wife. Where's Harriet?"

"In the cemetery at White Oak." Owen saw shock replace the sneer on his brother's face.

"Christamighty!" Paul opened his mouth to say something more, then closed it.

"She died giving birth to your child, but before she did, she asked me to tell you that she loved you. Doesn't that make you feel proud of yourself?"

"Believe me, Owen, I'm sorry about Harriet. But, shitfire, she followed me around asking for it." Paul started to get to his feet, but thought better of it and sank back down. "So the kid's mine. Hell, I'd like to see what he looks like."

"He's *my* son. Harriet was *my* wife when he was born. There's no way in hell you can legally claim him."

"I don't want to *claim* him. I just want to see him."

"You go near him, or mention that you even knew Harriet, and I'll break both your legs."

"It didn't take you long to get another woman in your bed. This one's a hell of a lot better looking than Harriet."

Shocked by his brother's callous attitude, Owen gazed at him in silence.

"You're just like Pa. All your brains are in that thing between your legs."

"What about you . . . brother?" Paul snapped angrily. "I guess you think you're *not* like him? The only difference is that you do with your fists what he did with the buggy whip."

"Shut your mouth, damn you!"

"I'll not shut up! You're as much of a bully as Pa. You're following in the old man's footsteps. He got his up by beating women and kids . . . all in the name of righteousness, of course."

"You should be horse-whipped for what you did to that girl."

"I don't suppose you've ever diddled around."

"Shut up," Owen thundered.

"I'm guilty of plowing a willing woman, but I've never beat someone smaller than myself. You're a hell of a lot more like that old bastard than I am . . . damn his rotten soul to hell."

Owen looked down at his brother for a long while and a chill replaced the heat of his anger. He remembered himself, a boy of fifteen, lying in the same place where Paul lay, looking up at the man towering over him and despising him, wishing he was big enough; and strong enough, to fight back. Self-loathing washed over him, mingled with a sharp tang of regret for what he had done, and regret for what his brother had become.

God help him! He had *wanted* to hurt him.

"You can stay the night—in the old house," Owen said tiredly. 'I want you gone from here in the morning."

"I wish to hell I'd never come back."

"So do I."

"Nothing has changed here. It never will."

"It's changed. So have you. Good-bye, Paul."

Owen shoved open the barn door and went out. He walked past Soren who was filling the water tanks for the hogs and on to the shed where he worked on his furniture. He was trembling so much that he needed to sit down. In the quiet of the shed, he sat with head bowed. The fists that hung between his knees were streaked with his brother's blood.

When Uncle Gus came in with the evening milk, Lily took the buckets from his hands. Ana followed him to the back porch.

"What's going on, Uncle Gus?"

"I ain't sure, lass. Owen worked young Paul over with his fists." He shook his gray head. "It plumb bamboozles me. If it'd been Soren, I'd not be surprised, but Owen—. I've never seen Owen like that. He always thought a heap of Paul."

"Where is he?"

"Paul? Soren took him to the old house to try'n patch up his busted nose."

"And Owen?"

"He's in his work shed. Just a sittin' in there."

"Did . . . Paul say anything?"

"He said Owen was mad about something that happened a long time ago. Somethin' not worth talkin' about."

Something not worth talking about. A slow, hot anger flowed over Ana, bringing a flush to her face. She forced herself to breathe evenly and not to let Uncle Gus see how much the careless words upset her.

"Supper's on when you want it."

"If it'll hold for a bit, lass, I'll mosey on down 'n' see if'n I can help Soren with Paul."

Ana watched the old man head for the house in the grove, then went back into the kitchen.

"Hettie, will you keep an eye on Baby Harry and give him his bottle when he wakes up?"

"I will. I'll take care of him real good. Are you going somewhere, Ana?"

"I'm going out to tell Owen that supper is ready."

"Why'd Owen hurt Paul?" The ends of Hettie's lips sagged. "Owen never hurts anybody."

"I'm sure Owen thought he had good reason. If you and Lily will take care of things in here, I'll go out and talk to him."

"When you come back, Ana, I'll take some supper over to Foster," Lily said, as she poured a bucket of milk through the strainer and into the crock to take to the cellar.

Worried about Owen, Ana hurried out to the shed. She found him sitting on a box beside his workbench. She closed the door. Without speaking she put her arms around him and pulled his head to her breasts. He drew her between his spread thighs and down onto his lap, holding her, breathing in the scent that was only hers, crushing her to him as though to draw from her strength.

Ana held him quietly. Her love for him was as deep as the sea. She rested her cheek on his head and waited.

"Ana . . . Ana—" He lifted his face, lined with soul-deep anguish. "I wanted to hurt him. Then I saw myself as he must be seeing me—standing over him with clenched fists—just like Pa used to do."

"Don't compare yourself with *him*! You're nothing like him."

"I realized that, sweetheart, as I sat here. Pa wouldn't have cared how many girls Paul ruined. He would have thought it the mark of a man."

Ana felt relief, mingled with a sharp tang of pain for his anguish.

"Did you tell him about Harry?"

"Yes. Then I told him that Harry was our son. He'll never try to claim the boy. It isn't in his plan to be tied down."

"Will . . . he be staying?"

"He'll be gone in the morning."

"Owen, I'm sorry, truly sorry you broke with your brother."

"So am I. I had hoped that there would be an excuse for what he did, a reason for deserting Harriet. But there wasn't. He never intended to marry her."

"Sometimes out of disaster a miracle occurs. It happened when your father took advantage of Hettie. Lily is Hettie's miracle. I lost Harriet, and you are mine."

"No, sweet woman. You are mine."

"We have more to do than sit here arguing about that," Ana said with a sassy grin. "In case you've forgotten, we have a son to raise, a farm to run, and we've got to decide what's best to do for Hettie and Lily."

"All of that? I don't suppose we have time for a few kisses."

"We'll take time."

His mouth was tender on hers, almost reverent, giving, yet taking. The soft utterance that came from her throat was a purr of pure pleasure. Slowly, deliberately, his mouth covered hers, pressing gently at first. She automatically parted her lips in invitation. The touch of his tongue at the corner of her mouth was persuasive rather than demanding. Caught in the throes of desire, she pressed herself against him, her arms winding around him with surprising strength.

The fervor of her passion excited him, forcing him to use utmost restraint. Resisting the pressure of her arms, he lifted his head to look at her. Her breath was cool on his lips made wet by her kiss.

"Whoa, sweetheart. I've got a feeling I shouldn't have done that," he confessed in a raspy whisper. "It'll be a while before I can go in the house without embarrassing the hell out of myself."

"You can wear my apron." Ana giggled happily and slipped off his lap.

They stood with their arms around each other. He turned his lips to her forehead. "I don't feel lonely inside anymore," he whispered.

"I don't either. Kiss me once more before we go in."

Epilogue

Christmas 1885

The sleighbells jingled merrily as the horse trotted toward home. Snuggled close to Owen and covered with a fur robe, Ana found it hard to believe that the temperature was twenty degrees below zero. The sun was bright, the air still. The sleigh pulled by two prancing, steaming horses glided noiselessly over the fresh snow. Ana's laughter rang out when a brightly colored cardinal flew out of a tree beside the road and crossed in front of them, and she flashed her husband a happy smile. Peace existed for him in this sweet woman. He had watched her with loving eyes as she shopped this last time before Christmas.

The store in White Oak had taken on a delightful new appearance since their last visit. Boxes, barrels, and sacks obstructed the passageways, and overflowed onto the shelves and counters. Crates of oranges were opened and leaned end-up against barrels holding nuts, fresh oysters and pickled fish. Boxes of candy vied for space with sugar and coffee. The counter was lined with a variety of firecrackers, torpedoes and Roman candles. Ana pointedly looked the other way when Owen had Hershel put some of each in a sack and he slipped it into his pocket.

Christmas in rural Iowa was a time for feasting and visiting with friends. The harvest was over, the cellars were full of food, the barns filled with enough hay and grain to last until spring. The week before Christmas, Ana and Owen had gone to the Christmas program at the church, and to a Christmas dance held in Oscar Hansen's new barn.

Owen and Ana were disappointed when, after the harvest, Foster left to go back to his haunts along the river. He had gained weight and put on muscle during the summer and had promised to return in the spring. Owen fervently hoped peace and contentment such as he had found would come to Foster.

A distant cousin of Owen's, Byron Jamison, had taken over running the Knutson farm after Foster left. Sophia Hendricks, a widow from Lansing, had moved into the house with Lily and Hettie to keep down talk in the community. As soon as it was discovered that Jens Knutson died a rich man, callers by the dozens had come to pay their respects to both daughter and granddaughter. Mrs. Hendricks was as protective of them as a mother hen with two chicks and had sent more than one ambitious suitor down the road with a warning not to come back.

Hettie had new pride. Lily had patiently taught her to write her name and to read a little. Ana had taught her to knit and to make rugs on a loom. Mrs. Hendricks mothered both Hettie and Lily and they had never been happier.

Lily was shocked, as they all had been, when Soren had departed with Paul the day after Esther's funeral. He had explained to Owen that matters between him and Lily had become too serious and he had to put some distance between them so that he could sort out his feelings. Ana wanted to shake Soren for leaving Lily without a single private word. The young girl had been broken-hearted for weeks, then gradually the sad look had left her eyes, and she began to take an interest in her new life without her grandpa and Esther.

Owen stopped the sleigh beside the back porch and helped

Ana carry the packages from the store into the house. While outside the fields glistened with snow and ice, inside, blazing fires gave the home a warm, hospitable glow. The sight and smell of Christmas was everywhere. The aroma of freshly made cakes, pies and candies filled the house. Handmade decorations added a touch of color in every room. A tree, adorned with red ribbon bows, strings of popcorn, and candles for lighting Christmas morning stood in the parlor.

Uncle Gus sat in the rocker with Harry on his lap. Both he and Hettie spoiled the child outrageously. The baby looked more like Owen each day, a fact that pleased Owen no end. Only Ana, Owen and Paul knew the truth about the baby's parentage.

When Owen came in after putting the horse away, he picked up the boy and held him high over his head.

"Owen, your hands are cold," Ana scolded.

"You don't mind, do you, son?" Owen flung the child up and down a few times. Harry went into spasms of laughter. Suddenly the baby belched and began to hiccup. "Oh, shoot! You little devil! You puked on me. Here, go to your mama."

"Serves you right for throwing him around like that. You're teething, aren't you, sweetheart?" Ana took the baby, wiped his mouth and cuddled him. The infant spit, cooed and smiled. "Your papa's got so much Christmas spirit, he can't settle down." Her eyes, soft with twinkling lights, rested lovingly on her husband's face. "You men had better get out of the kitchen or I'll put you to work." Ana sat the baby in the highchair and buckled the strap to hold him in.

"We have a turkey and a goose to pick, Uncle Gus," Owen said and put on his old work coat. "We'd better go or she'll have us rolling pie crust."

"There's no rest 'round here atall," Uncle Gus grumbled, pulling himself up out of the chair. "This Christmas thing is gettin' outta hand."

"Hush your fussing, Uncle Gus. Tonight you and Owen can pick out nutmeats and . . . pull taffy."

"Pull taffy!" Both men spoke in unison.

"Lordy mercy." Uncle Gus looked as if he were headed for the hanging tree, but his eyes were full of affection when they looked at Ana.

"That's bullfoot, huh, Uncle Gus," Owen muttered while ushering his uncle out the door.

Ana had caught the look Owen had given her. Their eyes had met, as they did many times during the day. He did not have to touch her, or hold her in his arms for her to know that she was wrapped in his love.

"It's snowing."

"It always snows on Christmas morning."

Owen came up behind Ana, pulled her back against him, and nestled his face in the curve of her neck. His nose tickled; she giggled and dropped the window curtain.

"Merry Christmas."

"You already said that—this morning—when I—"

"—When you told me about my Christmas present," he finished for her.

"It'll be a Fourth of July present. I shouldn't have told you until after the holidays. You haven't stopped grinning."

"When can I open my *other* present? The one you've been working on behind my back." His hand on her lower belly stretched from hipbone to hipbone and he caressed it lovingly.

"Owen Jamison, you've been snooping in my knitting bag! Well, you'll not see it until Lily and Hettie get here." She turned in his arms and put hers around his neck.

"If you're going to be mean to me, I'll not let you open your other present." He took a package out of his pocket and stuck it in the branches of the Christmas tree.

"Oh, what is it?" She made to snatch it and he caught her hand. "You know I hate surprises."

"You don't. You love surprises."

"Somebody better get in here. Harry's playin' in the punkin pie," Uncle Gus called.

Ana pulled herself out of Owen's arms and hurried to the kitchen.

"Uncle Gus! You're a tease," she accused when she saw that Harry was in the highchair sucking on a stick of candy. "Now I know where Soren got his devilish streak." She opened the oven and peeked at the huge turkey in the roasting pan. "Lift it out for me, Owen. I want to dip off grease for gravy. Oh, I wish Soren was here. Remember how he loved stuffing?"

"He's probably sitting in the sun on some island with a girl in each arm," Owen said drily.

"Humph!" Uncle Gus snorted.

Owen lifted the twenty-five pound turkey to the top of the range and went to peer out the kitchen window.

"I thought I heard sleighbells. Here they come. Jehoshaphat! That's some sleigh. The runners on that thing are twelve feet long. I'm going to race Cousin Bryon before the day's over."

"Owen Jamison! I declare. At times you act like a big kid." Ana ducked beneath his arm so she could see out the window.

The sleigh stopped beside the path leading to the porch. Lily and Hettie were helping Mrs. Hendricks, who was now like one of the family, up the icy path. There was much stamping on the porch as the visitors attempted to rid their feet of snow before they came into the house.

"Merry Christmas." Hettie's cheeks were red, her eyes bright and she had a huge smile on her face.

Lily was smiling, too. Rich brown curls that escaped from the bright-blue knit cap framed her face. Snowflakes rested on her head and shoulders.

"That was some ride," Lily exclaimed happily.

"I swan to goodness," Sophia said as she came into the house. "That horse is as frisky as a colt this morning."

"Merry Christmas, Sophia. Let me take your coat."

"Thank you, dear. My gracious! Something smells good. Mr. Jamison will bring in our basket."

"We made fudge, Ana." Hettie was shaking the snow from the hem of her dress onto the rug beside the door. "We got a coconut at the store. Did you know a coconut has eyes?"

Ana laughed. "I hadn't thought about it, but you're right."

"We got presents." Hettie dropped a kiss on Harry's head. "Got some for this sweet baby too."

"I've never seen anyone enjoy Christmas like Hettie. She's made gifts for everyone."

"Sophia! You're not supposed to tell."

"I'm sorry, love. I'm just so proud of you, I couldn't help but tell it."

When Byron Jamison came in, he brought a gust of cold air in with him as well as a large basket.

"Here's your basket, Soapy," he teased and knocked the snow from his knit cap and crammed it down in the sleeve of his coat before he hung it on the rack beside the door. The look he gave Sophia set Ana to wondering if a romance was brewing between them.

"Shall we go to the parlor?" Ana asked. "Owen will light the candles on the tree." She failed to see the look exchanged between Owen and his uncle.

"We've got to have our hot apple cider, honey," Owen said. "Sit down and I'll get it." He moved the highchair to make room at the table.

They lingered over the mugs of hot cider, talking not of Christmases past, but mostly about the race Cousin Bryon and Owen would have in the afternoon.

It was mid-morning when Owen cocked his head to one side and said, "Damned if I don't hear sleighbells."

Ana went to the window to look up the lane. "Who would be coming to call on Christmas morning?"

A sleigh, drawn by two steaming horses, circled the barn-yard and stopped at the door. A man jumped out and waved to the driver as the sleigh sped back down the lane. Ana looked back at Owen and his uncle. Both men had guilty grins on their faces.

"Tarnation! You knew he was coming!" She flung open the door.

"Hello," Soren yelled. "I hope you haven't eaten yet. I'm starved."

"Soren! Oh, Soren, this makes Christmas complete. And when *haven't* you been starved?" Ana flew into his outstretched arms, her dress getting wet from the snow on his coat.

"Give your favorite cousin a kiss, Cousin Ana."

"Oh, Soren. I'm so glad you're home."

"I'm glad to be here." He kissed her soundly. "Merry Christmas, Pa." Soren embraced his father.

"Merry Christmas, son." Uncle Gus sounded as if he had a frog in his throat.

Soren pumped Owen's hand, hugged Hettie and was introduced to Mrs. Hendricks. He pounded Cousin Byron on the back.

"You look almost human without that beard, cousin."

"Still mouthy. I'd thought you'd a out-growed that by now."

Everyone, except Lily, crowded around Soren. She stood at the back, in the doorway leading to the hall, looking on and smiling. Suddenly, Soren was looking at her.

"Hello, Lily."

"Hello, Soren."

"I'm back . . . to stay."

"I'm glad for Uncle Gus. He's missed you."

"And you, Lily. Have you missed me?"

"Of . . . course."

"Pa and I are going to build a broom and brush factory in White Oak."

Lily smiled, but made no comment. She had matured while he was away. It bothered Soren that she no longer hung on his every word and looked at him with adoring eyes, but with the cool, friendly eyes of a self-assured young woman. It suddenly occured to him that he might have lost his chance with Lily, and some of the joy of homecoming left him.

"Now that the family is all here, we can open our presents," Ana announced. "Isn't it grand, Owen?" she whispered as they led their guests to the parlor.

"Yes, sweetheart. It's grand."

Ana's heartbeat began to surge, and she could no longer speak for the tears in her throat. She smiled up at her husband. He smiled back at her, his face younger and rid of care; his mouth had lost its harshness months ago. He put his arm around her. She could feel the pump of his heart in her shoulder. She pulled his head down to whisper in his ear.

"You're a sneaky . . . piss-ant for not telling me Soren was coming."

He laughed against her cheek as his hand moved between them to caress her breast. "Yeah, I am."

"Owen! Stop that!"

Outside, big feathery snowflakes continued to fall.

If you enjoyed HOMEPLACE,
be sure to look for. . .

RIBBON IN THE SKY
by Dorothy Garlock

❧

You will be captivated by the hauntingly
beautiful story of a love that refused to die.

Set in Nebraska shortly after the turn of the
century, RIBBON IN THE SKY is a heart-
stirring novel with the power to make you remember it long after the last page has been
turned.

★　　★　　★

**Coming in December
from Warner Books.**